# Beauty Beheld

*To my husband, my devoted friend, fan, and supporter.*

*To Mom and Dad for demonstrating decades of timeless, unconditional love for us. I know you're excited, but please consider skipping the sex scenes.*

*For anyone who wears love's battle scars with pride and still possesses the strength and courage to fight again.*

# Chapter One

On a chilly Friday night thick with the promise of comforting food and familiar faces, I had no idea I was walking straight into the unraveling of everything I thought I knew.

After a long work day, my boyfriend, Daniel, and I walked into his parents' home. The only thing on my mind was relaxing and enjoying some delicious food with his family and loved ones. During their monthly "framily" nights, we played board games, listened to great music, and celebrated Daniel's family's Haitian heritage. The sweet and spicy aroma of simmering food and the lively tunes of Haitian singer Alan Cavé instantly arrested my senses. Not only was I salivating in anticipation of the zesty Creole cuisine cooking just feet away, but the loud music had my hips swinging loosely. My silver bangle bracelets rang out as I waved hello, clapped, and swayed my way toward the sea of welcoming faces.

"Aye, aye, aye," Daniel's younger sister, Princessa, chanted as I danced into their cozy living room. "The life of the party's here! Hey, Patience!" I hugged Princessa, who had also become best friends with my little sister, Chelsea, as a result of dating Daniel for five years.

"Hey, Cessa," I said, giving her a quick hug and kiss, while admiring her smooth, glowing mahogany skin. Her eyes danced as Daniel walked in behind me, juggling my homemade iced lemon pound cake and a chilled bottle of wine.

I kissed brief hellos with his father, Emmanuel, and each of their close family friends before removing my coat and taking it to the small hall closet. In the kitchen, I washed my hands before peeking beneath the lid of the tall, brass pot sitting on the gas stove. Much to my pleasure, my eager nostrils were greeted by savory shredded pork simmering in a tangy sauce with a medley of sliced onions, chili peppers, and...I sniffed. Was that lime juice? I swallowed a squeal, then peeked into the oven at an assortment of flaky pastries. I didn't need to break the crispy crusts open to know they held tender cutlets of beef, chicken, and pork. I was armed with a hearty appetite and primed and ready to dig in. Wanting to make this same meal for Daniel, I was disappointed when his mother still refused to share their family recipes with me. But nothing beats a try like a recipe knockoff, and that was what Pinterest was for.

As I closed the oven door, a penetrating chill hit me and I knew without lifting my head that her weighty gaze was on me. Lovelie, Daniel's mother. Her statuesque frame was led by her hips as she walked into the kitchen and over to the stove. Her long, jet-black hair was swept into a tight bun at the top of her head. She must have been in a good mood that evening because her smile actually reached her eyes as her gaze swept over my curvy frame, accented by a simple black dress and four-inch heels that added to my modest height. Her eyes creased warmly and sparkled from the overhead light.

"Mrs. Francois, everything smells great, as usual. Do you need help setting the table?" I asked, determined to start the evening on the right foot.

"Non, non, cherie, I'm pretty much done out there," Lovelie said, maintaining a warm smile as her thick accent rolled over the words. But something about her tone felt sickeningly sweet, like overripe fruit.

I took a seat on the stool beside the island, willing myself to relax.

"So, how is work?" Lovelie slid on a pair of oven mitts and pulled out the pastries. Her casual question carried just enough interest to feel like a trap.

"Great. I've had some nice new projects recently. I love what I do, so it never really feels like work to me," I replied, hoping my upbeat tone would defuse whatever was coming.

"Ah, I see." She nodded, but her eyes stayed fixed on me. "You still plan to attend graduate school, non?"

I shrugged, my shoulders stiffening. "Maybe. I've been kicking around the idea of getting my MFA for a little while, but I still haven't decided."

"MFA? What is that?"

I grabbed a carrot stick from the veggie tray and dipped it in ranch dressing. "It's a Masters of Fine Arts."

"And what is that for, exactly?"

"Many things. Photography, creative writing, performing arts..." I trailed off, aware of how unimpressed she looked.

She exhaled loudly, shaking her head slightly. When I didn't take her bait, Lovelie said, "Well, cherie, I was referring to a more practical degree program. You can probably advance rather quickly at that marketing agency if you would consider getting your MBA instead."

The air between us thickened. *Here we go again with the unsolicited advice. You need to focus on molding Princessa's life and stay out of mine.* I fought a strong urge to crack open the wine we'd brought. However, the last time I had a glass of wine before sitting down to dinner, Lovelie had asked Daniel if I had a drinking problem.

*Enough of this shit.* I met her eyes directly. "With all due respect, Mrs. Francois, I've been successful in my career, and I make great money. Everything's working out quite nicely, so please just be happy for me."

"Okay, darling," she said, flashing me that toothy smile of hers. But this one fell flat. "Noted."

*That was far too easy.* I popped a grape tomato into my mouth while heading toward the living room. Yet, the tension clung to me like static, crackling at the edges of my mind.

When I joined the small group, Emmanuel was wrapping up one of his stories about his father, an infamous Haitian farmer who grew the largest mangoes in his village. In Haiti, Emmanuel and Lovelie lived in a modest home in an upper-class community near Port-au-Prince. Descendants of hardworking families, they each held their familial status in high regard. I respected how hard Emmanuel's father worked to build his agricultural trade business and the obstacles he overcame while doing so. Emmanuel assumed control of the family business upon his father's death and the couple did very well for themselves before coming to America. They eventually settled in Cleveland, just before having Daniel and Princessa.

The warmth in the room should have been comforting, but my thoughts kept circling back to the strained conversation in the kitchen. I caught Daniel's eye as he smiled at his father, his pride radiating as Emmanuel gestured animatedly.

"And the beautiful Patience Hampton," Emmanuel's baritone voice boomed as he turned to me. "We were so proud of our featured panelist at the Cleveland Marketing Expo last week. You spoke so eloquently; it took all of my might not to jump up and yell, 'that's my future daughter-in-law!'"

I blushed, lowering my eyes as the group nodded and verbalized their approval. "Thanks, Mr. Francois. I appreciated you coming and showing your support."

Out of the corner of my eye, I caught Lovelie entering the dining room with a basket of yeast rolls. Her expression didn't betray much, but her disapproval pressed down on me like a lead weight. I shivered and seconds later, Daniel's reassuringly squeezed my hand. It helped, but only slightly.

I smiled at him, content with knowing that I at least had a stamp of approval from three out of four members of the Francois family.

Less than five minutes later, we were all seated at the table. As I scanned the setting, noting the extra plate and the unspoken tension that settled over the room.

Daniel's brow rose as his mother set a large ceramic dish at the center of the table. "Griot? Ma, you only make this on special occasions. Are we celebrating something tonight?"

Emmanuel, who was seated at the head of the table cut his eyes at Lovelie, his handsome face showcasing concern.

"Well," she took a seat, then after a long sip of wine, she said, "we have a lot to be happy about tonight."

"Do we, now?" Emmanuel's tone was curious.

Just then, the doorbell rang, breaking the awkward silence. My stomach sank as our eyes all shot toward the front of the house.

"Oh! I'll get it!" Lovelie stood abruptly, placed her napkin on the table, and smoothed her apron as hurried toward the door.

Daniel and I exchanged a glance, both of us waiting to see who this unexpected dinner guest could be. The sound of high-pitched shrieking and a flurry of English mixed with Patois floated in from the foyer. The guest was still standing on the porch, cloaked in the early evening shadows. "Bon swa, chérie," Lovelie said, which meant good evening.

In my spare time, I'd secretly began teaching myself Haitian Creole. What started as a surprise for Daniel soon turned into a personal curiosity. I couldn't help wondering what Lovelie was saying about me whenever she would slip back and forth between English and Creole.

When Lovelie stepped aside, a long-legged young woman strolled into the house. Lovelie rushed to remove her coat. Her classic beauty was so striking, it was almost alarming. She shook a thin coat of snow from her bust-length tresses which fell in soft waves over her cream sweater dress. As we all looked on in silence, her almond-shaped eyes quickly scanned the room. Her gaze held mine hostage for a long moment as we sized each other up. Then she glanced to my right and smiled as her focus landed on Daniel. He shifted in his chair, signaling that he recognized her, but I couldn't detect the level of familiarity between them.

"Everyone, look who stopped by," Lovelie announced, practically glowing as she ushered the woman into the room.

I sat frozen, my mind scrambling to place this mystery woman. Daniel's posture stiffened beside me, adding to my unease. *Who the hell is she?*

*Chapter Two*

**D**aniel's favorite aunt nodded with a faint smile of recognition.

"Fabienne," Emmanuel said as he slowly rose to his feet. "Ki jan ou ye?"

He was asking how she was.

"Mwen byen. Et ou, misye Francois?" she replied, her gentle voice barely above a whisper.

She was saying, "I'm well. And you, Mr. Francois?"

"Mwen byen," he responded.

I looked away as they eased into a comfortable hug. My mind was still reeling, scrambling to figure out who this woman was and how she fit into the family. I had been attending friends-and-family dinners for years, and not once had I seen her or heard of her. Could she be the daughter of a family friend? A distant cousin I hadn't met?

I glanced nervously at Daniel. He grabbed and squeezed my hand beneath the table. That's when I noticed Princessa's reaction. Her normally glowing complexion had gone slack. She avoided my eyes entirely.

What the fuck was going on here?

My gaze darted around the table, reading every face for clues as the silence thickened. I didn't realize my mouth was hanging open until my dry tongue nearly choked me. I reached for my water glass and drained it.

"Hello, everyone." Fabienne gave a dainty wave. Then she took the empty seat directly across from me and looked at Daniel. "Ki jan ou ye, Daniel?"

He gave a stiff nod and cleared his throat before responding in English. "I've been well. How have you been, Fabienne?"

Her face brightened, and she smiled as she answered, speaking English for the first time. "I've also been well."

Daniel looked back down at his empty dinner plate. That was it.

After a few more seconds of awkward silence, I realized no one was going to have the decency of formally introducing us. I leaned across the table and extended my hand. "Hello, Fabienne. I'm Patience."

Her eyes darkened for a moment. Then, with a small smile, she left my hand hanging. "Nice to meet you." She sat back as if the moment never happened.

After she reclaimed her seat, Lovelie turned to Emmanuel. "Honey, now that our last dinner guest is here, would you like to lead us in prayer before the food cools?"

Emmanuel hesitated before nodding. "Everyone, please bow your heads."

I promise I didn't hear a single word of that prayer. Emmanuel could've been speaking in tongues for all I knew. My eyes were locked on the woman across from me, who nodded and murmured her gratitude with closed eyes and a serene smile.

As soon as the prayer ended, muted conversations sparked around the dinner table while I sat there, stewing in my unbridled thoughts. *Why hasn't anyone explained who this girl is? She just popped in for dinner out of the blue like she was here last week. Princessa's over there looking like she needs a blood transfusion, Daniel's totally mute, and I feel like an outsider of a cruel inside joke. What's the story?*

The griot was on point, but after only a few bites, my stomach was a jumble of knots. I could barely keep down the little bit of food I managed to swallow. I sucked in a few shallow breaths to calm my raging nerves, as Daniel filled my wine glass. I shot him a grateful glance and took a long sip.

Then Lovelie spoke.

"Daniel, I forgot to mention—I ran into Fabienne at the grocery store this morning and invited her to join us..."

Judging from the expressions around the table, Daniel wasn't the only one she'd neglected to tell.

"...she's home for good now after passing the bar."

My brow lifted and I glanced back at Fabienne. She smiled shyly at Daniel and nodded.

There was scattered applause and praise around the table, and I added mine politely. "That's wonderful. What field will you be practicing in?"

"Immigration, particularly focused on helping refugees and asylum seekers."

"That's admirable. Daniel's also interested in law—well the healthcare side of it. He wants to impact overseas healthcare policy as a lobbyist. He's passionate about changing legislation."

Daniel gently squeezed my hand. It was only then that I realized I was rambling.

*Ugh. Why couldn't I stop talking?*

I peeked at Lovelie. She was beaming at Fabienne, like I hadn't even spoken. A combination of my nerves, the rising tension, and my anxiety caused my stomach to lurch.

"Eskize mwen," I blurted, rising to my feet abruptly. A hushed silence fell over the room. I hadn't realized my faux pas until moments later. My mind was a mess. "Er . . . excuse me."

Fabienne looked puzzled as she asked me, "Eske ou pale Kreyòl?" She was asking if I spoke Creole.

"No, she doesn't," Lovelie cut in, turning to Daniel, who had stood to steady me. "Daniel, have you been teaching her Kreyòl?"

He frowned. "So what if I have?"

"Sis . . . are you okay?" Princessa asked as we passed her.

My face and neck were hot, and droplets of sweat sprang onto my skin. Feeling light-headed, I swallowed and breathed slowly, trying to calm my queasy stomach. The last thing I needed was to have a meltdown in front of Fabienne.

"Yes, Cessa, I'm fine. Just need . . . some fresh air," I managed.

Lovelie scoffed. "Pure theatrics. The girl just can't handle someone more driven being in the spotlight."

Daniel released my arm and turned to face her.

"What did you say, Ma?"

"Lovey," Emmanuel warned.

"No, Dad, let her finish. I want to hear why she thinks Patience is trying to steal the spotlight. I've never met anyone more committed to making sure other people are recognized for their wins."

Lovelie's eyes flashed. "Can't you see what the rest of us do? She's threatened. That girl is always cheering for you from the sidelines, but she's doing nothing with her own life. That's why she's jealous of a woman with real ambition."

"Ma, that's not true. I'm finishing my doctorate, and I wouldn't have made it without Patience's love and support. And she's thriving, too. She owns a home, has a great career, and has a business."

"Son, she's complacent with her little entry-level career. She has no interest in getting an MBA. Hell, she's probably just waiting for you finish school so she can be a kept woman. But Fabienne as your partner . . . well . . . that's what a real power couple would look like."

"Welp, there it is," Emmanuel said under his breath, dropping his napkin. "I knew you had an agenda inviting Fabienne here tonight."

"Mom!" Princessa cried. "Daniel and Patience are happy. Why are you trying to ruin that?"

I closed my eyes, barely able to stand. "Daniel," I whispered, "please get my purse and coat."

"Power couple?" he repeated.

I wasn't sure if he didn't hear me or if he was flat out ignoring me.

Lovelie crossed her arms. "You've been using that girl to rebel against us. But it's time to stop playing in the sandbox and set your sights much higher."

"Ma, you're not about to stand here and tear Patience apart like this. You're speaking reckless like she's not even standing here . . ."

I wiped sweat from my brow. *Yes, I am standing here. And she's got one more "that girl" before I show her exactly who I am.*

"—when will you realize she's been my girlfriend for over five years, and I love her? She's not going anywhere. Fabienne and I have never been more than friends. I haven't even seen or spoken to her since high school."

"Sure about that?"

The comment was low, but I heard it. I turned.

Daniel spun toward her. "What . . . sure about what, Fabienne?"

"We may not have seen each other, but we've been talking and FaceTiming regularly for years."

Daniel stiffened beside me. "Yes. . . we've talked occasionally. Just checking in. What's your point?"

She frowned slightly. "So, complaining about not having anything in common with your girlfriend and how she has no career goals is 'just checking in?'"

I could barely hear her purring over the blood pulsing in my ears. But I strained to make out every word. I turned to face Daniel, eyes blazing. "You've been talking about me with her? Who the hell is this woman, anyway?"

"See, that's the thing, sweetheart," Lovelie said, her voice smug. "We've known Fabienne since birth. *She* comes from good stock."

"Lovey! Stop it this instant," Emmanuel's voice boomed throughout the room.

But her words still pierced me to the core. My eyes were trained on Daniel, my hands slowly clenching. Daniel had warned me that his family—especially his mother—was old school. Proud. Obsessed with appearances. For years, I'd ignored Lovelie's digs at my family. But I literally couldn't stomach it for a moment longer.

Seconds dragged on as Daniel and I locked eyes, standing stock still. He was stubborn, but so was I. I wasn't leaving until I got the truth.

"Tell her, Daniel," Fabienne coaxed.

His jaw locked. He broke our gaze to look at her. "Fabienne, just stop."

"Tell her there's no future. Just let her go."

Emmanuel rose and gave his wife a long, icy stare. "Congratulations, Lovey. You've outdone yourself. I really didn't think it was possible. Patience, dear, I don't condone any of this. But I need to excuse myself before I say something I regret. Goodnight, all." He stormed out.

"Stop being so dramatic, sweetheart," Lovelie called after him. "I made your favorite for dessert—coconut flan."

I dropped my head. Emmanuel's retreating footfalls echoed up the stairs.

Daniel stalked off toward the coat closet as I remained frozen with my back to everyone. I couldn't bear the sight of Lovelie and Fabienne looking so smug.

He returned and held out my coat, but I refused to move toward him.

I asked him, "What do you have to say about all this?"

"Come on, babe. Let's have this conversation privately."

My brow lifted. "So, there *is* a conversation to have. Why haven't we had it already?"

I found Daniel's bored expression offensive. "It's a long, irrelevant story. Let's just leave."

I slid into my coat and snatched my purse from him. "Your

long story is unnecessary at this point. What hasn't been said has spoken loud and clear on your behalf."

I rushed outside, and just as the crisp night air greeted me, I heard Lovelie's shrill voice through the storm door. "Now that that's over, let's all carry on with dinner, everyone. Fabienne, try this blackberry merlot. I don't know where that girl gets it, but it's divine."

I spun, marched back inside, and snatched the wine bottle out of Lovelie's hand so fast Princessa had to duck.

"You never thought I was good enough for Daniel. But let me tell you something—no one will know him, love him, or understand him the way I do. And he'll never forgive you for ruining the best thing that ever happened to him," I hissed through gritted teeth. "You think you know power? Real power uplifts, not emasculates. And, for the record, my name isn't *that girl, sweetheart, darling,* or whatever other condescending terms you've used for the past five years. You *will* remember the name Patience Christine Hampton from now on. It will haunt you in your motherfucking nightmares."

"Hol . . . hold up, Patience!" Daniel fumbled with his shoes as I stormed past.

Toting my reclaimed wine bottle, I let the door slam behind me. Just beyond the threshold of their front porch, my heightened nerves finally got the best of me, and I quietly heaved the evening's meal into a hydrangea bush. I wiped my mouth, flipped off their security camera, and stumbled down the long, curved driveway. I drained the wine and hurled the bottle onto their manicured lawn. Then I kept walking into the night, cascading tears blurring my vision as I ordered a rideshare.

Chapter Three

I stayed home for the rest of the weekend, nursing a pounding headache and crushed spirit. Stuffing my face with junk food and punishing myself by watching happy couples in an endless chain of romantic comedy movies were all I had the mental energy to accomplish. They say you spend half of your failed relationship breaking up. As I watched in disdain as people from all walks of life were rewarded with signature Hollywood happily-ever-afters, I replayed a mental loop of my relationship with Daniel. For the life of me, I couldn't pinpoint where things had gone wrong between us. Despite how hard I'd tried to give him the best of me, yet another one of my relationships had gone bad.

The problem was, I couldn't figure out how I'd screwed it up this time. For my entire life, my family and even some of my close friends claimed that I was far too emotional, too moody, and just too much. I admit that I hadn't had the best luck in my previous relationships due to hoarding emotional baggage. But I swear before God, I'd been so careful and had really tried to be on my best behavior with Daniel. I was selfless, attentive, loving, and supportive. I anticipated his needs and consistently satisfied them at the sake of putting my own needs last. I held him up each time his mother's constant criticizing, ridiculing, and berating behavior beat him into a pulp of a man. I was there to faithfully wipe his tears, speak life back into him, and prop him up to face another day. But I'd be damned if Lovelie hadn't still won in the end. Because I was willing to be completely done with Daniel if it meant having to put up with his mama for another moment.

My phone buzzed for the twentieth time that day, and I finally decided to just block Daniel's ass altogether. He was calling, texting, DMing, and sending courier pigeons, but I was in no mood to hear anything he had to say. He had tried to argue his case while I had stood and waited for my ride at the end of his parents' driveway on Friday night, eager to tell me whatever he felt was necessary in order to change my mind. His pleas fell on deaf ears. We'd been down that road countless times over the years. That wasn't the first time his mother had humiliated me in front of everyone, but it would be the last.

Normally, his smooth words worked because I didn't want to punish him for things out of his control. But when he had admitted to lying about talking to Fabienne for the full course of our relationship, something had clicked for me. That omission told me everything I needed to know about him. He was no different than the lying deadbeats I'd dated before him, except he was just a highly educated one. Turned out he had used me to sow his wild oats until he was done with school. Then he'd be ready to drive off into the sunset with his beautiful, soft-spoken bride. How could he have discussed me with her? How did she know all about his hopes, dreams, and fears while I knew nothing of her role in his life? I'd been waiting for his proposal while the idea of marrying me had probably never crossed his mind. One thing was clear—I wouldn't be Daniel's fool for another day.

I scrolled through the list of Daniel's followers on Instagram and quickly found Fabienne's profile. Then I studied picture after picture of her perfect body in bikinis while eating exotic foods and posing with other A-list-model-fresh-off-a-yacht-photoshootlooking bitches. She didn't even use filters because she was just as breathtaking in person. *Ugh!*

After using the bathroom, I poured a mixing bowl full of cereal. When I passed the decorative mirror hanging in my living room, I frowned, fingering my frizzy curls. I'd cried myself to sleep, barely slept a wink, then woke up with bags and puffy eyelids. Just when I sat down to dig into my Frosted Flakes, my phone buzzed again. The only reason I continued checking it was to see if Pop-Pop, my grandfather, had called. I always took his calls. When I saw it was my mother, I immediately picked up.

"Hello."

"Hey, Chrissy." She and Pop-Pop were the only ones who used the nickname from my middle name, Christine. "I got your message. Are you okay?"

"Hey, Mom. No, everything's gone to shit."

I could hear her tensely popping gum.

"Say less. I'm on my way."

About fifteen minutes later, she was ringing my doorbell. I looked through the peephole before letting her in. She strutted inside, looking like the complete opposite of how I felt. Her hair was styled in a big, bronze, curly 'fro weave and shaved on the right side. She wore a black bomber jacket, tight ripped jeans, and five-inch, laced-up, red booties. Her makeup was flawless, per usual. There were only seventeen years between us, so she was more like a big sister to me than a mother.

"Hey, Pooh Bear. These flowers were sitting on the porch. They're beautiful . . . oh, babe." She gasped when she took in my puffy eyes, disheveled hair, and rumpled clothing. Her hand shot up to her mouth. "I've never seen you like this!"

She pulled me into her arms, and we stood in my foyer for a long time. Silent tears leaked from my eyes, but I didn't have a single sob left to give.

She tossed the bouquet onto the foyer table. "Come on, sweetie. Let's sit. I brought gourmet popcorn and wine. I know you've probably had your rom-coms going all day."

We shared a comfortable silence in my living room for over twenty minutes. *Love Jones* played in the background, and I sat on the floor as she oiled my scalp. Once finished, she turned the movie off just before my favorite scene. "Ready to talk?"

*Hell nah,* I thought. But I offered a reluctant nod.

"So, y'all are really broken up? What in the world happened?"

I sat on the couch and shared the details I managed to remember from the evening before. All the while, my mom shook her head and took notes on her phone to avoid interrupting me. When I was done, she popped a long series of bubbles with her gum before speaking.

"Okay, so listen. We both know Lovelie's an insufferable asshole. And even though she had no right to attack you like that in front of everyone, I need you to help me understand how breaking up with Daniel was the right move. Did Bella put you up to that?" She referred to my best friend, whom I'd been trying to reach all day.

"I know you're team Daniel, Mom. And for good reasons. But I haven't spoken to Bella about all this yet. She's busy with the kids' sports activities all day today," I replied. "Daniel's a great guy, and I love him. But I curbed all my dreams to support his for years. I've spent countless lonely nights waiting for him to end a shift, finish studying, or wake up from a long nap just to spend a few moments together. I eat alone. I watch TV alone. I *am* alone. And I've never complained about that. But when I found out that he didn't even appreciate all of my sacrifice—that he's been trashing me to some random chick for lacking ambition because I'm busy emotionally supporting *his ass*? That just takes a whole caliber of nerve I'm not willing to excuse."

Mom nodded. "If that's true, that's some wild shit. I agree. You need to get to the bottom of why he's discussing his concerns about your relationship with anyone other than you. Especially with another woman whom he's failed to mention altogether! But is your issue with Daniel or with this woman? You mentioned she's beautiful, smart, and well-educated. But you're also all of those things. You can't allow anyone else to make you feel threatened in your own relationship."

I sighed, leaning my head against the couch cushion. She was always trying to make her relationship baggage mine. "I know that, Mom. I'm just . . . tired of constantly proving my worth to his mother. Then she brings this woman to dinner to intentionally make me feel a way and embarrasses me in front of everyone. What kind of self-worth could I have if I considered staying in that situation?"

"All I'm saying is, if you're in love with your man, be willing to fight for him. Don't just throw in the towel at the first sign of trouble."

"I *have* been fighting for him, Mom"—I tossed up my hands—"but I'm tired of all these defensive wounds. Healthy relationships don't involve all of this drama. Five years of this shit has exhausted the hell out of me!" More tears spilled from my eyes.

She pulled my head to her chest. "Okay. Come here, baby. *Shhh.*"

* * *

Calls continued from a hospital phone number long after Mom had left. I groaned and pulled my pillow over my head. The sooner Daniel let this go, the sooner I could move on with my life. Why was he calling anyway? He was almost done with his doctorate nursing program, and his arranged bride had returned from God knew where just in time to start their perfect life together. When the voicemail indicator buzzed, I picked up my phone to check the string of ignored messages, all from Daniel.

*Message One: Patience, love . . . I don't understand why you won't just hear me out. You have to know by now that my mother's opinion doesn't represent anyone else's. We all love and value you. You've been my rock, and I don't know what I would have done without you by my side for these past few years. I love you, Pae.*

*Please just pick up or call me back. I want to hear your voice before I go to bed.*

*Message Two: Good morning. I know last night was humiliating for you and that you're sick of my mom and her BS. That was underhanded and malicious, and I get why you're pulling away. But Pae, I swear to you, none of us knew about it. As far as Fabienne, I have not shared any personal details of our relationship with her. She's just someone I used to know a long time ago. She checks in from time to time, and yes, you've come up, but never in a demeaning way. I've told her far more good things about you than bad. I mean . . . I haven't told her anything bad about you. She pries a lot and just . . . caught me when we were having a bad day. It was just once. Please . . . just call me back and let me explain. Please, Pae.*

*Message Three: Patience. Did you get the flowers I left on your doorstep? I hope you read the card. I know it can't begin to explain things, but I'm hoping you'll at least give me a chance to tell you what happened. I would never do anything to hurt you. I love you too much for that. Please, just let me explain and you'll understand. Please.*

*Message Four: Hey. So, I guess you're flat out not going to call me back. You won't even hear me out. After all this time together, have I ever given you one reason to doubt my loyalty to you? Have I ever been anything other than respectful, kind, loving, and devoted to you? I mean, what more can I do to make you happy? Sometimes, it feels like I can never satisfy you. Real talk.*

*Message Five, the most recent one: All right, this will be my last message, then the ball is in your court. I haven't done anything wrong here. I didn't invite Fabienne to dinner. She's a non-issue. I barely acknowledged her when she arrived out of respect for you. I defended you to my mother. Like always, I was by your side when you needed me. And this is how you react? We don't do this, Patience. You know we barely even fight. Whatever you want, whatever you ask of me, I give to you with no questions asked. I'm always the one who folds, apologizes, gives in . . . I can't do it this time. If you still choose not to call me back after this, just know that you've let my mother win. The decision is yours.*

I squeezed my eyelids tight, and tears cascaded down my cheeks. That was where he was wrong. I'd witnessed how Lovelie had molded and manipulated everyone around her: her poor daughter, Daniel, and her husband. Her most recent behavior just proved that despite whatever boundaries I tried to set with her, I'd always fall victim to her ridicule, and there was nothing anyone in that family could do to stop that. So, she may have won the battle, but I clearly dodged my ultimate fear of being another hopeless, lifelong casualty in her war.

I hopped on my exercise bike to see if my girl Jess King could lift my spirits with a virtual thirty-minute R&B cycling class. I was officially single, sexy, and free, and it was time to work on getting summertime fine.

## *Chapter Four*

The large annex of Holy Messiah Fellowship Church was dark and quiet when I entered. I trudged over to the stage and plugged in my wireless speakers. Reality had hit me hard earlier that day. I'd devoted some of my best years to growing my relationship with Daniel and was left with nothing. It was hard to get out of bed, let alone lead a line-dance class, when my heart had been shattered just days before. But life goes on.

My mature group of line dancers—I was forbidden to refer to them as seniors—would be arriving in fifteen minutes. I held our weekly line-dance class come rain, shine, hail, or snow because canceling on them was not an option. So, I checked my vibe in order to keep up with their excitement for life. They loved on me hard and were always trying to get deep into my business. Although I loved every moment of being with them, I wasn't open to receiving advice on my love life, or lack thereof, that evening. I could hear them asking if I'd chased away that "fine, sexual-chocolate nurse-man," and he was the last thing I wanted to think about.

Grabbing a broom, I began sweeping up dust bunnies as I listened to the edited version of Kiana Ledé's "Mad at Me." When Pastor Kenneth Jordan first approached me about getting involved in ministry shortly after I joined Holy Messiah, I wasn't sure how I wanted to serve. I was not a "traditional Christian." I cursed, fornicated, and overindulged in wine on a regular basis, so I didn't want to feel like a hypocrite. As a twenty-two-year-old woman at the time, I wanted to fellowship with members and give back without being analyzed in front of judgey "church folk" eyes. Together, Pastor and I had decided to combine two of my loves—music and the mature generation—to create a recreational activity for some of our members. I'd been teaching weekly line-dance classes at my church for almost five years. The bonus was helping older members of the community stay fit and healthy with a regular exercise regimen.

During my sophomore year in high school, my late grandmother, Pop-Pop's wife, had suffered a mild stroke and eventually had required home health support. Twice a week, I'd stop by their house after school to relieve Pop-Pop so he could run errands or cook dinner. I'd paint her nails, do her hair, and read one of her historical romance novels, which later sparked my love for rom-coms. After we lost her, I began spending time with older adults every chance I got. Simply hanging around them made me feel alive.

Before long, my punctual, seasoned ladies and gents began entering the building, toting long coats, scarves, and Kangols. Just laying eyes on them put a wide smile on my face. I considered them extended family.

"*Hey,*" I sang, clapping my hands to the beat. "How's it hanging tonight, steppers?"

"It's hangin'," Brother Hill replied, bringing his wife a chair so she could change into her tennis shoes.

I turned on his favorite song of the moment, D'Angelo's "When We Get By."

"Aye! That's what I'm talking about," Sister Perkins said as she high-stepped through the door. She was seventy-three years young and as jazzy as they came. I laughed, high-stepping toward her to give her a hug.

Once the full group arrived, on time and turnt, we jumped right into action. I put on "Wobble Baby," our weekly warm-up dance, and the group got live. You would have thought we were at the old-lady nightclub versus an extension of the church building by the way those bodies were movin', poppin', and gyratin'. These definitely were not the same Mother Board members I saw poised in the first few pews behind the deacons each Sunday.

"And one . . . two . . . three . . . four . . . shift to your left leg. One . . . two . . . three . . . four . . . now cha-cha," I called out for a couple of new members over the music as I gazed at my class in the full-length wall mirror of the dance studio. "Yeah, that's it! Get it, y'all."

"Sister Perkins, you sho'll is wobbling that jam. Don't make us have to take you up to the altar for prayer on Sunday," Sister Chancellor panted.

"Or visit her on the sick-and-shut-in list," Brother Lewis quipped.

"Oh no, Matty. You must be referring to my jelly. 'Cause jam sure don't wobble like this!" Sister Perkins joked in return, adding a few extra shakes of her hips for good measure. Then she lost her place in our lineup and cracked up.

"Well, save some of that strawberry jelly for the buttermilk biscuits, chile," someone shouted from the back.

I shook my head, watching the gentlemen avert their eyes. Just like me, they would have to "unsee" all of this when these same ladies were dolled up in their dresses, hats, and lap scarves on Sunday.

Once the music had died down, I took a sip of coconut water and mopped my damp forehead with my hand towel. "Whew! That was a long one. Now, is everyone still interested in learning Ella Mai's 'Trip' next? It's an intermediate dance, so it will prob-ably take the rest of the evening to learn it, then run through it a few times."

"I say let's do it! My grandson's wedding is next month, and I plan to be on the floor all night teaching them a thang or two!"

Sister Perkins marched in place to keep her pulse elevated. "Unless you finally introduce me to that tall, fine grandfather of yours. That yummy snacc can be my date anytime!"

I stifled a laugh. "Sister Perkins, I'm not sure Pop-Pop can handle what you're servin'."

"Sho' caint! And don't you forget it!" She bent over and did her stiff version of twerking.

"Good evening, Pastor!" I yelled out, and she broke her neck trying to straighten back up. "Just kidding."

She clutched her pearls and shouted, "Oh, you're a hater!"

"Now that I have everyone's full attention, we can get started." I selected the mellow song from my line-dance playlist and took my place in front of the room. I began calling out the steps while demonstrating the dance for the group. They studied me in the mirror while swaying to the beat.

"Did that singer say, 'so I don't go shootin' where your heart be?' Oh yeah, I like this gal!" Sister Chancellor yelled.

Once we ran through the whole dance together, Brother Hampton grabbed his wife, Cessily, by the wrist and twirled her around. They fell in sync, gazing into each other's eyes and swaying to the sensual melody. Sister Perkins hooted and waved her arms in the air with her eyes closed, her feet expertly moving in time.

"Get it, Sister Perkins." I winked and said, "I hope your new man is ready for you."

She smiled and returned my gesture, then added an extra cha-cha before she twirled and whipped open her hand fan in one fluid motion.

"All right, don't break a cankle on me, now!" I called out over the music.

Just as I knew they would, my seniors distracted me from my problems as we laughed, twirled, and glided all evening long.

* * *

"Patience!"

I bolted upright, heart racing and chest heaving. The room was dark besides slivers of sunlight peeking through the gap in my drawn curtains. I rubbed my eyes and reached over to the night-stand to feel for my phone.

"Patience! Where are you, girl?"

I jumped, and my arm swung outward, sending the items on my nightstand clattering onto the floor. "I'm in here," I croaked, my voice thick with the remnants of deep sleep. I reached over and turned on my bedside lamp, which was suspended by its cord and teetering on the edge of a small table.

Trice strolled into my bedroom with her hands resting on her wide hips. "Patience Christine Hampton. I know for a fact you are not still lying in bed when we have a freaking flight to catch in two hours!"

I groaned, then rubbed my eyes. I knew I was in deep trouble when she refused to use contractions. "Cool your jets. I packed last night. I just need to brush my teeth and wash my face. My plane outfit's over there." I gestured toward the slider in the corner of the room.

"Ooh, that's nice, girl. You always wear the cutest stuff with your tiny self." She walked over to get a closer look at my tribal-print jumper and matching headwrap. "I knew those old biddies were going to cause you to oversleep! I should have gone with my first mind and given you that wake-up call at five. Making me use my spare key and thangs . . ."

I glanced at my phone and groaned loudly. I'd accidentally set my alarm for five thirty p.m. instead of a.m.

". . . dawgone mailbox is still full. You're going to mess around and make us miss this flight. And you know Gordon's cheap ass will kill us if we have to book another one."

"I know. I know," I said, stretching as I slipped out of bed. "I told you, I'm good. I just need to freshen up right quick. I took a bath right before going to bed."

"Well, get your ass on in there and take your little ho bath, then. Don't forget to hit those pits, tits, and slits! Ha *ha!* Hubby's waiting outside for us. I'll have him put your luggage in the trunk."

"Yes, dear. I'll be out there in a sec." I rolled my eyes and got dressed.

Patrice, who only went by Trice, was my work bestie. Her husband, Landon, always took her to the airport. Now I was a third wheel because Daniel had always been my ride. I let the thought linger as I rushed into the bathroom. While brushing my teeth, I scrolled through email and social media notifications on my phone. I normally preferred a quick yoga session before starting my day, but between oversleeping and my recovery from the last supper, I was off my routine and feeling blah. Broody and moody was the vibe. I deleted the recent voice messages from Daniel that I'd been holding onto to create more space in my mailbox. There was no use in keeping them when I knew things were over between us. His messages further proved that he saw me exactly as his mother had—his personal assistant, whom he "didn't know where he'd be without." He would soon find out "where" because I was closing that chapter of my life. I spat into the sink, then paused mid-brush when I saw a text preview from Princessa.

*Hey, Pae. I hope breaking up with Danny doesn't mean ur breaking up with me. Call me when u have time, sis.*

Tears sprang to my eyes as I stared at her words for a moment. I loved that girl like a second little sister. But I couldn't tell if Daniel had put his sister up to sending the text. As badly as I wanted to reassure her that I would never turn my back on her, I needed more time to process things. Although Daniel had kept his word in that last voicemail message and finally stopped reaching out, I wouldn't put it past him to have his sister contact me. So, I held off on responding. But I was certain of one thing: Daniel and his controlling mother were now in my rearview. Leaving the text message on read, I gathered my things and headed outside.

# Chapter Five

"What?"

Trice leaned in closer. "I said, I'm headed to the bathroom. Come with?"

I wrinkled my nose.

"Girl, bye with your germaphobic ass! I need an escort. We have a pact, remember? No homies left behind while we're out of town."

I rolled my eyes and nodded, then set my drink on the bar top before following her. I was momentarily blinded by the flashing strobe lights, and the baseline from the underground hip-hop music sent vibrations through my stilettos from the cement floor. I wobbled slightly on the toothpick-thin heels before reestablishing my balance. I'd been complaining about the watered-down drinks all night, but the bartender had mixed them a bit stronger than I'd thought. Trice disappeared into a sea of people for a moment, then came back and grabbed my hand, dragging me behind her. Clad in skin-tight midi dresses, all eyes were on us as we fought against the current of oncoming bodies.

Once we neared the restroom, we joined a line of at least fifteen ladies.

Trice turned to me and rolled her eyes. "Girl, you are such a killjoy tonight. What's up with you? When we first found out about this trip, you were excited to finally get a taste of Atlanta nightlife."

*Yeah, it was all good just a week ago.* I nodded. "I'm still excited."

She gave me a side eye before reaching into her strapless bra to retrieve a small pad.

"The hell is that?"

"A nursing pad. My boobs are full, and I need to pump and dump right quick. Follow me."

She passed up the ladies standing in line and headed inside the bathroom. Before I could stop her, she started hand expressing breast milk into the sink as casually as if she were washing her hands.

"Girl, these mamma-jammas were rock hard and throbbing. Shit, we're all ladies here . . . hopefully, and ya girl needs some relief! Anyway, are you finally going to tell me what's going on with you or nah?"

I blinked, staring at her for a moment. So, we were really doing this in this filthy bathroom? Trice gave a whole new look to brand-new breastfeeding moms. I shielded her from onlookers as I quickly broke down the details of the last supper at Daniel's house. I extracted the minor details that would likely get my ride-or-die friend locked up once we touched back down in Cleveland.

"Oh, hell no, P. Just who does his mama think she is?"

"Girl, I don't know. But I'm not with the bullshit. I separated myself from that situation immediately."

"I don't blame you. Does she just want him to marry someone Haitian or something?"

"No, that's not the vibe I got at all. His family just has high standards, and I'm clearly not meeting them—at least where his mama's concerned."

"Why would she think that?"

"Because I'm twenty-six and still don't have my master's

degree, and I haven't advanced in my role at work since starting it several years ago."

"What in the imposter-syndrome bullshit is that? Girl, you're the top performer in our department! You have your own house, a thriving side hustle, and your voice portfolio is amazing. What does Daniel have to say about all this?"

"Thanks, girl." I shrugged. "I wouldn't know, other than the BS he left on my voicemail last week."

She stopped mid-massage and looked at me. "What do you mean 'messages?' Girl. Do not tell me you're giving him the cold shoulder for what his fool mama's been doing!"

I sighed. "Like I said, I've been down this road with them before, and it leads nowhere. She invited another woman to dinner, for God's sake. She's clearly dead set against our relationship. And Daniel's a mama's boy, so even though he may not agree with her behavior, he still hasn't stopped her from treating me like a public enemy. I don't have a snowflake's chance in hell at being happy in that relationship with his mama at the center of his life."

She shook her head, flashing those large eyes on me, lips pursed. "This is *your man* we're talking about, P. If you don't see the relationship going anywhere because of y'all's pre-existing issues and thangs, that's one matter. But I don't believe his mama should be a factor in your choice to stay or leave your own relationship. Don't let that woman drive you away from your happiness."

Trice had no idea that not only had I been poring over my relationship with Daniel for years, but I was also struggling to build a firm foundation out of a mountain of scraps. I just wished people would be more supportive of me seeking my own happiness, regardless of what my choices looked like to them. I recognized my habit of processing my thoughts and feelings internally. So, I took a moment to articulate my feelings to my friend while she rinsed the sink and washed her hands, hoping she would see my point of view.

"Trice, I totally understand where you're coming from, girl.

No one wants to feel like they're being driven out of their own relationship. But that isn't the case here. There's no doubt that I care about Daniel. But between his long hours at work and school and the demands of my job, we've grown much further apart than I wanted to admit to anyone else or even to myself. Yes, we've been together for five years, but it hasn't necessarily been five *good* years. I loved him, but we lacked passion. And love alone can't coast us for another five mediocre years."

Trice sighed, then stared at me for a long moment. I could tell she was struggling with the idea of her "favorite couple" breaking up.

I reached out and took her by the shoulders. "I just need some time to focus on my own dreams. Figure out what I want from life instead of supporting someone else for once. And you don't have to fully understand that to love and support me."

She gave a sober nod and said, "Noted, friend. I'm always here for you." She gave me a firm hug, turned to adjust her bra and boost her boobs, then freshened her lip gloss in the mirror. "Now, are you ready to get that stick out of your ass? Never thought the day would come where I'd welcome that tired shoulder shimmy dance of yours."

I rolled my eyes at my friend while sidestepping a woman who rushed in, holding her mouth and making a hasty beeline for a recently vacated stall.

I decided I would consider taking Daniel's next phone call. Closure always brought an end to old things and, more importantly, the possibility of new beginnings. Regardless of what he had to say, I knew my clarity would come from studying his actions. Screw his pretty little words.

***

As the door quietly clicked closed behind me, I released a long exhale. I had successfully escaped the last workshop on the last day of our training unscathed. With another forty-five minutes of the training remaining, I knew I would make it to the safety of my hotel room before my coworkers—mainly Trice—could coax me into joining them for a night out on our last evening in Atlanta. We had spent the past four days attending an annual marketing convention. Exhausted and far too hangry to wait for room service, I opted to grab a quick bite at the hotel bar, then quietly head up to my room just before the workshop let out.

Wary of the never-ending "conference crud" germs that accompanied events like these, I sprayed the menu with sanitizer and let it dry before picking it up. Then I scanned it for a minute before deciding on angel hair pasta and shrimp and a glass of pear juice and prosecco. Savoring the quiet of the half-empty restaurant, I pulled out my phone to check my email when I saw a notification for a voicemail message from Princessa. Two weeks had passed since the ambush at Daniel's parents' home, and my nerves were still tingling. I knew I owed him some type of closure, but since I was busy attending a conference all week, I hadn't gotten a chance to call him yet.

"Thank you, Hunter," I told the bartender as he placed my steaming meal in front of me. I handed him back the silverware. "May I have a disposable knife and fork?" I wiped the perimeter of the plate with a napkin and grabbed a straw for my wine glass. I couldn't wait to dig in before heading upstairs for a hot shower and falling into bed. I had a 7:30 a.m. debrief before my flight back home. I was all set to eat when I was interrupted by someone speaking to me.

"That looks great."

I grimaced. Who knew three monosyllabic words could irk my entire soul? I paused before spreading my napkin on my lap. I was so focused on ordering my meal and catching up on emails that I hadn't noticed him sitting three seats down from me. After giving him an annoyed side eye, I reluctantly responded with a monosyllable of my own. "Thanks."

Once Hunter handed me the wrapped plasticware, I dug in eagerly.

The chatty stranger let a few moments pass before asking, "Are you attending the marketing conference?"

I hesitated before offering a curt nod, keeping my eyes on my plate and hoping he would get the blatant message that I wanted to be left alone. *Why does this always happen to me? I'm hangry and in no mood for Southern hospitality. Trice warned me this would happen if I opted to venture off among the locals on my own,* I steamed. After a slow sip of wine, I glanced up at the television, my leg jumping below the oak bar ledge. But I still watched him in my peripheral vision.

Seeming to finally take the hint, he stood and downed the rest of his drink before fishing his wallet out of his slacks. "Hunter, put her next glass on my tab and close me out, please."

I shook my head in protest. "Hunter, please don't do that."

"Miss, it's my pleasure."

Figuring he wasn't going to let it go, I decided to just take the drink and thank him. And that was when I got a good look at him. I froze mid-chew as I took him in. My breath caught in my throat for a moment. My eyes swept downward as I continued to give him a full once-over. He was easily the most striking man I'd ever laid eyes on. Dead-ass facts. I wasn't saying he was Kofi Siriboe, but since I'd never laid eyes on that particular chocolate masterpiece up close and personal, I figured it was safe to make that statement.

His brown skin and short dark curls shone under the overhead lights. He assessed me with smoldering dark brown eyes that could melt steel. And that body—cloaked in a light gray suit with a sky blue shirt and matching tie underneath that hugged his athletic frame—was immaculate. His suit jacket casually hung from his arm, and a brown leather shoulder bag crossed his chest like he was fresh off the cover of *Essence: The Sexy Black Men Who Commute Edition.*

I digress; he was *fine,* and although I wondered if he would look as yummy as Kofi fully nude while wearing a grapefruit . . . or two, I still wasn't interested in meeting anyone at that moment.

I recomposed myself and smiled weakly, unable to locate my voice, so I settled for nodding my gratitude before returning my attention to my meal. Thank God for small favors like top-notch poker-face skills because more than half of me was dying to lick my lips, throw back the rest of my wine, and yell, "Eff it! My room is right upstairs." The savory, sweet musk of his cologne hung in the air between us, and I fought to maintain control of myself—fully convinced he would somehow pick up on the cues of my raging internal battle.

I turned to take a slow, deep, composing inhalation. The thin straw in my wine glass met my eager lips, but the damn thing wasn't wide enough to allow me to slurp the remaining contents of my wine like I desperately needed to. I had to do something to stop myself from wondering what his body looked like beneath the freshly pressed clothes he had selected so carefully. Hunter must have picked up on my desperation because he topped me off without a word. Reeling from the thrilling power of what exactly could pop off if I only said the word, I slowly closed my eyes to relish the cool liquid cascading down my throat and attempted to redirect my unrelenting thoughts.

With force, I reminded myself that I was in Atlanta on my company's dime, not for a shameless sexual tryst—because that was all it could be. Besides, my room was adjoined to Trice's, and my other coworkers were a mere floor above us. Trice was cool, but I didn't need the others witnessing me stepping onto an elevator with a strange man and therefore inserting their pointy noses into my personal affairs. They weren't prone to starting rumor mills, but the office was small and full of women, so I wasn't going to supply them with any motivation.

I shoved another forkful of pasta into my mouth. As Hunter ran the gentleman's credit card, we listened to the muted buzz of collective background chatter, our thoughts undoubtedly forging separate paths. But mine ultimately led me right back to the fine specimen less than six feet away like a speeding boomerang. My mind went to the queen-size bed waiting for me upstairs. Cold and empty. Not unlike the empty bed that waited for me back home in Cleveland. I mentally counted the number of weeks since the last time a hard body was on top of mine, or beneath mine, or behind mine . . .

It wasn't until that moment that I realized I had actually lost track. Daniel had been so busy with school and work that our schedules had barely synced up for the weeks leading to the breakup. Had it really been more than a month since I'd last had sex? I groaned inwardly as I caught another peripheral view of him signing the slip of paper and sliding a cash tip across the bar top. *The seconds are winding down, Pae. What are you going to do? Hope and pray he'll say something else to your rude ass in the next five seconds? Highly unlikely. You've already ravaged the man's ego. Make a move; it's now or never,* my thoughts echoed in a frenzied crescendo in my head.

I forced myself to glance over at him, opening my mouth to finally thank him, but I was already watching his fine ass retreating as he casually strolled across the lobby and out of the hotel.

## *Chapter Six*

Grabbing my purse, I said, "Hunter, can you watch my belongings for a minute?" I didn't stick around to catch his response before bolting toward the lobby of the contemporary hotel. I weaved through the sea of people exiting the ballroom at the conclusion of the final seminar, the one I'd just cut short in search of food. *What the hell am I even doing? I should be heading upstairs to avoid this crowd, not charging right into it.*

Keeping my eyes on his retreating back, I pushed my short legs as far as they would go to lessen the distance between Mr. Charisma and me.

"Damn, that man can move," I puffed. *Of course, he's moving fast. You bruised his ego. A man's pride is a powerful drug.* I had no idea what I would say to him once I caught up with him, but something was urging me forward. I needed to keep him from leaving the hotel.

I caught sight of Mr. Charisma on the other side of the sliding doors. He was approaching a Land Rover that was waiting for him at the curb. I broke out in a full sprint, scared half to death of twisting my ankle in my five-inch stilettos. In hindsight, I realize I was undoubtedly propelled by long-ignored raging hormones as I moved like Flo Jo through the thickening crowd.

"Excuse me," I called just as the car's back door was opened for him by a short man wearing a uniform.

They both looked up, and I locked eyes with him.

His handsome face was stunned and curious. "Did I leave something behind?" He patted his pants pockets.

I shook my head, trying not to appear winded, although the impromptu sprint and Southern humidity—it was on a whole 'notha level—had me on the verge of collapse. "No . . . I . . ." I looked up at him and froze once our eyes locked for the second time. Just the sight of him was mesmerizing. It had been a long time since I had interacted with someone so poised, polished, and possessing an easy charm like his. Although I couldn't find another word, he must have read my mind.

"Seth, can you give us a moment?" he asked before leaning in to whisper something else into his driver's ear.

Seth nodded and turned to enter the driver's side of the car. Mr. Charisma extended his arm, ushering me toward a bench resting against the hotel's exterior wall. Then he stood, watching me expectantly. No longer trusting my knees, I took a seat. He followed suit and angled his long, lean body inward, giving me his full attention.

I fumbled with my fingers, still struggling to locate my next words. But my mind was a blank slate, and no words came. I suddenly felt like a desperate fool, running after this strange man. *You're not in a damn rom-com. Who in the world does this?* I thought.

He leaned down to get a better look at my face. "There's something on your mind."

I looked up at him. His eyes were so intriguing, and he actually seemed to care about what was going on with me. So, next, I was blurting out, "I'm reluctant to embrace new relationships . . ."

His brow eased upward, and I immediately regretted my rushed words.

"Not romantically speaking . . . just any new interactions with people I don't know. Opening myself up to even small talk just isn't me—especially after a long week of seminars, meetings, and training, which have left me drained. Nevertheless, I was rude to push you away when you were only attempting to carry on a little small talk. I want to apologize to you for that and thank you for your generosity." Floundering helplessly in my pool of vulnerability, I studied his face for the least bit of empathy.

His expression told me the last thing he expected was a forthcoming confession from me. I squirmed nervously as he took a few moments to process and respond.

"I can appreciate that. But I'm originally from New York City, so I'm pretty used brush-offs. I'm also not easily offended. I appreciate you coming out here to say that. You're all good with me." He gently patted my hand and stood.

Honey, when I say the electricity in that brief physical contact was enough to light up Times Square on New Year's Eve, I tell no lies. My heart soared for a moment without a care, right before it sank. I knew I didn't have anything else to offer him other than an unspoken apology, but I wanted so much more. I sucked at small talk, and although I knew exactly what I wanted from him, I had never pursued a man before. So, I was stuck between watching him walk off and sticking my neck out once again like a damn fool.

"Enjoy the rest of your convention and travel safely." He looked at me once more before slipping into the back of the truck.

Helpless, I watched from the bench as the driver started the engine to pull off. Seconds later, the hotel's revolving door slowly whirled, and a man, whom I quickly recognized as Hunter, walked up and handed the tall dark stranger a receipt through the car's cracked window. That was when I noticed that Hunter was holding my briefcase and a plastic bag.

I stood, puzzled, as he made his way over to me. "Ms. Hampton, Mr. Davenport requested that I close out your bill and box up your food so it wouldn't get cold. I hope it's okay that I also took the liberty of bringing your belongings out here to you, as I didn't know how long you would be gone."

Listening to Hunter, I glanced at the truck, which was still waiting curbside.

*Who in the world is this man?* My eyes rested on the car as my pulse throbbed wildly in my throat. *Why am I drawn to him like this?* I wanted to run to him and jump into that truck without a second thought. But I was in a strange city, and no one knew exactly where I was at that moment. I immediately thought of my no-girl-left-behind pact with Trice. What if something happened to me? She would find me, then kill me her damn self.

As if reading my thoughts, Hunter's eyes lit up. He gave me a subtle nod and a lopsided grin. "Mr. Davenport's in here all the time. He's really a great guy."

I didn't know a damn thing about Hunter's ass, either. I gazed past him as Seth stepped around to the back of the car. Then he stood, patiently waiting as he held open the car door. I offered my trust to those three strange men, and the last of my inhibitions gently blew away with the Southern afternoon breeze. I smiled my thanks to Hunter and took my belongings from him before pressing a cash tip into his palm. Then, on shaky legs, I walked over to the car and slid into the backseat.

The crisp air and butter-soft leather seat cooled my bare thighs. Mr. Charisma's eyes were trained on me, and his full lips pursed slightly as if he were fighting back a smile.

"Hello, again," I said, sweeping a tendril of hair behind my ear.

"Hello. Pleased you were able to join me."

"Yes, me too. Thank you for dinner. That was kind of you. Are you a guest of the hotel?"

He shook his head. "No, ma'am. Just wrapped up an all-day client meeting with my team. Our client is staying here."

"Oh, what do you do?"

"I'm a software engineer."

"That's a good look. We definitely need more minorities and women in the computer science industry."

I waited for him to ask me my name or what I did for a living but instead found myself wiggling under his thoughtful gaze. I asked, "So, are you headed anywhere in particular this evening?"

He turned and gazed out of the window for a moment and I took the opportunity to take in his short curls neatly trimmed into a fresh fade. Then he said, "No, not particularly. Now that you've joined me, do you have any requests?"

I thought for a moment and said, "I've always wanted to see Centennial Olympic Park."

He nodded thoughtfully, his eyes still pointed away from me. "First time in Atlanta?"

Why wasn't he looking at me? Once I realized I was kneading my hands, I rubbed them down the front of my skirt instead. "Yes. I've been stuck in meetings for the majority of my time here. It would be nice to actually get out and see a part of the city— other than clubs and bars—for a bit. That is, if you don't mind being my host for a little while."

When he finally turned to face me, the smirk was gone. That was when I noticed the intensity of his eyes. They were glued to mine, giving me nowhere to escape. I fidgeted a bit as he offered another small smile that I couldn't read.

"No, I wouldn't mind at all. Hey, Seth. You mind swinging us by Centennial for a few?"

"Not at all, Lennox."

*Lennox. Lennox Davenport.* The strength of his name shook something deep within me. It was unique, yet it rolled around in my mind with ease. I was desperate to experience the impression it would have on my tongue when I got the chance to speak it . . . or shout it. I gasped. What in the world was up with me?

His brow lifted, and I realized he'd just asked me something. "Sorry?"

He fought back another smile, and I was clueless about what

he found amusing. "I said, your timing is perfect because we'll be able to catch the sunset."

"Dope. I didn't figure you for a romantic."

He blinked. "How could you figure me for anything? We just met."

"Consider me checked," I said. "We haven't properly met. My name is Patience Hampton."

"Lennox Davenport," he said, extending his large hand to me.

I hesitated before slipping mine between his thumb and long fingers. He gave my hand a firm, brief shake, then a gentle squeeze. His skin was warm and surprisingly soft. I gazed down at his manicured nails. When he finally released my hand, I didn't know what to do with it, so I fingered my hair.

"Nice to meet you, Patience. Your name suits you."

"How could you know what suits me? We just met," I quipped.

His head rolled back slightly on his neck, and that was the only response I got from him. It was my turn to gaze out the window to hide my smile.

After a few moments of tapping on his phone, he broke the silence between us. "So, to further address your previous question, I'm not a guest of your hotel or any hotel, for that matter. I'm actually a new resident of this great city. I moved here from New York when my job transferred me last year."

"Oh." My heart sank. A small part of me was hoping he was attending the conference like me and lived closer to Cleveland. Then I admonished myself for even thinking about him that way, knowing I wasn't in the emotional state to entertain a new relationship. "That's quite a transfer. May I ask what you're currently working on?"

He nodded. "My company just acquired a smaller software company based here in Atlanta, so we're doing some troubleshooting and training staff. It was a bit of a culture shock for me. The sales process is definitely slower-paced, and there's a lot more relationship-building involved than with my New York clients. But I welcomed the opportunity and came here with an open mind. I've had a great time immersing myself in the history and customs here. Learning as much as I can while I can."

*A man of very few words . . . until you get him talking about something he's passionate about,* I noted. "Oh, so it looks like I chose the perfect tour guide. Or, rather, he chose me."

He pursed his lips thoughtfully.

"I must admit, I'm quite jealous of your recent transplant. I was born and raised in Cleveland, and although I attended college out of state and have done some traveling, I've always called Cleveland my only home."

He frowned. *Damn.* Each new expression of his stimulated something in me.

"I don't see anything wrong with that. Unless you've been outright denying yourself the pleasure of living elsewhere. What's kept you there all this time?"

I shrugged. "Mostly family. Friends . . ." *Complacency.*

It was his turn to shrug as if to say, *You like it, I love it.*

I avoided eye contact with him, quickly losing myself in the metropolitan scenery as we traveled northwest on Luckie toward Peachtree. We inched closer to our destination in the early evening traffic, and my thoughts consumed me. Shame consumed me, prickling my skin. He hadn't done anything to make me feel that way, but my own realization that I didn't have much to share with him regarding my career goals made me a bit insecure.

Compared with his ambition, I was embarrassed by my own lack of drive regarding my professional goals for the first time. There was a new job posted at my company, and I'd thrown my hat into the ring. But I was up against some steep competition from associates on the West Coast, so I didn't plan to lift my hopes up. I'd been so busy supporting Daniel for the past five years that I'd put my own professional aspirations on the back burner. Here Lennox was, living nearly a thousand miles away from his home, enjoying this beautiful city while I was wasting away at the same job for several years. It wasn't until that moment that I felt unfulfilled and . . . lonely.

My cheeks grew hot, and my pulse thumped in my ears as a montage of my dry-ass life flashed before my eyes, knowing I only had my own personal choices to blame for it all.

After a few minutes, I turned to him and asked, "How far are we from the park?"

He looked up from his phone and gazed out the window. "Probably about half a mile."

"I need to get out of this car. Let's walk the rest of the way."

Without hesitation, he said, "Okay, let's go."

# Chapter Seven

Once Seth pulled over to the curb, we hopped out of the car and headed back out into the humidity. I took a deep breath, filling my lungs with fresh air, and was immediately feeling better. I'd spent enough time cooped up indoors and was ready to experience what the city had to offer. Together, we set off toward our destination on foot. As we laughed and talked, I secretly took him in. With his hands in his pockets, he strolled down the busy sidewalk, fully comfortable in his own skin, not overconfident, just well aware of who he was. I listened intently as he talked about all of the cities he had lived in before Atlanta. He had a magnetic nature about him, and I immediately vibed with everything that fell from his lips.

"I have family all over, so I lived in Charlotte for almost a year, stayed in Houston for a bit, and even spent a few summers in LA and Cleveland with my relatives throughout high school and after graduating college."

"Do you have any favorite cities?"

"Probably Phoenix and San Diego. Every place is so different. I like visiting places where I know people so I can avoid the tourist spots. I want to see the places that make the city feel authentic. Later for the commercial stuff."

I just smiled.

After a few moments, he looked over at me and frowned. "What?"

"Oh, don't think I didn't catch that look you gave me earlier when I mentioned Centennial Park. That was light shade. You probably think I'm only interested in the tourist traps."

He kept his eyes ahead as we stopped at a crosswalk. "I never said that."

"You didn't have to."

He pursed those full lips yet again, and I imagined palming his head and planting a wet kiss on them. "Okay. You got me. I gave you a low-key side eye for that one."

"Try a high-key one."

He nodded and smirked again. "Okay, I see you've got a little sense of humor under that tough-guy exterior."

I smiled and proceeded as the walk signal illuminated. "Pop-Pop, my grandfather, attended the Olympics here in ninety-six. I remember how excited he was about witnessing Michael Johnson compete in the two-hundred-meter dash. He was the first and only person in our family to attend an Olympic event. Needless to say, I've been hearing stories about that experience since I was a little girl. It meant a lot to him to be a part of it all, so I just wanted to see it for myself."

After a few long moments, I looked over at him, unsure if he had heard a word I had said. His eyes were unfocused, and he seemed deep in thought.

"That's pretty dope," he finally said. "Is your grandfather still alive?"

I smiled. "Yes, very much so. I was hoping to get some pictures and text them to him."

He nodded as his long legs led him down the street. He caught me watching him and asked if I wanted to slow down. It was then that I realized I hadn't done a good job of concealing the struggle of pushing my short legs to keep up with his long ones. I was thankful that I'd changed into the flats I kept in my purse before we hopped out of the car, but I was still winded from the walk. I agreed that slowing down may have been for the best, and that was when he finally flashed a genuine smile. Not a smirk or a half grin. I caught sight of his right dimple, and good God, was it beautiful. He offered me his arm as we rounded the corner and entered the park.

The first thing I saw was the Olympic Ring Fountain. The dancing spring water glistened in the afternoon sun as music played on the loudspeakers. I was immediately sucked in to the park's upbeat energy. Young children laughed and chased each other as the water sporadically rose and retreated back into the rings in the ground. I looked up and saw the area was surrounded by international flags, and I tried to envision how it had looked back in 1996 at the Olympic games. The park was much larger than I had expected, heavily shaped by history and culture. As I gazed around in wonder, I noticed it was decorated with statues and monumental structures of all heights and sizes.

After a few minutes of spectating, Lennox asked, "Do you want to go over to the reflective pool?"

"Please."

We walked over to a large pool structure with embedded areas built in for sitting. We sat and looked out at the water for a few minutes, and it felt like I was sitting in the rippling water. I sighed.

Lennox chuckled. "Taking it all in?"

A gentle breeze ruffled my hair. "This place far exceeds my expectations. I love it here."

"I'm guessing this isn't your coworkers' idea of a fun evening."

"Not at all. I'm the only introvert in the group, and I'm often outvoted regarding our daily plans. So, it's been clubs, bars, and noisy restaurants all week. But this . . ." I gestured around us. "Experiences like this are what I live for."

He nodded, looking out at the water. "Same."

After a few minutes of quiet thinking, I turned to him and

said, "It's good to spend time with someone who's comfortable with silence."

He lifted a brow.

"I've been working and traveling with all women for the past four days, attending long workshops, eating out, and partying. All that involves a lot of damn talking. I'm . . ."

"Mentally and emotionally exhausted?"

I sighed again and closed my eyes for a moment. "You get me."

"It often seems like we're living in a world full of people who love to talk and are uncomfortable with silence. But you just have to find your people. We're out here."

"Exactly. I mean, I try not to be off-putting, but by the time I'm done with a full day's work, I just want a glass of wine, a book, and a warm bed."

Lennox nodded. "That's one of the perks of living alone. I get plenty of time to decompress."

"Do you consider yourself an introvert?"

He shook his head. "More like an ambivert. I'm energized by interacting with people, but I also highly value my time alone."

"I can respect that."

"How about we rent scooters and check out the rest of the park?"

"Scooters? What? Yes, that sounds amazing."

"Y'all don't have scooters in Cleveland?" he asked, offering his hand to help me stand.

"We have them downtown and throughout the metropolitan areas, but I don't usually spend a ton of time in those places. So, I'm ready to get the full 'tourist experience.'"

"I see you're not going to let me live that comment down." He smiled, shaking his head.

"Yeah, you can forget that."

We walked back toward the Olympic Ring Fountain and found two scooters. I offered to rent them, but Lennox refused. It took me a moment to get my bearings and my balance while riding a motorized scooter in a pencil skirt, but I was good after a few minutes. I followed his lead, and it seemed like we were headed out of the park for a moment. Then I looked up and saw the colorful life-size Olympic ring display. I smiled so wide my face hurt.

"Wow."

We set our scooters down, and Lennox held out his hand for my phone. Once a group of young guys finished taking pictures of each other, it was my turn. I stepped inside of the bottom ring and posed, smiling a mile wide. Lennox snapped, and I changed positions until he gave me a thumbs up.

"I think you'll like these."

I smiled as I swiped through and sent one to my grandfather. His response was immediate.

Pop-Pop: Yessss! 😜

I showed his text to Lennox, and he chuckled. "My mom uses emojis all the time. Hilarious."

"Just imagine how funny it is coming from my grandfather."

I wanted to see more of the statues and monuments, so we hopped back on the scooters to continue our tour of the park. Lennox was about ten feet ahead of me, but I was taking my time, soaking in the experience. The last time I was on a motorized scooter was at least ten years prior, and I was focusing on looking cute in case he glanced back at me. Just as I was about to speed up to close the gap a bit, I mistakenly hit the brake instead. The abrupt stop made me lurch forward, and I loosened my grip on the handlebars. I let out a pitiful little yelp as my right foot hit the pavement and dragged behind me on the concrete. As my body rolled to the right, I angled the scooter into the grass to prepare for a soft landing. The crash felt like it was happening in slow motion. I tried my hardest to avoid pulling the scooter down on top of me, squeezing my bare legs together beneath my skirt to hide my hoo-ha. All of this happened while praying to God that Lennox wasn't watching this gross humiliation unfold in real time. I landed onto the surprisingly hard grass and bounced twice, nipping my tongue as my teeth gnashed in anticipation of the impact.

When I opened my eyes a few seconds later, a tall blonde and her toddler son were standing over me, peering down with genuine interest.

"Oh, you poor thing. Let me help." She held her son's hand and extended the other to me.

I gratefully took it and slowly rose to my feet, brushing loose grass from my clothing.

"They just mowed the lawn," the woman said, reaching down to pluck several tufts of grass from my hair.

*Yep. Just my luck,* I thought, horrified, scanning the perimeter for Lennox.

When my eyes landed on him, he was still standing on his scooter a few feet away, his jaw loose and slightly agape. His brow was scrunched up, and it was hard to read his expression.

I thanked the woman and assured her I was fine before remounting my scooter and heading toward him. His mouth was still open, and his brows almost reached his hairline. I started to scold him for not coming over to help me up, but I realized he'd obviously been too shocked to move an inch.

"Are you good?" he asked, giving me a visual once-over when I approached him.

"Yeah." I sighed. "Just a bit of a user error back there. But I'm fine to keep going."

"Okay, good."

"Fine."

When he didn't make an effort to move, I stared up at him. As soon as our eyes met, his softened and twinkled. He reached down and pulled a blade of grass from inside my ear. Then his lips began to quiver, and I knew what it was. I glanced away sheepishly as he chuckled. At least he had waited until he had confirmed I was okay to do it. Hell, I wouldn't have even blamed him if he hadn't. It was exactly what I got for trying to be sexy in a skirt on a scooter for a stranger.

When I glanced back at him, I saw a tear escape the corner of his eye. I realized it was the first time I had heard him laugh. His entire face morphed into a carefree version of the mysterious, contemplative man I was getting to know, and I loved each second of it. I couldn't help but join him, even though it was at my expense. Seeing his softer side sent my heart leaping in my chest, and my stomach fluttered with intrigue and curiosity. Then I froze, fighting the urge to stick my pinky into his dimple as I stared at him. When he looked at me, realizing I was studying him, he paused, and his tongue darted over his lips. Time slowed, and I wasn't sure how long we stood there looking at each other in the middle of the walkway while others walked around us. But something definitely shifted between us, and we both knew it.

## *Chapter Eight*

Thirty minutes later, we called Seth to meet us. As we walked back to the truck, we fell deeper into conversation. Before my fall, he was a man of few words, so the weight of each of them penetrated me deeply. But now that the ice was broken between us, we were both feeling a bit more comfortable around each other. I was surprised by the raw feelings he stirred within me. I knew he was probably a textbook rebound case for me, and that part of the comfort and enamor I felt was likely due to the fact that I would never see him again. For that reason, I had no issue opening up and sharing some of my life goals with him. I was pleasantly surprised to find out about the similar things we both wanted for our lives. Our synergy was instant and electric, and I had never experienced an organic connection of such intensity with anyone.

By the time we pulled back up to the hotel, I was mentally spent, but in a good way, for the first time that week. I no longer recognized the type of thoughts I was having about him. The clock was winding down. My suppressed primal desires took a front seat and were demanding my attention. While we sat in the idling car, he studied my face for prolonged moments. My skin tingled as his brown eyes drank in each inch of me. The hunger in them was undeniable, and his lips spread into an easy smile as he seemed to pick up on my silent, reciprocated signal. Or maybe he sensed the pheromones shooting off of me like fireworks.

He finally spoke. "I had fun with you tonight, Patience."

I nodded and returned his smile. "So did I. Thanks for sharing your time and resources to show me a little piece of Atlanta."

"It was my pleasure. And I don't believe for a minute that you have trouble opening up to people. Our conversation was one of the best ones I've had in a while."

Every cell in my body ignited as blood rushed to my cheeks. I wanted to scream, *Boy, you're as far from "people" as a man could get!* I nodded again and replied, "Same."

He reached for my hand and held it firmly in his grip. His voice deepened. "I'm not gon' cap. I don't want our evening to end."

My mouth opened, and I paused, unsure of how to respond. Did he just utter those words with the sexiest Brooklyn accent I've ever heard, or had I imagined it? I'd never had a one-night stand before, but there wasn't a shadow of doubt in my mind that I needed to experience being with Lennox Davenport intimately before boarding a plane to Cleveland in the morning. I ran down a quick mental checklist: When was the last time I had ladyscaped? Did my bra and panties match? Did I leave my vibrator out on the nightstand this morning?

"How does your leg feel?"

"Oh, it feels fine. Thank you."

"Good. Do you like to dance?"

I blinked, then frowned before repeating, "Did you say dance?"

He nodded, still holding my hand in his. I pictured myself sharing a dance floor with Lennox all night, and I knew there was no way we would make it past the first song. My palm began to perspire, but he didn't seem bothered by it.

"Umm . . ."

"My colleague teaches a salsa class every Friday night, and

she's been inviting me for weeks. I've never taken her up on it because I don't have a partner. It starts in a couple of hours. I know it's last minute, but her studio isn't very far from here. Thoughts?"

Salsa? He was really reaching. I had multiple reasons to decline. First, he had just witnessed my ass falling off a scooter in a pencil skirt. Second, even though I loved to dance, I had never tried my hand at salsa. So, there was no way in hell I was going to attempt a sensual dance like that for the first time with him and risk embarrassing myself again in front of his fine self. I shook my head, but before I could protest, he hopped out of the car. I looked up to see him heading over to open my door for me. I grabbed my belongings and eased out.

"Why don't you head up to your room and change while I wait for you here in the lobby?" he suggested as we entered the hotel.

Terrified, I turned to him and placed a gentle hand on his chest. "Lennox, I'm sorry to disappoint you, but I'm not up for learning salsa tonight. It's been a very long week of training, and I'm dog tired."

He nodded, and his tongue slid over his lips. I watched it slip back into his mouth in what seemed like slow motion.

"I completely understand. I'm getting way ahead of myself, and I don't want to come off as too forward. Like I said, I just don't want our time together to end. But I respect your boundaries. I'm grateful for the experience of getting to know you a little better. Have a restful evening and safe travels back to Cleveland." He lifted my hand, grazed it with his soft lips, then squeezed it before releasing it.

He had said all that, and I still couldn't stop staring at his mouth. His lips felt good on my skin, and my yoni was raging with a pulsing heat so intense that it took all I had not to glance down to see if she was smoking beneath my skirt. Then that inner voice started in on me. *This is it, girl. After tonight, you will never see this chocolate-coated Adonis again!*

"Give me thirty minutes," I said before turning on my heel and making a beeline for the elevator.

After scrambling to gather the perfect outfit in a sweaty frenzy, I quickly groomed my lady parts, jumped into the shower to get off that sweat and outside smell, applied fresh makeup, and got dressed. My phone was going crazy, and I knew it was Trice. I'd just have to respond to her later. When I stepped off the elevator twenty-nine minutes later, each step felt like I was being hoisted up by cumulus clouds. I couldn't help grinning as my eyes scanned the lobby for him. When I finally spotted him, I saw that he was standing by a loveseat, gripping a bouquet of fresh red roses. His lips parted, but he said nothing as I walked up, giving him glowing goddess vibes. I'd plucked the remaining grass blades from my hair and swept it up into a loose bun, and a single stone hung from my necklace and matching earrings. My red high-low maxi dress hugged my hips a little tighter than usual since I'd thickened up a bit over the past few days while eating Southern cuisine on my company's dime. My outfit was finished off with strappy silver stilettos.

Mom always said to pack at least one sexy outfit while traveling because you never know who you might meet. I was sending her a virtual hug at that moment because Lennox looked like he was fighting to keep his cool in that hotel lobby as he took me in. He closed his mouth and ran his hand over his chin. I noticed his Adam's apple bob as he swallowed. Hard. Without a word, he took my hand and led me back to the truck, waving Seth off as he opened my car door himself.

I stepped in and was about to tease him about forgetting to hand me my flowers, but when he slid into the car, his rigid body language gave me pause. Homeboy was fighting a serious battle within himself, and I honestly felt sorry for him. I was fighting the same battle, but as a woman, I made it nearly impossible for him to tell. After taking a few moments to regain his composure, he looked over at me and offered a weak smile before giving Seth an address.

As we pulled away from the curb, I gazed out of the window, reluctant to make eye contact. The only sound was the crinkling cellophane of the bouquet that sat between us on the seat as the rising sexual tension in the car nearly suffocated me. I crossed my legs, then uncrossed them, and cracked the window, keeping my eyes pointed at the passing buildings until I heard my name.

"Patience, I apologize for not commending you on how beautiful you look. I guess I wasn't expecting you to emerge from that elevator looking like a gift from the gods. You looked great before, but you worked some serious magic in that half hour. Damn," he said, finally picking up the flowers and handing them to me. "These are for you."

I smiled and smelled them before saying, "Thank you, Lennox. I appreciate your kind words."

"We have a little time to kill before class. Would you like to stop for a quick bite to eat? I owe you for interrupting your dinner, and I could use a little liquid courage."

I nodded. "That sounds good. Do you mind putting the restaurant's address in my maps app? I just want to send my location to my coworker. She's been blowing me up and since I've been gone for hours without checking in . . ."

He smiled at me, and it easily reached his warm eyes. "You don't want her to get too worried about you. Sure, no problem. It's great having people who care about us."

"Most def."

As he tapped away on my screen, I asked, "So, liquid courage, huh? You sayin' you're not an expert salsa dancer?"

He laughed. "Nothing of the sort. In fact, I started to warn you not to wear peep toes because of these three left feet."

I would be lying if I didn't say I was thrown off by his response. His demeanor was silky smooth, so I just assumed he had the moves to go with it.

"Don't worry about that. We're just enjoying getting to know each other."

"Precisely." He winked and flashed a sexy grin as he handed me my phone. "But don't say I didn't warn you."

I swooned as I sent Trice a quick text.

Me: Met someone. Drinks, then dancing. Text you later.

My phone buzzed almost instantly.

Trice: Finally, a response from this broad! Ugh! I just wanted to see if you were still alive. Send me his first and last name and sneak a pic if you can.

I sent her the info she requested, sans picture.

At the restaurant, there was a forty-five-minute wait for a table, so we sat at the bar. Our appetizers arrived quickly, and Lennox ordered us a couple of Tito's with Sprite. When the bartender set them down, I sprayed my hands with sanitizer and removed the straws from our drinks. Then I replaced them with new straws.

Lennox watched me, then raised a brow. "What are you doing?"

"He cashed someone out, then didn't wash his hands before fixing our drinks and grabbing our straws."

His brow didn't lower. "Germophobe?"

"I don't like labels."

He laughed and said, "Okay, introvert."

"Okay, so I do allow some labels. Since you wanna judge me, tell me about some of your quirky habits or pet peeves."

He took a sip of his cocktail before asking, "Where do I begin?"

I laughed.

"How about we start with yours so I don't give you any inaccurate labels?"

I shrugged, squirting sanitizer onto his hand when the food arrived. "I don't know about quirks, but I have a pretty long list of pet peeves. But, at the top are people who don't respect my personal space, spit when they talk, and chew with their mouths open."

He chuckled, shook his head, then bit into a cheeseburger slider.

When he didn't say anything else, I asked, "Why are you shaking your head?"

"Noticing a pattern. They all confirm that you're a germophobe *and* antisocial."

I nodded. "All facts, but watch it. I don't like how you're trying to make me feel like I'm a stick in the mud or something."

"I can't make you feel like anything. That's an inside job."

"Well, I know how to have a good time." I huffed. "Wanna hear a joke?"

"Lay it on me."

"In a minute, but first, do you remember when I told you the one about my minor spinal cord injury?"

"What? And you just fell on your back at the park. No, I think I would have remembered that. When?"

I smirked and said, "About a weak back."

A few moments passed, then he stopped mid-chew, and I watched his eyebrows knit. After he swallowed his food he said, "Now *that* was the funniest joke I've heard in a minute."

"You need funnier friends," I said, dipping a piece of calamari in aioli. "Now, tell me about your hang-ups."

"I'm pretty laid back, so I don't have many pet peeves. As far as quirks, living alone for so long has made me particular about my household. My boys always give me a hard time when I make them take their shoes off at the door. I also don't wear street clothes around my house at all."

"I'm with you. Neither do I. Does that mean you also walk around nude?" That Tito's had me feeling bold tonight.

"If the mood hits. But I mostly wear sweats or pajama pants."

Now, that vision was one for my spank bank. *Ask a question and you'll get an answer,* Pop-Pop's voice rang in my head. And boy was I unprepared for that one. I held onto a shallow breath for a beat before responding.

"That's a reach. It's like listing a subtle strength when you're asked about your flaws in a job interview. Dig deeper, *Lennox.*"

He smiled. "Okay, *Patience.* I no longer pursue a woman if she talks shit about her ex or child's father during the first couple of times we interact."

"And why's that? Are you a shitty ex or baby's father?"

"Not at all. And I'm not saying there aren't shitty ones out there. I just like to focus on getting to know one another first before bringing up past relationships. Let me form my own opinions. Also, there's a way to approach every unfavorable part of our lives. But we have to own our role in what happens to us. So, badmouthing the person you chose to love or have children with to a total stranger just gives red flags for me."

I held my right hand up and said, "Preach."

"So, it's my turn to ask a question. What really made you come after me like that today? No funny shit."

Caught off guard by the direct nature of his question, I cleared my throat, then immediately reached for my own liquid courage. I had a feeling he'd ask about my motivation for pursuing him at some point, but I still wasn't ready to answer his question.

# Chapter Nine

fter a few long swallows, I turned to face him. "Initially, I came out there just to apologize for being rude. Like I said, I didn't have a real reason to shut you down like that. But, afterward, I realized I wanted . . . to get to know you better. I won't front. I believe there was undeniable chemistry between us from the start."

He offered a slight nod while intently holding my gaze.

As I gazed at him, I realized that locking eyes with Lennox was one of the most intimate experiences I'd had in a long time. I noticed that his eyes weren't dark like I had initially suspected. They were light brown with flecks of green, which popped against his mahogany skin.

I took a breath, then continued, "You know I have to leave in the morning, so I figured after spending all week focusing on work, I would spend my last evening here focusing on myself, my desires, and my . . ."

He continued to look right through me. "Personal needs," he offered, his voice thickened.

I glanced away, reaching for a piece of fried calamari. This was too much. I felt like he could see my soul. "You could say that."

He glanced at his watch and pulled out his credit card. "Let me text Seth to pull the car around. We need to leave out in about five minutes to get to the studio on time with traffic."

Less than twenty minutes later, we were walking into a contemporary loft on the upper level of an office building. I could hear the lively music in the stairwell, and it immediately pulled me in, spurring my inward shoulder shimmy. I pulled out my cell, opened the Shazam app, and learned the song was called "Cali Pachanguero" by Grupo Niche.

We stepped into the large studio adorned with shiny hard-wood floors, bright studio lights, and framed photos of salsa dancers—or at least convincing models in salsa attire. As we walked farther into the open space, an oil painting clad in bold colors caught my eye, and I paused to study it for a bit longer than the others. The muse was wearing a low-back red dress with her long, black hair pinned up into a messy bun. A red flower was tucked into her hair, and her left hip jutted out, showcasing her long leg through the side slit of her dress.

"Only thing missing is the flower," Lennox said, slipping behind me and pushing one of the short-stemmed roses he'd given me into my hair.

His hot breath left a misty imprint on the nape of my neck, and I suppressed an inward whimper. *What in the world is this man trying to do to me?*

I squeezed my eyes shut and took a long deep breath. "Thank you. She's striking."

"She can't hold a candle to you. Not even on her best day and your worst."

I turned to face him, and although we were standing amidst a sea of buzzing twenty and thirty-somethings, my eyes were fixed on him. His long, lean body was clad in a starched, white dress shirt and black pinstripe slacks. His smooth skin glowed beneath the overhead lights, and his brown eyes pierced me, silently daring me to doubt my feelings for him at that moment. Despite the vibrant, colorful music, my ears only noted his slow, even breath-ing, contrasting the rapid pace of my quickening heartbeat.

After a few moments, he cleared his throat and asked, "Shall we?"

Not trusting my voice, I bit my lip and nodded. He took my hand and led me farther into the studio. He introduced me to his colleague, Juliana, and all I could muster was a friendly smile, a finger wave, and a breathy greeting.

"So glad you could make it, Lennox! So nice to meet you, Patience. Your hair is beautiful!"

"Thank you," I said, "and I'm excited to be here."

After a few moments, Juliana called the class to attention, and we all assembled around her on the dance floor.

"I want to thank you all for joining us for another introductory salsa class this evening. I see some new faces, and although I won't call them out, please know that some of our more tenured dancers will step in and switch partners in order to expose you to a variety of styles throughout the evening. We're going to start out with a basic warm-up exercise, then we'll get into the instruction portion of the evening. Any requests?"

"Valió La Pena!" a lady with a dark brown angular bob, mini skirt, and legs that went on for days called out.

The crowd cheered, and Juliana replied, "You've got it, Carine."

Seconds later, the lively tune filled the room, and the dancers responded with trills and catcalls. I looked around self-consciously until I felt Lennox's hand on mine. I glanced at him and smiled just as Juliana took her place at the front of the room. Looking at all of us in the mirror, she began twisting her hips and stretching her arms out at her sides. We began stretching and doing some basic moves. I felt my nerves unwind a little and was grateful for the carefree nature of the group. It didn't feel like we were being watched or analyzed. Everyone seemed to be there to unwind and have a great time kicking off their evening.

"Now, it's time to begin a basic partners' exercise. Our beginners will start off with an open hold, and our intermediates will start with crossed holds. Advancers, feel free to start with a closed or crossed hold, whichever you prefer."

Lennox and I exchanged confused looks, and I assumed he was as unfamiliar with the terms as I was.

Juliana approached us and took Lennox's hand. "Lennox, you are going to lead Patience with a four-count step. But it will be three steps with a pause on the fourth. Forward three, backward three like this. Step forward and shift your weight forward on your left foot. Lift up on your right foot slightly, then bring your left foot back. Once your feet are back together, you will step backward with your right foot like this. Concentrate on your hip movement . . . Yes, that's it."

I watched him mirror her movements and was impressed by how quickly he picked them up. Then I studied Juliana's exotic hip and arm movements and wondered how mine would compare. While I watched them, a tall older gentleman with hazel eyes, salt-and-pepper hair, and a thick mustache walked up to me and took my hands without so much as a greeting. I started to say, "Excuse you," for invading my space, but before I could protest, he was taking a sideways step, pulling me along with him.

We stepped three to the right, then three to the left, and before I knew it, he was twirling and dipping me. I didn't know whether to haul off and slap him or thank him once I realized I was having the time of my life. He grinned at me and twirled me around again before delivering me to the next guy, who was short, diesel, and much younger. After dancing with him briefly, I realized he wasn't as experienced as my first partner. But he had some moves, and his cologne smelled great on him. He delivered me to Lennox almost five minutes later.

Standing beside each other, we fought to catch our breath in the brief pause between songs. But once an upbeat, romantic song called "Me Liberé" by El Gran Combo De Puerto Rico came on, I forgot all about my throbbing feet and the fraying edges of my silk press. Upon the opening trumpets and harmonizing male chorus, my body came alive.

As Juliana brushed past us, she leaned in, gave me a wink, and smiled as she said, "I believe, after tonight, this will be a song you two will never forget."

By then, I was grateful to find myself back in the arms of my handsome date. We faced each other, and he put his right hand on my hip. I placed my left hand on his right shoulder, and we began taking short, measured strides in time with the music. We were a bit shaky at first, still getting a feel for each other's rhythm and clumsily navigating our electric physical effect on one another. But the easiness of the spirited music, the laughter of the other enthusiastic dancers surrounding us, and the mounting sexual tension between us created the perfect storm.

By the time we reached the middle of the song, I rolled my shoulders, undulated my hips, and maintained deep eye contact with him as if my life depended on it. I swayed my hips rhythmically and kept asking myself, *Who the hell is this dude, and who in the world am I?* Judging from the way our bodies synchronized, any bystander would have assumed we'd been attending classes for weeks. His lips parted, and his hand slid lower and lower as the male chorus chanted, "Me liberé, me liberé. Me liberé, me liberé!"

Good Lord, I'd *never* felt so free.

My body loosened, and I arched my back to make my ass jiggle as I kept up with his tempo to the Latin rhythm with ease. Our bodies drew closer, filling the respectful gap we'd originally placed between us. He gripped my ass as I pressed my hips against him. I thought I felt a subtle poke from him right before he spun me out for a double twirl. When he pulled me back in to him, we strayed off course and began a custom slow grind. His hand caressed my backside as I gently wedged my short leg between his long ones. Yep, that was definitely a love tap I'd felt a second before, and I was serving him an open invitation to tap anything else he wanted . . . however he wanted. A trickle of sweat trailed the side of my neck before sloping between my breasts, but something told me that wasn't his focus as he stared at my bust.

He licked his lips and released a tortured groan. The brief

song concluded with a strong trumpet finish, and reality hit. I clamped my eyes in embarrassment.

"They're all watching us, aren't they?"

There was a momentary pause before his baritone filled my ear. "Yeah."

As the room erupted with applause and Juliana praised our efforts, I opened my eyes and gave a quick finger wave, then left the small studio in search of water. But when I spotted the table of refreshments, I rushed past it, opting for the bathroom. I locked the door and immediately stepped out of my soaked panties, wrapped them in a paper towel, and shoved them deep into my crossbody. Next, I wet another paper towel with cool water and mopped my neck and chest while exhaling loudly. I brushed more powder foundation onto my shiny forehead before freshening my lipstick and popping in a piece of gum. I wasn't sure how much time was left in the class, but in the words of Wanda from *In Living Color* reruns, I was "ret' to go." He was reading me like a got-damn *Dick and Jane* book, and I no longer possessed the strength to pretend like his pheromones weren't driving me insane. The whole evening was beginning to feel like self-torture, and I wasn't here for that—not for a moment longer.

Whatever was about to go down would occur with no resistance from me. And I was ready to willingly head in whichever direction he felt compelled to lead me. The ball was in his court, and I hoped he was feeling like Jordan because the clock was running down. I hoped against hope that he was ready to sacrifice a full night's sleep.

*Chapter Ten*

We stepped off the elevator, and the walk down the hallway to my suite seemed to last forever. But once my hotel door unlatched, we stumbled into the room, our collective weight causing the door to slam backward into the wall behind us. My eyes were clenched shut as his tongue caressed mine. Barely able to catch my breath and panting heavily and hungrily into his open mouth, I moaned openly, which seemed to spur him on. He gripped my ass so hard, I had no idea how I would manage to sit for a ninety-minute flight home the next day. One of my legs snaked around his back so he half walked, half dragged me through the dark room toward my bed.

When he broke the kiss and laid me down, my lips throbbed, swollen and pulsing. Both sets. I watched his silhouette in the moonlight as he gazed down at me and slowly unbuttoned his shirt. My composure was wearing away fast, and I fought with every ounce of my strength to keep from leaping off that bed and yanking the shirt from his back my damn self. Instead, I lifted my hips, pretending to slide off panties that weren't there. Hell, I didn't want to be judged for having long abandoned those bad boys, and I figured he couldn't see in the dark that they were long gone. Just as I was about to make a show of kicking them to the side, I felt his hand stop me.

I blinked. What now? I had endured every painstaking moment of the salsa class. I squeezed my thighs in anticipation while he stuck around to say goodnight to Juliana and offered to help her put up tables and chairs. This freaking gentleman. She declined, much to my relief. I had endured the tense, silent limousine ride while he rubbed light circles on my forearm with his long fingers. I'd played coy during the conversation in the hotel parking lot while we tried to determine if we should call it a night due to my early morning flight. I had patiently waited for him to make a move in the elevator after a young couple finally stepped off three floors before mine. But the moment his soft lips brushed against mine, something deep inside of me had snapped, and the floodgates burst at their seams like an IDGAF bomb had been skillfully detonated. So, his halting hand, at that moment, was about to be skillfully separated from the rest of his body if he wasn't careful.

"Patience." His throaty voice was coated with lust. "Are you sure you want to—"

I jumped up and mounted him mid-air, planting my hands on either side of his face. "Lennox, I understand you're trying to be a gentleman here. And any other time, or in any other situation, I would fully appreciate that because I'm a lady. But I don't know how else to show you that you have the green light from me. What in the world's stopping you?"

He stood quietly for a moment, and my mind raced as he gently set me back onto the bed and headed toward the door without a word. My face fell with disappointment, and I began thinking about how crazy I'd just sounded. I wished I would have just been real with him and let him know I hadn't felt this level of desire for someone in a very long time. I should have told him that, for once, I was finally choosing to allow myself some satisfaction by making love to him all night long. I should have let him know that our evening together had been the best time I'd had in years and that I was honestly considering canceling my morning flight just to spend the weekend with him.

But as I watched him take step after step, I knew I'd ruined everything. I knew it would be yet another night of nursing blue walls that even my vibrator couldn't satisfy. Story of my damn life. But my stubborn pride kept me muzzled. Once he reached the door, I squinted as white light flooded the room.

He turned to face me and said, "Well, if we're going to do this, I need to witness every moment of it."

I bit my lip, watching him like a hawk as he strode back over to the bed, his smooth chest peeking through the opening of his shirt. His eyes were on mine, and if I hadn't already snatched those suckers off, my lacy undergarments would have been drenched all over again.

Once he finally stood in front of me, he reached down and slowly twirled a loose tendril of my hair around his forefinger. Chest heaving, I took in the sumptuous feast standing before my eager eyes. He was poised, intelligent, interesting, but most of all, the man was just beautiful. All that shit I was talking mere seconds ago was dead as I watched his body lowering onto mine. I laid my head back on the duvet, my hands lying limp at my sides. His cologne filled my nostrils once again, and I scanned my memory, trying to identify the scent.

During college, I'd worked at the fragrance counter at a department store. Whatever it was, it was a quality blend. And he fully owned it. It wasn't like anything I had ever smelled before. The scent was masculine, sensual, and mixed with his bodily chemicals. It was blowing my damn mind. Then it hit me. Polo Red, the same scent Daniel wore. But the infusion of his pheromones recreated the scent in a way that did crazy things to me.

His hot, moist breath peppered my neck and activated a reaction in me that I hadn't felt in years. Daniel had been my only lover since starting undergrad. I'd been faithful to him from day one. Sex with him was faithfully uneventful, and he was a thin notch above mediocre in bed. When it came to pleasing me, he did just enough to get by. Head on my birthdays, our anniversary, and Valentine's Day—like it was some type of doggone privilege. Honestly, he could have used further instruction on how to hit the right spot. After hearing his soft snores, I always rummaged through my drawer, literally left to my own devices.

Wait, why was I thinking about Daniel's tired ass with this sexy man lying on top of me? I opened my eyes and looked into his, which were planted on mine. His brow furrowed, and his eyes began darting back and forth, seemingly searching for an answer. I reached up to stroke his head, but it was too late. He was already rolling off of me.

I sat up and looked at him. "What's the matter?"

"Where did you go just now?"

I shook my head. "Nowhere. I'm right here. With you!"

He stared at the ceiling for a moment before responding. "Patience, look, I have to be honest with you."

"That's the only way to be," I said, placing my weight on my elbow.

"I . . . it's been a minute for me. Since I've been intimate with someone."

I swallowed, fighting to keep my face from displaying the utter shock I felt. *His* fine ass? *How, Sway?* "Okay . . ."

"Actually, it's been about a year. And I don't really do casual sex."

I nodded slowly, disappointed in the direction this was headed. I'd somehow managed to cock-block my own damn self. *Damn, Daniel.* "I have to be honest—I've never met a guy who was abstinent by choice before."

He shook his head. "Oh, I'm not abstinent. I just try to avoid having one-night stands or sex outside of a relationship."

It was my turn to raise a brow. This man could easily have any woman he wanted. What type of willpower did he have to abstain from having sex as a young eligible bachelor in Atlanta? Now that

I was single, I knew I would be struggling with this back in Cleveland.

He reached for my hand, giving it a gentle squeeze. "My bad, Patience. I feel like I've led you on and wasted your time."

I shook my head and sighed. "Not at all. It's not like I expected you to greet me by saying, 'I'm Lennox Davenport and I don't have casual sex.'"

He shrugged. "That's one way of looking at it."

"Look, this has been the best night I've had in a very long time. I honestly feel like I've hijacked your evening, and I'm so appreciative of the time you've taken to show me a good time."

"No, this night was just what I needed. I get so swamped with work that I rarely give myself a moment to unwind."

I nodded again. "Sounds like we each served our purpose this evening."

"This wasn't transactional for me. In fact, I know you have an early flight, but I don't have anything waiting for me at home besides a mound of paperwork and a cold-ass bed."

I scoffed. "Well that's no way to spend a Friday night."

"You mind if I hang out here for a minute?"

I raised a brow, turned toward him, and asked, "That depends. You like rom-coms?"

"Pssh! I've seen *Coming 2 America* at least three times already. But if you like throwbacks, my only request is no movies with Bill Bellamy as the lead."

"The shade!" I laughed, laid my head on his chest, and reached for the remote. "But you got it, Mr. Davenport."

* * *

We chilled, laughed, and talked for several hours until the light from the television on our sleepy faces was replaced by rays of the rising sun.

"It's self-sabotage, quite frankly," I admitted, my head resting on his chest.

"Self-sabotage," he said, rubbing circles on the small of my back, and I fought to keep it from arching. "Yeah, I've been there."

"It really sucks. I went to therapy for years, so I've recognized the pattern and how unhealthy it is to sabotage relationships. Even though I'm aware how destructive it is—and cognitive dissonance is a dirty bitch—I still find myself circling the drain as soon as I realize I'm actually happy in a relationship. I still run at the first sign of trouble."

"Why do you think that is?"

I paused. As much as I was enjoying our time together and the candid tone of our conversation, I remembered what Lennox said about discussing exes during the first couple of encounters. I decided not to bring up my situation with Daniel. "I always hate to hear people say it, but I know it's just repressed, neglected trauma and baggage. Some of my past relationships have left residual hurt. I fell for the classic schoolboy move—thinking I had the wifey role when I was actually playing side chick. Unfortunately, it happened to me more than once. Over time, those mind games can impact a woman's ego, no matter how cold or valuable she thinks she is. So, I just find it easier to leave rather than stay and fight. The more you fight, the more emotionally invested you are. The more you set yourself up to get hurt."

He nodded. "I see your point. And I'm not going to respond like most dudes would and say, 'The only problem with that attitude is—'"

"I end up pushing away a good man once he finally comes around."

He gave a curt nod. "I'm just going to lie here and hold you because I know going through that must have been hard for you. And regardless of whatever baggage may come with her, when a woman is worth it, a real man will do whatever it takes to show her he's nothing like previous cats. Patience is a virtue, for real."

I wasn't expecting that response, and it had me at a loss for words. The butterflies in my stomach went apeshit. *This dude really gets me.*

I let his words sink in, one by one. They brewed while he rose from the bed and grabbed his suit jacket thirty minutes later. They simmered as he lifted my chin to place a sweet, long goodbye kiss on my lips. They steeped as I felt the impression of his business card pressed into my palm with his cell number scribbled on the back.

Then he bent down, and I savored the spearmint on his breath as he whispered, "This has been remarkable, Ms. Hampton. Thank you for your time, and have a safe flight home."

Still digesting his previous comment, I failed to grasp a sensible word. I offered a numb nod in reply, watching him stroll down the plush-carpeted corridor toward the elevator, my longing to be held in his strong arms for just a moment longer ripping me to shreds.

*Chapter Eleven*

I sat in the seven a.m. meeting in the hotel banquet hall that morning, blinking and nodding like a zombie. It wasn't due to lack of sleep, although that didn't quite help my situation. Mr. Charisma was to blame for hijacking my evening—and apparently, all of my subsequent thoughts. His smile with that stubborn little dimple. The way his large, possessive hands caressed my skin. His soft lips pressed onto mine. I didn't know how I had managed to shower, pack, dress, and make it downstairs in time. After the meeting, I checked out and grabbed breakfast. Trice offered me a wary side-eye, scooping a heap of instant eggs onto her plate. I slipped past her to grab a banana muffin.

After a few moments, she broke the silence. "Okay, Miss *Disappearing Acts.* What in the world happened to you yesterday? You slipped out of the meeting early, and that was the last I saw of you. You didn't answer your door and wouldn't pick up the phone when I called. If it weren't for that text you sent, I would have had the Atlanta Police Department put an APB out on your ass and thangs."

"Girl, you're so damn dramatic." I waved her off, grabbing a couple links of turkey sausage with tongs. "I just stepped out for a minute to clear my head. I took a long walk and got a chance to explore the city's arts."

"Well, I would have liked to clear my head last night, too. Lord knows my mind was fried after all those damn workshops and meetings."

I shrugged. "I just needed time to sort things out on my own. Think about what my next move will be once we touch down in Cleveland."

We sat down at a small table in the corner of the room, and Trice's light brown eyes settled on mine.

"Okay, broad. I didn't want to blow up your spot back there, but you're about to give me the damn tea. Where were you last night? And I don't want to hear about no walk! I saw your ass!"

In Sister Perkins's fashion, I clutched my pearls and gasped. "Whatever do you mea—"

"Spill it, bitch," she hissed.

I took a long swallow of orange juice before responding. "Okay, okay. First, what exactly did you see?"

"I was sitting at the bar when I saw you sashaying out the hotel lobby with a tall, fine-ass drink of water. You were dressed like a flamenco dancer or some shit. Talking about you have to figure out your next move. It looked like ol' Danny boy was the furthest thing from your mind last night."

My breath caught, and I nearly choked.

She handed me a napkin and said, "Gather your damn self, stop all this stalling, and tell me what the hell happened before our ride gets here!"

"I should have known your nosy ass saw something. You don't miss nothing. Damn!"

Trice stared me down, arms folded, and I knew I had to give her something. "Oh, fine. I met someone. He lives here in Atlanta and was kind enough to invite me out last night."

"That didn't look like a dinner outfit to me. And he had a big-ass bouquet of flowers! Who does it that big for a stranger they've only known for five minutes? Or is that just how they do thangs in the ATL?"

I shrugged, breaking apart my muffin. "He was just sweet. A really nice guy."

"More like a convenient rebound! I heard y'all talking all night with the TV on. Hell, I'm not judging you at all. I just hope you got it all out of your system so you can go home and work out things with Daniel."

"He was a complete gentleman. Yes, we had a good time and talked and watched movies all night, but nothing happened. We were just two lonely people enjoying each other's company on a Thursday evening."

"Oh, you're a good one. Had it been me, we never would have made it to that dinner. Judging from the way he was watching you walk up to him, you could have gotten it right then and there. That Southern man was captivated by that Midwest beauty!"

I rolled my eyes and stuffed the rest of my muffin into my mouth. My entire body was heating up just at the thought of Lennox moving on the dance floor. His smooth, effortless rhythm had me gone. I hadn't felt so free to be exactly who I was in a long time. He brought the realness out of me with no effort when it took most men years to get me that comfortable. I planned to hold on to that memory for a long time since it was all I had left of him.

"Did you hear me? Our ride's here." Trice stood up and grabbed her luggage.

"Okay," I said, standing up and throwing a tip onto the table. "I'm ready."

As we rushed across the half-empty lobby, I glanced back at the bar. I was grateful I had stopped by there yesterday afternoon, but it was time to move forward. I had to tie up loose ends with Daniel and figure out what I wanted in this new chapter of my life. As I stepped out of the automatic sliding doors, I pulled

Lennox's business card out of my wallet. I stared at it, smoothing my fingers over his name for a few moments.

"You're an amazing guy, Lennox Davenport. But, for the first time in my life, it's time to focus on myself with no distractions."

I tossed the card into the trash before handing my luggage to the driver.

## *Chapter Twelve*

I'd returned home three days ago and I still hadn't spoken to anyone outside of my family and coworkers. Once I had touched down in Cleveland on Friday afternoon, the only thing I wanted to do was hit the sheets because I knew a mound of work was waiting for me on Monday morning.

"Morning, sunshine!" My coworker Hilary sang as she set a white chocolate mocha latte on my desk.

"Thanks, love." I looked up from my laptop and flashed her an appreciative smile. Before I could return my attention to the screen, I noticed her usual business suit was replaced by a silk blouse and a pair of crisp slacks. Her business-casual attire was trendy but unexpected.

Taking in my raised eyebrow, Hilary shrugged and took a seat at her desk. "Just wasn't in the mood to be Corporate Barbie today," was all she offered.

I nodded, not pressing the subject any further. I took a cautious sip of the piping-hot latte, figuring she was feeling a way, just like me. After scanning my twentieth unread email of the morning, my brain fatigue led me to close my inbox. I pulled up an audio file for a local car dealership's radio commercial I had recorded a couple of days before. Our expected output was now twice as much since fast-talking Farrah quit a couple of weeks prior, making her the third intern we had lost in under four months.

Right after graduating college, I started working as a voice actor and communications specialist for a small agency. Trice, Hilary, whoever occupied the revolving-door intern position, and I worked on the west wing of a small office building that we leased. Our company was headquartered in LA. Although my job demanded a lot of what I loathed—talking—it was a lucrative career that kept my interest due to a wide assortment of projects. I lent my voice to radio ads, corporate training videos, audiobooks, and more.

"All right, ladies. My pitch and speed are good on this Honda dealership commercial, so I'll be sending it to marketing for final approval shortly."

Hilary nodded. "Good. I just checked out three projects from the team inbox. I'm heading downtown to the recording studio this afternoon, so hopefully, I'll be able to knock them all out."

I checked out two projects and printed the project details with specific requests from the client. While waiting for them to print, I sorted through the stack of papers sitting in the printer tray. I still had a message from Daniel from the day before, and I was trying to figure out how to respond to him. I knew I couldn't put him off any longer.

"You're clearly lost in those brainwaves this morning, P." Trice's rich voice jerked me from my thoughts. "Is that my press release in your hot little hands?"

I blinked. Somehow, I was standing next to her desk, clearly on my way to deliver her papers, but my mind had drifted miles away before I had gotten there. "Yeah, girl. My bad." I handed her the papers before returning to the printer to grab my own.

"What's with you, girl? You've been quiet this morning—even for you. Everything okay?" Trice's intense stare penetrated me, and I knew she wouldn't let me get away with a shrug.

"Yeah, I'm fine. Just a lot on my mind, but nothing I can't handle," I tried to assure her anyway.

She paused before responding. "You know you killed that Italian East Coast accent on that Pancake House commercial. Landon and I heard it on the radio last night and couldn't believe that was you. Who knew a sista could pull off a bit like that?"

I chuckled. "You know I grew up with a Sicilian best friend, and her mom was originally from the Bronx. So, I mastered that accent by eight years old. Whenever I visited her house on weekends, her extended family would be over there eating huge dinners, retelling old stories, and shooting the breeze. I guess a lot of their terms and ways of speaking just stuck with me."

Hilary walked over to the printer. "If I closed my eyes, I would think I was watching the New Jersey housewives. Oh, and Gordon forwarded an email from the client to the queue. It's for you."

"Okay, thanks," I said, returning to my desk.

I found the email from my boss and scrolled down to the client's feedback. Puzzled, I reread it for clarity. Then read it again. I slammed my laptop closed, then headed to a conference room, grabbing Trice on the way.

Once she closed the door behind her, she asked, "What's up, girl?" I was pacing the floor, still trying to process what I had just read. Trice shook her head. "Oh, this ain't good. What happened now?"

I walked over to the table and pulled the email up on my laptop. "Read that."

As she scanned the email, her arched eyebrows shot up. "Girl . . ."

I started pacing again. "So, it's not just me, right?"

She frowned. "Definitely not, P. The whole nerve of these people!"

"Read it out loud. I need to hear it again."

"'Hi, Gordon. We've all reviewed the submission from last week, and we'd like to offer feedback. As we stated in our previous email, we have a specific market in mind for this campaign. We plan to run this ad on urban radio stations to increase sales in that market. You mentioned having an assigned actor who is capable of creating content that would appeal to the African American community. However, on the submitted recording, it's difficult to determine her ethnicity. Would it be possible for her to use a more pronounced accent? If this request poses a problem on your end, please let us know. Warmest regards, Cathy.'"

My nails dug so far into my palms by this point, I felt pain shooting up my forearm.

"Something tells me we weren't supposed to see that email. Wait . . . did you read Gordon's comment? 'Patience, please see the feedback from the client below. They're requesting a heavier urban accent. If this makes you uncomfortable, let me know. I can ask Trice if she's willing to give it a go.'"

We locked eyes. "No, I didn't see that shit," I growled. "Girl, what in the . . . ? Excuse me if my 'African American vernacular English' isn't on point for you today, Cathy!"

"Girl, screw that. Ol' Cat wants straight-up blackspeak! Ebonics!"

I scoffed. "And to think, after attempting to tone down my urban accent for years in private-school and corporate America to fit in, I'm now not speaking Black enough for Cathy's taste. Like, what type of accent do they have in mind? Is this the only reason we were hired? To be tokens on hand for projects like this?"

Trice shook her head. "Wait, P. This is Gordon we're talking about. We've known him for years, been to his house, and have eaten with his family each year for the holidays. Although we definitely have to let him know how offensive the client's request is, I don't believe it was his intent to exploit either one of us. It's the *client* that's the damn problem!"

I scoffed. "You're right. Hell, Gordon is just about his coin. He's probably just shook over losing yet another project to Step It Up Communications. You know they'd sell their own mama for a client over there."

Trice guffawed and held her hand up for a high five. "P, you tell no lies!"

We were quiet for a few minutes. Then Trice looked up at me and asked, "So, sis, with your promotion on the line, I would totally get it if you decided to redo the job. And I wouldn't judge you for a single moment. Do you know what you're going to do?"

* * *

On the ride home, my mind was pulled in countless directions. As if I didn't have enough on my mind, the latest fiasco at work had me on edge. When I pulled up to a light, my phone buzzed. It was a text from Daniel. He was sending me a dinner reservation confirmation at my favorite restaurant for that evening. I shook my head. *Presumptuous much?* I was irked that he had the nerve to make plans for us without speaking with me first, but I guess he was tired of my stalling. Besides, we still had several things to discuss.

If I were being honest with myself, I really wanted to text him back. Despite things being over between us, I still missed Daniel. Riding home with Trice and Landon from the airport hadn't felt right. Whenever I traveled for work, Daniel picked me up from the airport with takeout from my favorite restaurant. We'd always stop by my house for a nightcap. Extended trips seemed to do wonders for our sex life.

I shook my head, biting my lip as I conjured up an image of Lennox's sexy ass in that dance studio. I almost sexually assaulted that man, acting desperate and dehydrated. I was actually stunned by my own behavior in Atlanta. I had a tendency to wait for a guy to make a move, even when I noticed him first and had never been that aggressive with a man before. The primal reaction Lennox evoked in me showed me that I was missing out on the sexually exhilarating, free, and unbridled side of myself. So, I was intrigued by my uncharacteristic reaction. Daniel had never roused any feelings like that in me. So how could I proceed with Daniel now that this newfound passion was ignited by Lennox? Seeing Daniel one last time could help me figure out if he was capable of doing anything like that for me. Because if I would be tasked with a lifetime of dealing with his mama, Daniel needed to be well worth the hassle.

Me: That's fine. I'm ready to talk. So, I'll meet you there.

Daniel: Bet. Wear that sexy black dress with those booties I like.

Later that evening, I handed the hostess my coat, smoothed my ribbed, kelly green midi dress, and glanced down at my gold sequin pumps because . . . no one tells me what to wear. I glanced around the perimeter of the restaurant and spotted Daniel sitting at the back near the open kitchen. The hostess guided me toward the table, and Daniel stood to pull out my chair. His eager eyes drank me in, lingering on my hips. Some guys like breasts; others like ass. Daniel was a hips and legs man. And since I had baby-making hips and my calves stay toned, due to being a volunteer line-dance instructor, he loved to see me in dresses. As I scooted my chair in and set my clutch on the table, he scurried back to his seat.

"Hey, gorgeous."

I looked at his twinkling eyes and fought the urge to smile. Although I was no longer interested in continuing a relationship with him, I was comforted by the familiarity between us. I nodded and offered a cool response. "Hello, Daniel."

"How was Atlanta?"

I sipped my water. "It was nice."

"You get a chance to visit Centennial Park?"

"I did. Pop-Pop's old pictures didn't do it justice."

He sipped his Crown and Coke. "I'm glad you got to experience that. I wish I could have shared that moment with you."

*Me too.* I had shared Pop-Pop's story of his time at the Atlanta Olympics with Daniel, and we had planned to make the trip once his clinicals were over. But life got in the way, and we never did. Instead, I'd experienced it with a total stranger.

I shrugged.

"You look radiant in that money green."

"Thanks."

"I've really missed you. I'm hoping our time and space apart gave you an opportunity to think about things."

Before I could respond, the waiter walked up to greet me and set down the prosecco and pear juice with a straw that Daniel must have ordered for me before I arrived. After reciting the evening's featured menu items, he took our orders and left.

I cleared my throat. "Yes, I took some time to think about things. Despite how I feel at this moment, we were together for a long time. I at least owe you the opportunity to speak your piece."

He frowned.

I assumed he was waiting for further explanation. I reached for a roll and buttered it in lieu of offering one.

He finally broke our silence. "Speak my piece . . . before what happens? Do you think *I'm* to blame for what happened at my parents' dinner?"

"No, you're not to blame for it, Daniel. But it's obvious you have some type of relationship with that girl—whom I've never even heard of. And she had a lot to say about how you feel about me for someone you haven't"—I used air quotes—"seen or spoken to since high school."

He started to reply, then glanced down and exhaled through his nose. "Okay, I wasn't expecting to get into all this before I finished my first cocktail, but here we are."

I sipped my wine. "No time like the motherfucking present."

"That's fine. The least I can do is explain. Fabienne is my father's goddaughter. Our fathers were best friends until hers died from an aneurysm eighteen years ago. He was a single parent, and his parents are deceased, so Fabienne moved in with an aunt who lived around the corner from us. She was over at our house often and spent a lot of time with our family. We practically grew up together, which is why I've never seen her as anything other than a sister."

I nodded, signaling for him to continue.

"After high school, we both left for college and lost touch. She went to Spelman, and I went to Hampton. The summer after we finished undergrad, shortly after I met you, she reached out via Facebook, and we caught each other up on things. She stayed in touch with my parents, so we knew most of the major stuff through them. We discussed surface personal things, and I brought you up often. She was aware that I was in a committed relationship, but I've never shared any intimate details about you or how I feel about you with her. You know I'm a private person."

"That, you are."

"The things she said at dinner were my mother's words. Not mine. You know I don't feel that way about you. I never have."

"What about when we were having a difficult time and you shared your feelings about me?"

"Oh, so you did listen to the voicemails I left."

"Just answer the question, Daniel."

"Like I mentioned, it was right after we had an argument and hadn't spoken to one another in over a week. Things were pretty dark for us at that time. She happened to reach out, and I vented to her about some minor issues I had with you, but I never talked badly about you. Turns out she's an opportunist, just like my mom, and threw it in my face the very first chance she got."

I felt the bite in his words; they were laced with disdain and regret. But I wasn't totally convinced about where he stood with Fabienne. One thing was sure—he seemed upset and maybe even disappointed by the recent behavior of the women in his life. I studied his face for a few moments longer, not trusting myself to speak. Overall, Daniel was a stand-up guy. Whenever I really needed him, he put his needs last and came through for me each time. I couldn't think of one time he had ever let me down. The problem was, I didn't want to always wait until I had a need for him to step up and see about me. I didn't want someone who was reactive; I wanted someone to be proactive. I held up my glass, signaling to our waiter that I needed more wine.

When I didn't comment, he took a deep breath and reached across the table, swallowing my hands in his.

"Pae, I know you were hurt by the stunt my mother pulled. Even though drama is to be expected from her, she went way too far this time. She and my dad had a long talk after everyone left, and he told me that she promised to work on her behavior going forward, whatever that means."

"What? You're not speaking to her?"

He shook his head. "Not since that night. I don't have anything to say to her right now."

*So, he put his mama on ice? That's a first.* I lifted a brow and took another long sip of my wine.

"But Fabienne's behavior was a total right hook for us both. If she always acted like that, I would have cut her off a long time ago. Should I have mentioned to you that I was in touch with her over the years? Yes. Was I hiding something from you? No. For the longest time, she was out of sight, out of mind, then she resurfaced right when you and I started dating. Despite what she said, our contact has been limited, and her presence hasn't made an impact in my life one way or the other. I haven't heard from her in over two years."

I fought back an eye roll.

"But, I'm not here to make any excuses for the role I played in this. The only thing that matters to me at this point is how you feel and whether I've lost your trust. I'm truly sorry for what happened that night, Pae. I hate that you had to experience that because you deserve so much more respect than that—from all of us."

His voice was thick, and it looked like he was struggling to maintain his composure. I listened to his words while searching his eyes. He resembled the same man I had loved and trusted for years, and I still felt something for him. I wanted to see him do amazing things with his life. But I knew I would no longer be sitting in the front row watching it all happen. The fact remained that his overbearing mother wasn't going anywhere, and that was a dealbreaker for me. I had dealt with her shenanigans for far too long, and she had gone further than any of us could have expected. Only a fool would stick around and continue to deal with all that on top of the issues we already had.

In the meantime, Daniel's lean mahogany exterior in that gingham button-down with dark jeans and suede kicks still looked downright edible. Our distance for the past two weeks had me wanting him in the worst way.

"Well, I guess I have no reason to doubt you. It looks like Fabienne and your mother are rather close, which means your mother has likely been brainwashing and priming her as her little puppet over the years. If you say I have nothing to worry about with Fabienne, I believe you."

He brought my hand up to his full lips. "Thank you, my love."

I cleared my throat, slipping my hand from his grip. "Like you said, I've had plenty of time and space to think things through. As far as you and I are concerned, you know I love you, Daniel. Part of me always will in some way. We've been through a lot together and have supported each other in tremendous ways. But after thinking about things long and hard, I've decided to walk away from our relationship."

His eyebrows raised, but he didn't look shocked. "Damn, I'm really disappointed to hear that."

I gave him a moment to process it. He squeezed my hand and said, "In the back of my mind, I've always suspected things between us were headed in that direction. I know you love my family and me, but I can't expect you to continue to put your dreams aside in favor of mine. Nor can I expect you to deal with all the drama from my mother. I guess a woman can only take so much."

I nodded. "I'm glad you see it that way, Daniel. I just wanted to meet up tonight to give you closure. I'm going to focus on getting my mind right, putting myself first, and doing things my way for the first time in my life. This experience, along with others, made me realize that I owe myself the chance to do *me* with no apologies."

He nodded and smiled. "Totally understandable. That's great, babe."

"I'm glad you understand."

A few thoughtful moments of silence slipped by.

I cleared my throat. "And part of doing me is seeking pleasure and gratification whenever and however I choose. So, if you're open to continuing a monogamous sexual relationship, I'm down. But, if you think it would be too difficult for you to separate your feelings, I totally understand."

I watched his eyes nearly double in size. "That wouldn't be a problem for me at all."

"Okay, I'm giving you the benefit of the doubt, and I'm trusting that I won't have to worry about any funny business with you and Fabienne because that's where I draw the line. Also, the moment you decide to be intimate with someone else, we cut all ties. We'll rely on the honor system, but if I ever feel the need to audit your ass, you better be ready with receipts and invoices. And I'm talking about a full transcript of DMs and text messages. I'm not for the drama."

Daniel held out his hands, and his face deadpanned. "Aye, not a problem at all."

I stood, gathering my things. "Cool. Get our food to go, and I'll meet you at your place in fifteen. Please don't keep me waiting."

"Mm. You know how much I love a woman who takes charge," he said.

"All too well," I replied. I walked out of the restaurant, rolling my hips without a backward glance.

*Chapter Thirteen*

After enjoying a quiet candlelit dinner of braised short ribs, mashed potatoes, and veggies by the fireplace, we could almost feel the thick sexual tension coating our skin. He fed me most of my dinner, but my sexual appetite only grew deeper. We locked eyes and, without another word, stood and made our way to his bedroom, wine bottle in hand, with every intention of devouring each other for dessert.

Once I crossed the threshold of the burgundy and black room, his hands were all over me. Clawing at the thick straps of my dress, he yanked them down so hard that I gasped. I searched his eyes, but they were hard to read. He was laser-focused on disrobing me, so I sat back on his bed and lifted my hips as he slid the dress over my ass and down the length of my legs. He pushed me down onto the comforter, lifting my left foot into the air. He slid off my gold pump before taking my toes into his mouth. He suckled them roughly, shooting currents of raging heat up my legs and directly into my yoni. I moaned, bit my lip, and gripped fistfuls of the comforter's silk material beneath me to keep from crying out. Disengaging from my feet, his eager tongue made a wet upward path over the length of my calves and inner thighs. I felt the gentle tug of his teeth against my satin panties. I instinctively lifted my hips once again, but he pressed them down, opting to push the thin material to the side instead.

His warm tongue nudged my labia apart before his entire mouth mounted my love below. No longer able to hold back my elation, I squealed out his name and arched my back. I palmed his head and pressed it further into me, eyes clamped shut as tiny stars began to dance behind my closed lids. His head bobbed rhythmically from side to side, and I joined him in his silent dance, bucking my eager hips to the beat of our unheard song. Listening to the solitary sounds of his tender kisses and suckles, we kept our timed pace. My hips rocked consistently, undulating to the pre-orgasmic waves that threatened to overtake me at any given moment. Hot tears leaked from my clamped eyes as a deep, familiar tremble began to brew in my loins.

I took a deep breath and tried to push him off in order to stave off the onrushing climax. He swatted my hands and tightened his firm grip on my hips, pushing his lengthy tongue deeper into my fleshy folds. As my body began to tremble, he slowly eased his mouth off of my swollen clit. Then he slipped a finger inside of me and began gently stroking my rooftop. I stiffened, slacked, stiffened again, and finally gave in to the relentless waves of passion that threatened to toss me off the precipice of my physical limits. Wild torrents of ecstasy rolled up and crashed throughout my entire body, and fireworks exploded in front of my eyes. I twisted, turned, and screamed louder than I ever had. By the time it was all over, I was hoarse, sweaty, and exhausted as all hell.

Damn, this brotha had stepped his head game up.

I lay there for a few minutes, attempting to gather my whole self. As I fought to even my breathing, the weight of the room's silence caused my eyes to finally spring open. First, I looked up at the ceiling and rubbed my eyes. When I glanced toward Daniel, who was kneeling between my legs, I saw his handsome face was chiseled with stunned concern for a few moments as he observed me. His confusion was justified because he'd never made me shout like that.

Then his eyes lit up, and a satisfied smile spread over his entire face. "I assume that was good for you."

"Boy, get over here," I growled, pulling him down for a deep kiss.

* * *

My barefoot, bowlegged walk of shame to my car in the rising sunlight after three exhilarating rounds of sex was well worth it. It had gotten my mind completely off of the bullshit I had encountered at my job. I hadn't planned on spending the night, but he completely wore me out with his new bag of tricks ready for me—beads, pillows, oils, toys, and a sex swing. I'd be lying if I said I wasn't willing and ready for every moment of it. Who knew all it took was dumping his ass to get the type of loving I'd needed for years?

I shivered as I started the car, waving back to him as he watched me from the front window. I turned on my heated seats, plugged in my phone, and backed out of his driveway, smiling wide and hard. April, the affectionate name I gave my yoni, was a bit beaten and bruised from a long night's thrashing, but she was fully satisfied. I'd have to ice her down a bit when I got home.

My phone powered up and began to ping. Who in the world was texting me at seven thirty in the morning? Once I reached a stoplight, I glanced down to check my notifications. I had missed a call and text from my little sister, Chelsea. Just before the light turned green, I voice commanded a call to her.

The phone rang three times, and I was just about to hang up and text her when she picked up and sang, "Whaddup, Munk?"

I smiled at her affectionate nickname for me. "Hey, Bunny. What are you doing up this early on a Saturday?"

"It's wash day, so I'm sitting under the steamer with a deep conditioner while reviewing this screenplay."

With the amount of hair my sister had, I knew she'd already been conditioning and detangling it for hours, just like I did for her when she was little.

"Damn, that's right. So, it's safe to assume your dance audition yesterday went well?"

"Oh yeah, I wrecked that boy!" Her voice instantly piped up. "I'll be getting the rehearsal schedule next week."

"Nice! Is this a traveling play, or is it just in Kent?"

"We'll be performing throughout Ohio. Four shows in Cleveland, one in Kent, one in Akron, and five in Columbus. I'm looking forward to this opportunity because as the lead dancer, I'll even have a few lines."

I pulled into my garage. "Not little Bunny testing out those acting chops."

"Yes, ma'am. The director of my last play highly recommended me. Since I've done some acting in a few high school plays, they decided to try me out. I'm nervous as hell, but I think this may play out well for me."

"Oh, I know it will. Let me know if you ever need me to run lines with you."

"Yes, you know I'm going to be relying on the actress of the family for a few pointers."

"Girl, please. I barely know what I'm doing out here. How's Tavares doing?" I asked, referring to her on-and-off boyfriend of several years.

She released an annoyed groan, and I knew little had changed between them. My sister had a solid head on her shoulders, made sound decisions, and would experience things in her life and career beyond what I ever would. Although she was intelligent, practical, thoughtful, and kind, the girl had shitty taste in men. She met Tavares at a performing arts summer camp before her eighth-grade year. They had been a part of every significant event in each other's lives since they first met. Whenever they broke up, they still kicked it as friends; when they were dating, they were inseparable. Their bond was unbreakable.

Although I knew Tavares loved and cared for my sister, he was not my first pick for her due to his poor money management choices and financial instability. It often interfered with my sister's life, distracting her from her studies as a junior at Kent State University. As her primary guardian, I had a serious issue with that. Despite my opinion of Tavares, I kept my nose out of my little sister's love life. Chelsea was now grown with her own life to live. As long as Tavares never physically abused her in any way, I would remain on the sidelines until Chelsea finally got the sense to walk away from him for good.

"Him and these damn payday loans are driving me crazy. His paycheck goes to insane fees every month, and he can barely keep up with his car note and helping his mother with bills. I had to help him get his car out of the shop yesterday, and now, I'm going to be short on rent. I'd rather not head all the way downtown to the credit union and dip into my savings if I don't have to . . ."

I shook my head so hard that my jaw shook. "No, there's no need to touch that account. I'll Cash App you. How much do you need?"

"Two fifty. I promise I'll get it back to you on Friday. I'm just so frustrated because I had an extra thousand in my account. But I was so thirsty to pay off my American Express card balance that I didn't factor in enough extra cash for emergencies this month. You know how important it is to me that I stay debt free. I just don't want to owe anybody anything."

"I know, sister. And you won't owe me anything for this. I don't want you worried about robbing Peter to support Tavares's ass. Just repay me by focusing on your classes and keeping your grades up." I wanted to add that she should stop enabling her boyfriend by loaning him money, but I knew it would be a waste of breath on my headstrong sister.

Chelsea was silent for a few beats, and I could picture a stubborn little pout budding on her face. "Munk, I'm definitely paying you back. So, thanks for the *loan*, sis."

"Anty-way," I said, rolling my eyes and dropping the subject with Chelsea before the Taurus in her reared its bullish head. I wasn't accepting any money from her, point blank period, but I saved that argument for another day. "I'm about to . . ." I stopped myself from saying I was about to hop out of the car, knowing she would go in on me fast and hard about my recent whereabouts, which were none of her concern. ". . . make some breakfast. Let me know once you get the schedule for your Cleveland shows."

"Yes, and I want Danny, Cessa, and Bel to be there."

I blinked. Bella was my best friend, but when she mentioned Daniel and his sister, it gave me pause. I still hadn't said anything to her about the breakup, and I wasn't sure how she would handle it since she was best friends with Daniel's little sister. "You got it, love."

Chelsea was nineteen years old, but she was convinced she was the older sibling. I loved her more than my next breath. Despite the eight-year age difference, our relationship was fun but complex due to a lifetime of inside jokes and the full spectrum of emotional trauma we shared.

Given the complexities of our parents' relationship, I spent most of my youth caring for Chelsea. My father had moved out when she was barely six months old, and my mother had taken his absence as an opportunity to focus on herself. She went from Sally Homemaker to gradually shirking her parenting responsibilities year after year, forcing me into the role of a pre-teen mother by twelve years old. I began taking care of myself and providing nearly all of my sister's care. On most mornings, I got Chelsea dressed, fed her, packed her book bag, and dropped her off at daycare before heading to school. Thankfully, my best friend, Bella's, older brother would drive us to and from school each morning.

The daycare wasn't too far from school, so he didn't mind taking us. Back in the day, security wasn't what it is today, so a twelve-year-old walking in a sibling and telling the daycare staff their mother was waiting in the car didn't raise brows like it would today. Apparently, my mother had no problem with minors taking care of her child while she slept off her buzz from the night before.

Today, she was thirteen years sober, and we were working on our relationship. Although my sister's relationship wasn't ideal, I had to learn to give her space and time to figure out what she wanted. After we hung up, I took a deep breath to center myself and redirected my thoughts to things I could control.

Sitting in the car, I scrolled through my Instagram feed. I checked out the suggestions of people to follow and my eyes widened. I slowed my scroll. There he was, standing in front of a row of lockers in a mirror selfie. I tapped on his profile and scrolled through his profile grid, feasting on the delectable assortment of eye-candy photos. I was disappointed to find that none were shirtless, but those tight-fitting tees that hugged his bulging biceps hadn't left much to the imagination.

He'd posted videos of himself doing reps with weights and pictures of his delicious-looking food. I studied several pictures of him posing in different color T-shirts bearing the same logo. Was it his business? I tapped on one of the hashtags in the caption. It looked like he was part of a collective cause promoting therapy services for Black men. I frowned, totally engrossed in my shameless cyber stalking of Lennox Davenport. How did he wind up in my suggested follows? I googled the metrics Instagram used, and he didn't meet any of them. Then I pulled up my contacts list and typed in his name. My jaw dropped as I stared at the screen displaying his name, email address, and mobile number. I tried to remember when he'd had access to my phone. The limo. Just before we walked into the restaurant. His slick ass.

By the time I opened my car door to get out, over thirty minutes had passed.

April damn near yelped in protest as I squeezed my legs together and stood. I fondly recalled Daniel's renewed dedication to our sex life. Our little arrangement might work out after all.

But the more I thought about how much I enjoyed my time with him, how fully invested I was during each second, how much I was looking forward to our next sexcapade, the more I realized the sex was only diabolical because Lennox Davenport had been on my mind the entire time.

Chapter Fourteen

My best friend of nineteen years invited me out to catch up over lunch, and it actually felt good to leave the house for a little while. Other than the occasional bedroom romp with Daniel, I no longer had time to hang with anyone. I was busy applying for jobs and researching graduate programs.

"I'm so glad I could finally drag your ass out of that house. You've been such a recluse for the past two weeks."

I rolled my eyes. "Well, it's not like I had a choice."

"Damn right, you didn't." Bella laughed. "Now give me the tea on you and Daniel. How did your dinner go? Are y'all still a thing or not?"

I offered a lazy shrug. "We're not. But it's . . . complicated."

"You guys broke up for real? I'm so sorry, girl. I know you've been on the fence about your relationship for the longest, and this last fiasco was probably the last straw." She lifted a brow while eating her chef salad. "But you said things are complicated between y'all? How so?"

I wiped my brow. My situation with Daniel was even more complicated now that I'd realized how Lennox impacted us. "He apologized for what happened and acknowledged that his mother's behavior is way out of line, which I really appreciated. But meeting Lennox showed me how the passion was missing in my relationship with Daniel. Being seen and cherished by a total stranger was just what I needed at that time. I realized the emotional intimacy between us had been long gone. And dating someone all the way in Atlanta isn't an option for me after that stunt Jerrod pulled when we tried long-distance dating the summer after high school."

"Yes, I can definitely see how you felt that way after that fiasco. But I'm still trying to figure out what's so complicated between you and Daniel right now," Bella prodded.

"What can I say? All of that taking accountability and standing up for me against his mama turned me on. So . . . I spent the night with him after dinner."

"Broad." Bella's eyes widened, and she set down her fork.

I shrugged. "I don't know how it happened. I broke up with him, then we made the decision to continue sleeping together. Like I said, it's complicated."

Bella grunted in disgust. "Damn, P. I mean . . . damn."

"I know it's crazy if your outspoken ass is speechless!"

"I'm always going to support you, no matter what move you make. If you're serious about doing you this time around, do you. However that looks."

"Thanks, Bel. Your support is so needed right now." I reached over and squeezed her hand. "Plus, I know this is only temporary. As soon as I figure out my next move, Daniel's out of here."

She nodded. "I feel you. Hopefully, you can find what you had with Lennox with someone here."

I shrugged. "Only time will tell. But for now, I'm staying low-key. So, how are things with you and Chauncey? And how are my little nephews doing?"

Bella was Sicilian and she and Chauncey dated off and on while co-parenting their biracial children. She tossed her long dark hair over her left shoulder and said, "Chauncey and I are doing okay for now. Little Vittorio is a handful, like his damn daddy. Bad as hell, but just cute enough to be worth the trouble."

"Every time I pull up Insta, there's his sweet little face. The camera loves him, and he knows just how to work those baby blues."

"Tell me about it. And little CJ's doing great. He's sitting up now. Vittorio watches over him like a hawk. He loves being a big brother."

"Well, give them both hugs and kisses for me. I'll try to get by there next weekend to see them."

"Sounds good. They're always down to spend time with their favorite ti-ti. Any updates on that new position you applied for at your job?"

"Not yet. I did the virtual panel interview last week, so I'm hoping I'll know something by the end of next week. But I'm glad you brought that up. Girl, let me tell you about what just happened."

I went into detail about the client's request that I use an urban accent for their radio commercial.

Bella's jaw dropped. "You gotta be shitting me. We still doing this racist bullshit in the twenty-first century?"

I shook my head. "Bel, I've never experienced anything like this in my entire career."

"I hope you let Gordon know you weren't doing that offensive shit."

I shook my head. "I haven't responded to the email yet. To be honest, I had to leave the office and work from home for the rest of the day."

It was her turn to squeeze my hand. "I'm sorry you had to go through that, sis."

"Thanks, but let me ask you something. And please be honest."

"Always."

"Does the Jersey accent I use on some of my radio commercials offend you?"

Bella sat back in her chair and gazed at me for a few moments. Her expression told me everything I needed to know.

Tears sprang to my eyes, and I was instantly disgusted with myself for being so hypocritical. "Bel, I am so sorry. I really believed that I was just acting. I never meant to be insensitive to you and your family. You know how much I love you all."

She waved me off. "Girl, I know you don't mean anything by it."

"But I need you to know that I'd never do anything to intentionally hurt you. It wasn't until that request came through that I realized how off-putting this all is."

She stared in my eyes and I knew she believed me. "Your apology means a lot to me. Thanks, P."

"Of course. Now, if I can just figure out what to do about this client's request."

"Sounds like you need to trust your instincts on this one. They won't lead you wrong." Bella slid on her leopard-print reading glasses. "So, your twenty-seventh birthday is coming up soon. I know you don't like parties, but this ain't about you. It's for me, bitch."

I sighed, knowing we were really past the issue now. Bella was a talented full-time wardrobe stylist. She recently started a business as an event planner and was building her portfolio. She already had beautiful pictures from her son Vittorio's third birthday party, her younger son CJ's christening, a gender reveal party, and a bat mitzvah. I guess she was planning to add an adult birthday party to her resumé, and I was her lucky next victim.

"I'm long past the days of trying to talk you out of anything, Bel. What do you have in mind?"

Her eyes lit up as she opened her planner. "I was thinking guests could come dressed as their twin celebrity. We can have a red carpet, paparazzi, and hold some IG live interviews. Whoever can stay in character the longest would win the fifty-fifty raffle. The other fifty percent would go to the birthday girl."

Taking a bite of my salad, I said, "Okay, that sounds dope, but you can donate my half to the HBCU Scholarship Foundation instead. This definitely sounds like fun, but everybody doesn't have a celebrity look-alike."

"They may not have doppelgangers, but even a slight physical or personality resemblance would be fun. I'm thinking of coming as Demi Lovato. What do you think about coming as Issa Rae?"

"Hmmm, not a bad idea. People say I favor her, minus the height. I'll have to think about what I can pull together over the next few weeks."

Bella clutched her hands and leaned in. "So, you're in?"

"That depends. Do I have to plan anything?"

"Nope, I'll handle every detail down to the decor, the custom invites, and the cake."

I gave her a thumbs up. "Then I'm in like Flynn."

After lunch, Bella went home to her kids. But I didn't feel like heading back to an empty house. I had been texting back and forth with Princessa for the past few days and smiled when she sent me a Tami Roman stale-face meme with a caption saying they were all over her mother's bullshit.

Princessa: I've been meaning to tell you that I met someone. I really like him. Call me later. U'll always b fam 2 everyone else in this house, sis. No matter what.

I smiled and texted her a purple heart and kissy-face emoji and let her know I'd call her that evening. Then I walked into the bookstore to use a coupon that was burning a hole in my wallet. I began perusing the latest African American literature releases at the back of the store. I was an avid reader growing up, but I hadn't gotten the chance to read anything lately. Now that I was single with much more free time, I was planning to snuggle up with a book in the evenings after work in lieu of binge-watching reality shows.

All of the choices overwhelmed me, so I pulled up my Goodreads app to look at my shelved list of books. As I scrolled through the endless possibilities and scanned some book reviews, a banner notification popped up with an Instagram direct message. I almost dropped my phone. It was an unread message from Lennox Davenport.

## Chapter Fifteen

My pulse immediately began thumping in my ears as my finger hovered over the notification to launch the app. I didn't know why I was so nervous to tap it. Once I finally did, I plopped down in a nearby easy chair.

Lennox: Hey, Patience. You were in my suggested follows, so I decided to reach out. How have you been these past few weeks?

Before I could stop them, my thumbs flew across my keyboard with minds of their own. He had sent the message a couple of hours ago, so there was no need to wait to reply for fear of looking thirsty.

Me: Hi Lennox. Good to hear from you. I've been well. And you?

I stared at the screen for a few moments before standing up and returning to the bookshelf. I decided on a copy of Phoebe Robinson's latest book and headed toward the cash register. In my car, I checked my phone again, and there was another message from Lennox.

Text me. My number's in your phone.

I sent him a quick text, then started the car. My skin prickled as I pulled out of my parking space. Now he had my phone number, and I wasn't sure where we were headed. My phone pinged, and I picked up my phone once I stopped at a light.

Your pictures are nice. I especially like your smile on the pier.

I lifted a brow. The pier? I hadn't been on the Flats Boardwalk downtown since the previous summer. Hell, how far had he scrolled? I must admit to you, I'd had creepers a time or two. Although, for some apparent reason, fine-ass stalkers were now in season. I smiled.

Me: Thank you. So are yours.

Lennox: Got a quick question for you. When's a good time to give you a call?

What did we need to talk about on the phone? I felt like the damn gingerbread man. This dude was trying to inch me further and further past my boundaries and into a tight situation. I'd thrown his business card away in Atlanta for a reason. Well, actually, seven hundred reasons, if you count the number of miles separating us. Now, I'd be damned if I ended up clutched in his greedy jaws.

The light turned green, and I put the phone back into the cup holder, pondering my response. I drummed my fingers on the steering wheel, then turned on the radio. I needed to take a beat to figure out what the hell I was even doing. This man drove me wild in my skin. When he was on my mind, there was no room for anything or anyone else. I was supposed to be focusing on my career and education right now, and I thought I had already closed the door with Lennox back in Atlanta. But here he was, popping right back into my life. It was a good thing his ass was hours away because the spark surging through me at that moment would have ignited an explosion if we were face to face.

I exhaled and replied.

I'm free now.

"Beauty." His baritone, booming through my car speakers, hit my ears in a delightful way and triggered a shy smile. "How are you?"

*Beauty? Oh, I like that.*

"I'm doing well."

"Good to hear your voice again."

"Thank you. I wasn't expecting to hear yours so soon . . . or ever," I blurted.

"Oh, really? Why not?"

"I just . . . thought we'd leave things where they were."

"Is that what you want?"

I paused. Ten seconds into the conversation and I was already squirming in the hot seat. "What other choice do we have? You're there, and I'm here."

"As long as there's a will and a way, we have plenty of choices, Ms. Hampton."

His response gave me pause, and I took a few quick breaths to recover. "Well . . . I guess that's true."

I didn't realize I was holding my breath until he responded moments later.

"Precisely."

"Well then, I guess . . ."

I heard his line click and I pause again. He asked if he could put me on a brief hold. Thank God for the reprieve because I was feeling all types of emotions and was at a loss for how to handle them. Did he enjoy making me uneasy, or was he always this intense? When he clicked over, I would find out what he had called for and then get his ass off the line. A few moments later, he clicked back over.

"Patience?"

My name on his lips was doing wild things to me. "Yes?"

"I apologize. This is a work issue that's going to take a little while to resolve. I'd like to call you back if you'll still be free in the next half hour."

"I should be. No problem." Actually, it *was* a problem. Now I had to wait for God knows how long to know what he had called for.

"Thanks. Talk soon."

I stopped and got some gas, then headed home. As my Teedra

Moses streaming radio station played in the background, I changed into leggings and a soft cotton tee and pushed my 'fro to the back of my head with a silk hair tie. Then I logged into my exercise app to do a quick virtual meditation session, attempting to get my mind right. Despite my sincerest efforts, I couldn't stop my mind from wandering. Lennox Davenport had really called me. I finally felt justified by his constant presence in my thoughts. I was also on his mind, and he wasn't too proud to reach out and get in touch with me, even though he left the ball in my court by giving me his business card, and I had dropped it by throwing it away. I knew he had plenty of beautiful options to occupy his time in Atlanta, but his mind was on me. I closed my app and turned my music back on, then started on the breakfast dishes waiting for me. I tried not to read too much into Lennox's call, but the underlying excitement had me shimmying my shoulders and shaking my hips to the upbeat tempo.

When the phone rang, I rushed to grab a towel and dry my hands before it stopped ringing. I slipped in my earbuds and said hello.

"Hey, Chrissy! Whatcha doing?"

"Oh hey, Mom. Just washing the dishes."

"Did you order something and have it sent here?"

"Yeah, that's for you. I saw you were low on shea butter the last time I was over there, so I ordered some from that small business I was telling you about."

She squealed like a schoolgirl, and I heard her ripping open the package. "Mmm, this smells amazing. Thank you, Chrissy!"

I smiled. It took the littlest things to make her happy. "Of course, Mom."

"How's your freelance business been going?"

"Steady. I'm actually finalizing a contract with an independent author to narrate a novel with a shared royalty arrangement."

Her exaggerated whoops made me smile. "Big Money Grip! You've really been grinding, girl."

"Yeah . . ."

"Uh-oh. I know that voice. You got something else on your mind."

I paused, wondering how much to share with her. "Well, yeah. At my main job, I'm working on a radio commercial project, and they basically said my voice isn't Black enough for the market they're trying to reach. They've asked me to rerecord it."

I heard her scoff. "What's that supposed to mean?"

"I guess they had a certain sound in mind to appeal to the urban market."

"Unbelievable."

"At first, I wanted to tell them hell no. But they told my boss that they'll request another actor if I'm not willing to do it. That won't be a good look for me."

"I'm just thinking about those god-awful radio commercials I hear. It's an embarrassment and blaxploitation to the fullest. Got us out here sounding like some damn fools!"

I began loading the dishwasher. "Yeah, I definitely don't want to contribute to that narrative."

"But at the same time, you're an actor. Although it's hitting closer to home this time, it's a role, just like all the other ones you've done, sweetheart. So, play it to the best of your ability while still representing our community well," Mom said. "You can add a little bit of twang to it—just enough to let them know you're a sista. But it could still be sophisticated, you know? Not full-on corporate or newscaster mode, but more like the voice you'd use in a relaxed environment with someone you're still getting to know."

I nodded. "Right. Relaxed but not *too* familiar."

"Exactly. That way you're still being true to yourself *and* making your boss happy. Remember, you're still up for that promotion, and he's watching how you handle situations like these."

The tension in my shoulders eased a bit. This solution may be a viable one that wouldn't compromise my integrity while meeting the client's expectations. "You're right, Mom. I think I'm pretty comfortable with that compromise. Hopefully it's good enough for the client."

"It will be. Well, now I know why you've been on my mind. I'm glad that's settled. I'm about to treat myself to a hot bath, then use my shea butter before my date tonight. Thanks, babe!"

"You're welcome. Have a good time tonight."

I finished the dishes and started cleaning the bathroom when my phone rang again. I was pleased to see it was Lennox calling back. I was hoping he'd finally put me out of my misery and tell me the reason he was calling.

"Sorry to keep you waiting. The phone hasn't rung all day; now, I'm getting back-to-back calls. Are you still free to chat?"

"Yes. Work stuff?"

"It never ends. Honestly, if they can't afford not to bother me on weekends, they need to be paying me more."

I nodded. "Cold hard facts. Time is money."

"Precisely. So, let me get to the point before we're interrupted again. I'd like an answer to my initial question before I ask my original question."

"Which question?"

"Patience, don't be coy."

"What makes you think I'm being coy? I honestly don't remember."

"Okay, my bad. Do you have an interest in continuing to get to know one another?"

I was taken aback by the direct nature of his question. We hadn't spoken since our time together in Atlanta and now he was talking about a relationship? "Well . . . if I'm being honest, I prefer not to start this off as a long-distance relationship." I didn't feel the need to bring up my recent breakup with Daniel as the main reason for passing on pursuing things with Lennox at the moment. Quite frankly, I didn't see a viable future with either of them at that point. The last thing I needed was to set myself up for another letdown.

"Okay. Is there a particular reason for this preference?"

"Well, from my experience, long-distance dating involves a lot of work and sacrifice and has lower success rates. So, starting a new relationship as virtual strangers that way would be quite a risk for both of us." *And I've gotten my heart broken when I learned I was a side chick to someone who claimed to be my man while living five hundred miles away.*

"That sounds like a pretty biased and pessimistic point of view."

I scoffed. "Well, it's no worse than your pretty opinionated and asshole-like point of view."

As soon as the words left my lips, my cheeks flushed. I wanted to tell him that his accusation was hurtful, but, feeling triggered and defensive, I'd snapped at him instead. There was a brief pause on his end, and although I was taken aback by my own reaction, I stubbornly held my tongue. A cramped silence hung between us for a few moments longer, and although I wanted to check if he was still on the line, my pride wouldn't let me speak up.

He spoke again in a measured tone. "Forgive me if that's how I've made you feel. It certainly wasn't my intent to pass judgment. I was only wondering if past events have made you reluctant to explore getting to know someone while long distance." When I didn't respond because I was terrified of blurting out anything else, he continued. "But I guess I have no choice other than to respect your view on this matter. But, like you just said, time is money, so I won't waste any more of yours or mine."

I sputtered before saying, "Well, may I ask what your original question was?"

"I believe that's water under the bridge if you don't see things going anywhere between us."

I scoffed. "So, I'm being punished for being honest with you?"

"No, but I'm not into childish mind games. I'm protective of my time, and I don't want to be selfish and cost either of us any more of it if this isn't going anywhere," Lennox said.

"That's exactly what I meant about being an ass. I can spot

one from a mile away. I refuse to let you gaslight me just because I answered your question honestly. Good day, Mr. Davenport."

"I notice a pattern of name-calling here, *Ms. Hampton*, when there's no need for it. Furthermore, the correct use of the term gaslighting applies to being manipulated into questioning your own reality or sanity by someone who's trying to gain power over you. That I did not do. I'm simply choosing to remove myself from a potentially toxic situation. Look, I contacted you because I enjoyed spending time with you a few weeks ago. But judging from your current disposition, something's clearly shifted between us since then, and I was unaware of that. No love lost. I hope your day and your mood improve soon, Beauty."

I was about to offer a snarky response when I realized he was no longer on the line.

# Chapter Sixteen

Four years after my father left us—also when my twenty-seven-year-old mother decided she no longer wanted to act like one—my grandfather stepped up in a major way. Once he found out that I'd assumed responsibility for raising myself and my sister at twelve years old, he took the reins so my mother could get the help she needed. Pop-Pop immediately moved us in with him, giving us the stability we both craved. Thankfully, my father was still footing the bill for our private school tuition, so our lives weren't disrupted further by having to switch schools. Each night, Chelsea and I had home-cooked meals, hot baths, and a sense of provision, protection, and consistency. So, whenever I stepped into my grandfather's house, I felt like I was coming home.

"Pop-Pop, I'm here," I called out after using a key to let myself in.

"In here, Munk," he called from the kitchen.

I walked right into one of his warm bear hugs. There was a full Sunday dinner spread on the kitchen table but on a Tuesday. Smothered pork chops, rice, collard greens, and . . . I sniffed. "Are you baking something?"

"You don't know my peach cobbler when you smell it? You were raised eating it."

I frowned, washing my hands. "I thought that could have been it, but it's March. And you only use fresh peaches."

He shrugged. "Yeah, I had a taste for it, so I went with canned peaches this time."

"Canned, frozen, or fresh, your cobbler's always amazing."

"You know it, Munk. Chelsea coming?"

"Yeah, a little bit later. I came early to help you set up, but it looks like you have things handled around here."

"Yeah, we're all set," he said, wiping his hands on his apron. "So, since we have a little time, tell me more about your trip to Atlanta."

I faked a smile, even though I knew talking about the trip would make me think of Lennox. "It was a great time. I enjoyed every minute of it."

"I loved that picture you sent me from the park. Printed it out at the drugstore." He gestured toward the picture of me on the refrigerator. "I sure do miss Atlanta. I'm going to have to get back down there sooner rather than later."

"Yeah, you definitely should. So, remember when I asked you to take me into your prayer closet last week?"

He nodded. "Yes, and I sent one up for you, just like I do every day."

"Well, it worked because I just found out I got the job!"

"What? That's dope, Munk. What's the position? Is it at your current company or somewhere else?"

"It's at my current company. After returning home from Atlanta, I had a long talk with Gordon, the owner, about my career goals. I let him know I was thinking about seeing what other options are out there for me. But he wasn't having that. So, he decided to bring recruiting in-house and created a role for me. Starting next week, I'll be the talent manager for all six of our offices."

"Outstanding! That's the perfect role for you. You've been

there for years, so he should have already done that. But everything happens in God's time."

I nodded, helping myself to a buttered roll. "Amen. I'll be traveling a little more, but I negotiated no travel during major holidays into my contract. And it's a significant salary increase."

"It better be!" He offered me a fist bump.

"I'm really looking forward to recruiting more diverse talent. Trice and I are currently the only Black women in the organization."

"You've got this, baby girl. Hit up those HBCUs."

"You know it."

Then his eyes softened. "Your mom told me about the whole blackspeak thing."

I groaned and took a seat at the kitchen table. "Pop-Pop, I've never experienced anything like that in my career before. My whole life, I was teased by the neighborhood kids for talking too white because I attended private school, but I never thought I'd hear that from a client."

He shook his head and joined me at the table. "Yeah, that's wild, kiddo. I know what your mom suggested, but what did you decide to do?"

"At first, I was ready to tell them to kick rocks and flat-out refuse to re-record it. But then I talked to Bella about how the Italian accent I used offended her. I even tried to learn Kreyól to feel included in Daniel's family. Those situations opened my eyes to the fact that I've been putting on an act my entire life."

A few tears slipped from my eyes before I felt the subtle sting of their presence. My mind flashed back to the role I was forced to take on as Chelsea's mother and father at a young age. I always had to put on a brave face and was never allowed to just be a kid, let alone focus on getting to know myself.

"Oh, Munk." The soft warmth of his hand landed on mine. "I had no idea you felt that way."

I shook my head, wiping my eyes. "Neither did I, apparently. Anyway, I decided to re-record it using my natural voice with a little flair. The clients were pleased with it, and so was I. It sounded great, and it felt rewarding to do it without compromising my standards."

"I'm glad it worked out. Yeah, life has done quite a number on you, Munk. But you've built so much character because of it, and I'm proud of you." He squeezed my hand, looking directly into my eyes. "Listen, family may not always come in the traditional form that most of us envision, but what matters most is having the right people around you when it counts. You have me, your sister, and your mother. And Bella is just like family. God has placed us all—even Daniel—in your life for a reason. But you have a family. You don't have to search for it or put on an act to feel like you belong. We're all right here, accepting and loving you and one another just as we are. You hear me?"

I released a shaky breath and nodded. "Yes, Pop-Pop."

"Good. Speaking of him, how have you been doing since the breakup?"

"Overall, I'm doing much better. Some days I wake up feeling great, and others, not so great. But I know I made the right decision, so I'm comforted by that."

"I was fond of Daniel and still am. But look at how much progress you've made since you two parted ways. No more grocery shopping for both of your households, prepping his meals, scheduling all of his appointments, and dealing with his mama. Now you have the free time to focus on your own career goals and live your life. That's all I've ever wanted for you girls. Life is too short to live it any way other than exactly how you want to. Remember that."

I nodded with tears stinging my eyes. Pop-Pop was right. I'd accomplished a lot since leaving Daniel. But I realized it was always up to me to pursue these things, and I was the one standing in my own way.

"Speaking of relationships, what in the world is up with that Sister Perkins? She called me this morning out of the blue and asked me out on a date. Talkin' 'bout she looked my number up in the church directory. That woman is outright bold. I mean, where they do that at?"

Chuckling, I said, "In her world, that's definitely the norm, Pop-Pop."

"You've got that right. Sheesh," he said, wiping his forehead.

After a few seconds, I lifted a brow. "So, you going?"

He blinked. "Going where?"

"On the date."

"Oh yeah, I'm going."

I slapped him five, and we cracked up.

"So, what else has been going on with you? You being low-key? Watching your rom-coms?"

"Yup. Just drinking my water and minding my business. Can't get into any trouble that way."

"Yeah, not much, anyway." He let a beat pass, then said, "True love really does exist outside of Hollywood studios, you know."

My head rocked back. "What you talkin' 'bout, Pop-Pop?"

"You know exactly what I'm talking about. Daniel was a pretty nice guy. But he wasn't the one for you, Munk."

"What makes you say that?"

"Well, you never really got that light in your eyes with him. You know, that glow women get when they're deep in love? The one from your movies."

"Love like that doesn't exist anymore. I'll never find what you and Dear had," I said, referring to my deceased grandmother.

"Oh, you'll definitely find it, Munk. With all that love in your heart, you're destined to find someone to give it to. And your obsession with those movies proves that deep down, you know you're worthy of it, too. You just need to find the right one you can feel comfortable to let your guard down with."

"Pop-Pop, how could I have been guarded with Daniel? I was with him for five years."

"You were guarded, all right." His voice was low and even. "You've been through a lot in your short lifetime. But, between what you've experienced and his mother's shenanigans, you wouldn't let yourself fully love that man."

"I don't know about that . . ."

We both jumped as the front door slammed. "Hold up! It's smelling good up in here!"

My mother walked in, toting a half gallon of vanilla ice cream and whipped cream. I leaned in to give her a kiss.

"What's up, Talent Manager?" She used a proper voice that made me smile. "Somebody's large and in charge. HNIC!"

"Why are you coming in here so hype?" Chelsea asked our mother, casually strolling in with her hands in her jogger pockets.

"There's my Bunny!" Pop-Pop's face brightened, stepping toward her.

"Oh, she gets a hug before I do?" Mom feigned a jealous look.

"What? I've got enough love for all my girls!" Pop-Pop held his arms out, and we all stepped in, planting firm kisses on his cheek.

* * *

Thursday morning, five whole days later, I was still trying to figure out what had caused me to lose my entire mind when I last spoke to Lennox. When I left Atlanta, I was ready to move forward with my life. I was done with Daniel and focused on finally accomplishing all the things I'd put off for the past few years. I also had decided that regardless of how I felt about Lennox, he didn't fit into that equation. After making the decision to step out of Daniel's shadow to live the life I had always dreamed of, I realized that I needed to focus on finding myself, finding my voice, and defining my purpose. But no matter how hard I tried, I couldn't get my mind off of Lennox.

He was invading my thoughts, and his mental presence was taking me off focus. Then, out of the blue, he reached out to me, and here I was, uprooting my entire day, waiting anxiously for his call. I was back to the unhealthy patterns I had developed over the course of a wide range of failed relationships. When Lennox voiced his opinion on my preference to avoid long-distance relationships, it came off as judgmental and triggered something deep inside of me. I hadn't meant to, but I had just snapped out of reflex. It could have been the pressure I was experiencing at work, or it could have been due to my habit of living in my feelings. Either way, Lennox had a point. The shit was toxic.

So now, the only thing I knew for sure was that I'd successfully burned yet another bridge in my life. I already had screwed things up with all of Daniel's family, so there was no way I would have the balls to show my face at another one of his parents' Friday night framily dinners again—even as a friend—after reading his mother like an alphabet book in front of everyone. I honestly didn't remember half of what I had said to her, but I knew it was bad because I felt great afterward, strutting out like a proud little peacock.

The only thing I had to look forward to anymore was my poppin' sex life with Daniel, which, to be honest, was only due to fantasizing about Lennox. I thought of him each time I was intimate with Daniel. So here I was, sleeping with a man I no longer wanted while fantasizing about another man I wouldn't allow myself to have. And my conversation with Pop-Pop was still on my mind. Did he really believe I was guarded and was never in love with Daniel?

I walked into the office after recording part of a computer-based sexual harassment training tutorial at our off-site studio. I had been talking for four hours straight, reciting the same dry-ass information over and over until the sound technician was satisfied. So, my plan was to complete a couple hours of online training for my new role at the office, then head home on time. My mind was already fast-forwarding to my date with wine, popcorn, and *The Real Housewives of Atlanta* that night.

As soon as I got to my desk, Trice stopped by and asked to speak to me privately. I looked at her like she had three heads. She knew my damn rule. The only thing I asked of my teammates on recording days was that they gave me at least ten minutes after I arrived in the office before they started making requests. When I tried to protest, she told me to get my ass up and to the bathroom, pronto.

Once we stepped inside the small restroom, I was prepared to let her have it.

"Heifa, I know you—"

"Ah! You may not want to start in on me just yet, Ice Queen."

I rolled my eyes at the nickname Trice used whenever I was in one of my moods. Then I checked myself and uncrossed my arms. "And why is that?"

"So, I started to text you last night, but I decided to wait until you got into the office for this pipin' tea."

"Well, come on, tea. What is it?"

"So, Landon and I were grabbing dinner at that new steak spot last night. The one you and I went to for happy hour a couple of weeks ago. We were about to leave, but on my way back from the restroom, I noticed some eye candy sitting at the bar. Girl, I'm talking about a FINE brotha. Suited up, clean cut, and tall, just like I like 'em. So, I tried to get a better look at him as I passed by, but low-key, though, because I didn't need Landon catching me and throwing one of his jealous hissy fits and thangs. Anyway, I glanced over at his equally fine friend in the meantime. You'll *never* guess who it was!"

"Daniel," I said.

"Nope."

"Raymond, the sexual-chocolate intern."

Trice laughed. "Yes, he *was* fine. But no. I said you would never guess."

"Well, since we've established that, now you can just tell me." I had already far exceeded my word count for the day and didn't have the energy to keep this up for much longer.

"It was the hottie from Hotlanta. Aye, aye," she said, twerking with her tongue hanging out.

I watched her for a few moments as her words registered. I swallowed back a scream before squeaking, "Say what, now?"

"Yes, you heard me, girl! Lickable Lennox was sitting at a bar in The Flats, casually chopping it like he lives here."

I cringed, holding up a finger. "First, make that the last time you refer to him as Lickable Lennox."

She giggled, wagging her tongue.

"Second, it couldn't have been him. I just talked to him a few days ago."

"What? You didn't tell me that! What y'all talk about?"

I frowned. "Wait, no. Tell me about last night's case of mistaken identity first."

"I've seen the man in person in Atlanta, remember? And I never forget a face. Especially when that face is taking my work wife out to dinner in a strange city."

I swallowed again, unable to find words. I just continued to stare at my friend's face in stunned silence, still fully believing she was mistaken. There was no way Lennox was in my city. He hadn't mentioned anything about making a trip up here when we'd last spoken.

"P . . ." Trice leaned toward me, bangles jingling as she waved her hand in front of my face.

Determined to get to the bottom of it, I fished my phone out of my coat pocket and pulled up Lennox's Instagram profile for the first time in over a week. His most recent post was of a jambalaya omelet with shrimp, toast, and Cajun fries. Although he hadn't shared his location, I instantly recognized the signature breakfast dish at a small restaurant up the street. It was locally known for delectable food.

*I like going places where I know people so I can avoid the tourist spots. I enjoy visiting places that make cities feel authentic.*

My mouth literally dropped as his words came back to me.

# Chapter Seventeen

"Oh, snap! He found our drunk brunch spot!" Trice leaned over my shoulder and moaned. "I would kill for a West Fourteenth special right about now."

Lennox Davenport was really here. That was probably what he had wanted to talk to me about last week, and I was too busy shutting him down about not wanting long-distance relationships to find out. *Fucking fool.* I dropped my phone back into my pocket and rushed out of the bathroom. Trice was on my heels as I snatched my purse and laptop case off my desk.

"You're leaving already, Patience?" Hilary looked up, her face etched with concern. "Is everything okay?"

"Something came up that she has to take care of. She'll be working from home for the rest of the day," Trice said, handing me the pair of sunglasses I had dropped in my haste. "See you later, queen!"

In the car, I pulled out my phone to call Lennox. There was no more time for being stuck in my head or living in my feelings. I had to find out if he was still in Cleveland and for how much longer. I dialed his number, praying he hadn't left without even letting me know he was here.

The phone trilled softly in my ear, and I inched around in my seat, antsy and anxious as hell. After the second ring, the call was sent to his voicemail. His baritone filled my ear, and I closed my eyes. I don't even remember what his outgoing message said because the next thing I knew, the tone was beeping.

"Hey . . . Lennox. This is Patience. Hampton. I . . . was hoping we could talk. When you get a moment, can you please call me back? Thanks."

I sat there for a few more minutes, dumbfounded, uneasy, and giddy. Then I headed home, planning to drown myself in paperwork to counteract my raging nerves.

I was in the laundry room, hair pushed up in a puff, rocking banana-print leggings and a *Purple Rain* T-shirt when my FaceTime tone rang. Figuring it was Chelsea or Pop-Pop, I picked up my phone off the dryer and almost hit accept until Lennox's name flashed across the screen. I jumped, dropping the phone on the floor. Yelping and cursing, I attempted to scoop it back up with wet, trembling hands. The ringing instantly stopped, and I wasn't sure if I accidentally pressed the accept button. *Please, God! No!* I looked at the screen, and it showed a missed FaceTime call.

I crumpled to the carpeted floor and sprawled out with a groan. "Boy, what the hell are you doing to me?" I screamed at the top of my lungs.

Lennox was tap dancing on my entire last frenzied nerve. But I also felt a tingle in my spine, relieved that he at least had attempted to reach back out after three painstaking hours had passed. I took a moment to catch my breath before stuffing the rest of my clothes into the dryer. I headed upstairs to the kitchen, grabbed a bottled water from the fridge, then sat down at the kitchen table to catch my breath. A chime alerted that a text had come through.

Lennox: My bad, butt dial.

I lifted a brow, then considered my response for several long seconds. Before I could hit send on my "no problem" reply, another text came through.

Lennox: How are you, btw?

Me: ~~Doing good. Did you get my voicemail?~~ (too thirsty)

Me: ~~Chillin like a villain.~~ (ugh)

Finally, I replied, I'm doing well. How about you?

Lennox: Can't complain. You at work?

Me: Working remotely, finishing up for the day.

Lennox: Cool, cool. What are you up to this evening?

Me: ~~A little bit of this, little of that.~~ (too aloof)

Me: ~~Just chillin' . . . watching some Netflix.~~ (Nope, no thirst traps here)

Me: Not sure yet. What about you?

Him: (Floating ellipses)

(Floating ellipses)

(Floating ellipses)

No reply.

After a couple of minutes of staring at the screen expectantly, I forced myself to set down the phone. I drained the rest of my water because, clearly, I was still desperate and dehydrated. I turned on the oven and pulled out some chicken tenderloins, a white onion, and a green bell pepper. Next, I grabbed some extra virgin olive oil and fresh herbs from the pantry.

My phone pinged, and I glanced over at the screen.

Lennox: I'd like to see you.

*He's here! He's still here!*

Lennox: FaceTime? This time, no butt dial.

I sighed, walking over to the sink to wash my hands. He wasn't still here.

Me: Give me a call instead? Cooking at the moment.

I slipped in my AirPods and continued seasoning the meat. A few moments later, the phone rang.

"Hey."

"Beauty."

*Wait, I'm still Beauty? Eeeeeeeee!* I felt my lips pull into a wide smile.

"What's for dinner?"

"Chicken fajitas with cauliflower rice and cilantro avocado lime sauce."

"Damn, woman! All that on a weekday? You're making me wish I was there to grab a plate."

My heart sank. He was no longer in Cleveland. I tried to keep my disappointment out of my voice. "Yeah, this is one of my favorites to make."

"Do you cook often?'

"Yeah. I guess you could call it a hobby."

"I enjoy cooking as well. As a foodie, I'm very particular about whose cooking I eat, so I mostly make my own."

"Same. I enjoy exploring different herbs and spices and mixing untraditional flavors."

"Sounds like my kind of cooking."

A few moments passed as I drizzled olive oil over the meat and vegetables.

Unable to stomach the tension for a moment longer, I spoke up. "So, Lennox. I just want to let you know how sorry I am for last week. There's no excuse for my behavior, so I won't even try to explain. Just know that I'm aware of how unbecoming that was to accuse you of trying to manipulate me. That's not what I think of you, and I regret speaking to you that way. I'm going to do my best to make sure nothing like that ever happens again."

"And I apologize for inferring that you were toxic. Like you, I got caught up in emotions and also didn't mean what I said. That wasn't cool."

"Well, thank you."

"But I'd like to hear your explanation."

I blinked, caught unaware. "About what?"

"About why you reacted the way you did about the topic of a long-distance relationship."

"Well . . . I . . ." I stumbled, wondering what his angle was. "I think I was just frustrated. You were so intense when asking about how I felt about potentially pursuing something with you. We don't know each other well enough yet to determine if that's worth pursuing at this point. So, I guess I wasn't ready to be grilled like that."

"I wasn't trying to wife you up. I simply asked a question to get clarity on what you wanted going forward."

I pulled out the cutting board and began slicing the onions and peppers. "Well, did you get it?"

"Somewhat."

"Okay, well, what else can I clear up for you?"

"What's held you back from your own happiness? I'm not arrogant enough to assume that I'm a factor in your happiness or fulfillment, so feel free to remove exploring anything further with me from the equation. But when we were discussing some of your personal goals while in Atlanta, you mentioned wanting to live somewhere besides Cleveland and making moves in your career. I'm just wondering what's stopped you from going after those things before now."

*Talk about a loaded fucking question.*

"See, that's what I'm talking about. You're so intense. We were just talking about cooking. Now we're already on to life goals."

"What's wrong with that?"

"I just . . . I haven't really taken much time to think about those things. I was in a long-term relationship with someone who was very focused on his career, and I guess I . . . used that as an excuse to put mine on the backseat. I chose to support his goals instead."

I blinked. That was the first time I had ever admitted that to anyone, let alone myself.

"Ah, there we are."

"But before you imply that I was forced into that situation, let me clarify that it was *my* choice to be complacent in my personal goals and career. I just enjoy supporting others. It's always been my thing."

"There's nothing wrong with that, Beauty. In fact, that's a commendable quality."

"However . . ." I prompted, sliding the food into the oven.

"If he truly loves and appreciates you, he will want to know about your goals and support you in return. Is he open to that?"

"I'm no longer in that relationship, but he never held me back from doing anything I wanted to do."

"Never holding you back is one thing. Actively encouraging and supporting you is another."

"Facts."

"So, we're back to square one, then."

"Yep."

"You."

"Yes, I guess so. You definitely gave me some things to think about in Atlanta. When I came home, I decided it was time for me to step up and stop blaming everyone and everything else for my shortcomings."

"Precisely. And the outcome?"

I smiled to myself, intrigued that he wasn't intimidated by my tendency to push back. For me, it wasn't about arguing; it was about having passion and making an effort to further the relationship. Lennox seemed interested enough in learning more about me and my well-being to weather the storm and get to the bottom of the issue. Mr. Davenport had just earned serious points with me.

"The outcome has been amazing. I'm starting a new chapter in my career soon with a handsome salary increase and a bigger platform to recruit diverse professionals into our organization."

After a long pause, he said, "I know how much diversity in the workplace means to you. You can't see me right now, but I'm smiling hard."

Picturing those dimples poppin', I said, "Yes, it does. I've already created a recruitment strategy that involves partnering with HBCUs and multiethnic student organizations at traditional colleges."

"I love it."

"Thank you for inspiring me to do more."

"That was all you. You just needed the opportunity to get out of your own way and see the options for yourself."

"So, I heard you were in my city recently," I said, taking a seat on the couch with a glass of wine.

"Yes, my first time in C-Town in a long time. My friend, Ginelle, has been showing me around. It's been real."

My cheeks flushed. *Ginelle. Who in the world is Ginelle?* So, he comes up to my city and chooses to kick it with another chick instead of calling me? Was he trying to make me jealous? I fought to keep my cool. She was probably just an old friend of his, or he wouldn't have mentioned her.

"Yes, people tend to sleep on Cleveland. I'm glad you were able to check it out. Did you have a good time?"

"I'm having a great time."

I swallowed a scream, keeping my tone even. "That's cool. Where are you staying?"

"Been here on business, so I had a corporate suite downtown for a few days. My aunt lives here, so I've been crashing with her and working remotely for the past couple of days."

*Damn, he's been here almost a week.* I held my breath and asked, "How much longer are you here for?"

"A couple more days."

"So, you were going to leave and not tell me?"

"Wouldn't *you*?"

I nodded. "You're right. I guess I don't really have a right to have any expectations of you."

He laughed. "After the way you showed your entire ass? You sure don't."

"That's more than fair."

We sat in thoughtful silence for a long while. I took a deep swig of my wine, rubbed my sweaty palms on my thighs, then asked, "So, are you joining me for dinner, or what?"

Chapter Eighteen

I opened the door and paused to take in each succulent inch of him. He seemed to have grown taller. He looked straight out of a high-end fashion catalog as his lean frame filled my doorway, donned in a gray peacoat, designer scarf, dark jeans, and leather boots. He effortlessly oozed sexiness from head to fucking toe. I squeezed my thighs for a quick moment before smiling at him and stepping aside to let him enter. "Hello and welcome."

He nodded and offered a small smile as he stepped into my home. And just like that, we crossed another threshold. Lennox was inside of my home, and I hoped with everything I had that he would soon be inside of me.

I caught a whiff of his cologne as he breezed by, respectfully removing his boots and placing them on the mat without my request. He removed his coat and scarf, and I held out my hands to take them from him. He leaned over and placed them on the banister, opting for a warm hug instead. With my head on his chest, I took the deepest breath my lungs could handle and brought my hands up to the middle of his back. He smelled and felt so damn good. His large palms rested lightly on my lower back. We stood there for a moment before he pulled away slightly and gazed down at me.

"You have a beautiful home. It smells good in here."

I looked up at him and didn't say a word. His face was perfect. I wouldn't change a single thing about it. Not his thick eyebrows or his smooth forehead that slightly wrinkled when he was thinking. Not his cute nose or his kissable lips. Not the fullness of his beard or his pencil-thin mustache. None of it. I licked my lips and squeezed my thighs once again. It was going to be a long night if he was expecting me to play the coy role. I wanted to devour this man right this very second. Wait. Were his lips moving? Shit.

"Beauty?"

I blinked, trying to rip my eyes away from his mouth. "Uh-huh?"

"Is that your timer? I think the food may be ready."

"I was just keeping it warm for us." I reluctantly stepped back, grabbing his coat and heading to the closet to hang it up. I heard his footfalls behind me as I rushed over to the oven and pulled out the food.

I jumped as his voice filled my ear from behind.

"That looks amazing."

"Thank you," I said, adding more parsley to the cauliflower rice and stirring it.

"Should I wash my hands in here or somewhere else?" he asked, gesturing toward the kitchen sink.

"There's fine."

I watched his shoulder blades glide under his fitted long-sleeved T-shirt as he washed his hands. I hadn't seen a body that defined up close and personal since . . . well, the last time I saw Lennox up close and personal. When he finished, I handed him a towel, and he leaned against the sink as he dried his hands. His eyes roamed over my body, clad in a red tie-dye tee dress. A red satin headband surrounded my curly 'fro.

"Lady in red. The color still looks nice on you."

"Thanks." I beamed. "Ready to eat?"

He nodded.

I fixed his plate and poured him a glass of rosé. "Sorry, I don't have anything stronger."

"Wine is just fine. Thanks for fixing my plate."

Before we ate, we bowed our heads, and he led a brief prayer. Then he raised his glass. "To our second meal together."

I nodded as we clinked glasses, maintaining eye contact. In fact, we barely broke our gaze during dinner as he discussed the details of his business trip and his time in Cleveland so far.

"So, you have friends here."

"Yeah, a couple from college and some old friends from my aunt's neighborhood. I used to visit her from time to time while growing up. My parents were always shipping me off somewhere. That's why I'm comfortable with traveling and moving around."

I nodded. "Is that what you wanted to talk about last week? Your trip here to Cleveland?"

He paused for a moment while he chewed. "That was part of it."

When he didn't offer any more information, I pressed, "So what was the other part?"

He shrugged. "I'm not sure if I want to ask you now."

I frowned. "Why not?"

"Let's see how the evening goes, and we'll revisit it later. You done?"

I nodded, and he stood and cleared the dishes from the table, leaving the wine glasses. As he loaded the dishwasher, I grabbed the bottle and glasses and headed to the living room. I opened my streaming radio app on the TV and selected my Andra Day radio station. The sultry melody of Zhané's "Sending My Love" soon filled the room. I went to the hall closet and strategically pulled out my Scrabble board game. While setting it up, I glanced over at Lennox rinsing off the dishes I used to prepare the meal and loading them into the dishwasher. I shivered. It was alarming how naturally we fell into this cozy, easy routine. I hid a small smile behind a sip from my wine glass.

When he joined me on the couch, I thanked him for cleaning up.

"Least I can do. Now, are you ready to get spanked . . ."

I raised a brow.

". . . in Scrabble?"

We chuckled, fully aware of the heavy cloak of sexual tension hanging around us.

"Goodbye, boy. You better come get this thrashing right quick."

As he picked his letters and arranged them on his rack, he asked, "So how long have you lived here?"

"Um, I bought this house about a year and a half ago."

"Congrats. Homeownership in your . . . what, mid-to-late twenties? That's dope."

"Thanks. I guess that's another reason I've grown roots here. Can't just up and leave without risking negative equity."

He lifted a thoughtful brow while laying his initial word, *muzjik,* on the board. "You could always rent it out."

My hips involuntarily rocked as I glanced down at the board. He was coming out the gate with a six-letter word for thirty-one points. I hadn't met a person who was anything close to competition for me in Scrabble. He was setting the bar high, and the exhilaration, along with the wine, was making me giddy . . . and horny. A Black man's flagrant intelligence was more powerful than any form of foreplay for me.

I sipped my wine and said, "I could . . ."

I carefully placed my letters on the board. *Quaky,* for twenty-six points.

He stared at the letters, then gave a slight nod as I fished more letters out of the bag. "But that's not something you're interested in at the moment?"

"No, maybe in a few years. For now, I'm good right here. The cost of living is great, and our city's been revitalized."

"Yeah, I heard about the new downtown life before I got here, but it exceeded my expectations. It's coming along. Great restaurants and clubs. I can definitely see why you stuck around."

His next word was *azides* for twenty points, giving him a twenty-five-point lead.

"Nice."

He sipped his wine. "Thanks."

After a few more plays, we decided to call it with me in a narrow lead of three points. "We both know who was going to win that anty-way," I boasted as we put away the pieces.

He smiled and stopped me when I tried to refill his empty glass. "No more for me, thanks."

"Would you like to watch a movie?"

He chuckled. "Another rom-com?"

I shrugged playfully. "I mean, is there anything else?"

"There is," he said, suddenly turning serious. His eyes fixed on me.

I squirmed as they swept all over my body. "Like what?"

He took my glass from my hand and set it on the table without breaking eye contact. Then he inched closer to me until his cologne filled my nostrils. Alicia Keys sang about touching her like it was the last time as my body beckoned him to inch closer. Closer. Closer.

I closed my eyes just before his warm, sweet lips landed on mine, bringing a waft of his cologne with him. He had switched from Polo, and I was thankful. I opened my mouth, and he slid his tongue inside, gently caressing mine. My head lolled on my neck as I angled to explore his mouth deeper. He tasted so damn good. His hands slid up my backside, over my rib cage, and stroked my swelling breasts. My eyes flew open, and I studied him. His eyes were closed, and I wondered what was on that brilliant mind of his. Then his eyes eased open, and we stared at each other as our hands hungrily explored each other's bodies. When his fingers landed on my hips, I lifted up my dress to straddle him. I began rhythmically grinding against him as he groaned and planted his hot mouth on my neck. My lips throbbed, still savoring the pressure of our passionate kiss.

He suckled my neck before moving down to my breasts. Popping open the front closure of my bra, he lifted my left breast into his mouth. His eager smacking stirred a heatwave within me. I clamped my eyes shut and palmed his head, bringing him closer to my body as we rose and fell in unison. My panties became soaked with evidence of my brazen intentions. Sensing my readiness, he slipped a finger into my slippery folds, and I bit my lower lip to keep from screaming out. The pressure continued to build, and I didn't know how much more I would be able to handle. He had already rejected me once in Atlanta, so I was impatiently waiting for him to make his move. But when? If he left me with blue walls again, I swear I would . . .

My hips spread as two of his long fingers penetrated me, working diligently against the strain of my damp panties. I rode his fingers like my life depended on it. Who knew if I would get any more than this? I opened my eyes once more to find him watching me attentively. I locked eyes with him, my mouth open and brow furrowed in sweet torment. The slow pressure continued to mount, threatening to tip past its peak.

"*Oh*. I'm going to come, Lennox," I moaned.

He continued to stare at me as he worked his fingers in a beckoning gesture.

"I-I-I mean it!"

He gave a slight nod, amusement creeping into his eyes.

"Shit funny to you?" I cried out, bobbing up and down on his hand.

"No. Shit's beautiful. Your face. It's incredible."

That was it for me. I threw back my head, arms outstretched like I was free falling. Lennox's hand gripped my waist tighter, stabilizing me as my hips bounced and bucked. My inner muscles contracted with a powerful force I didn't recognize. I still felt his fingers inside of me. By the time the orgasmic spiral retreated, I was horizontal, my head and hands resting on the table behind me, knees still bent on the couch, like a sexual acrobat.

A few more seconds passed before I heard his voice. "Patience?"

I opened my eyes. He was wiping his hand off on a napkin.

"I know you're in recovery mode, but we should get you upright before you end up with a stiff neck."

I grunted as he pulled me up by arms. We both smiled, face to face again.

"What. The actual. Fuck?"

Lennox nodded, a warm smile still resting in his eyes. "Yeah, shit was wild."

I climbed off his lap and plopped onto the couch beside him. "You got that right. Whew! Now, let's take care of you."

He stood and shook his head. "No, I'm fine. Don't worry about me."

"What? No, you're not leaving here like this."

"Patience, trust me. If we get something else started, I'll never leave here."

I twisted my lips. *Is that a bad thing?*

"I've told you how I feel about casual sex. Just because your fine ass is standing in front of me in that sexy T-shirt dress . . ." He planted a kiss on my neck. "Doesn't mean anything has changed. Besides, I have an early start and a lot to take care of tomorrow. But I had a great time with you this evening. Thanks for welcoming me into your home."

*People have premarital sex every day. Get into it,* I thought as I slowly rose to my feet. Instead, I mumbled, "Okay. I can respect that."

He stepped into the bathroom and washed his hands. "I'm headed straight back to my aunt's house. FaceTime in thirty?"

"Absolutely." I headed to the hall closet and handed him his coat.

He leaned down and planted a tender kiss on my lips, pulling away before I could slip him some tongue. "By the way, you got any red pumps?"

I gave a half-hearted laugh. "I'll dust them off just for you, Mr. Davenport."

*Chapter Nineteen*

We were two hours into our FaceTime, and I was hoarse from laughing. Turned out serious Mr. Davenport was pretty damn funny. Curled up under my down comforter with a pair of boy shorts and a ribbed tank, the red pumps beside my bed were the furthest things from my mind. We were enjoying getting to know one another, and the conversation was easy and light. I could tell opening up wasn't natural for him, but he was making an effort and I appreciated that.

"So, you really tossed my business card in the trash?"

I laughed. "I really did! I told you—I thought our time was over. Besides, long-distance relationships aren't my jam."

"Corny. Who says, 'my jam'?"

"I don't filter what I say based on what other people are saying at the time. *That's* corny."

He nodded. "Nah, I feel you. But 'my jam' was never what people were saying. It sounds cute coming from you, though."

I frowned. "Cute? I'm not a damn puppy."

"Okay, you're slurring your words. How many glasses of wine have you had tonight?"

I looked at my half-empty glass and replied, "About three and a half. I was nervous about having video sex for the first time."

"Well, you don't have to worry about that. I'm enjoying our conversation much more."

My cheeks flushed. "That's cool."

"But first time for video sex. I know you're a church girl, but what's that about?"

I held up a finger. "First of all, yes, I go to church, but I'm still human. I swear, drink, and party just like anyone else. It doesn't lessen my love for the Lord."

"Noted. No judgment here at all. I rarely make it to church outside of Easter and Christmas myself."

I nodded. "And that's fine. It doesn't make you any more of a sinner or less of a believer. Anty-way, there's a lot I haven't done. I admit I'm a bit on the vanilla side in the bedroom."

He just nodded while watching me closely.

I licked my lips and said, "So, I know you said you're only in Cleveland for one more day after this. That's disappointing because my bestie's throwing me a birthday party in a few days."

"Oh yeah? Happy birthday! When's the party?"

"Friday night."

His eyes went up and to the left while his brow furrowed. He was so sexy when he was thinking. "I don't have any in-person meetings scheduled at my home office, so I should probably be able to make that work. I can just push my return flight out a few days and work virtually for the rest of the week."

I felt my cheeks stretch as I smiled wider than I meant to. But he was doing everything right that night—except making sweet love to me. I felt the phone buzz and ignored Daniel's text, just as I had done with his two previous calls. "Thank you. I really appreciate that."

"To be honest, I'm surprised you even asked. Not being one to do long-distance relationships and all."

I rolled my eyes. "Hush, boy."

"So, what's the attire for this shindig?"

"Shindig? Now who's corny?"

He shrugged. "Just speaking your language."

"Funny you should ask. It's actually a celebrity look-alike theme."

He gave me a look.

"Now, that level of corniness I'd admit to. But it wasn't my idea. Bella just started an event-planning business and needs a creative theme for her portfolio. I normally skip celebrating it altogether, but I'm lending her my b-day this year."

"That was going to be my next question. How can someone so antisocial possibly enjoy throwing herself a themed birthday party? Who's the guest of honor coming as?"

"Issa Rae."

He nodded. "Okay, good choice. She's cold."

"Facts. I'm actually looking forward to it. I just have one small favor to ask."

"You want me to come as Jay Ellis. You got it."

"No, silly. Actually, it's a pretty big one."

His forehead wrinkled again.

"Since it's going to be my birthday and all . . . and we don't know when we'll see each other again, can you reconsider your stance on sex outside of relationships?"

His face dropped, and he looked away.

"It's just that the energy between us is so crazy, and if I'm going to see you again, looking all dapper as whoever you show up as, I know I'm going to be all over you. And like you just said, I'll be looking better than you've ever seen me before. Do we really want to do that to ourselves?"

I watched his face for a few moments, fully aware of how desperate that just sounded and terrified that he would instantly end the video call. But if he was judging me, I couldn't tell by his lack of reaction.

I took a deep breath and continued. "And Lennox, I don't know how many times I can handle rejection . . ."

He was quiet for a few moments, kneading his hands. I knew

for sure I was pushing him too far. Maybe I should have just let him return to Atlanta. But just like I had chased him out of that hotel lobby, the same pining to keep him close to me wouldn't let me wait a moment longer. I wanted him, and I was finally admitting it to myself. I knew I couldn't let another opportunity to get to know him better pass me by.

He looked to his right, I assumed toward a window, tilting his head upward. I studied his profile, eager to know what he was thinking. His chiseled jaw flexed. He seemed so convicted to abstain and, for the life of me, I couldn't figure out why. I wiped my sweaty palms on my sheets as I hung mercilessly in the balance, bracing myself for the worst.

He finally turned toward the screen and asked, "Have you still been having sex with your ex?"

Stunned by the blunt nature of his question, I chomped down on my lip. This was worse than the worst.

*Only while thinking about your fine ass!*

"Only sex. The last time was six days ago. But I no longer plan to continue a sexual relationship with him."

"Are you still in love with him?"

My response was easy and honest. "No."

"Patience . . ."

"Lennox, I'm being completely honest with you. Hell, I loved him, but I'm not certain that I was ever *in love* with him. We met in college, and it was my second long-term relationship. He had a good heart and was so passionate about helping others that he seemed like a safe bet compared to the guys I casually dated before him who cheated on me left and right. But over time, I just grew comfortable with supporting him and his vision because I believed in him. And it felt great to feel needed and useful."

I wanted to tell him that Daniel and I never had anything close to our initial spark. Daniel was very smart, but over the past five years, our conversations never intrigued me the same way my conversations with Lennox had. Although I hadn't known much about being in love, I was now certain that I hadn't been in love with Daniel. I was only in love with the idea of who he could become.

Lennox nodded. "I understand. And, once again, no judgment here. We all have needs."

"You know what," I said, "just forget it and come. Having you there to celebrate with me is way more important, and I don't want you to do anything that makes you uncomfortable."

"I won't feel pressured because I very much want to make love to you. Your sexual appeal is overwhelming. When I saw you step off the elevator that night in the hotel lobby, you looked so beautiful that I couldn't catch my breath. When you answered the door tonight in your casual outfit and no makeup, you looked even more beautiful. I now fully understand that the term breathtaking isn't just a romantic cliché. I struggle to breathe when I'm around you. It's a constant battle just to maintain my composure. I've never experienced anything like this before, and, if I'm being honest, it's alarming."

I gasped, stunned by his confession. No one had ever said anything like that to me.

"I just"—he sighed again, conflicted—"I have a biased view of casual sex that stems from my adolescence. One day I'll get into it with you. But, for you—for your birthday—I'm willing to make an exception."

"Lennox, are you sure about this? Do you want to think about it more first?"

"No, I'm actually relieved because something tells me what we have is going to be anything but casual."

I literally shivered from the chills.

Chapter Twenty

I was next in line to place my order at the drive-thru, listening to Daniel's outgoing message for the third time that day. I guess he was still upset about not being able to reach me the night before because he hadn't responded to any of my calls or texts. He mentioned he'd be working a double, but I could usually get a return text from him at least. I was determined to get in touch with him before the party—just in case he heard about it and planned on popping up. I wasn't willing to risk involving Lennox in any drama for my own selfish gain. I left another message requesting that Daniel call me back, then ordered a pecan chicken salad sandwich.

I drove to a nearby metro park and ate in the parking lot, savoring my time alone. Trice had tried her best to tag along so she could hear about my evening with Lennox, but I told her I had a dentist appointment. I hated lying to my friend, but the only thing on my mind was talking to Daniel and making it clear to him that our sexual relationship was over and I was moving on. There was no way I'd be able to do that with Trice there. It was time to put an end to it all. I realized after I left the office for the day, I would have to make a trip up to the hospital.

I left the visitors' parking garage and made my way across the skywalk to the main Cleveland Clinic hospital building. After visiting the cafeteria, I stepped off the elevator and onto his floor. I immediately noticed that I didn't recognize the receptionist. Then I remembered Daniel mentioned a couple of weeks back that Azure was out on FMLA with her daughter. I asked the young lady to see the outpatient clinic manager. She took my name, asked me to have a seat in the waiting area, and made a call. About six or seven minutes later, Daniel walked out in his scrubs and stood directly in front of me with his hands on his hips.

"Hey, Patience."

"Hello, Daniel. I'm sorry to interrupt your day. I thought I would stop by to make sure you're okay. I've been attempting to get in contact with you all day, and it's not like you not to respond."

"Well, I've been working for the past . . ."—he glanced at his smartwatch—"fourteen hours."

"Okay, well, I was only checking because even when you're working a double, I never have an issue getting a quick response text from you."

"We're down a person, and it's been really busy. Yes, I'm normally able to respond to your texts promptly, but I've been swamped today, Patience. What's going on?"

"I was hoping you could take a quick break to grab coffee and chat for a minute."

He sighed, then adopted a tone reserved for explaining something to a four-year-old. "If I couldn't find the time to check my phone and type a quick response before now, I'm sure it's obvious that I'm unable to take a coffee break."

I nodded and reached into my purse. "Well, I know you may have been tempted to grab a candy bar from the vending machine, and I don't want you to crash." I handed him a Greek yogurt and granola bar.

A hint of a smile flirted with his full lips but never quite made it to his eyes. "Thank you."

"No problem. You drinking your water?"

"I am."

"When do you get off?"

"Like I said, we're short-staffed, so it may be a double shift, or it might be longer. I knew it would be a zoo today. That's why I tried to reach you last night, but you were otherwise engaged."

"I know. I at least owed you a response text last night. I can acknowledge that, and I'm sorry."

He nodded but said nothing.

"Look, I know you're busy, and I didn't come up here to fight with you. I honestly just wanted to make sure you were okay and taking care of yourself. I also need to speak with you. So, if you feel up to it once you're done with your shift, can you please give me a call?"

"I will try my best."

The receptionist approached us with timid steps. "Excuse me, Daniel. A patient has been waiting for you in exam room three."

I grabbed my purse from the chair. "I'll go. Talk to you later?"

"Yeah, I'll try to give you a call," he replied, already on his way back down the hall.

Two days later, I stared at myself in my vanity mirror, smoothing out my strapless gold-sequin jumpsuit. I put the finishing touches on my eye makeup, then fluffed out my lustrous afro. I added a few tracks to make it fuller and cornrowed a few braids in the front, accenting them with gold rings. When my doorbell rang, I called out that it was open while fastening my rhinestone gold hoops. The door swung open, and my sister sauntered in, her wavy 'fro swaying and bracelets jingling as she moved her arms and hips to J Balvin's "Mi Gente" playing on the wireless speaker.

She leaned in for a kiss. "Hey, boo, hey! You cute, Goldie! And that metallic eye makeup is flawless!"

I did a full twirl, smoothing my hands over my hips. "Hey, darling. I had to accentuate them since I'm coming as Issa Rae. Those electric eyes and gorgeous smile are her best features. But I see you, Solange!"

"Ayyye!" She twerked and did a quick drop and pop.

"Uh-uh. Wrong sister. Solange ain't with all that."

"Oh yeah, I was giving pole dancer from her 'Almeda' video for a second there."

"Definitely what you were giving."

We high-fived and cracked up.

She walked toward my vanity. "Where did these gorgeous flowers come from, sister?"

"Er . . . uh . . ." Words failed me as I watched my little sister lean in for a quick sniff. I hoped to God that I had remembered to remove the card from the bouquet Lennox had delivered to congratulate me on my promotion earlier that day.

"Aww, Daniel's the sweetest. Definitely a keeper. Can you fasten these clasps for me?" She motioned toward her knee-length white fitted dress adorned in sequins and crystals.

Thank God for short attention spans!

"This dress is fire," I said, finally finding the courage to exhale. "What shoes are you wearing?"

She reached in her weekend bag and held up a pair of clear strappy stilettos covered with silver metal spikes. "I have these but was hoping you'd have something cuter."

"Those are sexy as hell. But you can peek in my closet if you think you can find something that may look better with it. Is Tavares coming tonight?"

"Yeah, he'll be there after he gets off work," I heard her muffled voice. She was already in my room.

I pulled out my phone to check if Daniel had called. I still hadn't spoken to him since I pulled up on him at the hospital. It irked my entire soul that he was blowing me off like this, but I could only get so mad at him. The fact that I had spent every free moment on the phone with Lennox was holding me back from unleashing on him like I normally would. Besides, it was my motherfucking birthday, and I was ready to kick it with my closest friends and family and hopefully end the evening with a nice little nightcap with the man I had fantasized about nonstop for weeks.

Having him in the flesh was the only thing on my mind since I first set my sights on him. As if mentally summoned, Lennox chose that particular moment to text me, verifying the venue's address.

Me: Yep, that's it. Parking is in the back lot. Get there early. It fills up quickly.

Lennox: Bet. I'll see you there.

I sighed in relief, thrilled that I would be able to see him that night. I had told him about my visit to Daniel's job and how he was MIA for the past couple of days. Bella agreed not to extend an invite to him, so Lennox agreed to attend. Lennox and I planned to be discreet with our interactions as a precaution. Although it wouldn't be ideal, I was just grateful he was going to be there to celebrate with me.

Chelsea strutted out of my bedroom rocking a pair of five-inch white stiletto sandals I'd long forgotten about. They had a Lucite strap with oversized studs and a dainty leather ankle tie.

"Sister, you must have been digging *deep* in my shit."

She twirled and said, "Like only a broke college student can!"

"Well, they're yours. And I see you found the matching clutch."

"Yes, it's perfect. Is Trice riding over with us?"

I shook my head. "She and Landon are coming together, so it's just you and me, kiddo. Let's do your makeup so we can get out of here."

Forty-five minutes later, the limo Bella had booked for us pulled up. We laughed and sang on live video, enjoying some dope music, chilled sparkling cider, and a champagne toast on the way to the hotel and conference center. When we stepped out of the limo onto the plush red carpet beneath our feet, we were temporarily blinded by camera flashes. We held hands and posed for the small group of photographers. We were the only ones outside as we strolled farther down the path leading up the driveway.

"Miss Knowles! Miss Diop! Over here!"

Chelsea frowned, looking at me. "Who they talking to?"

"Us, fool! Remember, we came in character." I laughed, nudging her toward the step and repeat.

"Oh yeah!" She giggled, then cleared her throat and gave a big wave. "Hey, y'all!"

I hung back and let her have her moment as she worked the cameras, doing live interviews for social media. She had Solange's easy tone and laid-back, humble energy down to a science. I was proud of her.

My phone buzzed and a text from Lennox popped up, stating he was five minutes away. I smiled to myself, refreshing my lip gloss. I stepped over to one of Bella's childhood friends, dressed to the nines and holding a microphone toward me. A short guy dressed in a tie, collared shirt, and slacks held out a phone for the Instagram live feed. "Issa, the guest of honor! Happy birthday, girlie! You're giving us Beyoncé *Goldmember* in that stunning gold-sequin jumpsuit tonight. Yes! Are you excited to see which of your celebrity friends will make an appearance for your special night?"

I smiled and nodded. She was far too hype for whatever Bella was paying her. "Thank you. Yes, absolutely."

"Any idea who will win the award for best dressed?"

I looked directly into the camera and flashed Issa's signature smile. "I'm rooting for everybody Black."

After a few more interviews, we posed for pictures in front of the custom Hollywood birthday-themed backdrop with the hashtag #PaeDay2021 before heading into the building. A sign bearing my name was in the lobby next to a large floor vase holding cream- and gold-dipped roses. We made our way to the dimly lit banquet room, and nothing could have prepared me for what was inside.

The first thing I set my eyes on was a floor-to-ceiling gold and cream balloon arch with a single gold and white throne and gold backdrop in the center. A dozen round tables with gold Chiavari chairs were spread throughout the room. The centerpieces alternated between multi-height crystal vases bursting with large white roses and shimmering tabletop chandeliers. *Happy 27th Birthday, Patience* was projected onto the shiny hardwood floor and the wall above the twelve-foot gift table. And don't get me started on the spread . . . There were hearty buffet stations with seafood, carved meats, salad, side dishes, cheese fondue, and a large dessert table. There was also a mobile 360 video booth, photo booths, a full open bar, and a DJ center stage whose voice I recognized from a local afternoon radio show. He announced my arrival, and I fought back tears as I took in what my best friend had pulled together in my honor.

As Stevie Wonder's "Happy Birthday" began to play, a host of my family members and friends rushed up to greet Chelsea and me with hugs and kisses. I barely recognized most of them because they were dressed to impress in wigs, professional makeup, and costumes. I enjoyed seeing them having fun while engaging with each other in full character.

My grandfather walked up in full Morgan Freeman mode—moles included—and gave Chelsea one of his huge bear hugs accompanied by a warm kiss before surrounding me in his arms. "You look beautiful tonight, Munk. Or might I say, you're looking hotter than July. Happy birthday."

I smiled at his Stevie Wonder reference. "Thank you, Pop-Pop. You're looking quite dapper yourself."

Bella walked up to join us, looking like the spitting image of Demi Lovato. She was rocking the singer's signature middle part with her long black extensions hanging down to her waist. She was stunning in a gold crochet peekaboo dress, serving us ample cleavage. "Hey, Gandalf the Grey Pop," she greeted Pop-Pop.

He smiled down at her and gave her a single-armed hug, fond of the nickname she'd affectionately given him. His towering height and slow, thoughtful cadence resembled *The Hobbit* and *Lord of the Rings* protagonist Gandalf Grey. "Well, hello, Lady Bella. This party's poppin'."

"Thank you. Anything for your darling granddaughter. But I'm going by Miss Lovato this evening, Pop."

"Gotcha." He leaned over and whispered loudly to Chelsea. "Like I have a clue who that is. You hungry, Bunny? Let's check out the hors d'oeuvres. Those fried macaroni and cheese balls are calling my name."

Chelsea gave Bella a hug and kiss before they headed off to the food station.

Once the rest of the crowd around me dispersed, Bella sang, "Happy birthday, boo!" We hugged long and hard.

"B, this is everything. You've really outdone yourself. Thank you!" Tears stung my eyes again.

She pulled back and wiped a tear from my eye before it could spill over my cheek.

"Girl, stop. You can thank Chauncey because he's footing part of the bill. His ass pissed me off last week, so I doubled the decor budget for my pain and suffering!"

I chuckled. "When is that man going to learn? Well, at least his screw-up was my gain this time."

"Here, let me take your coat. We're about to call some people up to the stage to play *The Price is Right* for the year you were born. Whatcha drinking tonight?"

"I'll have a fruity cocktail. Did you remember to order Anteel tequila for the bar?"

"Sure did. And we're using a Black female caterer. It's all black everything tonight!" Bella two-stepped away, and I cracked up.

"*Hey*, Issa! You look gorgeous, girl."

Before I could take a step, I was swarmed by another group of friends and associates. While hugging and kissing new and old friends, I kept my eye trained on the door. Relief washed over me when I noticed Lennox stroll in a couple of minutes later. When I laid eyes on him, I almost bit my tongue off while talking. I thought he was joking before when he had mentioned coming as the actor who played Issa Dee's love interest, Lawrence, from the HBO series *Insecure,* but it was obvious who inspired his look. Or maybe he just looked Hollywood scrumptious every damn day. Whichever the case, his slim-fit gray houndstooth suit and black button-down shirt were crisp and tailored to his muscular body like fresh paint.

"Please excuse me for a moment," I told a friend from high school before strolling over to greet him at the guest check-in table.

When he looked up and saw me coming, he stopped talking to the hostess mid-sentence. She was hanging on his every word like he was preaching the gospel. I chuckled, glad to know I wasn't the only one he had that effect on. His eyes studied my face before dropping to my bust, down to my polished toes, then up to my hair. I strolled over, taking my sweet ol' time approaching him as he took me in. We were so entranced with each other, unaware of anyone who may have witnessed the searing current of energy surging between us. Once I finally reached him, I placed a gentle hand on his chest before exiting the room to the hallway.

My heart's wild pace caused my pulse to beat louder in my eardrums than the bumping music's baseline. I couldn't hear a damn thing over my ragged breathing as my eyes quickly scanned the lobby's perimeter. I turned and stalked down a long corridor until I finally spotted an empty conference room at the end. I opened the door and slipped inside without a backward glance. Without a word, he quietly stepped inside a few seconds later, closing the wooden door behind him.

"Beauty . . . you look unbelievable."

He closed the space between us in three long strides. His cologne teased my nostrils, and I inhaled deeply. His large warm hands swallowed my waist, and his mouth immediately found my neck. I palmed his head, pulling him closer, sighing heavily in a sweet mixture of relief and pleasure. He picked me up and placed me on the table behind us. Feeling his body pressed against mine again was all I had been able to think about for the past four days. His hot breath on my skin amplified my throbbing pulse, and my legs spread, making more room for him. He expertly unhooked my bra sight unseen, freeing my breasts. Moments later, I felt his warm mouth surround my hardened nipples. I bit my lip to keep from grunting as white-hot currents shot through each limb of my body. April hummed, sang, and cried, threatening to pounce on him at any moment from inside my shimmering catsuit.

"Oh, Lennox."

"Yeah?" His voice was muffled.

"Mmm . . . don't stop."

He planted a trail of kisses up my neck and onto my chin before covering my mouth with his. It wasn't until then that I noticed he was chewing gum. His tongue was timid as it entered my mouth, exploring it, bringing a fresh taste of spearmint along with his sweet invasion. I savored the coolness, caressing his smooth tongue with my own. A gentle moan escaped my lips. I struggled to keep my hands clasped in my lap. I knew if they began exploring, they would be well off the beaten path in a matter of seconds. When we finally pulled away from each other, my lips were swollen and throbbing. I couldn't wait for the day that he finally kissed them.

"Just the sounds you make when we're kissing is enough to make me want to bend your sexy ass over this table and stroke you like my God-given life depends on it."

It was so good to hear what I was doing to him.

I nodded. "Lennox, I want to respect your decision. Let's wait until the time is right. I know you want our first time to be more meaningful than this."

He nodded, taking my hand and placing it on his protruding bulge. It was sensitive to my touch, immediately jumping in response. "Thank you, Beauty. I know this hasn't been easy for you. Trust, he can*not* wait to meet you. And when he does, I'll make it well worth the wait."

# Chapter Twenty-One

L ennox hung back for a few moments after I left the conference room. I stopped in the bathroom to check my hair and makeup. When I walked back into the banquet room, I almost collided with a broad chest. I looked up. "Err . . . excuse me."

"Hey, birthday girl! Almost didn't recognize you." Chauncey's deep-set brown eyes lit up, and he reached out for a hug.

I hugged him, smiling wide. "Hey, brother. Same! Who are you supposed to be tonight—a pimp?"

He held out his hands. "I'm Lucious Lyon!"

"Oh, snap! You picked the perfect character. I've always told Bella you look like a cross between Terrence Howard and T.I."

"Where have you been? I've been looking all over for you!" Bella stepped between us, grabbed my wrist, and began yanking me toward the stage.

I pushed my short legs to keep up with her long ones. "I was just freshening my makeup, and then I started greeting guests."

"You're such a shitty liar, girl. I saw your ass sneaking off with Lennox. Damn, that man is fine, by the way. I can see why he's got you open."

I ignored her comment and asked, "How did you know that was Lennox?"

"Because I stalked his social media page as soon as you told me about him. His name is unique, so he was easy to find."

"I'll definitely have to introduce you two later. But what's going on, B?"

She gestured toward the DJ area. "*That's* what's happening. I tried my best to stop him, but he wasn't hearing me at all."

The DJ faded out the music and handed over the microphone. I squinted and walked a little closer to see who was on the stage with him. "No." I shook my head.

"Yeah, it's me. Get on up here, girl." Daniel called, holding out his hand to me. He gripped the microphone sideways as he spoke into it, like a crooning '90s R&B singer.

I took him in as my timid steps inched toward him. He wore a pair of gray joggers and a fitted navy-blue thermal with a pair of Timbs. It was a contrast from his customary button-down and leather loafers. I tried to keep the fury from my face by biting the inside of my cheek and clenching my fists.

I didn't realize Bella was walking right behind me until she spoke. "Girl, just do it. I have security on alert just in case he gets out of pocket."

I glanced back at the doorway just in time to see Lennox stroll back into the room. *Just great.* Each part of my body collectively screamed in protest as I continued dragging my leaden legs toward the stage. As I joined my ex on stage, facing a room of about two hundred guests, my chest hurt from my heart's relentless thudding. I wiped my sweaty palms against my legs and accepted a hug from Daniel.

"Give it up for the birthday girl, y'all!"

His eyes were empty as he gave me a shallow smile and handed me a champagne flute. He whispered, "Happy birthday, baby. Thanks for the invite, by the way." Then he leaned over and made a show of placing a kiss on my forehead.

Assuming we were preparing for a birthday toast, I braced

myself for the worst. There was light applause from the guests as goose bumps sprang across my bare arms and back. I squinted below the overhead light to scan the room. My eyes landed on Lennox stuffing money into a tip jar at the open bar, a fresh cocktail in hand. His expression was unreadable.

When the applause and whistles died down, Daniel looked over at me for a long moment before speaking. For the first time in over five years, I didn't have the faintest clue what he was thinking. He wobbled a bit before lifting the microphone back to his lips, and I realized he was drunk off his ass. *This night just keeps getting fucking better.*

"What in the world can I say about this beautiful woman that isn't already painfully obvious? I mean, for real. Look at this gorgeous lady up here looking like a snacc tonight!"

I cringed as the crowd cheered, squeezing my eyes shut. *A snacc?*

"Patience is the total package—smart, sweet, supportive, loving, and she was an all-around perfect girlfriend."

I could hear scattered conversations in the audience when they picked up on Daniel's past-tense reference to our relationship.

He continued, "I know the past few years weren't easy on her. I can honestly say I wouldn't have made it through my clinicals, full course load, and endless work hours without her love and support. She is the epitome of a down-ass ride-or-die who is committed to seeing her man through it all. Without a single complaint. So, with that said, if you would all raise your glasses, I would like to toast this phenomenal woman and wish her a happy birthday." He turned to face me and raised his glass. "May all of your dreams come true, Patience. I mean that."

I nodded and mouthed, *Thank you.*

"Cheers!"

Daniel handed the microphone back to the DJ, and we left the stage together.

"Give it up for the birthday girl one more time, everybody!"

the DJ called out before playing our song, "Adorn" by Miguel, which I knew had to be by Daniel's request.

I tried to walk away from him, but he caught me by the wrist and pulled me in for an embrace. He began an upbeat two-step, and once I realized he wasn't going to give in, I fell in step with him to prevent a scene. I kept a healthy distance between us as he rested his hand on the rise of my ass.

My aunt came by to pin money on me and kiss me as he spun me out. Once he pulled me back in, I hissed, "Daniel, what are you doing right now?"

"What am *I* doing? I'm dancing with my cut buddy at her fucking birthday party that I wasn't even invited to."

"Yeah, that's right. You weren't invited. I haven't even been able to reach you for the past few days."

"Well, this shit looks like it took far more than a few days to plan."

"You know full well I haven't been reaching out to you countless times to discuss a party with you, Daniel."

His hands slid down the curve of my ass before giving it a firm squeeze. I quickly removed his hands, refusing to scan the room because I couldn't bear to catch Lennox looking at us. "My grandfather's here, Daniel. Have some respect!"

He kissed my neck. "What? He probably knows I'm still killing this."

"You're no longer my man, Daniel. So why would you show up here uninvited and drunk?"

"Well, I was online after dropping eight hundred dollars on your birthday gift. Then I got a notification that you were live. There you were, all gassed up on the Gram, riding in a limo with your sister."

"My birthday's tomorrow, so thanks for the last-minute gift," I said, removing his hands from my ass again.

"Pssh, that bitch'll be ready for curbside pickup at ten tomorrow morning," he slurred. "We also still have dinner reservations at eight tomorrow. Remember, I had to make them six months in advance to get us in there. I didn't bother to ask what you planned for your birthday because I *knew* you wouldn't exclude me. Hell, we just broke up a few weeks ago and just got it in last week."

"Okay, enough with the passive-aggressive bullshit," I hissed. "You haven't called me in three days, and I didn't take your booty call earlier this week. This is exactly where we are as a result of screwed-up communication. I told you not to catch feelings, but here you are, thinking you still have the right to crash a private event of mine."

"Look, I know you didn't want me here tonight, but I just want you to know that I meant every word I said up there. I've talked to my mom, and things with her are going to be handled differently from now on."

"Thank you for looking into that. And it only took five years and a breakup for you to see a need for that conversation."

"I admit, I definitely dropped the ball there. But I'm trying, Patience. I'm trying to show up better for you in the bedroom. I'm trying to do better with dealing with my mom. You mean everything to me, and I never meant to take you for granted all these years. Now that I know what I've done wrong, I want to fix it. Can't you see that? You were never an afterthought for me, baby." He pressed his groin into me, and I felt his erection.

I pressed against his chest to subtly recreate a respectable distance. "Yes, I've seen your recent effort. I really appreciate your recommitment to our former relationship. But it's all just too late, Daniel. I see that you didn't give a damn about how I felt until I was already gone. So, I'm going to tell you now what I've been trying to do all week. Things are over between us. The friendship. The sexual relationship. All communication between us has to end."

He stopped moving, his eyes dark. "So, you're really going to throw away five good years just like that?"

"You and I both know it wasn't 'just like that.' This has been a long time coming. Why can't you just be happy for me? I'm finally choosing myself and going after my own happiness instead of propping you up. If you really love me, this is what you'd want for me."

His mouth opened, but he said nothing.

"Look, Daniel. You're a good guy, and I don't want to make this any more awkward than it already is with a long, drawn-out goodbye. So, thanks for coming out, and good luck with everything. Sincerely."

I gave him a brief hug before walking away. I locked eyes with Bella, who had been standing nearby, hyper-alert with eyes on us. I gave her a subtle nod, and a minute later, Daniel was being escorted from the room by two off-duty police officers. I turned my head, unable to stand the sight of his drunk and horny ass being forcefully removed from my party.

"The people sure are getting a *show* and thangs tonight, honey." I turned to see my work bestie sashaying toward me and snapping into the air, and Landon was right behind her.

"Hey, girl. You look beautiful!" I hugged and kissed Trice before hugging Landon.

She twirled in her floor-length satin red gown. "Thank you. I took your advice and went for Aja Naomi King. How'd I do?"

"You are killing it, postpartum and all! Good thing you know how to get away with murder!" I snapped up twice and to the left.

"Meet my date, Damson Idris." She gestured toward Landon, donned in a black suit and a crisp white button-down, unbuttoned halfway.

"Happy birthday, Patience."

This time, I clutched my imaginary pearls. "Okay, *Snowfall*. And with the sexy British accent!"

Trice raised a brow and said, "So you know these soggy panties are sliding right off as soon as we hit the house, right?"

"Hell, they have a few vacant rooms up the hall, just in case you can't make it that long."

We high-fived and cracked up while Landon shook his head.

"I see Lennox is here," Trice said. "We've been chopping it with him for the past few minutes. I didn't want him to have to face that debacle alone."

I cringed. That shitshow was totally unexpected. "Ugh. How did he take it?"

"If it bothered him, he hid it well. But he left out a couple minutes ago, just after the first ass squeeze."

"Well, I really appreciate that, girl. This whole evening has been a damn mess. I officially broke off all communication with Daniel just now, but not as cordially as I originally planned. I was so angry with him for showing up here unannounced and drunk after ignoring my calls for days. I just wanted him gone. But after five years, I owed him better than that."

"Girl, I'm glad you let his ass have it. He was out of line tonight and drunk out of his mind. Groping you on the dance floor in front of your family like that. Don't be too hard on yourself. He really forced your hand on this one."

"I agree. The bloke had it coming," Landon said, deadpanning.

Trice and I met eyes and squealed like teenagers. His accent was spot-on; it was uncanny.

"Down the hall, last room on the right. And the door has a lock," I told her before walking off to find some liquid courage. After downing my cocktail in one long gulp, I exhaled and found my older cousin Nyla, who had my clutch. My hands were shaking so much that I almost dropped it.

"Cuz, what the hell was that?" she asked, her eyes laced with concern. "I thought you said you broke up with Daniel."

"Girl, I did. He said he saw me and Chelsea on live and took it upon himself to make an appearance."

Nyla frowned like the math wasn't mathin'. "But . . . how did he know where to come?"

"I . . . I don't know. Look, I'm mentally drained and emotionally exhausted. I'm thinking about just calling it a night."

"What? No, you at least need to wait until we sing 'Happy Birthday.'"

I nodded. "Okay, fine. Can you please let Bella know I'm ready?"

"I'm on it."

As Nyla went to find Bella, I pulled out my phone, walking out to the lobby to get a moment of privacy. I plopped down in an armchair, opening a message from Lennox.

Lennox: That was crazy.

I stared at his three simple words for a full ten seconds. After everything that went down, all he had for me were three words. Yeah, it *had* been crazy, but given the circumstances, that was a loaded statement. I had tried to be upfront with Lennox about what was happening with Daniel. His initial conclusion was that I was doing too much. So how did he feel about me now? Was he upset with me for engaging with Daniel to avoid making a scene?

Me: Yeah, it was.

I watched my guests line dancing inside the ballroom, having a great time without me. My eyes stung, and I fought the urge to cry. The whole night was ruined, and I knew I had played a big role in it. I wanted to have it all and was now at risk of being left with nothing at all.

Lennox: I'm chilling in the car. Let me know when they're about to sing Happy Birthday.

Me: In a few minutes, I think.

Lennox: Okay, heading back in.

I walked back in and finished the last half of the "Love on Top" line dance with a small group of girlfriends from church. Then the DJ announced it was time to sing "Happy Birthday." A three-tiered cake was wheeled out to the middle of the dance floor. It was white with gold confetti, a red carpet cascading down the side with a gold, sparkling *27* cake topper. The guests began forming a circle around me with Bella, Chelsea, Pop-Pop, and Tavares standing beside me. I looked over and saw Lennox standing at the edge of the crowd. His smile reached his eyes, which gave me hope. Just when they were about to start singing a cappella, the crowd parted. Someone else was making their way over to join our small group in the center. She wore an off-shoulder, frilly, light-blue dress with strappy, silver five-inch stilettos. Her chin-length wavy bob framed her oval face, and a modest smile rested on her full lips as she walked up and hugged Tavares, hugged and kissed Pop-Pop, then Chelsea. Once she made it to me, a gentle softness lit her face.

"Happy birthday, Chrissy. So sorry I'm late."

My mom was a true diva—always doing things on her own time, so I knew she was giving lip service. "Thanks, Mom. Better late than never." I closed my eyes and hugged her tight, inhaling her sweet floral scent. "But never late is better."

She nodded, and her shoulders shook with laughter as I lovingly poked her in the ribs.

I forced a convincing smile as my guests sang to me, as I cut the cake, and as I jumped onto the microphone to thank Bella for throwing the event and everyone for coming out. I smiled and laughed at the appropriate times as several people walked up to say goodnight. But I was simply going through the motions to save face. Inside, I was a total emotional wreck.

Fifteen minutes later, as guests lined up at the bar and hit the dance floor, I told Bella and my family goodnight before pulling out my phone to text Lennox that I was ready to leave. We left separately, and I walked down the well-lit street to a Thai restaurant half a block away, where he picked me up.

"Well, that was wild," I uttered, half to myself and half as an attempt to break the awkward silence that hung between us. I stole a glance at Lennox, who seemed immersed in contemplative thought as he navigated the downtown streets like a Cleveland resident. My nervous grip on the pad Thai caused my fingers to cramp. After Daniel showed up, my stomach was in no shape for party food.

Lennox licked his lips, then said, "Yeah . . ."

He sounded like he wanted to add something but didn't. I

knew he had a lot on his mind and was a man of few words, but I needed him to talk to me. Not knowing what was going through his head only caused my thoughts to run wild, and they always veered left. Was he planning to drop me off and never speak to me again? I couldn't take that. I needed him to know I wanted more. I was willing to explore the possibility of a long-distance relationship with him if he still wanted one with me.

He turned down the music, then reached over and squeezed my hand. "I know this was all hard for you. But I wanted to let you know how proud of you I am."

I turned to study his profile as he pulled onto the highway.

"Despite all the drama, you handled it all like a G while never breaking a sweat."

I continued to stare at him, hanging on each word and longing for more.

"Dude seemed very insecure up on that stage. 'Bout to cry and shit. He was overcompensating big time."

"Yeah, he was pretty emotional . . . heartbroken."

"Why? I thought it was just sex at this point."

"It has been, but there was still some residual emotion there on his part."

He lifted a brow. "Only on his end?"

"Yeah, only on his end. He didn't expect me to end things. But I already mentally checked out a while ago. I mean, I was hurt and felt disrespected when his mother tried to fix him up with a woman right in front of my face—one whom he lied about, then admitted to talking to all along. But, for the past couple of years, I'd just been priming myself to endure a passionless marriage for the rest of my life."

"Word?" When I didn't respond, he said, "That shit sucks."

We rode in silence for a few minutes, both processing things separately. To be honest, I was actually stunned by my own words. Everything I had said was true, but it was the first time I had admitted that to anyone else, let alone myself. I didn't love Daniel. I was going to marry him because I believed he was the best I could do. That I didn't deserve to demand more happiness or fulfillment for myself. I could tell Lennox picked up on the vibe I was throwing out because he pivoted the conversation.

"Yeah, well, Emo Ernie needed to chill during that slow dance because I was about to cut in between y'all. He knew things were over between y'all and that he lost everything."

I nodded, a weak smile on my lips. "I'm sorry you had to see that bullshit. I know we're just starting to get to know each other, but I'd never intentionally put you in an uncomfortable position like that."

"I'm just glad it's all over." He thought for a moment, then chuckled. "It was kind of cold how y'all had my man escorted out like that, though."

I could tell the evening's events really bothered him. I'd have to make up for all the drama I had put him through later. "That was all Bella. She prides herself on having drama-free events. I've never seen someone hire a full security team for a three-year-old's birthday party."

Another chuckle from him. "I saw Pop-Pop and your sister. Chelsea, right?"

I nodded.

"Was that your mom in the blue? You look just like her."

I should've known Lennox would catch that. "Yes, that's my mother, Etta Hampton."

Lennox nodded. I knew he picked up on the shift in energy when he brought up my mom because there was no way to mask it. Although my relationship with my mother had improved over the years, old scars don't fade easily.

"You look so beautiful tonight. I'm glad I could be a part of your celebration. Happy birthday, Beauty."

I thanked him and looked out the window. Although I was relieved things were finally over with Daniel, the adrenaline of the evening had waned. I was so wrapped up in being annoyed with Daniel for crashing the party and showing up drunk that I couldn't think straight. I regretted ending things with him that way. Despite his recent erratic behavior, he didn't deserve to be humiliated in front of everyone. I knew he was only acting out while trying to process what was happening between us. After five years, we were both owed proper closures, and I had chosen to be selfish instead. I had failed him, and now I would have to live with that decision.

<h1 style="text-align:center">Chapter Twenty-Two</h1>

It's amazing how a couple glasses of chilled blackberry merlot and a warm man on your couch can eradicate having guilt over another one. My legs were stretched across Lennox's lap as we cracked up at the late great John Witherspoon's fashion tips.

*"You've got to co-ordinate!"* John flashed the printed interior of his suit jacket that matched his collared shirt.

"Such a comedic legend," Lennox said, rubbing my feet.

I nodded, closing my eyes and soaking in the moment. No one could have convinced me even a month ago that I would be enjoying a classic romantic comedy and good wine with a fine but strange man loving on my tired feet after attending my birthday party.

Lennox glanced down at his watch, and I swallowed, concerned he was about to leave. He looked up and said, "Well, it's official. Let me be the first to tell you, happy twenty-seventh birthday."

I smiled. "Why, thank you."

He leaned over, and I closed my eyes, letting my lips part, prepared to receive his sweet tongue. Instead, I opened my eyes a couple of seconds after French kissing the cold air to find him reaching behind the couch. He pulled out a gift bag and handed it to me.

I frowned. "You got me a present?"

"Open it."

"Lennox, delaying your flight to attend my party was more than enough. You shouldn't have spent any more on me."

"Open it," he urged again.

I pulled out a white hoodie displaying a picture of me posing in front of a graffiti wall with my hands on my hips. Below my image in red sequins were the words, "I give dope voice."

I couldn't take my eyes off of it. It was gorgeous. "Lennox. This is everything. You had this made?"

He nodded. "Just arrived this afternoon. Grabbed the photo from your Instagram post from a couple of years back. I love the potency of your expression."

I laughed at the memory. "More like outright defiance."

"What's the story?"

"Bella took this about three hot seconds before we were tossed off of private property for trespassing. A very large, very angry man was yelling and charging right at us, but, as you can see, that sun was hitting my skin and curls just right. So, there was no way we were losing that shot."

He laughed, and the carefree nature of the simple sound filled me up.

I leaned over and slipped my pinky into his dimple. "Thank you for everything, Lennox. This all meant so much to me."

"I wish I could spend the day with you tomorrow, but I have an all-staff meeting first thing Monday at the office."

I straddled him, and his hands landed on my waist. "Well, why don't you spend the rest of tonight making up for it?"

I kissed him, long and deep, dragging my nails lightly over his scalp. He jerked a little, and his fingers sank farther into my ample skin and squeezed as a gentle moan filled our mouths. I couldn't tell if it was his or mine as I rolled the tips of his ears between my fingers. He pushed me back on the couch, and I lifted my hips as he dragged my satin panties down the length of my thighs. I rested my ankles on his shoulders, and he leaned forward, inserting his fingers into my dripping yoni. I pushed him back, jumping up from the couch and grabbing his hand. I pulled him down the hallway and into my bedroom before shoving him onto the bed.

He looked around the room, then paused when his gaze landed on my dresser. "What's with the stuffed chipmunk?"

I followed his gaze to the toy sitting there. "Oh, my grandfather and sister call me Munk. I used to store food in my cheeks for hours as a kid. Then I'd chew up my little snack at bedtime."

His face screwed up in disgust. "That shit's . . . disgusting."

I shrugged. "More like resourceful."

"Beauty, you wanted to leave your party before I even got the chance to sample the cake." He pulled me by the waist, bringing me down to the bed with him. "Now, it's time to cash in."

Before I could respond, he rolled over and sank his face between my thighs. I closed my eyes. *God, yes! We've finally made it to third base!* After a few minutes of him kissing, sucking, and licking my lower set of lips, I reached over and unzipped his slacks. I stared at his generous girth for a moment before mounting him in a sixty-nine position and taking him into my mouth. We took our sweet time exploring one another. I enjoyed the taste of him while working my hands on his shaft and hungrily absorbing inch by sweet inch of him. Meanwhile, he lapped me up like a precious oasis. The volume of our moans escalated, and we lost ourselves in the giving and receiving, the pleasing and pleasuring. I'd never felt so turned on by pleasing someone else. His climax became my only focus as I bobbed and sucked him with ease. His hands were gripping my ass cheeks, massaging them, squeezing them, and pulling them apart as he kissed my love below.

I was caught off guard when waves began to mount within me. They quickly crept up and threatened to consume me entirely. I pulled away from him and said, "I don't want to come yet. April wants to wait until you're inside of her."

He raised a brow. "April?"

I nodded downward.

He smiled, lips slick with my coating, and said, "Oh, she will."

I shook my head. "No, she can only come once. One and done."

He frowned. "No, I'm going to make you come now. Then I'm going to make you come again. And again."

"I'm telling you . . . I have never been able to come more than once per night."

Frowning, he tilted his head. "What'd I tell you about comparing me to previous cats?"

I shrugged. "I've never blamed anyone else for it. It's just how it is."

"We'll see about that. Spread your legs."

He slid his fingers inside of me and hooked them, stroking me vigorously. My hips moved forward on their own, as if beckoned. I clamped my hands onto his forearms, my face strained in a silent shriek. As the rhythmic waves staked an aggressive claim on my body, I locked eyes with Lennox. His eyebrows cinched as he studied me. His serious focus turned me on even more. *Ugh! Was there one imperfection on this man?* I succumbed to my orgasm, allowing the waves to carry me away. Releasing a soft moan, I allowed my body to drop back onto the mattress as I drifted, my muscles retracting.

"Rest up because I'm going to help you reach your second orgasm of the night. And I'm not leaving here until it happens."

I sat up and looked at him with a blank expression. "Well, I hope you packed your toothbrush. Because this shop is closed up for the night."

He leaned over and kissed my neck. "We'll see."

I closed my eyes and enjoyed the feel of his warm lips on my damp skin.

He stood and asked, "Where's the essential oil? I know you have some. I smelled it the second we walked in here."

"In the top dresser drawer on the right side. Light those

candles on the nightstand while you're up. The matches are in there, too."

I set my phone on the wireless speaker and opened my love mix playlist.

Lennox turned the lights up a bit while he poured oil onto his large hands. It smelled like ylang-ylang. He mixed in a few drops of jojoba, then smoothed his hands over the bottoms of my feet for the second time that evening. He moved them up the length of my legs and calves, then moved toward my inner thighs. As he worked the skin beneath his slick fingertips, he bent down and whispered, "Play with your nipples."

I flipped over and pulled my tank top over my head. I rolled my nipples between my fingers as he continued to massage my inner thighs. Then he bent one of my knees and began gently stroking my perineum. I moaned, enjoying the new sensation of being touched there.

"Breathe in through your nose, hold it, and release it through your mouth. Open up and fully welcome the erotic energy. Channel it."

I closed my eyes, concentrating on my breathing. He moved my left hand to my clit, and I began to stroke it slowly, still rolling my left nipple. It was still swollen and sensitive, so I let out a soft whimper.

"Yeah, that's right. Let me hear you, baby."

I tried to imagine his dick—my joystick—inside of me, pushing me past my limit with strong, confident strokes. But since I never had the experience, I conjured up the last time I had slept with Daniel, replacing his face with Lennox's, just as I had the past several times when I was with him. I bucked my hips as I continued to stroke and roll, stroke and roll.

"Unngh!"

"Yes, baby. I'm here with you. Louder," he coaxed me.

"That's so *goodt!*"

"Right there. It's coming. Just be patient. Keep making those sexy sounds. Get into it."

*His hips undulated, and his even strokes were slamming into me, quicker and quicker. He picked up the pace, and the headboard rocked to the music.* My imagination was running wild. "Yeah, yeah!"

"Submit to your erotic self. Let me know when you're close, baby. Don't forget."

My breath came out in forced pants. "I'm. Almost. There!"

He removed my hand from my clit before leaning over to kiss me. I was so hungry, I damn-near sucked his tongue out of his mouth. He disengaged and leaned down to suck on my right breast, massaging the nipple with his long tongue. He told me to begin rubbing my clit again. We did the edging process a few more times, and by then, I was almost screaming for him to allow me to come.

"I thought you said the shop was closed. Now, you think you're ready?"

"Stop fucking with me, Lennox Davenport," I growled through gritted teeth.

He chuckled. "Okay, let's go. Nipple and clit."

"And dick," I panted.

Instead, I got fingers.

He eased them back inside of me and stroked me again, much more furiously than before. This time, I kept my mouth shut as the waves arrived to reclaim me. But it felt much different than the previous one. My body was frenzied at the onset of this particular orgasm. Its power was so intense that I felt the wave welling up in every part of my body. First, my hands lost all sensation, then my abs began to pulsate, my legs spasmed, and my toes curled. I couldn't do anything but surrender as I tensed and yielded to the mini inner explosions detonating in each part of my body. My first reaction was to panic, but it felt so damn good that every bit of worry slipped beyond my reach. My back fell into a deep arch, and I tossed my head back before sinking into my pillow.

"*Oh*, gawd!"

By the time I finally opened my eyes and looked around, it was quite some time later.

My love playlist must have ended because Beyoncé was singing to us. *It's too much; it's too tough. He walk like this 'cause he can back it up.*

"You got that right, Bey," I whimpered.

I heard Lennox chuckle. "Welcome back."

I attempted to sit up and smile at him, but I was too weak to move.

"Just relax. I hope now you know there's no such thing as 'what you or your body can't do.' It's all in the mind, and you killed that shit." He held up two sticky hands illuminated by the candlelight.

My jaw fell. "I squirted?"

He nodded. "Everywhere."

I dragged my body to the edge of the bed.

He frowned. "Whoa, where are you going?"

"To get you a wet towel," I said.

"No, I've got it. I just wanted you to see it for yourself because I doubted you'd believe me."

"So, you've been sitting there waiting for . . ."

"Thirty-two minutes."

"Damn, did you check for a pulse?"

He laughed, and I leaned over to turn off the music.

"It's normal to be exhausted after your first full-body orgasm," he called from the bathroom. "It takes a lot out of you."

"So, that's what that was."

"Yup." He walked into the bedroom, drying his hands off on a towel. "Your face is captivating while you're coming. It's so complex, animated . . . radiant. I've never seen anything like it."

I blushed. "Lennox, that felt amazing. Thanks for being so dedicated to my happiness tonight."

"My pleasure." He sat on the bed next to me. "Beauty, I know things have gotten heated between us, and it hasn't been easy holding off on sex. There's no doubt we're attracted to one another, and we each want to take it to that level. And I've explained my reasons for not wanting to do so just yet."

I nodded. "You have, and I respect them."

"So, can I ask you a question?"

"Of course."

"Why the urgency? I mean, why was it so important to you that we connect on a sexual level so soon after meeting each other?"

I frowned, caught off guard by his question. Was he implying that I was thottish? It wasn't my intention to come off that way. I knew things were moving quickly between us, but I felt an intense connection with Lennox, and that was how I usually expressed it. But something told me he wouldn't settle for that response. He patiently waited while I took a few minutes to think. I didn't realize I was wringing my hands until he placed his on top of mine and squeezed gently. I bit my lip in frustration.

"Don't do that."

I smirked, knowing how it drove him wild. "I've just always cherished that type of connection with a guy I was seriously into. It allows me to express everything I'm unable to say out loud."

He nodded. "What is it you want to tell me that you don't feel comfortable saying?"

I shrugged. "I don't know. I just . . . I want you to know that I'm enjoying getting to know you. I appreciate everything you've done for me, and I think you're sexy. I really want things to work out between us."

"Why wouldn't they?"

"Because . . . you're all the way in Atlanta. I know you have family and friends here, but who knows how often you'll be able to make it up here or when I'll make it down there to see you."

He nodded. "So that brings us back to your concerns about long-distance relationships. Are you ready to tell me about that?"

I fell back on the pillows and gestured for him to join me.

"We having a little pillow talk?" he asked, lying down next to me.

"Yeah, this one's going to be a doozy."

He laced his fingers between mine. "I'm ready to listen."

I exhaled loudly. "I lost my virginity to my high school sweetheart, Roderick. I wasn't quite ready to take that step, but over the course of our relationship, I allowed him to convince me that sex was the only way to show him how much I loved him. After that, it became the only way we ever expressed love for one another. He stopped telling me altogether and only focused on sex. I was seventeen, and I figured that was just how it was in relationships. Once we graduated high school, we were supposed to attend Hampton University together. We made arrangements to move in a week before class started for a minority student orientation program. But, at the last minute, he told me he'd decided to enroll at Clark Atlanta University."

If Lennox was stunned by my little plot twist, he didn't show it. So, I continued.

"I was crushed because he hadn't even discussed his change of plans with me. I felt disregarded and abandoned, but he didn't think it was a big deal. My immediate reaction was to cut off all ties with him. But, after a couple of months, I agreed to a long-distance relationship. I'll admit, things seemed to be going great at first. He called me every day, and since his mother was a flight attendant, he would fly out to visit me on weekends. But once his coursework and work schedule got complicated, communication almost completely stopped on his end. When I suggested making plans to attend Roderick's homecoming, he mentioned he had to work. Soon, I couldn't reach him at all during the week or on weekends. I had a great relationship with his mother, so she agreed to book me a flight to surprise him during his homecoming weekend. I booked a hotel—honeymoon suite off campus—figuring we'd fit in time together when he got off work."

Lennox winced. "I'm guessing that didn't go as planned."

"Nope. Turned out, he not only attended the dance, but, judging from the pictures a friend of mine emailed me, he'd also coordinated outfits with his beautiful model girlfriend. When I told his mom, she was just as shocked as I was."

"Damn. Sorry about that."

I shrugged. "I guess it was just a lesson I needed to learn."

"What was the lesson?"

"For years, I thought it was simply to follow your gut. Roderick showed me what he thought of me when he began making ultimatums and pressuring me to make choices I wasn't mentally or emotionally prepared to make. He didn't think about me when he made choices about his future without considering my input. Then he lied to me about his intentions for the entire relationship. If I'd followed my gut and refused to be intimate with him, I'd have been much better off."

"You said that's what you thought for years. Has that changed?"

I nodded. "It has. After my breakup with Daniel, I began noticing a pattern over the course of my dating life. I have this intense fear of being cheated on and broken up with. To the point where I'll do whatever I feel is necessary to prevent it from happening. But the more accommodating I am, the more I attract people who use me. So, in a sense, I'm manifesting exactly what I want to avoid.

"After I ended things with Daniel, I was focused on spending time alone to help correct all that. I was dead set on getting to the bottom of what I was doing to contribute to my experiences. Then I met you. At first, I still had my wall up. I still wanted to focus on myself without starting anything new. The distance between us gave me the security I needed to open up to you. I figured we'd never see each other again, so what the hell?"

He nodded.

"Then, you showed up and awakened so many feelings inside of me. Shit was straight scary. I began feeling like anything was possible . . . with the right person. In Atlanta, I was sexually frustrated. But once we reconnected, the same old part of me longed for that physical connection between us because I thought that was how to seal the deal between us. When you turned me down, I was thrown because I'm just not used to men not wanting that from me."

"You and a lot of women," Lennox mumbled.

I frowned. "You've turned other women down?"

"Plenty. Women aren't shy about asking for what they want these days. For some of them, sex is as casual as a handshake. I don't judge them for it, but I've been called all types of emasculating names just for sticking to my principles. Shit's weird."

I rubbed his forearm. "Nothing like a bruised female ego. But I'm sorry you had to go through that. And I'm proud of you for sticking to your principles. Lastly, I apologize for making you feel like that's all I wanted from you."

He shook his head. "Not what I thought at all. Honestly, a big part of why I stopped things from going any further between us at the hotel was the look in your eyes just as we were about to get to it. You looked . . . conflicted. It just didn't seem like the right time for us."

I nodded. "Yeah, you're probably right."

He pulled me closer, and we just lay with our thoughts for a minute.

After a while, I sat up and gently cleared my throat. "So, before you go . . ."

"What's up?"

"Are you going to ask me the question from a couple of weeks ago?"

He smiled. "Oh, that."

"Yes, Dimples. *That.*"

"Well, I guess I can ask you now, since you were just being all transparent and shit."

"Okay . . . ," I prodded.

"My tenth high school reunion is in a few weeks, and I'd like you to accompany me."

My eyes widened. "To New York?"

"Yep."

"As your date?"

"As my date."

I tried to hide my grin as I asked, "So, does that mean we're dating now?"

"Well, that depends. Have you changed your mind about long-distance relationships?"

"After the magic you just cast on my body, boy? I'd follow your ass to Hong Kong."

He smiled, showing pearly white teeth. "Well then, yes. We're officially dating, Ms. Hampton."

I squealed before sinking my mouth over his.

Best. Fucking. Birthday. Ever.

# Chapter Twenty-Three

A few weeks later, I snapped pictures of the spectacular view as we drove over the Manhattan Bridge. The skyscrapers nestled against the East River were framed by bright sunlight. Once we reached the bridge's end, I was officially in Brooklyn for the first time. We pulled up to a contemporary hotel and parked in the garage. I was concerned about giving off an overly touristy vibe at first, but when I laid eyes on where we were staying for the next couple of days, I could no longer contain my excitement. Lennox was several feet behind me, helping the hotel attendant load our luggage onto a cart. I took that opportunity to let the moment soak in. Inside the hotel, reggae music was booming, and about a dozen people were nestled on plush couches, playing oversize Monopoly, Connect Four, and checkers. This was my type of vibe, and I instantly felt at home.

After checking in, we headed up to our suite. Once we crossed the threshold, I was reminded of the last time we'd been in a hotel room alone. I was hopeful for a different outcome because my man was looking fine in his open white linen cuffed shirt, light-blue harem joggers, and fresh white Air Forces. When I first answered the door the evening prior and saw him for the first time in almost a month, my mouth actually watered. His outfit fit his body to a tee. We both enjoyed driving, so we decided to do so in lieu of flying to get to know each other better along the way. But I knew then that pulling over at a rest stop and pouncing on him would definitely cross my mind a time or two . . . hundred . . . while behind the wheel. We took a nap for a few hours, then hit the road for the nine-hour trip. Since we were both music heads, we enjoyed some '90s hip-hop lyric battles and sharing fond memories while reminiscing about our childhoods.

The hotel room was bright, open, and breathtaking. The first thing I noticed was the view of the city. I rushed over to the picture window and stood there for a long time, taking in the slower pace of the residential area surrounding us. A few moments later, his hands gripped my waist from behind, and I leaned my head back onto his chest. I was looking forward to spending the next couple of days with him. I turned to face him.

"Lennox, this is perfect."

"Good. I figured you would like it."

I slid my hands over his broad chest. "Want to fit in a quick . . ."

He inhaled as I squeezed my thighs together.

". . . nap?" I breathed.

We chuckled, well aware of the mounting sexual tension raging between us.

He nodded. "That would be nice. I was thinking we'd go see Mom Dukes for a minute before going to grab dinner."

"Sounds good. I'm looking forward to meeting her."

"She can't wait to meet you, either. Halo, my father, is out of town on business, so it'll just be the three of us."

"Is your brother in town?" I asked, heading over to my bag to pull out disinfectant spray and wipes.

"Yeah, Prez may actually pop in at the reunion for a minute with his girl, Mia."

"That would be dope."

"Yeah, he was a few years behind me, but he still talks to a few people from my graduating class."

"You said you moved to Atlanta from here, right?"

"Yep."

"But you also said you haven't been home to visit your parents since shortly after graduating high school . . ."

He unpacked his toiletries. "Yeah, I had a spot out in the Bronx with Prez for a few years after graduating college."

"It must've been interesting living with your brother on your own for the first time."

"Yep, never a dull moment with that dude."

I noticed his shoulders tense a bit, so I eased off the subject. "So, what's on the itinerary tonight?"

"It's going to be a series of events. They designed it so you can pick and choose which ones to attend." He reached into his messenger bag, then handed me a flyer.

I took a break from cleaning to lie on the bed and review the itinerary. "Looks like we'll be starting off with appetizers and throwback games here at the hotel. Nice. We can just head right downstairs for that. Next, we'll be heading to dinner."

He nodded. "I thought we could grab a private dinner with Prez and Mia instead."

"Yeah, that's fine with me." I continued scanning the flyer. "Then we're heading to the aquarium for appetizers and socializing. Fun! Then Alpha Space for . . . excuse me. Does that say roller skating?"

Lennox nodded, his eyes dancing. "That's going to be fun. It's called Soul Roll. Super cool vibe."

Despite the enticement of his sexy smile, I couldn't bring myself to return it. "Bae . . . she does not skate."

"Why doesn't she?"

"Have you ever seen Bambi the little fawn trying to stand up for the first time? That's me on skates. All legs and limbs."

He chuckled. "Oh, I'm sure you're not that bad."

"You can laugh all you want, but know this . . . if I go down, so will you."

"Don't worry, Beauty. I've got you."

I glanced back down at the sheet. "Then we're grabbing late-night ice cream. Mmm, I want to try this vegan piña colada."

A few moments of silence passed before I looked up. Lennox was leaning against the dresser, eying me carefully. My breath caught in my throat, and I dropped the flyer on the bed. I was lying on my back with my legs bent. From there, I couldn't tell if his eyes were planted on my legs or my thighs, but the vein bulging in his neck looked like he was battling a strong compulsive urge.

"Lennox."

His voice was low and measured. "You're my girl now. You can call me Ox."

I tilted my head, teeth clenched, and a surge pressed through me. I didn't know if the excitement was due to hearing him call me his girl or hearing the nickname Ox. I was used to calling him bae and rarely used his name at all. But *Ox*. Ox was strong. Ox was powerful. Ox fit him just right.

As shivers ascended my spine, I closed my eyes, scraping my lower lip beneath my teeth.

"Say it."

I gazed at him and exhaled, unable to trust my voice at the moment.

He pushed off the dresser and began crossing the room toward the bed. Once he stood right beside me, I struggled to sit upright. His eyes swept over my body before penetrating my own. "Beauty."

I nodded, otherwise stock-still.

"Let me hear you say it."

I swallowed, trying my best to ignore April's silent plea while submitting to his command. "Ox."

I was surprised by my assertiveness as it rolled from my lips easily. I left them parted as I drew out the ending sound. His eyes closed, and he balled his fists. I noticed subtle movement in his joggers, which incited a full-out riot inside me. My joystick was crying out to me. I gripped the comforter beneath me and yanked, hips wriggling.

"*Ox . . .*"

He stared down at me and I at him, silently daring him to take action while refusing to break eye contact. He stroked my hairline with his fingertips, then fingered one of my coils. I eased my head back against the padded headboard, keeping my eyes trained on him.

"Oh, *Ox.*"

He grunted and dug his hand deeper into my hair, gently massaging my scalp in small circles with his thumb. The pressure was stimulating, but I refused to give in to the distraction.

"Yes, *Ox.*" I began rotating my hips slowly. "I've missed you."

"I've missed you too, Beauty."

"*Mmm*, and we've got a couple of hours to kill."

His eyelids drooped a bit. "We need rest."

"Making slow, sweet love can be very relaxing."

"Not the way I'm going to do it." His voice thickened with lust.

April shrieked, and I flattened on the bed, clamping my eyes shut and forfeiting our staring contest. I was mentally fried and spent, envisioning all the things he would do to my body that night. We mutually agreed before he even touched down in Cleveland to pick me up for our trip that we would wait until that evening to experience each other for the first time. In anticipation, I'd spent the previous day waxing, plucking, exfoliating, and priming each inch of my body. I had every toy, lube, and prop known to man sitting in my duffle bag. Mr. Davenport was in for a treat.

I'd be lying if I said it didn't feel good to see how difficult abstaining had been for him as well. Since day one, I'd worn my lust for Ox on my sleeve, but we were now equally matched when it came to untamed desire and suspense. That little fact gave me the edge I'd need to survive the evening. Knowing I wouldn't be getting any type of nap until I had a release, I shimmied out of my leggings and slid on my house shoes before retrieving my bag of tricks from the dresser. I pulled back the comforter and tossed it onto the floor, knowing it likely hadn't been laundered between the last few guests.

"Take off your shirt and lie on your stomach," I commanded, drawing the curtains.

As I put my chill-mode playlist on, Ox undressed, then lay his bare chest on the fine Italian linen. I straddled his thighs, rubbing jojoba oil on my hands. As I slowly pushed my hands up his lower back, I massaged each vertebra with my thumbs. Once I reached the top of his broad shoulders, I returned my attention to his lower back and worked my way up again in a circular motion.

I leaned down and whispered into his ear, "How's that feel?"

He grunted . . . face buried in the pillow. I assumed he was enjoying it and continued pushing my hands up to massage his upper back and arms. I slowly worked my way down to his palms and fingertips, stroking them one at a time. The tension in his taut neck and shoulder muscles slowly melted away beneath my fingertips. I told him to turn over before taking his engorged manhood into my hands. I stroked him with both fists, moving them upward before rubbing my thumbs over the glistening tip. Once he recovered from his happy ending, his breathing grew deep and rhythmic. After cleaning him up, I covered him with the sheet and headed to the shower—waterproof rabbit vibrator in hand.

"How do I look, Mr. Davenport?" I stepped out of the bathroom, face beat and curls hydrated. I smoothed my hands over my navy and white striped tank dress, doing a little twirl to show off the ruched waist and asymmetrical hem.

My smile faded when my eyes landed on him. He looked like a *GQ* model in a navy linen Havana jacket with a kerchief, a pale-blue polo, and white linen pants. I glanced down to check out his . . . tan boat shoes. I still couldn't believe he was mine, all mine.

"You're breathtaking, babe."

I blinked, then swallowed. "Thanks. You look so handsome."

He leaned down to kiss my forehead. "You ready to head downstairs?"

I nodded, grabbing my jacket and clutch.

Once we ensured he had the room key and the itinerary, we stepped into the hallway, holding hands all the way to the elevator.

"You smell good. Citrus?"

I nodded.

"And I love the red shoes." He gestured toward my strappy ankle-tie sandals. "You manage to wear something red every time I see you. Dress, shoes, headband, nail polish."

I shrugged. "Hmm, does that color do something to you?"

He cleared his throat, and I saw that jaw clench, but he said nothing. We stood in front of the elevator, but he didn't press the call button. After a few moments, I reached out to press it, but he stopped me while still holding onto my other hand. I gazed at him just in time to catch his left eye twitch.

"Are . . . you all right?"

He stared straight ahead, and his Adam's apple bobbed as he swallowed. "Beauty, please don't do this to me, okay? Not tonight."

Now I was really puzzled. "Do what?"

"We're going to see my mom in an hour, and we have a long night ahead of us." He cleared his throat. "I've been fighting this—this losing battle. Ever since I first laid eyes on you. You're so fucking sexy. I can't even begin to describe what you do to me."

I blinked and thought, *Did he just say 'fucking?' Damn, he even makes cursing sound sexy.*

He continued, "As you know, I haven't had sex in well over a year. I promise you that tonight will be well worth the wait for both of us. But if we're going to make it through the rest of the evening, we've got to work together. So, you've gotta do your best to dial the sexiness back a bit. I need you to help me out by being on your best behavior."

My first thought was to mess with him a bit more, just for kicks. But the pained look in his eyes told me that he was seriously struggling with self-control. It was the first time I'd seen him lose his cool. I didn't see it as a weakness. Seeing this honest, open side of him evoked compassion, respect, and understanding in me. So, I sighed and nodded. "Okay, Ox. And I'm sorry. I just tease you because you always seem to have things all under control. Every time I see you, I can't think or react. It's almost like my mind's slate is wiped clean."

He took a step toward me, and I stepped back. Then he took another. As my back brushed the wall, he planted his hand against it, towering over me.

"And you don't think you do the same shit to me? I've been fighting an internal war since day one." His minty breath penetrated my nostrils, and I inhaled deeply. "You don't think every time you beg me to make love to you that I don't have to fight through heaven and hell to refuse your sexy little ass? While you thought I was asleep after the massage, I heard your moans from the shower. They ripped me to shreds. I was so fucking helpless and defeated while lying in that bed. I had to pull the pillow over my head to drown out your voice. You can't possibly imagine how hard it was for me to resist ripping that shower curtain off the rod and coming to thrust myself inside you."

My thoughts abandoned me. I could only focus on maintaining my breath, which came in forced pants as I gazed up at him, not daring to move an inch.

"But making our first time special for you is worth more than a quick screw for me. I want you to look back at our first time together as your favorite romantic memory. I want it to be something out of one of those rom-coms of yours. Like that shit."

He pushed his groin against me, and I felt my joystick throbbing. Heat rushed my body, and I squirmed against the wall, whimpering.

"So, I'm begging you, Patience Christine Hampton, to stop this shit right now. Before I say fuck this reunion, fuck my brother, later for Moms, and hoist your little ass up against this wall, driving myself inside of you right here . . . right now, then continue to sex you brainless for the rest of the night."

A door opened down the hall as my widened eyes burned. But I couldn't move my head or blink. Instead, I soaked in every beautiful moment of the passionate fury raging inside of him. His harsh words, escaping through clenched teeth, hit me hard, and I recognized, right then and there, exactly what he was contending with. I wasn't a damn fool. I fully understood the type of danger I was in. This man's sexual energy had been pent up for at least a year, and he'd been saving himself exclusively for me for the past twelve weeks. All this time, I'd been prodding a starving lion. And at that moment, I realized that I wasn't the hunter. I was the motherfucking gazelle.

*Chapter Twenty-Four*

Framed pictures of Biggie, Aaliyah, and Lil' Kim in her infamous squatting pose lined the walls as we walked into the event hall. Late '90s hip-hop music blasted, slightly amping up our tense mood. Before we could grab a seat, someone was calling out from behind us.

"Lenny! Lenny, baby. What's up, brother?"

*Lenny?* We turned to see a tall, brawny redhead holding a beer in each of his outstretched hands.

Ox chuckled, tilting his head back. "Ahh, what's good, man?"

Muscle Bound set his beers down on the bar, then gripped Ox in a bear hug, clapping him on the back, saying, "Man, you got super smooth on us. Looks like you grew a few inches, too, bro! What the hell?"

Ox stepped back and crossed his arms. "What's been up, Brendon? How've you been?"

"Been good. Started a brewing company a couple of years back, and we're working on expanding our local distribution. Was just meeting with the food and beverage manager at the hotel to see if I can deliver a few sample cases here."

"Is this it?" Ox gestured toward the bottles Brendon had just set down.

"Yeah, I was just bringing Sheldon one, but take it. It's yours. Let me know what you think."

"Definitely. Hey, Brendon, this is my girlfriend, Patience Hampton. Patience, this is my classmate, Brendon Phillips."

Brendon held out his hand, and I shook it, despite the moisture from the beer bottle's condensation. "Pleased to meet you, Patience. How did you and Lenny meet?"

"I was attending a conference in Atlanta at a hotel where he was meeting a client."

"Yeah, that's right—you're living in Atlanta now. Are you still in the software industry?"

When Brendon turned his attention back to Ox, I took that opportunity to exit the conversation. "Excuse me." I pressed my hand into Ox's back before slipping away to the bar.

A cocktail or two would be necessary for me to endure being grilled by total strangers all night. I laid my clutch on top of the bar before taking a seat. There were only two bartenders serving the growing crowd. I was relieved to have a few minutes to wrap my head around the bomb Ox had just dropped on my ass. I had no idea how we were going to make it through an entire day of activities without busting at the seams. I was knee-deep in my thoughts when two women in skimpy dresses took the empty seats beside me. The cloud of designer perfume they brought with them caused me to clear my throat.

I tuned out their loud laughter and high-fiving for the first thirty seconds or so, but when their tones became hushed, I couldn't resist listening in.

"Mmm, girl. Yes, his fine ass is here," the one next to me said.

"I told you. Prez let me know last week."

"He bring a date?"

"Don't know. I just walked in five minutes ago and was talking to a few people. But if he did, the bitch better be on her A-game tonight!"

They cackled and high-fived again.

"Now that I think about it, I haven't seen any pictures of him with females on social media. As far as I'm concerned, he's fair game."

"Well, I know that doesn't surprise you. The only thing he ever cared about was winning at everything he did and being the best. The only marriage he's committed to is his damn goals."

"Dead-ass. Dude was a beast."

"How long Prez say he'll be back here?"

"He didn't mention it. You know how tight-lipped he is about his family. But Prez did say he'd be stopping by at some point tonight, so maybe we can all kick it like old times."

"That's cool. When you making your move, though?"

I kept my eyes on my phone but couldn't keep my brow from lifting. My eye began to twitch, and I struggled to even my rapid breathing, knowing they were casually discussing my man while sitting right next to me.

"I'll go talk to him after a good, stiff drink."

"Well, it's a good thing you got that baby weight off because you used to be a skinny hoe in high school."

"Bitch, I will never not be his type."

The bartender came over and placed a napkin in front of me. "What can I get you?"

I licked my lips and said quietly, "I'll take a prosecco with pear juice and a Tito's neat. Make that a double."

The woman closest to me turned toward me and asked, "Oh, hey, sis. How are you?"

I kept my eyes low. "Good and you?"

"Are you alum? I think I'd remember you. I'm Kennedi, and this is Jazmine."

I looked up, taking her in before responding. Her large doe eyes bore dramatic lashes, and she had a cute button nose and full red lips. "I'm Patience . . . a plus one."

"Oh. Well, nice to meet you. You from the Brooklyn area?"

"Ohio."

"Wow, you've come a long way to be here. My cousin lives in Akron . . ."

*No, bitch.* I quickly dismissed her, turning my attention back to my phone and hoping she would take the hint and refrain from speaking to me. When the bartender brought over the drinks, I slid him a twenty-dollar tip, tucked my clutch beneath my arm, grabbed the drinks, and dipped.

Instead of heading straight over to Ox, I found a nearby table and sat down. Every time Ox left a group and took a few steps, he was pulled into another group by someone else. He made eye contact with me, shrugged, and smiled. I smiled and nodded, encouraging him to do his thing. His former classmates engulfed him in hugs, dapping him up, and greeting him with smiles and laughter. It made me smile to see him in his element, the only brown face in a sea of white ones, and totally comfortable in this crowd. I scanned the room and noticed Kennedi, Jazmine, and I were the only Black women in the room at the moment. That was pretty typical of private schools in affluent communities, and I was sure we'd all learned to master code-switching in our own ways. I sipped my wine and waited patiently for the highly anticipated moment to arrive.

After a few minutes passed, it looked like Kennedi was ready to shoot her shot. She stood and smoothed her dress. Jazmine reached over and fixed her friend's hair before giving her an approving nod. Reaching for her fresh martini glass, Kennedi made a beeline for my man. I sat back in my chair, sipping my wine and watching Ox's face.

It looked like he was in the middle of telling a story to a small, captivated audience. Kennedi hung back, patiently waiting for him to finish. When the crowd broke into uproarious laughter, she stepped up and said something, placing a hand on Ox's forearm. He glanced over and held out an arm for a friendly hug, much like the ones he gave to many of the other females he'd encountered. She placed her hand on his upper back, and it remained there for a few moments before Ox removed his arm from her shoulder. Their body language looked respectful enough. Ox continued his conversation with the others for another minute or so before excusing himself from the group.

I glanced at Jazmine, who watched them from the bar, undoubtedly rooting her friend on from afar. *Mm-mm. Sorry, girl. Shot blocked. Time to find another hoop on another court.* Shortly after disengaging from the group, Ox visited the buffet area. A few minutes later, he was leaning over and kissing my cheek.

"You left your jacket at the bar." He hung it on the back of my chair. "Sorry about all that. That was my varsity basketball team. We were catching up and reminiscing. You okay?"

I smiled up at him. "Yes, I'm good. No worries, bae. It's a reunion. That's why you're here."

I felt four little holes burning into the side of my head, but I refused to balk under the scrutiny of those women. I never even looked up to gauge their reactions as Ox took a seat.

"Is this cool, or you want something else?"

I gazed down at the plate of hummus, veggies, and pita chips. "This is perfect, bae. Thanks. I don't want to ruin my appetite for dinner. You're not having anything?"

"Naw, I'm cool." He took a slow sip from his cocktail.

"So, I see there were a few sistas who attended your school," I said, subtly motioning my head toward the bar, where Kennedi had just rejoined Jazmine. My peripheral game was mean.

Ox nodded without looking in their direction either. "Yeah, it was Kennedi, Jazmine, a younger dude named Chaz, another younger guy named Antonio, me, and Preston. That was pretty much it."

I nodded. "Same. I can count on both hands and a couple of toes how many of us were in the entire school."

"Yeah, I definitely would have liked to have seen more diversity. It was a nice cohesive vibe, though. Staff and faculty were adamant about making it an inclusive atmosphere. Besides, the Black student body was close-knit and worked hard to make sure we always had a voice and a platform. We started the Black Student Union my sophomore year, which is still thriving today. They're much larger now and have invited alumni—including a few NBA and NFL players and Fortune 500 execs—to return and speak and network over the years. I've also spoken to them a couple of times with some of the other founding members since graduating."

I thoughtfully bit into a carrot and nodded, but inside I was burning with pride for my man. "Damn, bae, that's so dope."

He studied me for a moment, then broke into a smile. "So, when are you going to ask me?"

"Ask you what?"

"Something's been off since I came over here. I'm guessing you're wondering if I've ever been involved with either of the sistas you just referred to."

My arm hairs stood at attention. Was I that obvious? I thought I was playing it cool, but he clearly saw right through me. I shrugged. "I figured if that was the case and you felt it was vital information, you would let me know on your own."

He shrugged as well. "Naw, I didn't have a girlfriend in high school. Chicks were too much of a distraction for me. I was too busy playing ball and trying to get an academic scholarship to attend school out of state."

I nodded. "Okay, MVP. Didn't know you were a star athlete."

"And a debater and a mathlete."

My eyes bugged. "Come again?"

"Yeah, I was into everything—robotics, sports, student council. Had a lot going on."

I guess he really was a beast, as Jazmine had so eloquently put it.

"Let me find out my sexy babe was, in fact, a sexy little nerd." I did a shoulder shimmy.

He rolled his eyes as a slow smile crept onto his lips, highlighting that cute little dimple.

"What? Black men who are confident in showcasing their intelligence are an aphrodisiac like no other for me."

"I've seen everyone I was hoping to, so we can head out in a few."

"Cool. So, Preston and Mia are meeting us at your parents', then?"

Ox's smile slipped, and he cleared his throat before taking a long drink from his cocktail. I saw that eye twitch again. After a few tense moments passed, I was about to ask if I'd unknowingly said something wrong.

His voice was strained when he replied, "Nah, babe, we'll just see them at dinner."

His reaction triggered a few more questions, along with a bit of uneasiness. Did their mom dislike Mia? I wanted to press Ox further so I could know what I was about to walk into because I was already nervous as hell about whether his mom would like me. The last thing I needed was to walk into another Friday night framily dinner type of situation and be ambushed with family drama like what had happened at Daniel's house. But I realized I had struck a sore spot somehow. Not at all used to hitting a brick wall with him, I eased up and reached across the table for his hand, giving it a reassuring squeeze instead. I was confident he would tell me about it whenever he was ready.

That was how I'd failed to notice we had unwanted company.

"Hey, good people!"

I jumped when her squeaky voice invaded our space.

"I don't mean to interrupt. Just wanted to stop by and say hey."

I looked up at those doe eyes again and fought off the impulse to knock those shiny new veneers down her throat.

Ox seemed slightly relieved by our eager little intrusion. "Hey, Jazmine. How's it going?" He stood up to give her a quick hug.

"I'm doing well, Lenny. I had the pleasure of meeting Patience at the bar earlier. She's lovely. How'd you guys meet?"

So, since I shut her down at the bar earlier, her puppeteer was sending her over to get the scoop. I studied her frozen smile and smirked, not saying a word.

Ox sat down and finally spoke up, but I could tell he was a bit put off by her forwardness as well. "We met on a business trip."

"*Oh* . . . that's nice. Well, you look cute together."

*Uh-huh. Bitch over here trying to save face. You know I heard every word of your friend's thirsty little plot. And yes, this here bitch stays on her 'A-game.'*

"Thanks," Ox said, squeezing my hand and eying me with that same look that sends me spiraling. He better cut that shit out before I canceled the whole night and dragged his ass right upstairs.

"Well, like I said, I just wanted to stop by and say hello. Will you guys be at Soul Roll?"

"Yeah, we'll be there. Should be like old times."

*There they go with that "old times" shit again*, I thought. Then an image of my awkward ass wobbling on roller skates flashed in my mind. I bet those heifas were nice with the skates. But I'd be damned if they were about to finesse my man on the floor without me on some New-New and Star from *ATL* type shit. Over my dead damn body. I'd have to figure this situation out.

"Babe, we should get going," Ox said, standing up suddenly. He must have read my facial expression, my vibe, or my "energy," as he liked to put it. He didn't have to tell me twice. I grabbed my purse and jacket and stood.

He turned to Doe Eyes. "Jazmine, we'll be having a private dinner, so we'll catch you and Kennedi a little later."

Something flashed in her eyes, but it was so quick that I couldn't pinpoint it. Then she smiled and nodded, turning on her heel and prancing away without another word.

I felt Ox's arm snake around my waist, resting on top of my ass as we headed out of the room. He waved to his former class-mates with one hand and gave my rump a firm pat with the other. I couldn't help but giggle. No backward glance was necessary. I knew I was the envy of every woman in that room.

When we entered his parents' luxury apartment building, it felt like we'd just walked into another hotel. The elaborate, expansive lobby was gorgeous. The closer we got to the elevator, the more my stomach flipped. When the doors opened, a young couple stepped out, arguing passionately and paying us no never mind. I stopped dead in my tracks.

"What's wrong?" Ox asked.

I turned to him and placed a hand on his chest. "Hey, I saw a Whole Foods not too far from here. Do you mind if we grab a bottle of wine or fresh flowers or something else your mom may like right quick? I'd hate to meet her empty-handed."

His brow furrowed for a moment before his face melted, giving way to a warm grin. "You're nervous to meet Moms, aren't you?"

"What? No! I just want to be polite. When it comes to most mamas, first impressions are critical. I just want this to be right."

"Well, my mom isn't like that. But we can head over there if you want. It's just a three-minute walk."

We clasped hands as we turned to leave, buying me a few more minutes of peace. As we stepped back out onto the street, a gust of warm wind greeted us. We set out on our path, enjoying the day's final rays of sunlight.

After a few minutes of comfortable silence, I said, "So, you said your dad is out of town on business this weekend, right? I hate that I'm going to miss meeting him."

Ox nodded, then squeezed my hand, checking for traffic before we crossed the street. "Yeah, he spends a lot of time on the road. Neither of them was home much when I was younger, but my mom's retired now."

"What did they do?"

"My mom owned a hair salon and a couple of small beauty supply stores. Halo's a sales manager at Marriott. So, they could afford to send me to private schools, but between both of their busy schedules . . ."

"You were a latch-key kid. Yeah, I know all about that. More than I'd like to."

He nodded, keeping his gaze straight ahead. "Spent a lot of time after school at friends' houses and plenty of summers with relatives."

"So, who came to all of your games and tournaments?"

"They alternated. I have an uncle here in Brooklyn who's a truck driver. So, he made them whenever he was in town. Once my mother made enough money with the salon to retire and hire more employees at her stores, she started coming to a lot more of my games and spending more time at home. That was when I hit my junior year. We've been extremely close ever since. My father stopped making them altogether once I made varsity."

I waited for a beat, and when he didn't offer anything further, I asked, "How's your relationship with your dad?"

He cleared his throat and stepped aside as I entered the grocery store ahead of him. It was busy inside, and I got a bit distracted by all of the hustle and bustle. I scanned the perimeter for signs directing me to the wine aisle.

"You may want to get her flowers instead. She has expensive taste in wine."

"Well, I've never met anyone who doesn't love blackberry merlot or a good prosecco with pear juice. But I'll take your word for it." I headed for the floral department and picked out a bouquet of bold gerbera daisies and white roses.

"Nice pick. She'll love these." Ox leaned over my shoulder, and I brought the bouquet up to his nose for a quick sniff.

After a second thought, I stopped by the wine section. I grabbed a bottle of rosé when I couldn't find my merlot. I looked down when I felt my phone vibrate. I didn't recognize the phone number, but it was from a 216 area code. Something told me to grab it.

"Hello," I said, stepping into the self-checkout line with Ox.

"Hi, Patience. It's Mrs. Francois."

*What in the entire hell?* "Hold, please." I muted the call

before turning to Ox. "Bae, I need to take this call. Can you check out, and I'll meet back up with you in a moment?"

He frowned, reading my expression. "Sure. Everything good?"

I nodded. "Yeah, this shouldn't take long."

"No problem. Meet me out front when you're done."

I headed toward the bathroom before resuming the call. "What can I do for you, Lovelie?"

# Chapter Twenty-Five

She paused and cleared her throat. I know she was used to me referring to her as Mrs. Francois, but that was a salutation of respect. And the game done changed.

"It sounds like I've caught you while you're out, so I'll be brief. I'm reaching out regarding Daniel. Ever since the two of you parted ways, he just hasn't been himself. He's been picking up far too many shifts at the hospital, and he hasn't been getting enough sleep or studying time. I'm afraid he may not pass the APRN exam if he continues at this rate." She paused. "Patience, are you still there?"

*Yes, trying to figure out what the hell all this has to do with me.* "Yes, I am."

"I now understand that I wasn't always supportive of your relationship. But one thing I never doubted was your loyalty and devotion to Daniel. You've always kept him on a balanced routine, and now he's really struggling to keep it all together. Princessa and I have tried to offer our support, but he's not accepting help from either of us."

Another pause. It sounded like she was putting me on speakerphone.

"I'm asking if you can reach out to Daniel as a friend to help him get himself back on track. It would be greatly impactful for him to hear from you right now."

I had initially tried to pursue a relationship with Lovelie to fill a stable mother-figure role that was void in my life. At first, her approval meant everything to me. I thought that if I changed the way I dressed, walked, or talked, she would accept me. I was a lot younger then. Over the years, she showed me that no matter what I did, she refused to see me as anything other than another tool for manipulating her son. As long as she kept the insults coming and refused to accept me, the wedge would prevent us from taking the next step in our relationship. But I jumped off of that toxic merry-go-round and wasn't interested in joining her for another ride. She no longer had me to manipulate and harass on end, and now she *needed* me. Lovelie was trying to shove her bunions into my stilettos. The shoe of being Daniel's primary cheerleader, supporter, and caretaker was now on the other foot. She finally saw just how critical I was to his success. I'd be lying if I doubted enjoying this moment.

"Thanks for reaching out, Lovelie. I'll be sure to keep Daniel in my prayers. But my answer is no."

I heard her sharp gasp, followed by her muffled voice stating, "*She said no.*" A few seconds later, she said, "I beg your pardon?"

"I said I won't be reaching out to Daniel today or any other day. If I were to do that, it wouldn't provide anything more than a Band-Aid on a deep mother wound. What Daniel has always needed is stitches, and those can only come from you. I'm sure you've called me out of genuine care for your son. But instead of putting the task of addressing his brokenness on me, use that energy to accept and embrace your son with unconditional love. He may not have made all the decisions in his life that you wanted, but he deserves your love and support nonetheless. And most importantly, your respect for whatever his life choices may be. That's what will help him the most right now."

"Amen, sis!" I heard Princessa yell in the background.

"Best of luck with everything," I said, then ended the call.

I studied my reflection in the mirror. Up until that moment, my stomach was doing flip-flops about meeting Ox's mother. I was concerned that she may judge me or misunderstand me the way Lovelie had. But I realized she would be meeting an entirely different woman. I knew what I brought to the table, and I was prepared to show up as my authentic self. And that would have to be good enough for her. I washed my hands, refreshed my lipstick, and walked out.

I joined Ox outside, and we headed back to his parents' apartment. "See, just a fifteen-minute detour. We'll be back at the apartment soon."

Ox shrugged. "Our dinner reservation isn't for another hour, so we have plenty of time."

"Thanks for working extra time into our itinerary. You know I'm always throwing us off schedule."

"No problem. How are you enjoying yourself so far?"

"Brooklyn is beautiful. How long have your parents lived in their apartment building?"

"Not very long. They're hipsters at heart, so it didn't surprise me when they sold the house right after I graduated high school and opted for apartment living. It fits their lifestyle a lot better. I think this is their third apartment in the past decade."

"Have they been down to visit you in Atlanta yet?"

"Not yet. I'll get them down there before the end of the summer."

We returned to the lobby and took the elevator. Ox leaned over and pressed the sixth-floor button. I smoothed my dress and slid my hands over my hair.

"You look stunning."

"Thanks, bae. I can't wait to meet your mom."

"I've already told her all about you. She can't wait to meet you, either."

"Yeah, I bet she's been waiting for this a long time. Your first real girlfriend. This is going to be interesting."

"Please stop doing that."

"Doing what?"

"Parting and puckering your lips like that. You do it when you're overthinking, and that shit turns me on."

"Oh, I didn't realize—"

Before I could finish my sentence, his lips were on mine. His oncoming weight pinned us against the wall for the second time that evening. I reached down, gripping the handrail to steady myself. His hot breath spasmed as his sweet tongue massaged my lower lip. I reached up and palmed his head, hungrily sucking his full lips as the gentle push of our ascension exploited the tingling sensation between my thighs. Still gripping the wine and flowers, he slid his free hand up my dress. A low grunt slipped from his lips as he fingered my thong's dainty lace. He stroked the fabric lightly, causing me to purr as he pulled away and stared at me. I couldn't read his eyes.

Then with a raspy voice, he said, "I should stop this elevator."

"Don't you dare, Lennox Davenport," I shrieked.

He walked over to the control board, and I glanced down to see my joystick standing at full mast.

"You're being so unfair. I'm meeting your mother in a few seconds."

He pulled the stop button. "You don't have to. We can just tell her I wasn't feeling well . . . head back to the hotel."

I balked as he reached into his pants and began massaging himself.

My eyes scanned the small space for a camera.

<h1 style="text-align:center">Chapter Twenty-Six</h1>

I fought to even my breathing, still not trusting what I saw unfolding in front of me. Had this boy waited until we got to New York to totally lose his damn mind? Especially after he'd given me a speech in the hallway?

I hissed through clenched teeth, "Ox! You're buggin', boy. Stop. It."

He grinned, retrieved his hand, and gave my ass a firm squeeze. "Fix your lipstick."

I shot him an evil glare, then fished in my bag for my lipstick yet again. "All that talk about being on my best behavior. You need to take your own damn advice!"

He winked at me, then pulled the button, and we resumed our ascension. "I'm telling you . . . I can't resist your fine ass no more."

I huffed, using the mirrored wall to finish adjusting my hair and makeup. How did he think telling me this was helping our situation? He needed to get control of himself because sex was the furthest thing from my mind. I had the opportunity to start fresh and make a great impression on his mom, and he was messing it all up for me.

"You're so tight. Not at all like the horny little Beauty I know. That's okay. The rosé will help you relax."

Fuming, I pressed hand sanitizer into his palm. Why he would pick this particular moment to fuck with me, I did not know. "Be quiet and clean your filthy hands. You're about to hug your mother, for God's sake. You're definitely from New York with your gully ass."

He chuckled as he complied. I refused to make eye contact and stared at the elevator doors until they opened. The last thing I needed was to see that sexy smirk of his.

When Lorna greeted us at the door, my annoyance instantly melted away. Her soft, smiling face held luminosity, making me want to melt. So, when she held out her meaty arms, I walked straight into them and closed my eyes as she pressed me to her ample bosom.

"Patience! Hello! I'm so excited to meet you," she said, rocking me from side to side.

"Hello, Mrs. Davenport. It's such a pleasure to meet you as well," I said.

She pulled away and examined me at arm's length. "Please. Call me Lorna. Such a pretty, petite little thing and all that gorgeous hair!"

"Thank you." I smiled, stepping aside as Ox entered the apartment.

"Hey, Ma."

I took in his boyish grin as she covered his face with kisses.

Out of respect for the white oak floors in the spacious and immaculately clean apartment, I slipped out of my stilettos and grabbed my footies from my clutch. Lorna gestured toward the dining room, where a large spread of cheese cubes, fresh fruit, and whole grain crackers were waiting for us on the table.

"Have a seat. I'll be right there." She walked over to the kitchen while examining the wine label. "*Oh*, I love rosé!"

*See?* I mouthed to him, snaking my neck.

*She's lying,* he mouthed back, grinning.

She joined us at the table, toting a wine cork and three glasses. When she plopped down, a gust of lavender and orange blossoms surrounded us. I closed my eyes and enjoyed her sweet scent. I loved this woman already.

Her eyes landed on Ox. "So, El, would you pray over the food?"

I immediately bowed my head, and Ox began to pray.

"Father God, we thank you for our safe trip here. Please bless this food we're about to eat for the nourishment of our bodies. In Jesus's name, amen."

I hadn't fully lifted my head when Lorna started talking.

"So, Patience, how was the trip up here? Is this your first time in New York?"

I smiled, nodding thank you as she handed me a chilled wine glass. "Yes. It's also our first time on the road together. I'm loving what I've seen of New York so far. I'm looking forward to seeing more of it."

"That's so nice. And you have such a velvety and soothing voice."

I could feel my cheeks warming as I glanced down at my hands. I wasn't used to receiving so many compliments. Especially not from a perfect stranger.

She continued. "Halo and I aren't originally from here. I'm from Toledo, and he's from Cleveland. I actually attended Cleveland State University, but we didn't meet until our graduate program at NYU. After graduation, we both landed local internships. The initial plan was to return to Ohio, but we both fell in love with the Brooklyn area and ended up settling down here."

"That's wonderful. Lennox mentioned you're retired and own several businesses."

"Yes, it's been eleven years, and I'm already bored, honey. I spend a lot of time popping into my stores and attending hair shows with my stylists."

I smiled. "Gotta love a woman with an entrepreneurial spirit. Lord knows it isn't easy."

She shook her head. "No, it's not, but I wouldn't have it any other way. Where are you guys headed for dinner? Oops, El just gave me a look, so I guess it's a surprise."

"That's cute that you call him L."

"Yes, El is short for his middle name, Ellington."

I raised a brow and stole a glance at Ox. *Lennox Ellington Davenport.* Turning back to Lorna, I said, "I love that name! Are you a fan of Duke?"

"Yes, big time. In fact, El was conceived to 'In a Sentimental Mood.'"

I giggled, reaching for a grape. "Makes perfect sense."

Ox rubbed his forehead and said, "Ma."

"Anyway, Duke and Stevie were all we played around the house when El was a child. In fact, he knew how to play most of Duke's songs on the piano by the time he was eleven."

I turned to face him. "So, you're a piano prodigy?"

Ox sipped his wine. "Not hardly."

"Stop being a modest mouse. You know you can play, boy. If we didn't sell our grand piano before moving here, I'd make you prove it right now."

I squeezed his hand. "I would love to hear you play one day."

He just shook his head, popping a cube of cheese into his mouth.

"Don't act like I'm embarrassing you, El. It's only a matter of time before Patience finds out your dirty little secret."

I glanced at him, then Lorna, trying to decipher their code.

After a few tense moments, Lorna threw up her hands. "You were a cute little nerd. So what? I always told you it's the nerds who are successful in life and get all the beautiful women." She reached over and squeezed my hand.

Nerd, huh? Well, that awkward little duckling sure did blossom into a majestic black swan.

Lorna turned toward a small corner shelf behind us and pulled out an old photo album, and I noticed Ox shifting in his seat.

"Ma, you promised you wouldn't do this."

"I'm only going to show Patience your swaggy pictures. You know, the muscle-bound basketball and dapper prom ones."

I scooted closer to her as she opened the back of the album, eager to get a glimpse of what I assumed would be a tall, inept version of my man. I gasped as my eyes landed on the first image. Ox was about four years old and clutching a basketball, sitting on the shoulders of a tall, striking man. Ox's short arms were outstretched toward the hoop. I could almost hear his squeal, and his ecstatic, plump little face warmed my heart. I immediately pictured what our son would look like. Keeping her promise, Lorna hurriedly shoved the picture back into the book and turned the page.

"Ahh, here we are. El's junior year on the varsity team. My baby had it all—height, good ball-handling skills, a great mid-range jumper, consistent grit and hustle for rebounds and assists, and he was nimble on the court."

I sat back and stared at his mama for a second. "Either you're a hardcore sports fan, or you've been moonlighting as a sportscaster."

"Oh no, neither." She laughed, placing her hand on my knee. "But when it comes to my El, I'm dedicated to learning the ins and outs of everything he takes an interest in. He's my pride and joy, and I've always tried to make each of his passions my own."

Turning a smiling face to Ox, I said, "No wonder you turned out so great with a mama like her."

He nodded. "She was always the loudest one in the stands. It didn't matter if it was basketball, the chess club, or the debate team. Everyone in the room knew my full name."

"Oh, boy, you loved it!" Lorna swatted at Ox.

I took in his downcast eyes. Was he . . . blushing? "It was great having you there, Ma."

"I know it wasn't always that way. But we did the best we could, sweetheart."

My heart sank as I realized they weren't talking about who

was there but who wasn't. I reached over to rub his leg beneath the table and felt his muscle tense beneath my palm. I wanted to give him a hug but kept my eyes fixed on the album. Lorna continued flipping through the pictures, stopping at a basketball team photo. I instantly recognized Brendon and a couple of other guys I had recently met at cocktail hour. They were all overly tall, lanky, and awkward looking. I spotted Ox looming in the back row, donning his custom smirk and seemingly amused by something no one else on the team knew.

"Did you meet any of these boys at the hotel?" Lorna asked me.

"Yes, a few of them. They pretty much look the same, except for facial hair and a few more muscles . . . or beer bellies."

Lorna chuckled. "I believe it. El would invite those boys over after practice, and they would nearly eat me out of house and home! '*Ooh*, you got some new snacks, Mrs. Davenport?' They were all good boys, though."

Then her fond expression darkened and her jaw hitched. I watched her eyes linger on the team photo for a few prolonged moments but couldn't pinpoint who she was looking at. Ox cleared his throat, and she quickly moved on. When Lorna turned the page to his prom pictures, I froze. Ox was decked out in a tailored black suit, vest, shirt, and tie, looking down at his watch. He. Looked. Edible. *So, this man has always been this smooth.*

The effect a year of growth and maturity could have on a teenage boy was amazing. In another picture, his arm rested around the waist of a girl standing in front of him. I blinked once I realized it was Kennedi. She was stunning in a black ball gown with a sweetheart bust that fit her then tiny waist. It spread out into a dramatic floor-length organza skirt. She laughed as she adjusted her sparkling black tiara. I tried to read Ox's expression, but he was speaking to someone in the background.

"Oh, you went to prom with Kennedi," I said, focused on keeping my voice even.

"Yeah," was all he offered.

Why hadn't he mentioned that before? Did he have something to hide? *Bitch, I will never not be his type,* her high-pitched voice rang out in my head.

Lorna disturbed the uncomfortable silence. "Well, there weren't many other choices at that school. And El wasn't exactly popular with the ladies outside of school. So, since he and Kennedi were friends, they decided to go together. You've met her?"

I shook my head, reaching for my wine glass to calm my nerves. "Not officially."

"She's a nice girl. A bit thirsty for my taste, but nice all the same."

Lorna's remark caught me off guard. Not the comment I was expecting from a woman in her mid-fifties, but spot-on all the same. For this reason, the chilled wine hit my windpipe, and I choked. I fought back the urge to cough and tried to breathe through my nose with my mouth still full of wine.

Ox reached over and began slapping my back with unnecessary force. "Really, Ma?"

Lorna stood and began fanning me, shooing Ox away. "Move, boy. You're not helping her! Are you okay, Patience?"

I finally managed to swallow, then cleared my throat and took a deep breath. I squeaked out, "Yeah . . . wrong pipe."

"Good. Now, sip your water." Lorna turned to Ox. "Now, what do you mean 'really, Ma?' That child was calling here for you around the clock asking, 'Is Lennox home, Mrs. Davenport?' Why didn't she ever just call your cell?"

"She did. But it was always off during basketball practice or rehearsals, and I'd forget to turn it back on. I told her I just wanted to be friends, but she wasn't trying to hear that."

Lorna and I exchanged knowing glances. Then she said, "Yes, honey. You were very focused on your studies and activities and didn't have time for anything else. I'm proud of you for sticking to your guns and not allowing any distractions to interfere with your plans. Speaking of distractions, did you hear that your cousin, Torrey, is on his fifth child already? Ain't even thirty yet."

Ox shook his head. "I tried to tell him."

She turned to me. "He was at Morehouse on a full basketball scholarship. His first baby's mama was a nice girl from Spelman. The rest of them . . . well, let's just say he hasn't been as selective." She wrinkled her nose.

"Did he finish school?" I asked.

"Yes. He's an electrical engineer. Never married, travels all over the world," Lorna said.

Ox shrugged. "Different strokes. It's not up to us to gauge that man's success."

"True. I'm just glad you didn't go down that path." She turned back to me. "So, Patience, El tells me you work in the marketing industry. How did you get started in your career?"

"It's actually a funny story. I was focused on applying for public relations positions in corporate America when my grandfather's godson asked if I could intern with him for the summer. He had a successful voice-acting business and needed help with some projects. In addition to a decent salary, he gave me private voice-acting lessons. By the end of the summer, I'd recorded my first book trailer, multiple intros for a famous YouTube influencer, and a few internet radio commercials with his company. That fall, he found me the job that I have now. I also take on freelance projects whenever I have time."

"Outstanding. It sounds like you have a very supportive grandfather."

"Yes. I don't know what I'd do without him."

"Do you have any siblings?"

I nodded. "A little sister, Chelsea. She's a junior in college. And two half siblings, who are sixteen-year-old twins."

"Nice little age difference there. How's your relationship with Chelsea?"

I popped a grape into my mouth. "Very good. She's responsible and mature, so the age gap doesn't impact us much. Plus,

I've been a mother figure to her for a great deal of her life. Our father walked out on us when she was six months old, and our mother struggled with alcoholism shortly after."

Lorna's brow raised, but it seemed out of shock, not judgment. After a beat of processing, she placed her chin in her palm, eyes warm, and asked, "My dear. That means you were, what . . . ?"

"Seven and a half years old when my father left and almost twelve years old when my mother officially checked out on us. It was rough. But, it's life."

Lorna shook her head, placing her hand on mine. "No, darling. That isn't life. And it shouldn't have ever been yours. El rolls his eyes when I say this, but I studied child psychology at Cleveland State University before moving here. Dear, it's quite likely that you've suffered from emotional trauma since a very young age."

"Yes, I understand that."

When she turned to face Ox, I kept my eyes on her. "El, can you give us ladies the room for a minute?"

I felt the sudden warmth of Ox's hand landing on top of my trembling one. He squeezed it as if to say, *If you don't want me to leave, I won't.* I squeezed it back to let him know I was all right. I was grateful Lorna had the discernment to continue our conversation in private.

Ox stood. "I'll be downstairs, babe. Text me when you're ready to go."

He leaned down and kissed his mother's cheek. "Behave, Ma."

Then, as the door clicked shut behind him, it was just the two of us, the air between us heavy with unspoken words.

*Chapter Twenty-Seven*

Lorna turned to me and said, "May I ask you a personal question, Patience?"

*We weren't just getting personal a second ago?* Although I normally considered being grilled like this by virtual strangers off-putting and a gross invasion of my privacy, there was something about Lorna that made me comfortable with opening up. Her demeanor was naturally warm and endearing, and I felt like I could trust her almost instantly. Besides, it was time for me to get comfortable with sharing more of my past with Ox since I was learning about his. Talking things through with Lorna would be the first step. "Yes, that's fine."

"Have you ever sought therapy?"

"Yes, I have. It was complimentary during undergrad, so I took advantage of it during all four years. But not since graduating."

"I hope you're continuing to make monitoring your mental health state a priority."

I nodded. "Yes, ma'am, I am."

She smiled and patted my hand. "That's great to hear. I have another personal question. If you're not comfortable answering, please let me know."

Perspiration sprouted on my palms. I swallowed, then said. "Yes, go ahead."

"Did you ever receive a diagnosis?"

"Yes, I did. And I don't have a problem discussing it. The therapist mentioned the possibility of fear of abandonment along with something called scarcity mindset."

Lorna nodded and exhaled. Just when I thought she was going to move on, she seemed to change her mind and continued. "Patience, first and foremost, I commend you for being courageous enough to seek therapy for your childhood trauma at such a young age. Second, El didn't share much information about you with me before today. He wanted to respect your privacy and allow you to tell me yourself. As I'm sure you can tell, I'm a hands-on and touchy-feely kind of gal. I enjoy getting to know others and what makes them tick. I hope that's okay with you."

I nodded, wondering what she was getting at.

"Patience, I want you to know that I would *never* use anything I learn about you against you. We're still getting to know one another, but you have my word on that. But those who suffer from fear of abandonment and a scarcity mindset often attract people who treat them poorly and eventually leave them, which only reinforces their worst fears and deepens their distrust of others. So, I know you've been through a lot in your personal and romantic relationships, baby."

I offered another numb nod. Her gentle eyes pulled me in deeper, and I hung on each word.

"I assure you that Lennox is *not* that kind of person. I'm not accusing you of having walls built up, but if you do, you can let them down with him. He's not perfect, but he's a good man. We've raised him to be empathetic, caring, kind, and to have the utmost integrity, and he hasn't wavered from it."

"Yes, ma'am, I agree. Getting to know him better has been wonderful."

She patted my hand again. "That's so great to hear. I have a good friend who is a therapist in Cleveland. If you have any privacy concerns, she can refer you to another local therapist in her network, and the sessions would be complimentary for as long as you need them. Please take advantage of them, if you ever see fit, on your healing journey."

I nodded. "Lorna, thank you. That's a kind offer."

"Of course, dear. Is there anything you want to ask me?"

Thrown by her question, I was unable to think of anything in particular. "Not at this time."

She nodded, holding my gaze for a few long moments before continuing. "I know you have a dinner to get to. I really enjoyed meeting you, Patience. Thanks for making time to stop by, and I hope to see more of you in the near future."

She stood with her arms outstretched. But my mind was still whirring, so I struggled to stand up on wobbly legs to hug her. I was glad when I finally managed to because when I folded into her arms, it felt just like the home I'd always searched for. I closed my eyes and allowed her words to move through me, tapping into dormant emotions and unleashing subdued memories and thoughts from the past. I bit my lip, holding my breath, but it wasn't long before a dam burst from deep inside. Before I knew it, what had started as sucking in a deep breath to cool my nerves morphed into a deep, guttural sob.

Lorna rubbed small circles on my back and hummed softly. Her low, soothing voice in my ear calmed me and coaxed me to let go of the weight I'd been carrying with me for years. I clutched her back and shoulders as if my life depended on it, and she gently rocked me from side to side, just like my grandmother used to before she had died. She whispered sweet affirmations into my ear, telling me it was okay to finally release my fears, doubts, and concerns. She reminded me that I was brave, strong, and enough. Her reassuring words sounded so foreign, so new, and so wonderful to me. I hadn't heard anything like them spoken over me before with such certainty and conviction. I never wanted that sweet moment in her dining room to end.

My tears fell freely. I believed Lorna. And because of that, I knew that I could trust what my instinct was telling me. That I could step out on faith and fully trust that Ox would not hurt me like so many others had before.

# Chapter Twenty-Eight

About twenty minutes later, we were seated by the window at a romantic riverside restaurant just below the Brooklyn Bridge. The calm water reflected the lights from the surrounding skyscrapers, and the serenity coaxed me deeper into my racing thoughts. After fixing my makeup in the car, I hadn't said much. I knew Ox was respectfully giving me time to process everything I had discussed with Lorna. He didn't pry, and if he had, I wasn't sure what I would've even said to him. What I did know was after such a heavy conversation, I was mentally and emotionally drained. The daunting task of putting on a bright and chipper attitude for his brother, Preston, and his girlfriend loomed over me. So, I took the last few minutes before their arrival to zone out and reserve my energy while taking in the incredible view.

"Excuse me, miss. I'm Javier, your server. I've brought you a bottle of Sémillon, per the gentleman's request. Would you care to sample it?"

He extended an oversize glass toward me, which I eagerly accepted while shooting Ox a grateful smile. Inhaling deeply, I savored the aroma of the full-bodied wine before sipping it. It was perfect. I nodded, and Javier filled my glass halfway before setting down the bottle and stepping away to give us more time with the menu. After a few more sips, my muscles relaxed, and a welcomed warmth spread throughout my body. I noticed a stocky man in a suit take a seat behind a grand piano and assumed he was preparing to give us a live show. Here I was, sitting next to my handsome date in a romantic restaurant that he probably had reserved for us weeks prior, enjoying fabulous wine in a beautiful city . . . and I was brooding. I offered him a small smile, deciding to become better company for the rest of the evening.

Reaching over, I squeezed my man's hand. I said, "Bae, this is beautiful. How'd you know I've always wanted to come here?"

"You're a foodie and a wine enthusiast. So . . . an educated guess."

He leaned over and placed a sweet kiss on my lips. I closed my eyes, savoring the moment. Ox was everything I needed. Everything I'd prayed for. I sent up a silent prayer, thanking God for sending him to me. Then I was nearly jumping out of my skin.

"*Yer!* Look at my big brother all boo'd up."

I looked up as a shorter, stockier version of Ox approached the table with a bronze beauty in tow. Ox and I stood, and I looked on as the brothers embraced.

Then Ox stepped aside and said, "Prez, this is my girl, Patience. Patience, this is my baby bro and his girlfriend, Mia."

"So nice to meet you." I stepped forward and hugged Preston.

"It's even better to meet you. Ox always has such great things to say about you." Preston had his brother's same relaxed demeanor. His hazel eyes held my gaze for a few prolonged seconds, and I could tell he was likely just as intense.

I offered my hand to Mia, and she yanked me in for a hug. "Girl, we're dating brothers. We ain't doing no handshakes around here!"

I didn't have to ask if she was a New Yorker. That accent was thick and unapologetic. I laughed, taking in her short and busty frame. Her zesty energy was larger than life, and I immediately knew I was going to like her. I took a mental note that the brothers both liked short women.

"Boo, I already told you this is a nice place. You're going to have to tone it down in here," Preston warned, pulling out her chair.

I took a seat, amused that this was coming from the same one who had walked in here shouting a second ago.

"Don't act like you can't take me nowhere. I know how to behave myself," Mia said, eyes closed while popping her gum.

I stifled a laugh while pretending to peruse the American cuisine entree options on my menu.

"So, Patience. I don't mean to go in on you right away, but I have to learn more about this mysterious woman who finally convinced my big brother to make some type of commitment. I mean, he wasn't on no player-type shit. But he was a major strait-laced, laser-focused hermit. Do you know that guy Randall from the show *This is Us*?"

I gasped, and Mia cracked up. Ox joined right in.

Preston continued. "Dude was just so driven. Chicks could barely get his attention. And believe me, many have tried."

"So I've heard. And I get what you're saying about his drive. He's disciplined as hell, too. Was he in the Junior ROTC? Y'all can tell me," I joked.

Preston laughed. "Bruh. She really does know you!"

Ox nodded. "She certainly thinks so. But she don't know me, bay bro. I've just been married to my career. Nothing wrong with that."

Mia reached over and high-fived Ox. "I know that's right. There's nothing better than BMW."

"Amen to a Black man working." I did an air toast and sipped from my glass.

Javier reapproached the table. "Hello and welcome. Can I offer you two anything to drink?"

Mia said, "I'll have a glass of the Sangiovese blend, please."

"And I'll have the cabernet sauvignon."

After Javier took our dinner orders, Ox shared the edited version of how we had met in Atlanta and his first trip to Cleveland. The couple must have really been mystified because they hung on his every word.

"If my brother was still sitting on your couch after being called out, I know you're in good with him. 'Cause this dude don't tolerate disrespect in any form or on any level. Hand to God."

I nodded knowingly. "Oh, I definitely believed he was done with me after that. But once I heard he was in Cleveland, I knew I had to make a move, and quickly, if I ever wanted to see him again."

Preston shook his head. "Well, this dude holds grudges like a mothafucka. But you weren't too prideful, so that shit ended up working out. That's what's up. When the ups and downs come, it's all about give and take."

"And you guys are super cute together. You got Ox looking all dapper, and he's showing all thirty-two of his teeth and shit," Mia cooed.

"Y'all really don't know me like that," Ox said, low-key smiling behind a glass of Tito's and Sprite.

A few seconds after the laughter died down, I raised my hand timidly like an elementary school student. "So, permission to address the ivory elephant at the table?"

Preston chuckled and nodded. "Granted."

"Lennox introduced you two as boyfriend and girlfriend, but the view over here's hitting a little different." I leaned back in my chair and served them side eye.

Ox's gaze immediately landed on Mia's left hand. His eyes lit up. "Bay bro . . ."

Preston's handsome face spread into an easy grin. "Yeah, man," he imitated Usher. "After three years of dealing with my ass, I figured it was time to make this shit official."

Ox stood, and his little brother did the same. Mia and I

followed suit, embracing each other as the brothers dapped and hugged one another.

"Congratulations, Mia. You're going to be a beautiful bride!"

"Thank you. I hope you guys can make it back up for the wedding. We're aiming for the May after next to give us enough time to save up."

Stunned by how optimistic she was that I'd still be around in almost two years, I grinned even wider and replied, "Of course! We wouldn't miss it for the world."

Once we were all seated at the table, Javier walked up on cue with chilled flutes of champagne.

I asked, "Javier, how did you know we were celebrating?"

"I'm psychic," he said, smiling. "Just kidding. Mr. Gómez let the hostess know when he and his fiancée arrived. Best wishes to you, madam."

I raised a brow while Mia flashed him a dazzling smile.

"Thank you!"

We each accepted a glass, and I had to force my eyebrow back down. I accepted a champagne glass from Javier, and Ox led the toast.

"To my little brother, who's ready to tie the knot at only twenty-five years old to a beautiful, amazing woman. I've always respected your union, and I look forward to seeing you continue to grow together. Great things are in store for y'all. Welcome to the family, Mia."

We met eyes and clinked glasses. As I brought the glass to my lips, I noticed a shift in Ox's expression. I reached over and gripped his thigh beneath the table.

After a sip of champagne, Preston looked at Ox and said, "Now, bro, I know you're all the way in ATL and super busy with work, but I need you to be my best man. Can I count on you to stand beside me on the happiest day of my life?"

Ox's jaw repeatedly pulsed before he set his glass on the table. "Nothing would make me prouder, Prez."

Mia squealed, clapping her hands excitedly. "Yes! Now I can start asking my bridesmaids. Prez refused to let me start the wedding planning process until he secured his big brother as his best man."

"Aww, that's sweet," I said, touched by the sentimental moment, but I kept a close eye on Ox. "So, how did the proposal happen?"

"Oh, it was just a quiet evening with close family and friends. He invited my mother, father, and sisters over and proposed while we were having dessert. They dimmed the lights, and he put our song on, 'Encantadora.' Then his mother led me into a room filled with white rose petals. He got down on one knee and asked for my hand. He had already asked my father for his blessing, and my mother just loves him."

Completely speechless for a moment, I just smiled. Reading the table and judging from the averted eye contact, I knew the tension I felt wasn't my imagination. Why did it feel like I was the only one left in the dark about what was really going on here? When it became apparent that no one was going to break the uncomfortable silence, I said, "Mia, that sounds wonderful. Would you two excuse us for a quick moment?"

They nodded as I stood. When Ox still didn't get the hint, I nudged him and jerked my head toward the exit. "Come on, babe."

He slowly stood and followed me outside.

Once the fresh air hit us, he took a deep breath and seemed to snap out of his trance. His voice was upbeat when he asked, "That's great news, huh, babe?"

"Yeah." I pulled my sweater over my shoulders. "It sure seems to be."

He shoved his hands into his pants pockets. "He hit me up last week and said he had something to tell me. I figured this was it. I'm really proud of him."

"Yeah, they both seem very excited about including you in their wedding. How do you feel about Mia?"

"She's a great girl. Smart, funny, driven, and loyal. Prez was a wild boy, but she stuck by his side through all the bullshit he put her through. So, some of her gentleness has rubbed off, and she's edgier now. She needs it, dealing with his ass."

*Oh, so he's one of those types.* The more I thought about it, the more it made sense. Extremely good-looking, charismatic, outspoken, and attention-seeking. But since I didn't have anything valuable to add to the conversation, I just hummed, keeping my thoughts to myself.

I didn't think my silence made much of a difference to Ox. He was miles away, looking out over the shimmering water with unfocused eyes. That same vein bulged near his eye, and I knew he was struggling with something. I had a million questions of my own because things just weren't adding up. And it was only our first night in New York. But if my own experience with family drama hadn't taught me anything else, it was to have compassion for others by respecting their privacy regarding family affairs.

So, I pulled his hand out of his pocket and pressed my palm against his, silently reassuring him that I was there for him. I stood and gazed at the water beside him, confident that he would eventually come around and tell me all about what was bothering him. In his own time.

# Chapter Twenty-Nine

The event center looked small from the outside, but I was pleasantly surprised once we walked inside. The bass from a Cash Money song was booming, and purple lights swirled on the open hardwood floor. The music and ambiance took me right back to the summers I had spent with friends during my teenage years. Bella and I would hang out at the skating rink on Friday and Saturday nights with a group of friends from school, sitting on the painted brick wall and dancing as the skaters whizzed by. Neither of us knew how to skate well and wouldn't be caught dead trying to learn in front of the fine boys who came from all over the city to frequent the large rink. Instead, we focused our attention on makeup, sexy outfits, and learning our angles in the mirror to perfect flawless resting faces. Unbeknownst to us, it was the perfect formula for attracting the guys who would bring unapologetic drama and heartbreak to our lives.

Ox ordered our skates and then guided me over to a chair. I cringed at the thought of how many other sweaty feet were crammed into them before mine. Along with my footies, I pulled antibacterial spray out of my purse and disinfected the inside and outside of both pairs. As Ox bent down and laced my skates, the mounting apprehension suffocated me.

When I stood and put my weight on the skates, I was wobbly at first. But I caught myself and began to slowly move forward. With his hand on the small of my back, he trailed me as we inched our way toward the back of the large room where skaters sailed around in an oval, rocking their hips, rolling their shoulders, and dancing to the pulsing beat. I reached out and gripped the neighboring wall, and when he sensed my hesitation, I felt his warm breath on my ear.

"Babe, I got you. You may fall a few times, but I'm not going to let you hurt yourself. Just take your time."

Oh, there was no way I was falling in front of Ox tonight. I had to gather myself and face my fear of looking like a fool head-on. I sighed, then pushed forward to join the racing crowd, feeling like a brand-new driver joining a highway fast lane for the first time. But I had committed to doing this, so there was no turning back. On wobbly legs, I pushed and glided, pushed and glided. Almost immediately, my legs went their separate ways, awkwardly spreading my hips apart. I fought to bring my right leg back in since it was stronger. But it was difficult to will the skate wheel to go against the grooves in the worn hardwood floor. My legs began to shake, and my ability to maintain my balance began to slip beyond my grasp. I let out a whimper and reached out for the wall. Ox swung out in front of me, skating backward as he faced me.

"You got it, Beauty. You got it," he said, grabbing my hands and gripping them. "You need to take shorter strides to accommodate those short legs. Your feet should be shoulder-width apart . . . Good. Now slightly bend your knee on your gliding foot. Squat . . . Now go! Nice!"

Okay. I was actually managing to glide. I gave him a feeble smile, still feeling insecure but a bit hopeful. I wasn't trying to master this shit in one night. I just wanted to have a good time with my man. I kept my eyes trained on him, although I was mortified thinking about how Kennedi and Jazmine were prob-ably nearby, cracking up at my awkward ass. Determined to prove myself, I switched legs, lengthening my stride and rolling faster. I felt pretty good until I broke eye contact with him.

"Oh shit, Ox," I shrieked. "We have to round the corner ahead. We have to turn!"

"I'm right here with you. We're doing this together," he said, spinning out and skating beside me without letting go of my hand. "Come on. We're doing this."

As we rounded the corner to complete our first full loop, I loosened my death grip on his hand.

"Okay, now that we've made your first loop, let's go to the side and practice stopping in case you need to avoid someone in your path."

He guided me, and we edged along the wall. "There's a brake on the toe of your right roller skate. When you need to stop, you're going to squat and lean forward just a little bit. Then ease your right skate forward slightly and press down hard on the toe. Let's practice."

We practiced starting and stopping a few times, and once I felt confident enough, we joined the flow of skaters around us. He caught me each time I started to fall, and we laughed as I scram-bled to maintain my balance. Before long, I was gliding on my own and even managed to work in a few shoulder shimmies when "Anything" by SWV came on.

"We see you, Lennience!" A Caucasian dude I didn't recog-nize high-fived Ox as he skated by.

"You're doing great, babe. I'm proud of you," he leaned down and whispered into my ear.

It felt good to let go of my worries for a while, sailing among the large crowd with his arm around my waist. We shared a rhythmic flow that felt natural and easy. Each time I glanced over at him, he was looking at me and smiling. If it wouldn't have been at the risk of falling flat on my face, I would've reached up and poked that dimple.

I hadn't spotted Jazmine yet, but I had caught sight of Kennedi zipping past us a couple of times in a cropped tank. Her belly ring glistened above the high-waisted skinny jeans that accentuated her long legs. She spun in a quick circle, then switched her weight from leg to leg, bopping to the beat after she passed us. My mind conjured up the image of her and Ox dressed to the nines and posing for prom pictures. I wondered if anything had gone down on their prom night. Did he deny her like he had me so many times? Suddenly, I didn't feel like skating anymore.

I patted Ox's chest. "Bae, thanks for being so patient with me. But you don't have to babysit me all night. Go be with your friends. I'm content with kicking off these skates and resting my legs for a little while."

He looked at me for a long moment, then said, "Come on." He led me to a chair, unlaced my skates, and slid them off my feet.

I put my shoes back on, all set to grab a drink while he returned our skates. When he came back, I stood, preparing to witness the party from the sidelines, when he took my hand. Together, we walked back out to the floor, weaving between oncoming skaters.

"Ox! What the hell are we doing?"

Once we reached the center of the floor, with the traffic of skaters encircling us, he turned to me and whispered into my ear, "My boo ain't watching nothing from the sidelines. We *are* the motherfucking party."

I just stared at him as the "Love in This Club" remix by Usher and Beyoncé played. His arms snaked around my waist, and he leaned down, nuzzling his nose into my hair. We fell into a slow bop beneath the swirling purple lights. Perfectly content, I rotated my hips and allowed my eyes to flutter closed as the duo serenaded us.

"And we're not gonna stop just because the people in this crowd are watching us," he sang into my ear as his hands eased up my ass.

*Shit, my baby can sang!* I blushed and grinned, nearly

stretching my cheeks to capacity. I focused on being present with this beautiful man. The man who completely stopped having a great time to make me feel included and loved at *his* class reunion. Normally, being in the center of the floor with all eyes on me would have driven me crazy. But just being there in his arms erased any concerns other than our perfect moment coming to an end. Oh yeah, he'd definitely be getting the works later on.

Three songs later, a small group of us were gathered on the makeshift dance floor. The DJ mixed in a new song at the tail end of the existing one, and as soon as I heard the percussion of Tamia's "Can't Get Enough," I squealed, wiggling in his arms.

He placed a warm kiss on my forehead, released me, and said, "Go get it, babe."

Without hesitation, I stepped aside and began rocking on the balls of my feet to the sensual beat, waiting for the mixing to end so the song could begin. Once Tamia began singing, I looked up and saw three other women also rocking and swaying beside me. We stepped to the right in unison, then the left in sync. Between twirls, we tossed each other smiles as we stepped in our heels. When I glanced at Ox, he was watching me closely, gripping his chin. His eyes were trained on me, following each movement as I glided across the dancefloor. I then led the "Blurred Lines" line dance when a confused group couldn't get the steps together. After the third line dance, I was fully hype, sweaty, and ready to kick my stilettos off my throbbing feet. Just as I was about to go find Ox, I felt a hand land on my shoulder. It was Jazmine.

"Hey, do you know this one?" she asked, her big eyes twinkling.

I nodded. "Sure, I can show you."

She handed me chilled bottled water, and we headed back out to the middle of the floor. I taught the group the simple line dance to the chill tempo of Toni Braxton's "Long as I Live."

"This one is cute," Kennedi said, swaying her hips and snapping her fingers.

Once I successfully left the dance floor, there were more

people standing in the middle of the floor than skating on the perimeter. The crowd was vibing, dancing to '90s R&B in shoes, skates, and bare feet.

Ox stepped out from a crowd of bystanders, handing me a drink. "Figured you worked up a thirst. You can move, babe."

"I can do a little somethin'."

"Mmm. Look at this crowd all around us. I told you we were the motherfucking party."

Dawn Penn's "You Don't Love Me (No, No, No)" came on and we grinded for a few songs, lost in each other and not giving a damn who was watching. Ox bit his lower lip as he pushed his hips into me. I turned around and pressed my behind into him, enjoying the sensation of my joystick between my cheeks. When a Biggie song came on, the whole building got hype, and we shouted out the lyrics in unison. The DJ fed off our energy and continued his playlist of Brooklyn lyricists, including Jay-Z, Nas, Mos Def, and Busta Rhymes. I was high off the music, buzzed from the wine, and amped for what was still to come that night.

After a few more songs, we slipped our hot, sweaty, and horny bodies out the door and up to the rooftop. By the time the cool air hit us, my vocal cords were done. Ox stood behind me, and we stared out at the magnificent view of Brooklyn's skyline.

He placed soft kisses along my damp neck before asking, "You good, babe?"

I nodded. "Ox, I'm having such a great time. Thank you for inviting me."

"Of course. Sorry for all the pressure that's come along with it. I've never brought a girl home before, and my people have lost their damn minds."

I chuckled. "It's clear they love you, and they're excited for you."

I felt him nod, but he didn't say anything else.

A few quiet moments passed, and we were content with letting the distant sounds of city life fill the silence for us. Then I turned to face him, reaching up to press my lips against his. He parted his lips to accept mine. I moaned as he gently sucked them before massaging my tongue with his. When our kiss ended, I kept my eyes closed, savoring the moment. His arms rested comfortably around me as if they'd always easily found a home there. The familiarity of his embrace was uncanny, like we'd been together in another life.

"You know, that hoarse voice of yours is kinda sexy," he said. Before I could respond, his fingers were under my dress, tracing the lacy material of my thong.

"Mmm. What's next on the itinerary?"

"I think we can call it a wrap for tonight."

"You okay to drive?"

"Yeah, I haven't drunk anything since the restaurant. And I've been drinking water."

"Say less. Let's dip."

"There you are, Lennience! You guys ready to roll?"

I jumped, looking over at Brendon's bulky frame taking up the entire doorway.

I frowned. "Why does everyone keep calling you Lennience?"

Ox chuckled. "Apparently, my thirsty teammates have been waiting for over a decade to attach me to a couple name."

"That's some straight white-boy shit."

"Precisely."

I wrinkled my nose. "Paenox definitely sounds better."

He reached over and pinched my nose as we headed back inside.

Chapter Thirty

By the time we returned to our hotel, it was almost dawn. We'd done everything from shark watching at the aquarium to eating ice cream at two a.m. to having an impromptu parking lot dance party complete with a drunken twerking contest. It didn't take much liquid courage for me to win that one. All I had to do was channel exactly what I planned to do to my man that night and it was a cinch.

Finally, we were crossing the threshold of our suite, and I was primed and ready to take full advantage of his fine ass. I reached for the light switch, but he stopped me. When I looked up, I saw why. My breath caught in my throat as my eyes landed on the stringed lights hanging along all four walls. When Ox turned on the bedside lamp, I noticed scattered red, pink, and white rose petals lying on the white down comforter. A bottle of champagne rested in a bucket of ice on the desk next to a tray of white-choco-late-covered fruit. The arrangement was surrounded by lit tealight candles. He placed his cell into the docking station and moments later, "Mornin" by Dawn Richards began to play. It wasn't until he walked back over to me that I realized I still hadn't moved an inch since entering the room.

He took my hands. "You like it?"

"Babe, I love it. There are at least eight bouquets of fresh flowers in here. How . . . ?"

"Mia has an interior design and staging business. They also do hotel room decorations for lovers. I called her the day after your birthday to set this all up. Come inside."

As I walked farther into the room, I could tell that someone had just been in the room because I smelled a hint of perfume.

"Ox, this is beautiful."

He led me to the bench at the end of the bed. I sat and absent-mindedly leaned over to remove my shoes.

"Uh-uh." He gazed at me, licking his lips. "Keep those on."

He knelt and propped my legs on his shoulders. I drew in a ragged breath as his head disappeared beneath my dress.

His voice was muffled, but I still heard his three-word command. "Lift your hips."

I complied, then released a sigh as my skimpy thong slid over my hips and over my thighs. He emerged with a grin on his face as the fabric dangled from his teeth. I couldn't do anything but toss my head back onto the bed, but he had other plans.

"Stand up."

He helped me to my feet, and we walked over to the sliding door. The early morning breeze kissed our damp skin as we walked out to the patio. "Why are we out here?"

He responded by sliding his hand between my thighs, stroking my clit, and steadily increasing his speed. The friction stoked the growing heat between my legs, and I moaned, "I thought we were done with this fingering shit, *Ox*."

"I'm just getting April primed and ready."

*Shit, she stay ready.*

He turned me around to look out at the street below us, then fell down to his knees again. His bold tongue penetrated me from below, and I lifted up on my tiptoes. He stroked my clit with passionate laps of his tongue, his hands gripping my ass. I enjoyed my view of the rising sun. It boldly split open the sky and spilled its fiery rays onto the river below as Ox split my love open and gratefully drank from my flowing river. My breasts bounced, and my hips rocked as I rode his lovely face. Moaning with pleasure, I gripped his bobbing head. He worked my labia in his mouth, swirling his tongue over it with ease and precision. A cool breeze kissed my face, doing little to quell the fire burning inside of me. Just before I could reach my climax, he disengaged and stood, wiping his glistening lips with the back of his hand.

"Come."

"I was trying to," I growled.

He chuckled, leading me back into the suite. We followed a petal trail leading to the bathroom. As the shower water heated, I slipped his jacket off of him and took my time unbuttoning his polo. Once he was stripped naked, I stared at him for a full minute. His body was flawless. It wasn't free of scars or birthmarks. His smooth skin definitely bore those. But I fully appreciated him and wouldn't change one thing about him. Everything ebbed and flowed and came together to form a masterpiece of a dynamic man. I collapsed to my knees and saluted his manhood like it was owed my allegiance right there on that tile floor. He fed me one inch at a time, and I received him with anticipatory moans.

I kept my eyes open, taking in every detail of his face as I pleasured him. He watched me for a few moments but eventually jerking his head back, eyes clamped closed and mouth slightly ajar. I gripped his ass, bringing him farther into me as I savored the full length of him in my mouth and down my throat. I hungrily consumed him, unabashed by the desire I felt for housing him inside of me—in any possible way. He stepped back, then scooped me up in his arms. By then, we were both breathless, yearning and burning from our eyes as we stared at one another. Placing me on the bathroom counter, he undid the straps of my shoes with his eyes on me. Reaching behind me, he unzipped my dress, then picked me up and set me back down so I was standing on the floor. I lifted my arms as he pulled my dress over my head. His eyes roamed my body, and he studied me like displayed art, seeming to memorize every part of me.

My eyes landed on my joystick, marked with my red lip prints and still bobbing up and down in appreciation. Ox followed my gaze and smirked, then entered the walk-in rainfall shower. The water cascaded around his broad shoulders and chest in a downpour.

"Have you ever made love in the rain, Beauty?"

I shook my head.

"I get to be your first."

I stepped into the shower, joining him beneath the streaming water. His hands were all over me. One was rubbing my nipple while the other explored my curls. Our mouths met, the warm water spilling over my upturned face. I tapped him on his chest, letting him know I was ready to go. He reached behind him to the soap rack and handed me the foil wrapper. I ripped into it with my teeth, then squatted down to slip the condom over his length.

"Gentle or . . . not gentle?"

I paused. I'd never been asked that question before. "I want it rough."

He hemmed me against the wall while looking down at me. "Last chance."

I confirmed with a nod, and he squatted to line his hips with mine before shoving into me without another word. I gasped, shocked by the amount of space he demanded inside of me. Reflexively, I dug my nails into his back, scraping the skin as I planted my mouth on his neck. He thrust upward while lifting me completely off my feet and grasping my ass in his large palms.

"Ungh, I'm right here, babe. You ain't gotta fantasize about this shit anymore."

I exhaled a soft moan, releasing months of sexual tension, anxiety, and relief. He retrieved himself three-quarters of the way, then slammed back into me. Pressing my teeth into my bottom lip, I grunted. He deepened his squat and began swirling his hips clockwise as the falling water spilled over our faces. With bullseye precision, he hit each spot and angle hidden deep inside of me, strumming up a beautiful storm of sensations in me.

"*Ox*, it hurts so good!"

He himself pulled back out before slamming into me again. The pain was so delicious, I didn't know whether to scream in pain or cry in delight. My yoni was pulsating and simmering and singing to the gods. Despite my overwhelming elation, I kept my eyes trained on him, allowing him to read every etch of satisfaction on my face and finding the same expression painted on his.

"Lie down," he growled.

This time, I didn't ask questions. I obediently lay on my back, right there down on that shower floor. He lifted my hips a couple of inches from the floor and spread my legs wide. Then he knelt down, slipping my ankles over his shoulders. I studied his shadowy face as his back blocked the falling water. His expression was unreadable as he gripped my hips and entered me at a new angle that hit so far inside me, I jumped.

"Ohh! You're so deep. Shit!"

"You still want it rough?"

"No. Please. I . . . can't take it," I whimpered.

He slowed his strokes, still nearly retrieving himself after each one, teasing me and sending me over the edge at the same time. He felt like no one I'd ever experienced. But what did it for me was his face; he was intent on studying me the entire time to ensure I was pleased. I knew he was committing my body, my rhythms, and my orgasmic pattern to memory. We edged a few times, first him, then me, then me, then him. Torment was prominently displayed on each of our faces while flirting with the coaxing boundaries of an explosive climax. We were denying ourselves pleasure in order to elongate the fleeting experience of uniting for the first time.

My hips continued to lift and press into him as he gyrated, now in a counterclockwise motion. Our rhythm was so easy, like we'd been lovers for years. After a few minutes, I tapped his chest, and he pulled out before helping me onto my feet. I wrung out my hair, and it hung over my shoulders under the weight of the clinging water. Without a word, he picked up the shower gel. The peppermint and rosemary oils blossomed, activated by the shower steam. Instead of using my loofah, he opted to rub his large hands all over my body, working up a healthy lather.

He massaged my neck and shoulders, slipped his fingers over the slope of my breasts, then let them slide over my abs. He paused to gather some more gel, then let each hand descend in parallel paths down my hips.

When our eyes met, he immediately aborted the mission.

He picked up the wand and quickly rinsed the suds off my body. Next, he carried me out of the shower, grabbing a towel on the way to the bed. Pulling back the sheets first, he laid the towel down before setting me on top of it. I wrapped myself in it and began drying off.

Once I dried my hair, he handed me a glass of chilled champagne.

"To our first time together."

We clinked glasses and sipped.

"It's better than I ever could have imagined."

He lifted a brow. "You haven't even come yet."

"You've got me more than ready to."

He nodded toward my duffle bag of tricks. "What you got in store for me this morning, Beauty?"

"Nothing in that bag comes close to what you're serving."

"And here I was, all ready to be open-minded."

"Trust me, you've got me open enough for the both of us. It's not needed."

He reached for another condom. "I'm glad you're satisfied."

"How do you want me?"

"Right there. Open your legs."

I set down the glass, then lay back on the pillows. He slid right into me, immediately filling every crevice, and we released a collective sigh of contentment.

He moved both of his legs outside of mine, straddling me. "Squeeze your legs together."

It seemed awkward at first, but once he began stroking me between clenched legs, he felt incredible. He snaked his way to my rooftop, knocking at my door. I moved my hips in sync with his, and we fell into a steady rhythm. Within seconds, stars were bursting before my eyes, and April was pulsing violently. Feeling completely weightless, I must have begun shrieking because I felt him jump. He clamped his hand over my mouth, muffling my voice in consideration of our neighbors. Or maybe it was to make sure they didn't call 9-1-1.

As I felt myself descend back onto the bed, his voice was gruff when he asked, "Was it good?"

I took a few moments to gather myself before responding. "So good, bae."

"Good. Now, get on top."

Without hesitation, I dropped my towel and straddled him.

"Hold up. You say you've been taking barre classes, right?"

I nodded, confused. "Yeah, to help build leg muscle strength for line dancing."

"Well, I want you to barre on this dick."

I giggled. "Boy, stop."

"I'm not laughing. Show me how you get down in those virtual classes."

I sobered up quick. "Okay . . . uh, go sit on the chair."

Once he did, I stood in front of him, briefly stretched, then balanced myself on the balls of my feet in the relevé position.

Once I straddled him, I shifted to a wide-legged stance with my heels lifted six inches off the floor. I bent my knees and sank down onto the head of his dick in a nearly seated position. We both groaned as I engaged, then lifted up slightly, pulsing my heels in slight up and down movements. Each time, his dick pressed past my lips gently before I pulled away. My eyes were trained on his gorgeous face, but I felt his penis jerking around, excited by the thrill of the tease.

My fingertips grazed the back of the chair, treating it like a bar to help maintain my balance. I kept my shoulders straight and chin level, channeling my inner ballet dancer.

Up.

Down.

Up.

Down.

Up.

Down.

Up.

Down.

*Double time,* my trainer, Ally Love's, voice rang in my head.

Up. Up.

Down. Down.

One inch up.

Two inches down.

By then, we were both sweating, gasping, panting. I pushed myself to maintain control. The pleasure of my pulsing yoni far outweighed the pain burning in my stretched hips and calves.

Up.

Down.

Up.

Down.

The squeeze of his hands on my ass was firm and unyielding.

Up. Up.

Down. Down.

Up. Up.

Down. Down.

I had a death grip on the squeaking, rocking chair.

"Be still! You wanted this," I chastised as he tried to push himself up into me.

"*Ungh!* I know," was his response.

Up.

Down.

Up.

Down.

April screamed at me, *Bitch, please!*

I gave my head a slight shake, focusing on his handsome, tortured face.

Up.

Down.

*Hold, hold.*

"Enough of that shit." He grabbed my waist and slammed me downward.

"*Oof!*" He knocked the wind out of me.

He stood, bringing us both over to the desk. My ass knocked over the champagne bucket, sending cubes and champagne spraying everywhere. I kissed him hungrily, and he drove into me like he was fresh out of prison.

"Ooh, Beauty. Shit!" he spat through clenched teeth.

Our bodies jerked and rocked, our rhythm was off, and I couldn't keep up with his quickening thrusts.

I looked into his eyes and realized the romance period was over. The hunt was now on. The lion was prowling for the kill after a prolonged fast. He was famished. And, quite frankly, I was surprised he'd lasted this long.

He pulled out, bending me over. Instinct made me grip the desk's edge as his crazed pounding increased in speed and intensity. I relented and sprawled across the desktop; my breasts smashed against its smooth service. His thickness stretched me wider than I'd ever been stretched. His unabashed moans were turning me on something fierce. His pheromones mixed with his sweat, teasing my flared nostrils. I lifted my head and watched him in the mirror before me, only to discover he was doing the same. But his eyes weren't focused. In fact, they were glazed over, his mouth slightly agape as he released his pants in forced bursts. He pulled out again and jammed his fingers into me. I bucked my hips as I rode them, grateful for the reprieve. Then I gasped as a sudden new sensation invaded my body.

His thumb was pressing against the rim of my ass.

My eyes widened, and he paused, waiting for my consent.

I nodded. When he proceeded to enter, I screamed out, caught off guard by the strange feeling. He kept his finger there while reentering my pussy, stroking each entry simultaneously.

I shut my eyes and cried out, attempting to still my frenzied mind, still fighting to process the fact that I was being doubly penetrated. Everything swirled around me in a sinful haze. It all hurt so good. I elevated to the ceiling and was looking down at myself. This man was making me feel countless new sensations and emotions in a short time, and I was hitting every peak possible. I never wanted it to stop.

On cue, my selfish vagina began to pulse once again. *No, April. Not now,* I admonished.

I tried my best to stave off the oncoming orgasm, but my will was weakening by the second.

"Shit, Beauty. You feel so damn *goodt!*" When I heard the richness of his thunderous roar, relief washed over me, and I succumbed to the swelling waves, letting them wash me away as I felt his throbs sync with mine.

It was at that moment that I fell hopelessly in love with Lennox Davenport. *Good dick'll do that.*

# Chapter Thirty-One

"Wake up, Beauty."

My eyes, feeling like they weighed a ton each, fluttered open. I frowned and squinted under the bright sun rays cast over my face. Ox was lying on his side with his soft eyes staring at me. With his handsome face illuminated in the morning light, it felt like I was seeing him for the first time. After witnessing all his physical vulnerability as he lost control and climaxed inside of me just hours before, I was enamored with this relaxed version of him. It was quite possibly the most beautiful thing I'd ever seen, and I was looking forward to seeing more of that side of him.

"Hey."

He smiled. "Hey."

"What time is it?"

"A bit past noon."

I bolted upright. "For real?"

"You passed out around seventy-thirty, and I didn't fall asleep until around a quarter after eight."

I cleared my throat and leaned against the padded headboard. "Well, I guess we missed the continental breakfast."

"Mia stocked the fridge with juice, water, and snacks. We

don't have to leave this room until we're ready." He headed to the kitchen and poured a glass of pineapple juice, then handed it to me before kissing my forehead. "How do you feel?"

I took a long sip before replying. "Is there mint in this?"

He nodded.

"Wow, that's good. Sore."

"Yeah, about that. I apologize. It's been . . . a while for me. I wasn't too rough, was I?"

I shook my head.

"Good. I enjoyed myself. Did I meet your expectations?"

"You exceeded the fuck out of them. You're pretty laid back, but I was pleasantly surprised to learn that you're a beast in bed."

"Well, to be literal, we did it there the least."

I chuckled. "Touché." I turned on my side to face him, propping my head in my palm. "What about you? Was it everything you dreamed?"

He stared at me for a few seconds, his eyes darting back and forth as he studied mine. "Patience, that was the best sex I've ever had."

My head tilted back. The sex was mind-blowing for me, but I was stunned to hear those words from him.

He reached over and laced his fingers between mine so our hands were palm to palm. "I've never felt that type of emotional or physical connection with anyone."

I let his words sink in for a moment, then realized it was the same for me. Even in the roughest moments, it felt like we had shared something sacred.

"Me either. Now I understand why waiting was so important to you. Everything about it was beautiful, and I'll always remember this. Thanks, bae."

He leaned toward me, and I jerked back.

"Whoa, mister. What are you doing?"

"Kissing you . . . ?"

"But . . . I haven't brushed my teeth yet."

"We were having a moment, babe. Why are you even thinking about your breath?"

"Oh, I . . ."

He leaned in again and placed a sweet kiss on my lips before pulling me on top of him. Looking up at me, he said, "Patience, you're an amazing woman. I knew it from the moment I saw you sitting at that bar in Atlanta. I knew it when I drove eleven hours to a client meeting in Cleveland that could have easily been virtual. I knew it when I saw you in that dude's arms that night on the dance floor. I knew I couldn't wait another moment to make you mine."

Something in my stomach fluttered as I thought of him watching me with Daniel. I couldn't imagine how that must have felt. Although I hated that he'd had to see that, I knew there was no way I would have wanted to experience that evening without him. He was the guest who mattered most to me that night. If that made me selfish, so be it.

I looked down at him. "So, you don't regret bringing me here to meet your family and friends?"

"Not in the least."

"Good. I'm glad I came. Your mom and brother are really nice."

"Yeah . . ." He nodded, a wistful look in his eyes.

"What *is* that?"

He looked at me and frowned. "What's what?"

"That sad look you get in your eyes every time I mention your family. I've patiently waited for you to open up about it because I know there's something there."

He squirmed beneath me, so I rolled off of him, refusing to release him from my gaze. He was quiet for a long while, his pensive stare fixed on the ceiling. I waited patiently as he sorted through his thoughts. When he finally sighed and turned toward me once more, his eyes were glistening.

My heart sank. It really hurt me to see him hurting, but I remained silent, reaching out to stroke his arm.

"My family's fucked up, babe."

That was the last thing I was expecting to hear from him. I stared at him for a long moment before responding. "There's no judgment here, Ox. Ever. Just tell me what's on your mind."

"My father spends a lot of time on the road, and like I said, my mother was always working hard to help pay for my education. Whenever they were home, they made time with me a priority. In hindsight, I guess they never invested much time into their marriage."

I nodded, watching him closely.

"Once my mother semi-retired and was home more, my father stopped placing a priority on being home with us. He started taking even more 'extended trips,' and we saw less and less of him. You know that Toni Braxton cut, 'Seven Whole Days?' My mother actually lived that shit. He'd disappear for weeks without checking in with her, and she rarely knew his travel schedule or when he'd be home. I figured they were just having average marital problems and never had the courage to ask my mom about it."

He sighed before continuing.

"I was at the end of my junior year of high school when a freshman on the basketball team cornered me in the locker room. I'd just stepped out of the shower and was drying off when he asked if he could speak to me. I told him to just say whatever he needed to say, and he was really blunt with it. 'I'm nice on the court, and I think I can make varsity. But I need your help.'

"I admired his tenacity, so I agreed to work with him. We trained for months together, and I taught him everything I knew. We grew closer, and I enjoyed getting to know him. Like I said, there wasn't much diversity at our school, so I always made it a point to get to know young brothas as they came in. We were on the court late one night when he said he had something to tell me."

I winced, knowing where this was going.

"My world completely stopped, babe. Shit rocked me to the

fucking core. He was only *three years younger* than me! My parents were married for nineteen years by the time I found out."

"Did your mom know about him?"

"Naw." He shook his head, letting a tear fall. "I had to be the one to tell her. That shit nearly broke her."

His Brooklyn accent was getting stronger by the second.

"Ouch." I winced, sitting up and pulling him into my arms. "So . . . you're telling me that your father conceived another son when you were only two years old and never told anyone?"

"That's what I thought at first. But once Moms confronted him about it, we got the truth. Apparently, he was messing with a Latina chick around the way for a little while. They fell off after a few months and never spoke again. She reached out to him again when Prez was fifteen. By then, he was unruly. Acting out, in and out of juvie, just out of control. She said she needed my father's help with getting him together."

I couldn't do anything but shake my head for a long while. Things were finally making sense. Preston and Mia's absence at Lorna's house before dinner, Preston's surname, Gómez, no mention of Ox's parents in their proposal story, and Lorna staring at the basketball team picture all played like a montage in my mind. "So, he enrolls him at the same school as his firstborn son with no explanation?"

"He said he was meaning to talk to us about it but conveniently never got around to actually doing the shit."

"Classic."

He sniffed. "So, here I was, dealing with not having a father in the house as a teenager when I needed him most, consoling a lonely mother, trying to keep my grades and a ton of extracurricular shit together, and now figuring out how to be a big brother to a little dude I barely knew who was literally off the hinges."

"So, you stepped the fuck up," I said, tightening my grip on him and rubbing his back.

"Damn right. I mean, the shit threw me for a serious loop at first. I struggled with whether I should even have a relationship with Prez because I didn't want to disrespect Mom any further.

"Eventually, I decided he was just as blameless as I was in all this. So, yeah, I took him under my wing and began introducing him to everyone as my little brother. For the next year and a half, we were inseparable. I got his grades together, helped him make varsity, and applied to trade schools with him. All that."

"That's boss, Randall," I joked through my tears.

He chuckled, then sniffled. "Everybody's been pressuring me to bring a girl home to meet the family since high school. But the truth is, I've never wanted to bring somebody back to this dysfunctional shit. Not unless it was someone I knew I could trust."

By then, my tears were soaking the sheets. My heart hurt for the seventeen-year-old I saw in those pictures whose whole world had suddenly collapsed around him. The one who, despite all of the disrespect, chaos, and turbulence introduced to his family, decided to stand taller and become the man his father hadn't been in his or his little brother's life.

"How did your mom manage to handle all this?"

He frowned. "I'll give it to her—she's a real one. If she ever broke down, she never let me see it. Hell, she had a full-time job just keeping me from jumping on that dude on sight whenever he walked through the door."

"Did it ever become physical between you and your father?"

"Oh, yeah. I was young, dumb, and raging with hormones. I definitely tested his ass a time or two, and it even came to blows once. That was when the extended summer trips started. Like Prez said, disrespect isn't something I can ever tolerate, especially toward females. My mother constantly went without proper rest and self-care just to make sure my father and I were good. So, for him to pull that shit . . . man, I just don't understand it."

"How close are your father and Prez now?" I asked, tracing circles on his bare chest.

"Not very close. Since he didn't have much of a relationship with Mariposa, Prez's mother, Halo treated him more like a responsibility than anything else. Halo seems like a real stand-up dude on paper. He voluntarily reimbursed her for back child support without getting the courts involved. He showed up for his high school graduation and helped pay for his trade school education. He's also present for all of his milestone events, but that's about it."

"Does your mom ever attend those events with him?"

He shook his head. "Naw. And Halo doesn't press it, either. That's one line he'll never cross with her again."

A few moments of thoughtful silence passed between us. Then I said, "Sorry for all the questions, bae."

"You're good, babe. It feels good to finally talk about it." He gave my thigh a reassuring squeeze.

"So, have you and Prez always been close?"

He nodded. "Yeah. He's a wild one, so I still have to keep close tabs on him. But he's got a good heart. He's also really driven. He has a tow truck business with quite a few city contracts, and he's planning to hire his fourth employee."

"That's dope. For real."

"Yeah, I'm proud of him. He's come a long way."

"Well, he had an excellent role model."

He stared at me for a moment before kissing me. It was a deep, passionate kiss that left me breathless.

He got up and used the bathroom. The sheets slid off his nude body, and any thoughts other than feeling him on top of me again slipped from my mind. When he returned, he lay right back in my arms.

I played in his dark curls for a few moments. "Bae?"

"Yeah?"

"Tell me about your reaction to their engagement announcement at the restaurant. You said you like Mia, but I noticed your whole mood shifted when you heard the news."

He licked his lips and sat up in bed. "I'm about to grab some water. Want one?"

"Yeah."

Returning to the bed, he handed me a bottle and sat on the edge of the bed. When he leaned over to kiss me again, his cool lips tasted clean and sweet. He swirled his tongue over my lips and sucked on them gently before releasing them.

"Mmm, so many sweet kisses. What are they for?"

"Giving a fuck."

I frowned, puzzled.

"It took a minute, but I finally got you comfortable enough to ask the tough questions."

He had a point. It wasn't my nature to press issues. But I wanted to know as much as I possibly could about Lennox Davenport.

I shrugged. "I've always wanted to. I just wanted to give you time, bae."

His hand caressed my thigh. "When it comes to you, I'm always an open book. You can ask me anything you want to know."

A few moments of silence passed, and I snuggled against his chest. "Wow, I finally understand why you refused to have casual sex before now."

Ox nodded. "Yeah, man. I'm still dealing with the aftermath of careless sex and reckless choices."

*And that's why you feel such a need for control,* I thought. *You've probably had so little of it up until now. Stuck trying to clean up everyone's mess and pick up all the shattered pieces of your childhood.*

He sighed. "Now, about Mia and Prez. Although he's my little brother whom I love dearly, I have to admit . . . there's a bit of resentment there. Hell, I pretty much resent all three of them."

*All three of them? Even his mother?* My brow lifted, but I didn't speak.

"Of course, I resent Halo for creating this whole situation for all of us. I resent my mother for staying with him after everything he put her through with barely any consequences. And I resent

Prez for expecting me to be his older brother, his father, his thera-pist, his wingman, and anything else he can think to ask me for. I try not to let it affect my relationships with my mother and brother, but half the time, I feel all alone. Like nobody really has my back in all this."

I nodded, leaning up to kiss his cheek and rub his back. "It's crazy how parallel our lives have been. I think that's a big reason why we were drawn to each other."

"Precisely. Shit's magnetic as hell. I couldn't resist you, no matter how much I tried."

I leaned back, feigning disgust. "Oh, you've *tried*?"

"Hell yeah, I've tried. Have you met your ass?"

We laughed, and I was happy for the temporary reprieve from the tense subject.

"Well, let me assure you. You are not alone in this, Lennox Ellington Davenport. You're everything I didn't even know I've been searching for. So, no matter what you need, I'm just a phone call or road trip away *whenever* you need me. I'd move heaven and earth to be there for you."

He stared into my eyes for a long moment, then held my face in his large hands, kissing my forehead. "Same. And I believe you, Beauty. I really do."

# Chapter Thirty-Two

I rubbed my hands as I sat down at the dining room table at the Davenport residence on Monday afternoon. After a full day of lounging and loving with Ox, I was ready to nourish my body . . . in other ways.

"This spread looks amazing, Lorna. What do we have here?"

"This is shrimp scampi, tilapia with lemon herb butter sauce here. This is avocado, corn, and tomato salad, and this is broiled orange roughy in a sweet and sour pineapple ginger sauce over here," she said, gesturing to each dish.

I scanned the lavish apartment for a moment.

"Did I forget something? What're you looking for?" Lorna asked.

"The small army you obviously prepared this meal for! How do you expect the three of us to eat all of this? Not saying I won't give it my best shot."

Lorna smiled. "I've always cooked in large portions like this. Ask El. I came from a large family. So, please dig in and get your fill."

I noticed Lorna's energy was a bit off. It was hard to determine whether it was due to the fact that I'd cried like a newborn baby on her shoulder the last time I'd seen her or because Ox and I had just spent time with Preston.

I began helping myself to the shrimp scampi. "Well, thank you for going to all this trouble."

"No problem. Thanks for bringing dessert. I can't wait to get into this key lime pie." Lorna poured us both fresh-squeezed lemonade and asked, "So, how was the reunion, and what did you guys end up doing yesterday?"

Ox and I exchanged quick glances, knowing we'd barely left the bed the day before. Other than briefly FaceTiming my little half-brother on my father's side, Xander, I hadn't spoken to another soul all day.

"The reunion was great. Lennox managed to get me on a pair of skates. That was epic."

"Not your thing?"

I shook my head. "Not at all. But he was very patient with me. We went to the aquarium beforehand, then out for late-night ice cream. It was a great time. I haven't been out kickin' it until dawn since my early college days."

"I'm so glad you guys had a great time. Was that ol' thirsty girl there?"

I blinked, holding back a laugh. "Yes, Kennedi was there, skating around in a skimpy belly shirt. I have to admit, I was a little self-conscious about my subpar skating skills. But Lennox went out of his way to make sure I was comfortable and enjoying myself."

Lorna gave a firm nod, scooping up a piece of tilapia. "That's my boy. How was dinner? I caught the look from El the other day, so I didn't ruin the surprise. Wasn't it just gorgeous dining by the water like that?"

*Oh, hell.* What else did he tell his mom about our dinner plans? I didn't want to make things uncomfortable by bringing up Preston's engagement. "Yes, it was very romantic. The food and wine were delicious."

"That's our favorite special occasion restaurant."

"Yeah, they've been going there since I was little. I always said as soon as I got a girlfriend, I'd take her there on our first date," Ox said, taking a bite of salad.

My cheeks flushed, and I nipped my cheek while chewing. When I pulled my eyes up to gaze at him, he was casually chewing his food as if he hadn't just dropped a huge bomb on me. "So, you've never taken a date there before?" I asked him.

He looked up and shook his head, confused by my stunned expression. "Nope."

A few moments passed, and I didn't realize I was lost in my thoughts until Lorna placed her warm hand over mine.

"El has always been a man of few words like his father, but his actions are intentional and thoughtful. The key to best understanding him is to watch, not listen."

"Thanks, Lorna." I mentally tucked her words away because something told me I would need them later.

I was busy fidgeting in my seat, battling the urge to jump my man right in front of his darling mama. The surging white heat between my legs lit up my entire body like a Christmas tree. *He's been waiting for you.* My heart thumped like crazy, and I had trouble hearing the rest of her gentle words of wisdom. So, I just nodded, wiped my sweaty palms on my dress, and shoved salsa salad into my mouth.

"So, you two are leaving for Cleveland today, right?"

Ox nodded. "Yeah, I'm staying there for a few days before heading back home."

"Mmph." She nodded and paused for a beat. "You know, Halo and I were in a long-distance relationship while he was in his hospitality management leadership development program."

I watched Ox's brows lift. "Y'all were?"

Lorna nodded. "Yes, for two long years. He was sent to rotations in various cities all over the country. Flights home each weekend were too expensive, and he was often too far from here to drive back home. So, he spent a lot of his downtime in hotels. Of course, that was long before FaceTime or even video phones.

We were engaged for less than six months and were head-over-heels in love. So, it was rough. We relied on old-school ways to keep things fresh."

"Okay, this is where I check out." Ox stood, wiping his hands on his napkin. "Going to the bathroom."

"Now, that's one way to clear a room." Lorna winked at me, and we shared a laugh. "So, anyway, I was new at my job and couldn't take much time off to visit him. I was insecure that he'd eventually find someone else to keep him company while on the road. I knew I had to do something."

I leaned in. "What did you do?"

"I said and did whatever I had to keep my man satisfied. We learned how to please one another and keep each other engaged from afar. We used our vivid imaginations to accomplish what we couldn't do to each other in person. And I popped up on him in a sexy trench and heels whenever I could." She leaned closer, holding my gaze. "Most importantly, I became *whomever* he needed me to be."

I blinked and had another Sister Perkins moment, clutching my pearls. What in the fifty strands of gray hair was going on here? Was I really getting sex-life advice from my man's mama?

Ox walked back into the room. "Y'all done in here?"

Lorna smirked and said, "Yes, honey. I was just letting Patience know the value of keeping things interesting while the two of you are apart."

Ox glanced at me, his warm eyes apologetic. I offered him a weak smile in return, still trying to give myself a brainwash. The visuals dancing in my mind were definitely not it.

"So, I hear your brother got engaged," Lorna said as Ox sat down.

"Yeah, he told us at dinner the other night."

"Good for him. Are they planning to have a big wedding?"

Ox shrugged. "I'm not sure. But he asked me to be his best man."

Lorna nodded and closed her eyes momentarily. "Well, it's wonderful that you'll get to be there for your brother's big day."

I shoved more food into my mouth, wondering why she'd chosen to initiate such an awkward conversation while I was there. From what Ox had shared with me, Lorna preferred not to discuss Preston or his mother, Mariposa, at all. I didn't doubt that all three of us were thinking about the guest list for Preston and Mia's big day. Would Lorna's name be on the invitation, or would she be a plus one? Hell, would she even be in attendance at all? Ox mentioned she hadn't attended Preston's high school graduation, which was understandable. That was just too soon. But had time healed her wounds after a decade of getting used to Preston's existence in her husband's and son's lives?

"Yeah, Mia's quality. She's really good for him."

Lorna turned to me. "What did you think of Mia, Patience?"

"She seems very sweet. It was easy to tell how much they love each other."

"Good, good."

We all ate another forkful of food in unison. Then a heaviness descended on the room, and I could feel the tension mounting. I braced myself, unsure of what was about to happen.

"So, with the wedding coming up and after we've met this wonderful girlfriend of yours, do you think we'll be able to see more of you, El? Maybe around the holidays this year?"

Ox frowned. "I wasn't aware I was the reason the three of us haven't been spending time together."

"You weren't?"

"Dad still spends a lot of his time traveling for work. It's normally difficult to align our schedules outside of the holiday season."

Lorna smiled and shook her head. "El, darling, we both know that's not the case here."

"What do you mean, Mom?"

"I'm saying you've been outright avoiding us since you left here for college. I know you're busy, but we're lucky if we see you twice a year. And when we've offered to come and visit, there's always some type of excuse on your end. You've been in Atlanta for over a year now, and we still haven't seen your place."

Ox sighed. I guess she was taking advantage of having her son here face to face to discuss what bothered her. I just wished it hadn't been while I was there. Their exchange was making me apprehensive and uncomfortable. As sweet as Lorna was, every mama had direct access to her child's buttons, and she was pounding each of those bad boys like they owed her money. Although I knew how Ox really felt about how things had transpired with his family, the question was whether he'd choose to be upfront with his mother about it.

Ox rubbed his forehead and sighed again. "I haven't been avoiding you, Mom. I just didn't want to deal with the drama of being back home. After everything I dealt with during my last two years of high school, I just needed time away from everyone."

Lorna reached over and squeezed his hand. "I know, baby. But it's been over ten years since you graduated from high school. Don't you see how your choice to stay away has driven a wedge between all of us? All of this could be resolved with a simple conversation."

Ox recoiled, disgusted. "Mom, do you really believe that *I* drove the wedge between us? That all it will take is a *simple conversation* to fix all the turmoil *he's* caused? I don't mean to be rude, but I believe our issues are well beyond the scope of an undergrad psychology degree."

Lorna held up her hands. "I'm not assuming I have all the answers or solutions, El. I'm just saying the first step is sitting down and talking about it."

"Is that what worked for you and him? Is that why you now have the model marriage twelve years later?" He scanned the room. "Because I'm looking around, and it looks like more of the same. He still ain't here."

I flinched, stunned that he'd spoken to his mama like that. I bit my lip to refrain from saying something or kicking him under the table.

"Yes, El, as a matter of fact, it *has* worked for us. We've had countless candid conversations and reached an understanding."

"Well, that's good to hear, Mom. I'm glad things worked out for y'all, and if you're happy, I'm always going to be happy for you."

"And what about you and your father?"

His jaw clenched. "I'm afraid it's going to take a lot more than a conversation or two to heal things between us. He hasn't even apologized to me."

Lorna leaned in, resting her chin in her hand. "Okay, what exactly would you like him to apologize for?"

Ox scoffed. "Betraying our family, for one. Not having enough respect for me, as his firstborn, to let me know he was enrolling my half-brother—whom I knew nothing about—in the same school I was attending. Having to find out we shared DNA on a street basketball court. Then I was expected to put all that shit aside, step up, and be the big brother he never had. Instead of enjoying the last couple years of my adolescence, I was focused on sticking my neck out for Prez, keeping him out of trouble, and fathering him—like I had any clue what that looked like."

Stubborn tears teetered on the brims of Lorna's eyelids. Her bottom lip trembled, and she took a breath. It was obvious she felt empathy for her son. She loved him, and she was trying to be strong for him. "El, I agree you shouldn't have had to worry about any of those things. Looking back, I can definitely acknowledge we made some critical parenting mistakes along the way. We were so busy tending to our own feelings and emotions that you were robbed of many things and weren't given the chance to be heard or to even get a proper explanation of what occurred from your father. For that, I'm truly sorry. I really am."

She paused for a moment, and the air grew denser between us.

Then she continued, "I also know you've openly questioned my choice to stay with your father, despite what he's done to us.

All I can say is it can be difficult to try to understand a situation until you're in the midst of it. At the time your father's transgression came to light, we had been married for almost twenty years, had raised a child together, and shared a lifetime of memories. You were small when it happened, and once we all found out, many years had already passed. Yes, it hurt me to the core to learn what he had done all those years ago, and I felt deeply disappointed and betrayed. As you know, I asked your father to leave, and I took the time I needed to process it all. I tried to understand your father's actions and where they left things in our relationship. Ultimately, I concluded that what he had done wasn't a deal-breaker for me. El, he's my best friend. You have no idea how it feels to love someone like that. But I really hope you will one day."

I stole a glance at Ox but couldn't decipher his expression as he steepled his fingers and gazed at his mother.

Lorna continued, "In the end, honoring my vows and choosing to forgive him was more important than walking away from it all on the matter of principle. We've had years of therapy, and we're in a really good place now. I still have boundaries, and your father goes out of his way to respect them. And it's been working well for us."

Ox continued to stare at her, but I knew he was soaking in every word.

"Although you're a victim in all of this, too, your need to control everything has interfered with your ability to be reasonable, empathetic, and compassionate toward other people regarding choices and situations you don't understand or agree with. It's stunted your maturity and your mental and emotional health, baby.

"Sometimes, when I look at you, I still see the resentful little boy I could never coax into turning the other cheek when someone hurt or betrayed him. The truth is, I now have thirty-one mostly happy years of marriage under my belt. And before I can expect you to fully understand the complexities of 'grown folks' business,' you still have far more growing up and living to do."

I refused to release my breath in fear of disrupting the moment. My empathy and compassion for Ox had to take a backseat. He needed to hear this from his mother. He still needed to heal, and she knew exactly how to help him get there.

She leaned forward again and squeezed his hand. "I want you to support my decision to stay with your father, baby. Do I have that from you?"

He was dead still for such a long time. It seemed like he wasn't going to respond to her at first.

Then he finally blinked and said, "You say you've moved on. You say you've both grown from all of this. But you still refuse to develop a relationship with Prez. So, have you really healed from all the pain Dad caused us? When it's all said and done, this is your life. But I believe you deserve better than having to continually turn a blind eye to all of this."

What sounded like a pair of keys clinked on the glass table in the foyer, and I jumped, looking up.

I did a double-take as an older version of Ox closed the apartment door and strolled into the dining room. Damn, those genes were strong. His gray beard and wavy hair shimmered with sweat. He was in basketball shorts and a white tee, so I assumed he was either just coming from a workout or from hooping on the basketball court.

He bent down and placed a gentle kiss on Lorna's forehead. Her eyes lowered, and I realized why she'd been a little off. She had known he would be joining us today. That was why we were having this conversation right now. That was why she had invited us over again.

Halo offered me a warm smile and nod, extending a hand. "You must be Patience. I'm Halo, Lennox's father."

My mouth opened, closed, then reopened as I struggled to choke out a response. Not only was this man gorgeous, but his chiseled features, muscular arms, and salt-and-pepper goatee were showing me just how fine my man would still be in twenty years. "Hello, Mr. Davenport. So nice to meet you." I smoothed my damp palm over my dress and accepted his hand.

"Same. I apologize for my appearance. I'm just coming from the gym downstairs. Hello, Lennox."

Ox released a grunt, shifting in his seat and taking a long swallow from his bottled water.

"I couldn't help but overhear a bit of your conversation with your mother. Looks like my timing's just right, huh?"

Ox huffed, then scoffed. I looked on, taken aback by his childish behavior. It was a version of him I never imagined witnessing. His mother's comment about maturity rang in my ears. I guess she knew her child.

Halo took a seat at the head of the table and sighed heavily. "Listen, son, you've felt comfortable enough to question me and my decisions for quite some time now. But I need to let you know, right now, just who you're dealing with. Since you wanna be a big man dabbling in grown folks' business, I'll give it to you straight."

He took a quick swig of water, and my eyes lowered. Halo wasted no time getting down to business.

He continued, "I've made some poor choices, and I'm still here, dealing with every one of the consequences. Hell, I'll be doing whatever I can to make it up to your mother until my dying day. But your brother wants to nail me to a cross because he believes I abandoned him. And you want to keep me up there over a transgression I made twenty-five years ago because you don't agree with how it was handled. But what you've failed to understand is, I only have one man to answer to—that's God. I've repented to Him, I've reconciled with my wife, and as far as I'm concerned, I've done my due diligence.

"Now, I've provided shelter for you, put you through private schools, helped pay your way through college, and secured your safety for the first twenty-two years of your life. So, as far as I'm concerned, you've only officially been 'a man' for, what . . . the past six years?"

I swallowed my gasp, but I couldn't prevent my eyes from widening. My gaze lowered to my lap once again in an attempt to conceal my shock. My heart went out to Ox because both of his parents were blowing down on him. Hard.

"That's not true, but you're entitled to your opinion," Ox said quietly.

"That's right, son. We all have our own opinions, and you and your brother haven't been shy about expressing yours. As a result, you've been causing my wife to be in the middle of all this drama for years instead of having the courage to step directly to me and talk man to man. Like she hasn't already been through enough."

Ox's jaw clenched. "What about what your sons have been through? Why haven't you prioritized making shit right with us? Writing checks for tuition and child support won't magically eradicate all the bullshit you've put us through. The absences in both our lives. The selfish way you've put your own needs and desires before ours. What do I have to step to you for? A real man would have sat his son down and let him know what the hell was going on before he found out from a virtual stranger."

Halo leaned back in his chair and crossed his arms. His steely eyes were fixed on Ox, but he offered no response.

While I hated every moment of the drama I was being forced to sit through, I was proud of Ox for standing up to his father. But I also knew he'd struck a nerve. For the third time that afternoon, I wiped sweaty palms down my legs and shifted in my chair. I glanced at Lorna. Her lips were clenched, and she kneaded her hands while her eyes darted nervously between her husband and her son.

No one spoke or moved for nearly two excruciating minutes.

"You're right, son. And that's another one of my deepest regrets. I should have taken the time to sit you and your mother down before making my next move. You two had every right to know what was going on before anyone else. The fixer in me just wanted to take action to try to make up for the fact that I missed my son's first fifteen years of life. But what's done is done. I can no longer live my life stressing about what I should have and could have done.

"So, since you need to hear it, I'll go ahead and say it. Whenever you're ready to talk about things and sort out how to move forward, I'm always going to be here. In the meantime, may God show you the same mercy and grace He's shown me when it's your turn to ask for this young lady's forgiveness. Because if you make it long enough in your relationship, you *will* fail her in a major way at some point."

Ox shook his head, swirling the ice cubes in his glass of lemonade. "Naw, that won't happen."

"Don't think so? Just keep on living. Although I don't ever want to see it happen, it's almost guaranteed. In the meantime, I'll continue to pray for an increase in your maturity and a decrease in your ego to help get you through it, if it does. Because, quite frankly, the view over here still shows me a little boy struggling to fill a grown man's shoes. Good luck with that, son."

He stood, clapped Ox on the back, and left the room without a backward glance.

# Chapter Thirty-Three

The tension was still heavy over two tense and uneventful hours later on the ride back home. I offered twice to put on the playlist I'd curated, and Ox denied it twice. So, I accepted that he simply wanted to drive in contemplative silence. I was almost six chapters into a New York Times bestselling thriller, but I couldn't attempt to summarize what I'd read for the life of me. My mind soon joined his, floating a thousand miles ahead of us—or maybe lagging just as far behind. Either way, I felt for Ox because his tender ego was bruised. I was sure it had been hard enough to hear his parents' tough love without having his brand-new girlfriend there to witness it. I was also sure that his mind was still processing the bittersweet message from his mother and the nearly one-sided conversation with his father. Lord knows the weight of their frank words still haunted me. I shivered.

Ox's warm hand immediately slid down my leg, and he asked, "You cold, babe? Want me to turn down the air?"

Relieved by the welcome break from his brooding, I offered a weak smile and said, "Nope, I'm fine. I just get those from time to time."

He nodded but kept his hand on my knee. "I'm taking the next exit to fill up and use the restroom."

"Okay. Want me to take over? I love driving."

"Yeah, if you don't mind."

After he filled the tank, we used the restroom and grabbed some snacks. Several minutes later, we were ready to get back on the highway. I adjusted the seat and synced my phone to CarPlay. We pulled onto the highway with my Road Trip playlist in progress.

Ox asked, "So, you created the Road Trip playlist just for this trip?"

"Actually, I created it years ago, and the title is proverbial because it's mostly throwback hip-hop songs."

"Ahh, so it's more like a mental road trip."

I nodded. "Yep. But it also happens to be a great highway soundtrack. I enjoy the monotony of being on autopilot and just letting my thoughts drift."

"Precisely."

Ox sat with his head on the headrest for a while, and I thought he was sleeping until "International Players Anthem" came on.

"My bitch a choosy lova, never fuck without a rubba!" We rapped in unison as the beat dropped.

I smiled as we rapped along with the lyrics and bounced to the beat. By the fifth throwback gem by Pete Rock and CL Smooth, I noticed his tension had begun to ease, and he was halfway back to his natural, laid-back self. He was a music head like me, so I knew throwback hip-hop hits would do the trick. I rested my hand on his leg, and he took it, bringing it up to his lips.

"Thanks, Beauty. I needed this."

"Yeah, we both did. That shit was intense as hell."

"Agreed."

"Are things always like that between you and your dad?"

"Naw, that's actually the most he's said to me in years. We've been avoiding that conversation since I was seventeen."

I grimaced. "Well, it certainly sounds like he's been preparing to have it for just as long."

"A big part of me thinks he still sees me as that same teenager. He hasn't seen much of me since then."

"I'm sorry."

"Shit's wild because my mother mentioned she had asked him to leave right after we found out. I straight forgot about that shit. Now that I think about it, he was gone for a couple of months right after we confronted him about Prez. But dude was gone so often, I guess I didn't really feel his absence much. I was full of rage. That shit was toxic and all-consuming. I just couldn't understand how he had time for a whole other family when he barely had time for us."

"Do you believe his claim that he initially didn't know about Prez?"

"Yeah, I later found out that part was true from Mariposa. But at first, I didn't believe anything my father had to say. Once Mariposa reached out and they got a paternity test, I remember he volunteered to pay her back child support. Then he covered all of Prez's expenses from that point on. But that wasn't what Prez or I ever really needed. All we wanted was for our dad to be active in our lives. To come to all of our games, to teach us about life . . . be there to help us figure this shit out."

I nodded, knowing exactly how he felt.

"I really bonded with Prez over that. We both felt the weight of his absence in our lives and vowed to never let our brotherhood falter."

I smiled. "Bay bro. I'm glad you have him."

He nodded. "But if I got nothing else out of today's conversation, it's the fact that I definitely need therapy. I've got cognitive dissonance like a mug. All this time, I thought my mother had just lain down and taken Halo's shit without a fight. She kicked that dude out of the house, and from what they each said, it sounds like she's still putting him through it. I thought her decision not to pursue a personal relationship with Prez was a sign that she was stuck. But she's fine. It's just a hard boundary for her. She's a lot stronger than I gave her credit for."

"Yeah, she's a good one. She handled it all with grace. I don't know what I would've done in that situation."

He squeezed my hand, turning to face me. "Look, I know he was talking all that crazy shit about me betraying you one day, but I need you to know that ain't happening. I would never do anything to make you experience that type of pain. We're still paying for it, all these years later, and I'd never put anyone through that."

*Never say what you won't do,* Pop-Pop's baritone voice warned in my head.

I swallowed. I was still thinking about Halo's words as well. Ox betraying me the way Halo had done to Lorna would be my literal worst nightmare. It was the main reason why I avoided emotionally investing myself in relationships to this day. But I had faith in Ox. I knew how much he loved me and that his strong discipline wouldn't allow him to betray me like that.

After the weight of his anticipation for a response got the best of me, I finally relented. "I know, babe. I see it. But I wanna help you heal from this. How can I support you?"

He shrugged. "Hell if I know."

I let a few beats pass before I said, "I think you were onto something with the therapy. Not to get too personal, but have you ever gone before?"

He squeezed my hand again. "After witnessing both my parents go in on me like I was a toddler, I'd say nothing about my life is off-limits to you at this point."

We laughed.

"But no, I haven't gone before. Although I've seriously considered it. A good friend of mine in Chicago started a national therapy initiative focused on breaking the stigma of seeking counseling in Black communities. He mostly focuses on promoting the benefits of therapy for Black males. I believe in it, and I support his cause by wearing the shirts and posting about it, but it's time to put some action behind it."

"I think it would help you come to terms with a lot of things and with rebuilding your relationships with your parents."

He nodded. "I'll definitely look into it. Soon."

"And I'll do my part as the supportive girlfriend by holding you to it."

"Bet."

We rode for a few minutes in silence. He was massaging my palm and fingers, and it felt great.

"What about you?"

His voice was so soft I barely heard him.

"Hmm?"

"So, what's the story with your folks? Are you close with them?"

Even though I knew we'd have this conversation at some point in the near future, I still had hoped I would have more time to think about how to respond. Having these types of conversations face to face wasn't easy for me. I preferred relying on phone conversations as a crutch for stalling or changing the subject altogether. But he was looking at me expectantly again, and I knew I didn't have the heart to bullshit him after all he had just gone through. I owed him the truth.

"I . . . well, uh." I gripped the steering wheel with my left hand while trying to keep my right one from trembling in his grip. "I have a good relationship with my mom now. She's a recovering alcoholic, so I had to live with a lot of her poor choices as a small child. But she got the help she needed, and we've since rebuilt our relationship. I don't really speak to my father. I only see him at big family events. According to my mom, he continued to pay my tuition and chipped in on braces and other major expenses, but he wasn't present in our lives at all. My father's situation is similar to yours, except he flat out left us, then started his other family. Like I told your mom, he has twins, Lexi and Xander, who are three years younger than Chelsea. He's been married to their mother, the woman he cheated on Mom with, for almost eighteen years now."

"Damn. Do you communicate with the twins?"

"Oh, yeah. Fortunately, I'm super close to all of my siblings."

"What about your stepmom?"

"We're cordial. She keeps me in the loop regarding the twins. They were all invited to the party but weren't able to make it because my dad got sick."

"That's too bad. Is he good now?"

"Yeah, he's good."

"What about the rest of your father's family?"

"I keep in touch with my aunts, his younger sisters. His parents are both deceased. But whenever I speak to my dad, it's because he initiates it. He actually reached out before we left to ask if he could take me out to lunch for my birthday when we got back."

"You going?"

I shook my head. "The only day he's free before I go back to work is tomorrow."

"Then go. I'll just hang back and get some work done while you're gone. Besides, my friend Ginelle wanted to grab drinks before I left."

There was that name again. Who exactly was this chick he seemed to link up with every time he came to Cleveland? Instead of making assumptions or getting jealous, I decided to just come right out and ask about her.

"You've mentioned her name a couple of times. How do you know her?"

"Oh, she's a childhood friend. I've known her since visiting my aunt in Cleveland over summer break. She lived on her street, and a large group of us played together all the time. Out of everyone, Ginelle and Stacy were the only ones I've stayed in touch with. Stacy's a dude, by the way."

"And Ginelle clearly isn't . . . ," I mumbled.

A few seconds later, I glanced at Ox and noticed he was smiling. "What?"

"Are you jealous?"

My cheeks flushed. "No . . . I'm just wondering why I had to ask you about her. You've brought up spending time with her multiple times without explaining who she was. I just thought that was odd."

He squeezed my hand and said, "Well, you have nothing to worry about. Ginelle and I are strictly platonic. She's just excited about seeing me since I haven't been to Cleveland since a few years before we started kickin' it. Besides, she's been bugging me about introducing the two of you. So, hopefully, we can make that happen soon."

I nodded. "I'll just reschedule with my dad. We only have a little more time together."

"Beauty," Ox uttered with a firm grip on my hand. "Go. You need this."

I stared at the road ahead for a long time before I replied, "Okay, I'll go. But come with me."

He hesitated for a moment, and I wondered if I had misread his interest in learning more about my family.

Finally, he said, "I'd rather not be a distraction, but if that's the only way to get you to see him, I'm fine with that."

I nodded again.

We were quiet for the next mile, then he asked, "So, is there anything I should know going into this? I don't need any more dudes blowing down on me with that old-man strength."

Caught unaware, I snorted, then continued laughing so hard that tears eventually streamed down my face. The image of Ox being brought down to size by his old man was awkward to witness at first, but his words finally allowed me to find the humor in it.

Ox still had not. He just sat there, quietly shaking his head.

When I recovered, I said, "Naw, he'll be excited to meet you. I've never introduced him to anyone I've dated, so he'll be grateful to have access to that part of my life."

Ox turned to face me. "No one? Not even Emo Ernie?"

I smirked and said, "Not even Emo Ernie."

"Didn't you say y'all kicked it for five years?"

"Yeah, we did. It wasn't because I didn't take our relationship seriously. It just never aligned quite right since things have always been touch and go with my father. Daniel's family was so damn perfect, and I already felt judged by his mother for coming from a 'broken family.' Although Daniel never made me feel a way about it, I didn't need him to see any more dysfunction than he needed to."

Ox chuckled. "Ahh, I get it. So, you saw my shit up close and personal and figured, 'Hell, even I can't top that shit.'"

I joined him in laughter. "Exactly!"

"I just want to meet him and hopefully learn a little more about the stunning Patience Hampton before I leave."

I smiled, grateful that Ox would be by my side to take off a bit of the edge of meeting up with my father. I knew my father would like Ox, and hopefully, the two of them would spend that time getting to know each other and leave me completely out of the conversation. As far as I was concerned, the less I said to my father, the better.

"So, you seemed shocked that Daniel never met my father after five years, but you haven't brought a girl home for the past ten. Catch that irony!" I shot him a hard side eye.

Ox seemed at a loss for words for the first time since I'd met him. I turned the music down and continued to navigate the open highway. There was no way he was getting any relief from the hot seat I'd tossed him in.

"Yeah, about that . . . ," he said, swiping a hand over his brow. "What Prez said was definitely true. I wasn't out here being a player or anything like that. I was just focused as hell, and from what I witnessed in my friends' relationships, females seemed to be a lot of drama. I didn't need the distractions."

We rode for a few minutes in silence before I responded. "Okay, I was trying to give you the opportunity to amend your statement, but I see now that you're sticking to it. I'm going to have to call bullshit on that one, Ox."

His mouth opened, and I looked over to catch a hint of a smile pulling at the corner of his lip. "What do you mean 'bullshit'?"

"I mean, what you just said sounded like bullshit. Yes, unhealthy relationships can distract you from your goals. But you don't seem like the type who's easily distracted or deterred from going after what you want—females or ambitions. You're inquisitive, and you never settle for anything less than an authentic answer from me. So, try again because that one just didn't do it for me, bae."

He shook his head. "Here you go, thinking you know me again."

"I actually have gotten to know you. You're someone worth getting to know, and I'd like to know as much as I can. Let me in, bae. I promise not to use anything you share against you."

He sighed. "All right. I can't argue with that. I wouldn't have accepted that answer from you, either. And after all you've witnessed, you deserve nothing less than the whole truth from me."

"Right. I don't think either of us expected or wanted to experience any of that, but it eliminated all formalities between us. Feel free to keep it one hundred with me from this point on." I squeezed his hand.

"So, my parents' situation really did a number on me. I think seeing everything go to shit with no warning has destroyed my faith in the stability of relationships. So, I've casually dated, and it's led to sex here and there. But as soon as either of us started catching feelings, I would back off. I decided that whenever I did decide to settle down with someone, I was going to do it the right way. No games, no lying, just an honest relationship."

"That's not the vibe I got in Atlanta. You wanted much more than casual sex."

He shrugged. "What can I say? Your aura pulled me in instantly. But, if I'm being honest, the distance between us made the idea of exploring a relationship a lot more comfortable for me.

We have the space to miss each other, we appreciate our time together a lot more, and we're getting to know each other at a slower pace. Just imagine if I lived here. There's no way we would've been dating for a full month before being intimate."

I nodded. "Great point. But distance can also create room for insecurities surrounding infidelity."

"Only if we let it. I'm honestly not concerned with that at all. I believe it's really over between you and Daniel, and I don't peg you as the cheating type. Have you ever been unfaithful in your past relationships?"

I shook my head. "No, I've always ended one relationship before starting another. Even with our situation, I'd already decided to break up with Daniel. I did seek closure from him, and we continued a physical relationship later on, but, as far as I was concerned, we were no longer a couple when I met you."

"Then I'm just going to continue to trust my gut and believe that we've got it right."

"I still can't believe you chose me."

He leaned back in his seat and looked at me. "Why wouldn't I choose you? You're smart, ambitious, and beautiful."

I just shook my head and shrugged.

"And once I got to know you, I learned how passionate you are about the people and causes you care about—family, friendships, and equity. You're not good unless everyone around you is good. I love that about you."

I gave his hand another squeeze. "Thanks, Ox. I know we didn't have a perfect start, but I'm glad you stuck around through all my drama. Now that I've met your family and know more about you, I'm even more intrigued. You've been through so much, and no one would ever know it by your character. You're a stand-up dude. Thank you for inviting me into your life and for such a beautiful weekend."

"Of course. I'm looking forward to meeting some of your family and learning even more about you."

I cringed, thinking about who I could introduce him to. My

family was small and complicated. We only had time for a lunch date with dad on this visit. Maybe I could introduce him to Mom, Chelsea, and Pop-Pop on his next visit, although I was nervous about how they would handle the news about our relationship after my recent breakup with Daniel. They were all very fond of Daniel, and Mom and Chelsea each had expressed their hopes that we were on track for marriage.

I knew all my mom would need to know was how happy Ox was making me to be on board with our relationship. I also knew once she laid eyes on him, it would be a done deal. She was a sucker for a handsome face. For Chelsea, her attachment to Daniel was mainly due to her relationship with his younger sister, Princessa. Over the course of our relationship, Daniel and I had gotten our sisters together often since they were so close in age. They'd quickly developed a relationship of their own and had been inseparable ever since. I smiled, thinking of how I affectionately referred to them as "Frick and Frack."

As for Pop-Pop, I had no doubt that he would be even crazier about Ox than Daniel, but I was fully aware that relationships and building trust took time. Most importantly, I wanted to give them all enough time to mourn one relationship before introducing another. Things were already unstable and unfolding fast enough for me without forcing my chaos into everyone else's lives.

"You seem deep in thought over there. You've gone from grinning to frowning to chewing your lip in a matter of seconds. You good?" Ox squeezed my hand.

I nodded, never taking my eyes off the open road. "I am. Things are better than ever with you by my side."

# Chapter Thirty-Four

My favorite part of waking up for those next few days was opening my eyes to find Ox staring lovingly at me. I was already accustomed to his handsome face being the first and last thing I saw each day. Once my groggy eyes became focused, I noticed there was no smile on his lips and his face held a fixed expression, like he was carefully studying me. His eyes lingered on my legs, still entangled in the satin sheets, then swept over my hips and stomach. Only when we locked eyes did he grant me the pleasure of seeing his lips curve into a gentle smile. With a soft moan, his mouth covered mine as his hands palmed and squeezed my breasts. Cradling his head, I savored his lips, and my hips eased up from the mattress as if drawn toward him at their own will.

Making love to Ox was an incomparable experience. The full command he had over my body was astounding. No matter how I tried to prolong my climax and deny myself the ecstasy of succumbing to him fully, my body disregarded my mind's plight like it was on a whole other wavelength. Completely obedient to his demands, April willingly yielded, self-detonating beneath his coaxing strokes, time after time. Ox took his time and loved me attentively as if his life solely depended on my endless gratification. And when I shouted his nickname in the throes of passion, I willingly put respeck on that shit.

That man made it his mission to get to know me from the inside to the outside. So, while on the walk from the car to the restaurant to meet my father for lunch, I shouldn't have been surprised when he stopped in his tracks and suddenly turned to face me, taking in my pensive expression.

"Hey, you okay?"

I frowned. "Yeah, I'm fine. Why?"

"I felt your arm tremble. Did you catch a chill? It's eighty degrees out here."

I shrugged, unaware of my physical reaction to the impending doom awaiting us. "I'm good, bae. Let's just get this over with."

He searched my eyes for a moment longer, then nodded.

When we walked into the small pancake house, I barely heard the chatter of patrons and clanking dishes over the thudding pulse in my ears. I scanned the dining room for my father's signature brown Kangol that he donned year-round. As soon as I spotted him sitting in a back booth, I pushed myself forward, squeezing Ox's hand in my sweaty palm. Ox released my hand and placed his at the small of my back. The subtle gesture comforted me, and I exhaled the breath I'd held captive, forcing a smile onto my face.

"Hi, Dad," I greeted him as we walked up.

He looked up from his menu, his forehead riddled with deep thought lines. As soon as he laid eyes on me, his expression warmed with recognition. He stood, pulling me into a hug, and my body stiffened instinctively.

I disengaged and stepped aside. "Dad, this is Lennox Davenport, my boyfriend."

"Lennox. Nice to meet you. Alex Hampton."

"Same, sir."

They shook hands, and Ox maintained eye contact with my father until we slid into the booth across from him. I avoided it, immediately reaching for a menu to scan. There was food on it, so I sprayed it with sanitizer and wiped it with a napkin. The server, who introduced herself as Stephanie, came for our drink orders. Grateful for the water she provided, unprompted, I almost drained the glass in one long gulp. When I lifted my eyes to make eye contact with my father for the first time since arriving, I noticed him looking back and forth between Ox and me with a proud smile on his face.

"Well, you two sure make a handsome couple."

When I said nothing, Ox responded with, "Thanks, sir."

Dad waved off his comment. "No need for the formalities. Alex is fine."

Ox nodded and asked, "So, what's good to eat here?"

Dad raised a brow. "First time here? How so? It's a community staple."

"Oh, I'm originally from Brooklyn, but I live in Atlanta. Before meeting Patience, I hadn't been to Cleveland in years."

Dad's smile deepened. "Brooklyn, huh? How'd you two find one another?"

Ox gave the abbreviated, PG version of how we had met while I dipped our silverware into the cup of hot water the server provided.

"That's some story," Dad said, eying me closely but keeping his opinion on it to himself. "Well, you can't go wrong with the oven-baked German pancakes. Is that still your favorite, sweet baby girl?"

I fought back an eye roll at the nickname he insisted on calling me. It was funny how things changed. I practically lived to hear him call me by that name as a little girl. Hell, I lived for anything he did or said back then. He couldn't do anything wrong in my eyes at that time, as far as I was concerned. "Yes, they're great. But I'm getting a veggie eggs Benedict today."

I placed our sanitized silverware on fresh napkins just as the server returned to collect our orders.

Once she cleared the menus from the table, my father asked, "So, how was your birthday? Sorry I wasn't able to make the party. I was in the hospital. You know I wouldn't have missed it for the world."

I met my father's eyes for the first time. His rich brown skin gathered in soft folds beneath his round face, but his eyes were bright and joyful. My mother had always told me we looked alike growing up. I initially disagreed, but there was no denying it anymore once I had entered adulthood.

"What? Lexi never told me that! I thought you were just a little under the weather. Hospitalized for what?"

"Just a bad asthma flare-up from an allergic reaction. Lexi tried a new fragrance and used damn near the whole bottle on herself. I fought it for a while, but it eventually did me in. She felt terrible. Probably why she didn't mention it to you."

Frowning, I mumbled, "It seems like your allergies have gotten worse over the years."

"I'm fine. Don't worry about your old dad. So, did you have a good turnout?"

I nodded. "Yeah, it was a great time."

"I had my T'Chaka costume all decked out and ready. Brenda found the exact replica on eBay."

At the mention of my stepmother's name, my throat tensed involuntarily. I took a deep breath and reached for Ox's water glass.

He squeezed my thigh and said, "So you're a *Black Panther* fan, huh?"

I rubbed his hand to assure him I was fine.

"Oh, who isn't? I saw that movie three times at the theater decked out in African attire from head to toe. And at least half a dozen times on DVD."

Ox chuckled. "Same. It's a classic."

"You went to the theater in full African attire?" I asked Ox, stunned.

"No, but I wore my Avengers hoodie. I'm a hard-core Avengers fan."

"Hmm," I said, sipping my hot cocoa. I didn't know that about him.

Stephanie brought our food, and I immediately dug into my eggs. Dad cleared his throat, and I straightened up, setting my fork down. We joined hands, and he briefly prayed over the food.

After a few minutes of silence, Ox said, "These German pancakes are pretty good. They remind me of the ones at Richard Walker's in San Diego."

"Oh, that place is phenomenal," Dad said. "I've stood in line outside for an hour just to get their baked pecan pancake."

Ox nodded in agreement. "The smell when you walk in there. I almost considered taking out a loan to start a franchise after my first visit. Babe, I have to take you there when we go."

I smiled at him but continued to focus on my food.

A few more moments of thoughtful silence passed, and my father asked, "So, what's been happening in the life of my now twenty-seven-year-old?"

"Nothing much. Just working and getting to know this amazing man better."

"Do either of you have plans to relocate, or are you planning to keep it long distance for a while longer?"

We looked at each other for a moment, unsure how to answer since we hadn't discussed our long-term plans before then.

"Since I have more flexibility in my job and have friends and family here, I plan to visit Cleveland as often as I can," Ox said.

My father lifted a brow and sipped his coffee. I glanced over at Ox, and he offered a weak smile. I could tell he was wondering what my father's non-reaction meant as well. A few moments passed, and my anger quickly escalated until I was steaming.

I set my fork down. "If you have something to say, please just say it, Dad."

There was Ox's firm squeeze on my hand again, but I ignored it. The whole audacity of this man. Who was he to pass judgment on our situation or try to give *me* relationship advice with a failed marriage and child abandonment glaring on his fuckboy resume?

"I was only thinking that early on in a relationship when you're initially getting to know one another, there are quite a few things to learn about each other. For example, learning how to communicate and even argue correctly and how you really feel about each other. Those components all set the foundation for a long-lasting, healthy relationship."

I bit the inside of my cheek until the copper taste of my warm blood leaked on my tongue. I was doing a poor job of fighting the rage and resentment boiling inside of me. Trembling, I literally saw red as the urge to flip the table over, send him flying back on his pompous ass, and scream his hypocrisy into his face surged over me. Ox slid his arm around my shoulder to quell my hysteria, but I was inconsolable.

"*You?* You want to give us advice on healthy relationships? What exactly do you think gives you the right to do that?" My voice came out calmer than I expected.

My father's eyebrows shot up again, and his feigned shock sickened me. He stumbled before managing to say, "As your father, I believe I have the right to be invested in your happiness . . ."

"What about all the years your unapologetic absence crushed my chance at happiness? And all of my precious dreams? How it diminished my self-worth and my belief that I deserved to be loved. Were you 'invested' back then?"

Ox leaned over and whispered into my ear, "Patience, this isn't the time or place to do this. Let me—"

My father held up his hands. "I understand you're working off of a biased point of view, and I—"

"Biased? I lived every waking moment of the shit! *Please* tell me how it's biased."

"I was referring to you only hearing your mother's version of what happened between us. We were adults doing adult things, and you were a child without the capacity to understand what happened between us, so—"

"Oh, I understood, all right. You selfishly walked out on your seven-year-old and six-month-old daughters without so much as a goodbye in the middle of the night to go start your brand-new family! So, please tell me, what's left to understand?"

Ox slid out of the booth, standing to his feet. "Mr. Hampton, I think we should call it. This conversation isn't going anywhere productive."

My father's eyes remained on mine, housing tears that refused to fall. "Sweet baby girl, I've tried for over two decades to explain my side of things to you. For ten long years, my access to you was blocked by your mother and grandfather. And since you've been an adult, you've built so much resentment toward me that I can't even get through to you for a moment. I've tried time after time to foster a loving relationship with you, but you refuse to let me in. I was hoping that having your boyfriend here as a mediator would help things, but . . ."

"Who blocked you? You *left* us, and we never saw or heard from you again! So, later for your tears and sad-ass excuses. There's nothing left to say on that. Your actions have already spoken for you!"

"Is everything okay here?" An older male wearing a shirt and tie suddenly appeared beside Ox.

Our waitress, Stephanie, trailed him wearing a concerned expression.

"Everything's fine. I was just leaving," Dad told them. He reached into his wallet and tossed money for the bill onto the table. Then he reached beside him and retrieved a bundle of frayed envelopes bound with twine rope. The thick stack clunked onto the table and rolled toward me. As my father stared at me, his eyes were still soft but laced with disappointment. "I've made my share of mistakes, Patience. I won't ever deny that. But I've spent the past twenty years trying to make up for them, and I'll do my best to continue to try to get through to you."

Numb and emotionally spent, I watched him stand and shake Ox's hand before striding out of the restaurant without another word.

Ox knelt beside me with worried eyes searching mine. He handed me a glass of water. "Babe, are you okay?"

One thing was for certain—I couldn't be further from okay at that moment. Once again, my anger took over, making me unrecognizable to myself. I felt trapped and buried beneath all of the fury my father stirred in me. His aloof demeanor made me want to scream. His happy-go-lucky attitude made me want to cry for the little girl in me who could have used his positivity—even from afar—while carrying the weight of the world on her shoulders. His disregard for my feelings and well-being made me want to crumble right there in Ox's arms. I was coming apart at the seams under the scope of a stunned audience when all I wanted was to be whisked away.

My bottom lip trembled, and I couldn't find the words to tell him what I needed.

Right on cue, Ox added a few bills to my father's, grabbed the stack of envelopes, and ushered me out of the silent restaurant before the first tear could fall.

# Chapter Thirty-Five

When Ox pulled into a parking space at the Metroparks and turned off the engine, I was still trembling. My nerves had calmed a little, but bits and pieces of my conversation with my father were still bouncing around my mind. I was stunned by his audacity to analyze my relationship with the first person I'd introduced to him. Now, after years of neglect, he wanted to be Daddy freaking Dearest.

When I felt Ox's hand cover mine, I jumped slightly. He gently squeezed it, and I squeezed his back. He cracked the windows, and we watched a small flock of Canadian geese. The baby goslings trailed their mothers as the small group sailed across the fishing pond. I envied their collective peace at that moment.

"Why couldn't I have just been a damn bird?" I mumbled, reclining my seat and throwing my arm across my forehead.

Just when I thought he wasn't going to respond, Ox said, "Geese are pretty smart."

"That's great."

"They have a good memory for recognizing harmful people or events." He paused and turned to me. "And they get pretty aggressive when they cross paths with them again."

I tried to ignore him, but he reached over and turned my face toward him, locking eyes with me for a long moment.

"You wanna go for a walk, Beauty?"

I sighed, then nodded before stepping out of the car and slipping on my shades. The heat hit us hard and strong, so I removed my jean jacket and tied it around my waist. Ox took my hand once we hit the trail circling the large pond's perimeter.

"So, I caught your reference about being overly guarded, and I know you have something more to say about it," I said, sidestepping goose poop. "Speak your mind."

He looked over at me. "I'd rather hear what's on yours."

I groaned. "If my ex is Emo Ernie, you're Talk-It-Out Teddy."

When a few seconds of silence passed between us, I was hesitant to look over at him. The last thing I wanted to do was take my frustration out on him when all he'd ever been was supportive of me. I snuck a peek at him as we stepped onto a small wooden bridge. He stopped to peer over the creek flowing below it. When I walked up beside him, the first thing I saw was that dimple.

He turned to face me. "You think you're funny, don't you?"

I shrugged. "Actually, I'm hilarious, but I'm not trying to be right now. My father brings out the worst in me, and I'm not ready to talk about what happened."

He nodded. "After my encounter with Halo, I wasn't, either. So, I'll grant you the same courtesy you gave me in New York. But, coming from Talk-It-Out Teddy, I learned a long time ago that not talking it out hurts a hell of a lot more. And, since you asked me to speak my mind . . ."

I stepped off the bridge. "Nope. Changed my mind."

He followed me, and I stopped to snap a quick picture of a monarch resting on a milkweed plant.

"What I was going to say is I totally understand where you're coming from. You just saw the same thing play out in New York with Halo. It's actually uncanny how similar our situations are."

I nodded. "Yeah, what are the odds we're both suffering from daddy issues?"

"But as far as your behavior at the restaurant, Beauty . . ." He waited until he had my full attention before continuing. "That was rough to watch."

I started walking again. "I know. Not my proudest moment."

"That escalated so quickly. What exactly brought on all that anger?"

I evened my breathing, folding my arms tightly across my chest. "*Again.* Don't wanna talk about it."

I kicked some pebbles with my Converse, refusing to look up at him. Maybe he'd understand if I told him to drop it en Español. I just didn't know how much clearer I could make it for him that I was uninterested in continuing this conversation.

However, he continued, "Do you think your reaction could have been a little exaggerated?"

I shrugged, keeping my eyes straight ahead as tears perched on my lower eyelids behind my shades.

"Hell, I've done my share of lashing out at my father. That's why I was hoping to avoid seeing him altogether in New York, but he and my mother clearly had other plans. But from my point of view, you were guarded from jump and didn't even give him a chance to speak his piece. Why even agree to see him if you're not willing to at least be cordial?"

I spun around to face him with slitted eyes. "Because he doesn't deserve cordial from me!"

His voice lowered as he reached out and held my forearms. "Beauty . . . it seems like he's trying to make up for his past mistakes. And you forgave your mother for checking out on you and your sister. So, I'm just trying to understand . . . why not him?"

I shrugged out of his grasp, fighting to speak against the knot lodged in my throat. "My mother fell victim to a disease beyond her control as a result of being abandoned by her husband with two small children. My father, on the other hand, *chose* to walk out on his responsibilities and never looked back. What's hard to understand about that?"

"You're right, Patience." He lifted my chin and stared into my eyes again.

When I finally looked up at him, I wanted to give in to his gentle expression. I knew he wasn't judging me or questioning my choices, but I felt cornered by his insistence on having this conversation.

"Don't forget I experienced all of that, too. But when you told me in Atlanta about your tendency to self-sabotage healthy relationships, I thought you were ready to let go of the pain you've been holding on to. Not forgiving your father doesn't just impact you. It's stunting your ability to feel secure in your relationships, to allow yourself to experience happiness, and it's mentally tormenting you, babe. I'm always here to support you, but first, you have to face that shit head-on."

The pleading in his voice was ripping me to shreds. I knew he desperately wanted the best for me. But he was being unrealistic about the depth of my issues with my father. Brushing hot tears from my cheeks, I removed my shades and plopped down in the grass in a huff. A few moments later, Ox sat beside me without a word. He pulled me into his arms, ignoring my resistance until I sighed and laid my head on his chest. After fifteen minutes of wrestling with my thoughts in silence, I tapped his chest.

We stood, and as he hugged me, he said, "Listen, babe. I may not get how you're feeling every single moment, but I'm committed to understanding you more each day. I'm sorry if that feels like I'm coming on too strong."

I looked away, and he pulled my face back to his.

"I also realize that I need to respect your healing journey, however that looks. We don't have to talk about this again if you don't want to. But if you want to, I'll be ready to listen."

I nodded, lifting up on my toes to kiss him. Then we strolled to the car, hand in hand.

## Chapter Thirty-Six

By the time I had worked up the courage to unwrap the bundle of envelopes, Ox was back in Atlanta. I knew I wasn't in the emotional state to process the content of those letters with a clear mind. So, I had shown Ox my old house, where I had attended school, and some of my old stomping grounds, temporarily taking my mind off things. I was grateful that we concluded our trip on a good note.

The envelopes sat on the foyer table for almost seven weeks before I even thought about touching them again. In the meantime, to zone out of the shitstorm components of my life, I devoted my precious time and attention to the things that made me feel happy, alive, appreciated, and celebrated. And to my heart's delight, it just so happened that most of those elements were wrapped up in one tall, wonderful package. I also completed training for my new job, which I loved.

I had selected a master of fine arts program and would be starting in a few weeks. I still taught line-dance classes to my church members, and I prioritized spending more time outside of the house with Chelsea and Bella. Outside of those activities, I FaceTimed and spoke on the phone with Ox. We talked every morning on the way to work, texted throughout the day, called each other while driving home, and FaceTimed as soon as we walked through the door, often chatting until we fell asleep each night. He came back to Cleveland a couple more times, and I made it out to Atlanta once.

With all that communication, we had learned a plethora of things about one another. We discussed everything that crossed our minds, and no topic or subject was off-limits, with the exception of my father. I told him everything, and he never hesitated to answer questions about his childhood, his proudest moments, and his deepest fears. After the drama of New York and the breakfast with my dad, I felt comfortable letting him see each side of me. Our personal worst nightmares had already played out, and we'd never left each other's side. He had faced the storm beside me and stayed behind to help me pick up the pieces. He had carried me when I lacked the strength to stand on my own, and his loyalty spoke volumes to me. It was just like Lorna said: his actions showed me everything I needed to know about him.

When I walked into my house on a rainy Wednesday evening and saw that stack still awaiting me on the entryway table, I paused instead of walking by. Ox had a late client meeting that evening, and I had grown tired of all the tormenting, unanswered questions coursing through my mind about the content of those envelopes. Almost two months had passed since the pancake house, and I still hadn't spoken to my father. With each day that passed, I had more questions about what made him so insistent that what I believed about him was wrong. I was tired of the confusion I felt and of carrying the burden of acrimony inside of me. I finally had found happiness with a good man who was protective of me, adored me, and made it his daily mission to ensure that I was aware of how sensational he thought I was.

I wasn't willing to sacrifice my happiness for suffering in the baggage of my past any longer. I was ready to release all of the unforgiveness and fully experience the joy right in front of me. I knew it wouldn't happen until I finally heard my father's side of why he suddenly had gone missing in my life. After that, I'd have to address the things he had to say with my mother and grandfather.

Settling on the couch with a glass of wine while holding the stack of envelopes, I took a deep breath, knowing that nothing but God would help me face the demons waiting ahead of me. "Dear Lord, please grant me clarity and a clear heart so I can fully receive the words on these pages. Help me recognize the truth and not fall for the lies of the enemy. Block any unfruitful emotions or clouded judgment from distorting my thoughts. Help me remain close to You and easily adhere to Your guiding voice. Please cast all negative thinking—or anything that is not of You—from me. Help me remember my goal of forgiveness. In the name of Your son, Jesus, I pray. Amen."

I exhaled, then untied the bundle with trembling hands. The first envelope was cotton-candy pink. My name was at the top, followed by the address of the home I grew up in. The first thing I noticed was the red *Return to Sender* stamp at the top. The post-marked year was 1999, a few months after my father had walked out on my mother, sister, and me. That confused me because we were still living at that address at the time. So why would the letter automatically be returned? I quickly googled the return address and found it was for a Holiday Inn that was now closed. That was probably where he had gone after walking out on us and before marrying my stepmother.

I instantly recognized my father's tight handwriting. It was the same handwriting from the personal notes on the inside covers of all the children's books he had bought me as a little girl. I studied those words for years, wondering how someone who took the time to buy books and inscribe them while his wife was still pregnant with his first child could abandon that same wife and his daughters without a backward glance. I slid the card from the envelope, and a piece of paper floated out to the floor. It was an old ten-dollar bill wrapped in wax paper. He had tried to send me cash the same old-school way my family from out of town had. There was a huge eight on the birthday card.

Tears stung my eyes as I read his message.

*Sweet Baby Girl,*

*I'm sorry I couldn't see you on your birthday. I had some chal-lenges getting to you. But I promise to come get you this weekend. I love you more than life itself. I hope you enjoyed your day and always remember that Daddy loves you.*

Challenges. Wondering what kind of challenges would prevent him from seeing me on my birthday, I moved on to the next envelope postmarked one month later. It was a letter.

*Sweet Baby Girl,*

*How have you been doing? Boy, how I miss that darling smile of yours. It was the first thing I saw each day. I miss you waking me up every morning—my little personal alarm clock. I've been trying to get to you, but it hasn't been easy. I'm not going to give up, though.*

*Do me a favor. Make a list of all the things you want to do this summer, and when I get you for a few weeks, we'll make them happen. I can't wait to take you on a trip and buy you all the pink cotton candy you can eat!*

*I'll see you soon and always remember that Daddy loves you.*

I frowned, wondering why he hadn't mentioned Chelsea. After reading a few more letters, brimming with what seemed like empty promises, I looked through the rest of the stack and counted over eighty envelopes in total. They were all marked as *Return to Sender*, spanning from 2000 to 2011. Then I noticed a bulky legal envelope holding photocopied child support payment stubs and legal documents starting in 2002 for sole physical custody hearings on which I was the only name listed. I thumbed through the rest of the envelopes, and my heart sank when I came across court-ordered DNA test results.

Had my father really tried to deny my sister? I always looked exactly like him and my paternal aunts, and Chelsea favored my mother's side of the family, but it hurt me to know that he had put my mother through that type of ridicule. When I scanned the paperwork for details, I gasped, nearly dropping them believing there was no way the information could be accurate.

*The alleged father is excluded as the biological father of the tested child. This conclusion is based on the non-matching alleles listed above with a direct index equal to 0. Probability of Paternity: 0%.*

My eyes floated to the top of the page, desperately searching.
*Mother: Etta Hampton*
*Alleged Father: Alex Hampton*
*Child: Chelsea Loren Hampton*

The numbing shock that resulted prevented me from moving for at least ten full minutes. I wanted to scream and rip the paper into tiny pieces. Silent tears streamed down my face as I grasped for some sort of meaningful conclusion while staring at the test results. The more I studied the words on the page, the less sense they made. This paper told me that Chelsea, the love of my life, my ace boon coon, was my half-sister. That we didn't have the same father. That my mother was with another man while my parents were still married.

How long had that been happening? Did they have an open marriage? If not, who was the transgressor? Who had betrayed whom first? I remembered thinking about how easy it was for my father to just move on and start his new family. But my mother already had a child outside of their union by the time that had happened.

I conjured an image of Chelsea in my mind—her narrow face, pointed chin, and large brown eyes with freckles dusting her cheeks where my facial features were full and round. Her tall ballerina figure and fine, dark-brown hair easily hung past her bra line where my frame was short and curvy, and my hair was thick, black, tightly coiled, and refused to grow past my shoulders. We were both beautiful in our own ways, and we celebrated those beautiful, pronounced features as part of our unique identities. But those physical differences had always served as a subtle mystery for me since she was born. Just like my mother, Chelsea never had mentioned those differences. *Had she known all this time?*

She would always be my sister, and nothing would ever change that. That, I was certain of. But I couldn't help but wonder how knowing this information would impact the rest of my life. Exactly who else had been in on the "Keep the Wool Over Patience's Eyes" campaign for the past twenty years? It was time to find out exactly what was going on.

Suddenly, my father's words hit me, and my stomach lurched.

*For ten long years, I was blocked by your mother and grandfather.*

I wouldn't put a damn thing past my mother. She had resented my father with a passion I'd never seen. But was Pop-Pop in on this hoodwinking shit, too? What kind of benefit could they all possibly expect to come from hiding what my mother did and allowing my father to take the fall for it all?

Chapter Thirty-Seven

I'd been blowing up Chelsea's phone all day, but I still hadn't heard back from her. I knew she was balancing a full schedule of work, summer classes, and play rehearsals, but it wasn't like her not to at least respond to my texts. I texted Tavares to check in on her whereabouts, but he must have worked an overnight shift the day before because I still hadn't heard back from him, either. I planned to stop by Chelsea's apartment if I didn't hear from her by that evening.

I broke my spotless attendance record by calling off work that morning. Even though I never called off, I knew I wasn't in the frame of mind to face anyone in the office, and I knew I wouldn't get anything done while working from home. I still needed time to process everything and figure out how I felt about my newly revealed family history. It seemed like everything I had thought I knew about my family, my life, and even myself was a lie. Everything I had built my foundation on was crumbling into sinking quicksand. I didn't even trust the ground I walked on anymore.

Even Ox's morning text, which never failed to bring a smile to my face, hadn't cheered me up. He had worked pretty late the night before, so we only got the chance to hop on a quick goodnight video call. He was beaming, happy about helping land a huge new client for the company, and I didn't want to sully his mood. When he texted that he would be FaceTiming me in twenty minutes, I applied some concealer and brightener to disguise my puffy eyes and began sipping hot tea and honey to coat my throat, which was raw from crying. Ox was modest and hesitant to acknowledge his own accomplishments. So, I was careful not to let my brooding overshadow his big moment. With a perky voice that betrayed my breaking heart, I offered him sincere praise and enthusiasm because I enjoyed putting my problems aside to celebrate my man.

His morning text, which I knew would read: *The woman who's stolen my heart, and Beauty is her name,* sat unread in my message box. Each of his morning texts started with a line from one of my favorite songs, "Beauty" by Dru Hill. Ox always accused me of turning him into a sappy cornball, but those consistent texts made me feel seen by him, even from hundreds of miles away. But that morning, I didn't feel beautiful. My eyelids were puffy, and my eyes were bloodshot from crying myself to sleep the night before. I felt like I'd been run over by a train, and not even a romantic text from the love of my life could help pull me out of the funk I was in.

I called off work that morning and originally planned to use the day to get a head start on narrating the fiction novel for my personal client. But my voice was hoarse and raspy from crying all night. So I lay on the couch, watching my fifth consecutive episode of *Dish Nation* with bacon crumbs resting on my bare stomach. My hair was piled on top of my head, and a heap of used, balled-up tissues was beside the couch. Worst of all, I couldn't reach Chelsea, my voice of reason, to see if I was overreacting about everything. So, needless to say, I was an entire mess.

Once my nose stopped up and I could no longer breathe while lying down, I reluctantly sat up. My phone began to ring, and I jumped up, grabbing it and staring at the screen. I sighed heavily. It was only Trice.

"Hello?"

"Hey, girl, hey. What has you playing hooky today? Lennox back in town?"

"No, he's still in Atlanta."

"Oh, so a legit sick day? You soundin' all nasally and thangs."

I sniffed and one of my nostrils deflated. *Ugh.* "Something like that. More like a cross between a personal and sick day."

"I get it, girl. Well, it's already Thursday, so you may as well kick your weekend off now. You get all that extra PTO time with that new role, boss lady."

"Not like I'll ever be able to use it. Girl, this workload is bananas. Gordon should have hired someone for this position years ago. But I'm blessed that person is me."

"That you are. I'm on my lunch hour. Want me to bring by peppermint oil, chicken noodle soup, and some herbal tea?"

I shook my head. "You're sweet, girl. But no, I'm good."

"Okay. Let me know if you change your mind. I could easily stop by after work."

"No, get home to that beautiful baby. Give him a kiss for me and tell Landon I said hey."

"Will do. Feel better."

"Thanks, work wifey."

My joints crackled and popped in protest as I slowly rose to my feet after what seemed like hours of lying horizontally. I wiggled my stiff legs and stretched, reaching for the ceiling. On the way to the bathroom, my fuzzy socks got tangled up in the hem of my robe, causing me to lose my footing and slip. I screamed, and my arms flew out reflexively. Before I knew what was happening, my body slammed into the wall with my left wrist striking it at an awkward angle.

"*Ow!*" I wailed. Hot tears sprang to my eyes. What the actual fuck was going on with me today? I couldn't even manage a fifteen-foot walk to the bathroom without jacking myself up.

While sitting on the bathroom floor, crying, I took a moment to think about my life. I realized that in order to grow and manifest the things I was asking of God daily, I would have to get comfortable with giving up a few things on my end. I was done holding on to resentment of my father. I was done hating my step-mother and holding each of them responsible for my unhappiness. If I wasn't satisfied with how my life had turned out, I was the only one to blame for that. It was time for me to take full ownership of my own joy. And getting up and dusting myself off in order to do the work necessary to manifest the life I wanted was exactly what that would look like.

Four and a half hours and two X-rays later, I walked out of the emergency room with a sprained wrist diagnosis. To top it all off, I had spent so much effort trying to get myself dressed and out the door with only one good wrist that I accidentally left my phone at home. So, I was stuck with nothing to do but stare at the wall and think while waiting for hours to be examined, then for a doctor to review my X-ray results. I was so over this day and ready to climb into bed, pop a painkiller, and hit the reset button. I trudged across the parking lot, fumbling around in my purse to find my keys with my good hand.

I unlocked the door, and just before I slid into the driver's seat, a firm hand landed on my arm. I jumped, jerking my arm back.

"Hey! Get the hell off me!"

When his hands shot up, I got a closer look at his face, and my keys slipped from my fingers, clattering onto the concrete.

"Pae, it's me. I didn't mean to scare you. I called out to you, but you were out of it."

I cleared my throat, fighting to even my breath. In an even tone, I asked Daniel, "What are you doing here?"

"I've been calling your phone. We have an emergency."

I held up my wrist. "It's at home, and I've been inside, getting this treated. And I've already told your mother I can't help you. How did you know where I was, anyway?"

He stepped closer. "What happened to your wrist? Are you okay?"

"I'm fine."

"Wait. You've been talking to my mom?"

I rolled my eyes. "Daniel, you haven't answered my question. Did you follow me here?"

Daniel gave me a sheepish look before showing me his phone. "I've been waiting in the parking lot for you to come out."

I jumped in his face. "Daniel, I know you don't have a tracking device on my car!"

He backed away, scanning the parking lot to see if we had company. "As much as I'd like to defend myself right now, I can't. Just know it's for your own good. I'll let you know more about it on the way."

"I'm not going anywhere with your psychotic ass! Get that shit off my car right now!" I yelped in pain after gesturing toward my car with my injured wrist.

"Are you okay?"

"I'm fine. I said get it off my car, Daniel."

"Look, I'll take it off once we get back. But we have to go. Now."

"I just said I'm not—"

"Pae! Just listen to me, dammit," his voice boomed, piercing the evening air.

I stiffened. "Okay, I'm listening."

"Princessa called me. She and Chelsea got into a bad car accident out in Berea! They're at the hospital."

# Chapter Thirty-Eight

My eyes narrowed, searching his carefully as I processed what he had just said. I was still trying to figure out how he'd put a tracker on my car without my knowledge. Then he told me my sister had been in a car accident? How exactly could I trust anything he had to say?

"What did you just say to me, Daniel?"

He reached for me, but I shrank back from his grasp, nearly losing my footing.

"Just. Tell me. What are you talking about, Daniel?"

"You okay, sis?"

I turned around to see a petite woman in scrubs walking up, wearing a deep frown. I gazed down and noticed her hand was discreetly tucked inside her messenger bag. She obviously didn't care that Daniel was also wearing scrubs. Sis code overrides everything.

I nodded and gave her a weak smile. "Yes, I'm good. I know him."

She studied us for a few more seconds before nodding. "Okay, be safe."

Once she crossed the lot to her car, after shooting us a few backward glances, Daniel lowered his hands, which had been raised like he was being read his Miranda rights.

He said, "Princessa was still pretty shaken up, so I couldn't get much out of her. But she called forty-five minutes ago, crying. Apparently, Chelsea gave Princessa a ride down to the campus this morning. They were rear-ended and then hit another car. Chelsea's okay, but she's suffering from whiplash, back pain, and a bad headache. She's been released from the ER. Princessa said she's been calling your phone because she doesn't want to worry your mom or Pop-Pop. We can get there in thirty minutes if we leave right now."

Without another thought, I ran over to his truck, yanking on the passenger side door. "If you're fucking with me, you'll regret it."

"Why in the world would I lie about something like this?"

"I need to know what you know. Why is Chelsea all the way in Berea? She's supposed to be at play rehearsal right now. And Princessa's on summer break, so why is she going down to Baldwin Wallace?"

Daniel eased out of the parking lot. "She said they were visiting a guy she's been talking to online."

My thoughts went back to my last text conversation with Princessa.

Princessa: Sis, I met someone.

I groaned, and Daniel caught the look on my face.

"You knew about this dude and didn't tell me? She said he's twenty-three years old!"

My mouth fell open. "What? She never told me his age. Just that she'd just started seeing someone." That was when my chest tightened. "And Princessa said she's doing okay? I feel terrible that I didn't ask about her."

Daniel reached for my hand, and I didn't pull back that time. "Yeah. She's a little banged up, but she's going to be fine. Apparently, Princessa called this twenty-three-year-old while the EMTs were examining them. Chelsea rode in the ambulance to the hospital, and they followed her."

I rolled my eyes in disbelief. "What in the world is happening today?"

We pulled up to a red light, and Daniel turned to me. "Pae, that's my little sister, and you already know how I feel about Chelsea. We're going to get to them and make sure they're okay. Then we'll handle the details of the car situation and bring them back home safely."

I nodded, choking back the sobs welling up in my throat. "I've been trying to get in touch with her all day, and as soon as she needed me, I wasn't there. If something more serious had happened to her, I never would have forgiven myself for letting her down."

Daniel shook his head. "I'm not going to let you do that to yourself. Your situation couldn't be helped. And Chelsea is just fine."

"Thank God." I tried calling Chelsea's phone a few times from Daniel's phone, but she wasn't answering. "Hey, before we hit the freeway, I need you to stop by my house so I can grab my phone right quick. I don't want Chelsea to panic and end up calling my mother or grandfather."

"Yeah, no problem."

"Thanks. I'll run right in and out. I just need Tavares's number from my phone so I can have him meet us down there."

"That's a good idea. More than likely, the car isn't drivable."

He pulled up in my driveway ten minutes later, and I jumped out of the car and ran inside. I took the stairs two at a time and grabbed a pair of leggings, a T-shirt, and an extra pair of flip-flops from my bedroom just in case Chelsea needed a fresh change of clothes. Next, I ran downstairs to hunt for my cell phone. It wasn't in the living room or the kitchen, so I ran back upstairs to look on my bedside table and search the bathroom. I spent the next five minutes running around in frenzied circles, wanting to yank my hair out and scream in frustration. Just when I was about to run back outside and tell Daniel to call my phone so I could hear it ring, I found it wedged between the cushions of the couch, slick with bacon grease and dead. Shortly afterward, I burst out the front door, clutching my overnight bag, and jumped into the passenger seat.

"Go! And don't think all this has let your ass off the hook. As soon as my phone powers up and I talk to my sister, you're going to tell me why you have a tracking device on my got-damn car and for how long," I said, plugging my phone into his car charger port.

Daniel set his phone down with a smirk, but not a damn thing was funny. He pulled out of my driveway without another word as I stared down at the screen, silently willing my phone to come back to life.

*Chapter Thirty-Nine*

## LENNOX ELLINGTON DAVENPORT

When the letter arrived, I almost tossed it out by accident. It was wrapped in a bundle of grocery store fliers and manufacturer coupons. But when I saw an envelope sticking out with a *The May Cleveland* return address, it immediately caught my attention. The letter stated my application was approved and welcomed me as their newest lessee, starting on August 1st. When I informed them of my transfer to our Cleveland office, my team was sorry to see me go, but they were all eager to assist me with my transition. I had met most of the IT team I'd be working with while working in Cleveland earlier that year, so the transition would be pretty smooth. I was able to bring the majority of my belongings with me and put the rest into storage for future retrieval. A group of close friends in Cleveland was ready to assist with the logistics of my move, and I looked forward to surprising Patience with my arrival.

I must admit, the idea of committing to a long-term relationship for the first time was a bit intimidating for me. I hoped Patience would appreciate the grand gesture of moving cities to be closer to her and take it as a symbol of my devotion to exploring things between us further. Over the past several months, she had shown me who she really was. Her vulnerability was raw and appealing, and I immediately knew she was the one I wanted to do this relationship thing with. My choice to abstain from casual sex before meeting her was the result of years of pent-up frustration. The females I was physically attracted to were beautiful on the outside but left much to be desired otherwise. They all seemed to be focused on the wrong things. Eventually, their lack of drive, morality, and focus led me to believe there wasn't much hope for me when it came to finding a potential life partner. Consequently, I decided to refrain from having sex until I found a connection worth pursuing long-term. A year later, I met Patience. Boy, had she tested each and every one of my morals and principles.

From the moment she had charged her sexy little body right into the center of my life, I knew she was exactly what I'd been waiting for. I'd chosen to abstain from having sex with her because I sensed something was broken in her from jump. I didn't want to complicate things between us any further, so I decided to focus on getting to know her better instead.

I understood how hard it was for her to abstain, but I just wished she had understood that sex has a deeper meaning and substance for me than most people. It symbolizes the level of our love we have for one another. Even through our little tiffs, she remained on my mind and in my heart. But after witnessing the turn of events of my parents' marriage, I knew I had to be sure before making a permanent play with Patience. After our trip to New York, I felt reassured, but it was what happened at the diner for me. Seeing her crumble and wanting nothing short of stopping the world on its axis before letting a single tear escape her eye was a life-changing experience for me. I'd never felt that level of conviction for protecting a woman other than my moms before. That shit was unnerving . . . and scary as hell.

When Mom and Pops were visiting me in Atlanta a few weeks ago, Mom let me know how she really felt about Patience. Not only did she adore her, but she had brought my paternal grandmother's ring with her. The one Pops had given her. Said she'd be proud for Patience to rock our family jewels. We all had a long talk, and they believed my choice to relocate to Cleveland was certainly the move.

That was why after grabbing the keys for my new luxury apartment downtown, I stopped by a wine cellar and copped a bottle of their finest champagne. Then I spent several hours at the mall purchasing a suitcase, lingerie, bath salts, seductive body wash, massage and body oil, and vegan bath and body items for an amazing evening. I made dinner reservations and couldn't wait to break the news to Patience over our meal that we were only ten minutes away from my new home. And I'd only be a twenty-five-minute drive away from her. No more flights, FaceTiming, or falling asleep holding the phone each night.

But she didn't respond to my morning text like she usually did. I stopped by her job to catch her when she walked out to her car, but her car wasn't in the parking lot. Figuring she had worked from home that day, I headed to her house. When I didn't see her car parked in the driveway, I assumed she had just pulled it into the garage. I was nervous and excited while waiting on her doorstep, but she never answered the door. I parked on the street and waited while calling and texting her with no answer. I figured she may be teaching line dancing at the church or visiting her grandfather.

Almost an hour passed before a white Lincoln Navigator with a license plate that said DNP4ME passed by and pulled into her driveway. Confused, I watched my girlfriend jump out of the passenger seat and run into her house. She looked upset, so I hopped out of the car. I crossed the street and made my way across her tree-strewn lawn before I stopped dead in my tracks.

Daniel's face was in the side mirror of the idling SUV, scoping my every move. I called for him to step out of the vehicle, but he didn't budge. Instead, he cracked the window, emphatically suggesting that I check my Instagram messages. I wanted to yank him out of his truck and wipe that smug smirk clean off his face, but curiosity got the better of me. I patted my pockets and realized I didn't have my phone. I turned around to head back to my car, ready to settle things with Emo Ernie once and for all. My head was swimming in a sea of random thoughts.

Why was ol' boy telling me to check social media like he knew something I didn't? I hopped inside my rental car to grab my phone, leaving the car door ajar. When I pulled up the app, I immediately went to Patience's profile. Her last post was three days ago, which I liked. Then I noticed a direct message request from Daniel from almost a month prior. I opened it.

*What's up, my man?*

*I know trying to move in on my woman has kept you rather busy, so I'll get right to the point. Since you didn't have any respect for my relationship, I thought I'd be kind enough to let you know some things about our girl, Patience, that you may not have learned yet during your brief little encounter. I bet you're thinking everything y'all have going on between you is real special, right? Yeah, that's cute. It's probably because she led you to believe that shit. But I know for a fact without even being there with y'all that everything you've experienced with her is old news. She's been doing the same shit for years.*

*She probably took you to the vacant lot overlooking Valley View. Did y'all watch the sunset in the valley and talk all night in the car during your time up here? Did she take you to the Pancake House for brunch? I bet she drove you by the house where she grew up and told you all about her childhood memories before her father left. Did she show you the private school she attended as a little girl?*

*How do I know all these things, you ask? Because she did the same shit with me and the guy before me and probably the guy before him. So, we'll see how long it'll be before she loses interest in her little rebound relationship with you. Before long, you'll be tossed out like yesterday's trash, my G. Remember, I had five long years with her. She's just getting her little rebellion out of her system right now. Soon enough, she'll be right back home where she belongs.*

*When she leaves your pretty-boy ass hurting, don't hold it against her. We all know she's just damaged goods, doing the toxic shit damaged goods do. Besides, the apple never falls far from the tree. And even if it tries, that shit can't roll but so far.*

*Peace,*

*DF*

I reread the message, trying to figure out who the hell he thought he was. It was difficult to sort the facts from the bullshit.

Fact: He knew all the places Patience had taken me during my trips to Cleveland, which was weird.

Fact: He had touched on her tendency to self-sabotage which was a known pattern for her. But Patience and I had already discussed that.

Fact: She just pulled up with this dude after falling off the grid all day.

Fact: She told me she had broken things off with this dude, but she also wasn't aware I was in town.

Fact: Her father did set a precedent of abandonment for her, regardless of having his reasons for leaving their home and later being denied access to his daughter for doing so.

Fact: I really had no way of knowing how the hell she passed her time when I wasn't here.

As the facts continued to stack against us, my fists clenched. I closed the door, leaned back on the headrest, and closed my eyes, taking a few moments to even my breathing to keep from going apeshit on Daniel's ass. Thankfully, I gained a little clarity after a few moments.

Despite how factual parts of his message were, I wasn't trying to hear any of that noise. I clicked on Daniel's profile page, and thankfully, it was public. His most recent post caught my eye. It was a picture of him with his back to the camera. My eyebrows rose as I tapped on the post for a closer look. This fool had a fresh tattoo of Patience's face and name etched across the top of his back. The caption read, *Happy birthday to my queen.* It was posted the night before Patience's birthday party. There was a clear adhesive bandage over it, indicating it was brand new. That was probably why he had shown up at the party all sauced up. He was probably self-medicating because that shit looked like it had taken several hours . . . or possibly days. *Thirsty ass*. I shook my head.

I needed to get to the bottom of things with Patience. I still didn't understand why she hadn't returned my calls or texts all day, only to pull up with this dude. Before I could calculate my next move, I glanced up to see her rushing back out of the house. She hopped into his truck, carrying the same overnight bag she had brought with her to New York. I frowned, my confusion momentarily paralyzing me. *An overnight bag? The fuck?* They peeled off together seconds later, headed back out of the development.

As much as I didn't want to believe what this dude was saying to me, I couldn't help but trust what my own eyes were showing me. Patience didn't even look up as they passed right by my rental car. But Emo Ernie made it a point to lean over, making direct eye contact and flashing that corny-ass grin of his as they passed by. That same one from all those now-deleted, booed-up pics with Patience I had seen on her social media profile a few months back. I hit him with the hardest Ice Cube mean mug I could muster in return. As they turned the corner and merged with traffic on the main road, my sneer melted, and hot rage singed my veins.

I had gone through hell and high water to uproot my life and move up here to be with her, only to watch her pulling off with him going God knows where. Is that what went down when I wasn't in Cleveland? She was still dealing with this guy while I was busting my whole ass just to be closer to her? No, that couldn't be it. Not Patience. She could never be capable of no foul shit like that. It was apparent that this dude was manipulative and undermining. His slick little message said it all. I knew something serious must be at stake for her to be rushing to get back into his truck. I saw the worry etched on her face and the way she ran in and out of the house. The question was, what was this dude, Daniel, up to?

I pulled off, busting a U-turn in the middle of the street. There was no way I was letting Patience ride off somewhere with this lunatic. As I navigated the twists and turns of the development at high speed, I thought to myself, *And here I was planning to spend the evening breaking in my new digs by making love to my woman in every single room. This can't be life.*

I shook my head.

After being a Clevelander for less than three hours, I was already taking massive Ls.

Chapter Forty

DANIEL HENRY FRANCOIS

My heart goes out to her as she speaks on the phone with Chelsea's dude. Patience is a good-hearted woman and could always be counted on to drop what she was doing to help someone else—especially her little sister. As unfortunate as the circumstances were, it was good to lay eyes on her up close again. I loved this woman with everything I had, and I'd stop at nothing to prove it to her. That was why I had agreed to her little sex-only agreement after our breakup. I knew it would only be temporary, and I'd eventually win her back. I wasn't even mad when she'd had me escorted out of her little party. I gave her that one. I was being an asshole to her when she came to my job and by refusing to take her phone calls. I was just pissed since she had that dude at her house. When I had stopped by with a bottle of blackberry merlot and some gourmet popcorn, she'd been letting his ass inside. And, come to find out, it was the same dude I'd spotted at her party—the one I wasn't invited to. If I hadn't caught Pop-Pop's Instagram live and the 360 video he'd posted with the tagged location, I wouldn't have even known anything about it.

Anyway, new dude stood out like a sore thumb because he was the only face I didn't recognize at first. After dating her for five years, I knew damn-near everyone in her life. So, when I saw him smirking at me like he knew something I didn't, I knew what it was . . . old clown-ass dude. When I'd seen him walking out of her house a few days prior, I was so hot, I didn't even trust myself enough to ring her doorbell. I knew I would end up hurting him. But when I'd started blowing up Patience's phone afterward, she wouldn't even pick up for me. Probably figured she didn't need my ass anymore.

I still couldn't believe she would betray me like this. She was the one who'd set the rule that we would be exclusive in our physical relationship, but clearly, it hadn't applied to her. I had even tried reaching out to new dude before with no response. That was exactly why, the moment I saw him waiting on her in his car like a simp, I slowed down to made sure he saw with his own eyes that I was back in the picture. Because I knew if Patience had seen him when we pulled up, it would've been game over for me on sight. And that was a risk I could no longer afford to take.

For some reason, she had it bad for this dude. In a matter of months, he'd managed to penetrate those same walls that took me years to break down. Even fresh off the breakup of our long-term relationship, she'd been carefree with this guy, like they'd been kickin' it for years. At first, I'd figured it was a classic rebound situation and planned to wait until she got it out of her system, especially with him living out of state. But now I saw that this dude was actually serious about her. If I waited too much longer, I might mess around and lose Patience for good. Nah, that wasn't happening. After all the time I'd spent molding her the way I wanted her, I'd be damned if I would let him swoop in and claim what was mine.

Now he was back up here, visiting her again when he was just here two weeks ago. Shit was getting really hot and heavy between them, and I had to admit, I was a little shook. I hadn't been able to sleep or eat, and I'd been messing up at work. To top it all off, it was looking like I may really be losing her. But dude had better be ready to fight for her because I had nothing left to lose at this point.

She hung up from a second phone call; it sounded like it was with my sister. Then she turned to look at me. I recognized that look in her eyes. I had pushed her too far this time.

"Daniel, what the hell is wrong with you? Why in the world have you been using a tracking device on me?"

I tightened my grip on the steering wheel while remembering all the interactions I'd witnessed firsthand between her and ol' boy. How she'd made love to him at our favorite spot in the park, how she'd taken him to our favorite restaurant, and most importantly, how she'd driven him around her old stomping grounds, sharing special childhood memories with him—ones she hadn't shared with me until multiple years into our relationship. I'd put in real work to get where I was. Honestly. I mean, what grown man actually wants to spend his Saturday night doing jigsaw puzzles and drinking wine? On a college campus? Certainly not me. Especially not while I was patiently waiting to get her in bed. She had made me wait almost three months to hit that. I doubt that was the case for Rico Sauvé's ass.

So, what was it about this pretty boy that had her forgetting who'd held her down for all these years? Tolerating her mood swings, daddy issues, and meddling family, all while juggling a rigorous graduate program and a hectic work schedule, had been exhausting. Although she was definitely worth any and all sacrifices, I could admit that I'd had moments when I didn't appreciate her fully. But now that we'd spent this time apart, she was all I could think about. That was why I was even willing to maintain a no-strings-attached physical relationship with her on her terms. Having any part of her was better than having none of her. Now, there was nothing I wanted more than to hold her and make love to her again. But I had to spend my time watching her all hugged up with this guy instead.

And all for what? My controlling mama screwed things up for

me once again. Right when we were at the finish line. I was almost done with getting my doctorate, and I had a good position lined up at The Cleveland Clinic. Life was just about to start for us. Then, instead of leaving bad enough alone, my meddling mama called Patience after shit had blown up and tried to smooth things over. In what universe could that possibly have worked?

Princessa kept telling me to leave it alone and let Patience return on her own. But I couldn't do that. Too much time had already been wasted. Precious time with her that I couldn't get back. I'd trained her to become a perfect, supportive potential wife. Our plan was for her to remain at home—maybe grow her voice-acting side hustle, have our children, and hold me down so I could provide for all of us. As little as six months ago, Patience was perfectly fine with all that. Now, this new dude has started dropping all types of crazy ideas in her head. She'd updated her LinkedIn profile to a Talent Manager position, and she had a college bumper sticker on her car. Where in the world had all of this come from?

She shoved my shoulder, and I blinked.

"Huh?"

"*Huh?*" She mocked. "You heard me ask you a question!"

"Pae, it's for your own good. You're running around with this random dude I've never seen before. He's coming into your house with luggage. Staying the night and taking my place. Whatever happened to us against the world? You forgot about me already?"

She stared at me for a long moment, and I realized I'd let it slip that I'd been watching her house.

"What the fuck, Daniel? Really?"

It was time to pivot. "What do you really know about this guy? You're moving way too fast, and it really ain't safe out here. You know you can't possibly have anything real with him this fast. Leave this little rebound relationship alone and come back to what you know."

She shook her head. "Daniel, you have no idea how crazy you sound right now. If we didn't need to get to the girls—" Her phone buzzed, and she looked down at it. "Hold on. I need to take this."

"Hello," she answered. She stiffened, then listened for a few moments before responding. "Hey! Yes, I just called. Princessa said you were in the bathroom. How are you feeling?" She nodded, paused, and nodded again. "Yes, I'm on my way . . . no, don't worry about the car. We'll handle that later. Yes, Tavares knows, and he's right behind us. No, I promise I haven't called Pop-Pop or Mom."

They talked for a few more minutes before she ended the call. She tapped at her screen for a few minutes, and I was tempted to ask her who she was texting. Before I could, she glared at me. Just like that, I was back in the hot seat.

"So, you've been sitting outside of my house. Do I need to serve your ass with a restraining order?"

"Pae, you know good and well that I would never hurt you. I'm just trying to figure out how you've moved on so quickly. After all we've been through together, you're really willing to walk away like this?"

She closed her eyes and sighed. "Daniel, we've had some really great times, and I honestly value some of the things you've brought to my life. But there's no future for us because we're each heading down different paths."

I scoffed. "Since when?"

"Since I've actually spent some time thinking about what I want."

"You mean since you've spent time letting him brainwash you."

She sat back in her seat and stared at me. I stared at the road ahead and pretended not to notice. "No, Daniel. That's just what support looks like. Get into it."

I gripped the steering wheel again. "You're saying I don't support you?"

"No, you eagerly supported anything that supported *your* master plan. But that's just not what I want anymore."

I shook my head, carefully selecting my next words. "We . . . we came up with the master plan together, Pae."

"Yes, back when my main goal in life was to see you thrive. But, if I'm being honest with myself, there was no room in our relationship for my success, too. I just want to be happy, Daniel. Ultimately, isn't that what you want for me?"

"So, this guy makes you happier than I do?"

She sighed. "Lennox is a great guy who I'm still getting to know. Does he support and encourage me to do more things for myself? Yes. Do I rely on his support and encouragement to be happy? No. Did I rely on you for those things? Absolutely! Our codependency was toxic. I just couldn't . . ."

Holding my hand up, I said, "Whoa, whoa. Back up. Codependency? Since when did I try to manipulate or control you?"

She threw up her hands. "Daniel, you put a tracking device on my damn car, for God's sake! You used to have me sit and wait in your dorm room for you while you worked so I wouldn't attend frat parties or go barhop with my roommates."

I frowned. "Why you talking about old stuff?"

"You DM'd my man!"

*Damn, I knew he had* snitch *written all over him. Probably sent her screenshots.* I heard her voice catch and glanced over at her. Tears were streaming down her face as she swiped a trembling hand across her cheek. I wanted to reach for her, but I was so stunned and hurt that she'd accused me of being controlling, I couldn't move.

"In college, you used to check my odometer when you got home from work to make sure I didn't go anywhere. Do you remember requesting my cell phone records from T-Mobile to review them line by line, just to see who I was calling when I wasn't with you? Or has your selective memory decided to kick in?"

Her eyes were razor sharp, and my face grew hot. "Wait a minute. Don't try to put this all on me. If it was so terrible being with me, why didn't you just leave?"

She shook her head again. "I'm not sure. It could have something to do with the fact that I'd been through three consecutive failed relationships, and I desperately wanted *something* to work to prove that I was lovable. Honestly, I think I just needed a win, Daniel."

It was my turn to look at her with fiery eyes. "Oh, so you never loved me? I was some type of fucked-up trophy for you to put on a shelf or some shit?"

"That's not what I'm saying. Look, don't think I've been going around badmouthing you to everyone because I haven't. You know that nearly everyone in my life has been Team Daniel over the years. You haven't been a bad boyfriend—you just did the best you could with what you had."

I could tell she was intentionally avoiding bringing up my mother.

"And I'm one hundred percent willing to accept my blame in this, too. In a lot of ways, I was self-serving because I enjoyed feeling needed by you. It made me feel useful to play an active role in your success. It was the validation I needed at that time to replace the emptiness I felt from my father's absence. But now, all of that is over."

I reached over and grabbed her hand. "Pae, listen to me. It doesn't have to be. I'm more than willing to support your new career goals and everything else you want. Let's do this together. We can still have it all."

I heard her mumble, "You just don't get it."

I played dumb. "Huh?"

She sniffed, wiping away another tear. "Pull over."

I looked over at her, frowning. "What?"

She looked at her phone, her thumbs flying over the screen. "Get off at the exit and pull the car over. Now."

I did as I was told. Once I pulled into a gas station parking lot, I turned to face her. "You gotta use the bathroom or something?"

She wiped away her tears, and her expression was one of resolve, which scared the hell out of me. "Look, I really appreciate you saying that, Daniel. For real. When we met, we were two damaged people looking for love and acceptance from one another, which should have come from the people who were most important to us. Over the course of our relationship, we received and provided those things for one another. But you need to get clear on one thing: I'm no longer interested in being in a relationship with you. Can you or can you not respect and honor that decision?"

I released the breath I'd been holding since she had begun speaking. Her mouth formed a line, and her eyes darted back and forth, carefully searching mine. I recognized that look. It was the look she'd get whenever we discussed her father. Closed off, dark, and unforgiving. At that moment, I realized that no matter what I had to say in my own defense, no matter how I tried to convince her that I'd change into whomever she needed me to be, she was done listening. Cold prickles of fear washed over me as I witnessed her conviction. She'd really chosen to leave me.

Her phone buzzed once, twice, then a third time, but she didn't take her eyes off mine. I took her hand and raised it to my lips, savoring her smooth skin on mine for the last time. Then I slowly nodded.

She removed her hand from mine. "I need to hear you say it."

I bit my inner cheek, then forced out the words. "Yes, I can respect and honor your decision to end our relationship."

She gave me a curt nod and said, "Okay, then. Please take care of yourself, Daniel."

Her phone buzzed again, and she finally glanced at the screen before grabbing her overnight bag from the backseat. Then she asked me to unlock the door and stepped out of the truck. I watched her walk over to a blue sedan pulling up beside us. Without another glance my way, she and Lennox pulled away. Moments later, I noticed Tavares pull off behind them.

And after over five glorious years of loving that beautiful woman, just like that, she was out of my life for good.

Chapter Forty-One

PATIENCE

After making sure Princessa was okay, Tavares, Chelsea, and I left the emergency room just before Daniel arrived. I didn't feel right leaving Princessa with a total stranger, but Ox was waiting outside, and limiting any further interactions between him and Daniel was completely necessary. So, the four of us watched from the parking lot as Princessa safely left the building with Daniel and her twenty-three-year-old boyfriend.

The police had ordered a tow for Chelsea's car since it couldn't be driven from the accident scene. Tavares checked it out of the tow yard and had it towed to a local mechanic. Lennox and I trailed them to the car shop. I slid into the driver's seat of Tavares's car and waited with Chelsea while they checked her car in to be serviced.

Her skin was bruised and there was dried blood above her right eyelid. "Oh, Bunny."

"Sis, I'm fine," she grunted, adjusting herself slightly in her seat.

"Careful."

"I'm just glad Daniel was finally able to reach you."

I nodded, not bringing up the tracking device. She had enough on her plate with the recovery ahead of her, so the less she knew about anything I'd been through over the past twenty-four hours, the better.

"Yeah, me too. So, you said Princessa got the insurance information of the person who hit y'all?"

"Yeah. It was a girl around our age, about nineteen or twenty. She said she her flip-flop slipped off the brake. But the impact was too hard for me to believe that. She was probably distracted."

I just shook my head. "I can't believe this. Your first accident after four years of driving."

"Right. The wild part about it was Princessa's phone died, so the radio came on for a second while she was connecting my phone to the Bluetooth to stream music. We were struck from behind just before your radio commercial came on. Your voice was in the car with us when it happened. I was scared, but hearing your voice made me feel better."

My natural voice. No Italian accent, no urban twang, just the soothing voice she'd known from birth was what had calmed my little sister during one of the scariest moments of her life. I blinked back tears and squeezed her hand.

She sat up. "Munk, what's that on your arm?"

"Oh, it's just a temporary brace. I tripped and slammed into the wall, but I'll be fine."

"Damn. Is that where you were? At the hospital with no reception? That's how Daniel found you?"

I nodded, hating to omit the truth. "Yeah. Once he let me know what happened, we left right away."

"So, how did Lennox end up here?"

I blinked, scanning her face for a moment before responding. I hadn't formally introduced them yet. Tavares and I had rushed into the ER, and I'd asked Ox to stay in the car to prevent him from running into Daniel. "How do you . . . ?"

"Sis, if you think for one second that I wasn't going to look into that man after I saw him walk into your party, you don't know me at all. I grilled the hell out of Bella after you left. She tried to play it off like he was Chauncey's friend, but the way you started glowing once you laid eyes on him told a different story."

This was the first time I'd ever been speechless with my little sister. My mouth opened, closed, then opened again. "Okay, grown ass. He's here visiting for a while. He surprised me and showed up at my house while I was at the hospital."

She nodded. "Well, he fine-fine. But he betta know I don't play about my sister. So, as long as he treats you with the utmost respect, we'll be good."

"You have nothing to worry about, sis."

She winked. "Good. Then neither does he."

I dapped her up with my good arm. Several minutes later, I stepped out of the vehicle, meeting up with Tavares and Ox in the parking lot.

Tavares gave me details on the estimate and how long they would need to service Chelsea's car.

"Thanks for taking care of that, Tavares. After you take Chelsea home to gather more of her things, can you make sure she's at my house before nine?"

He frowned. "I'm sorry, why would I bring Chelsea to your house?"

I blinked again. I knew she'd be sore in the morning, and I wanted to monitor her overnight due to her mild concussion. "To spend the night."

Tavares shook his head, looked me in the eye, and said, "Nah, Patience. Respectfully, I've got this."

I studied him for a moment. "What do you mean? Got what?"

"I mean, Chelsea will be just fine staying with me tonight. I'm going to pick up her prescription on the way home, then give her a nice warm bath and make sure she eats something before getting a full night's sleep. I've been asleep for most of the day, and I've already called off from tonight's shift, so I'm all set to monitor her overnight."

I glanced at Ox, but I could tell he'd chosen to remain neutral. "Tavares, I . . ."

"Patience, I've been in love with your sister for a long time. No one's more important to me. I know how much you love and care about her, but Chelsea works very hard to show you that she's responsible and independent. It's time for you to learn to trust that she'll be just fine on her own. This can be the very first step . . . if you're ready."

*If* I'm *ready?* My mouth was suddenly dry and I could feel my palms sweating as I struggled to come up with a reply. As I stared at Tavares, I realized he'd never failed to drop whatever he was doing to come to my sister's aid, loved her unconditionally, and had been right by her side through all of her major life events. This young man was stepping up and telling me that I needed to step aside. What could I do other than respect him?

"Okay, I see I've clearly misjudged you. You do have this, Tavares. Thank you for offering to take care of my sister."

He nodded. "It's what we've always done for each other. Nice to meet you, Lennox. Take care, Patience. I'll have her check in with you once she wakes up tomorrow."

I watched him get back into the car with my sister as I fought a strong urge to pull open the passenger door and give my sister a laundry list of dos and don'ts. Instead, I leaned my head against Ox's shoulder and blew her a kiss as they drove away.

Ox rubbed my arms. "You gonna be okay?"

I nodded. "I think I am. Let's go home."

# Chapter Forty-Two

PATIENCE

Three weeks passed, and I was still shocked that I could see Ox without hopping on FaceTime or a plane. He'd managed to orchestrate a full relocation strategy and move without so much as mentioning it to me. Quite honestly, I had nothing to lose and everything to gain from this arrangement. If I ever needed to feel those strong arms around me or twist my pinky in that darling dimple, he was less than a twenty-minute drive away. Now that he was in Cleveland, we were spending a lot more time actually dating each other. Enjoying trips to wineries, catching Cavs and Browns games, going on double dates with friends, and doing puzzles while drinking wine. Except now I had a boyfriend who didn't have to pretend to enjoy doing all of those things with me. So, I was very happy Ox had chosen to make that play.

Last week, I'd invited Chelsea, Tavares, Pop-Pop, and Mom over for dinner. It was difficult facing all of them initially, knowing what I did. I still had many unanswered questions about my family's choices. With the most recent events, I didn't have much time to determine how I felt about the people I thought I knew best. But, for the time being, I chose to focus on the fact that family was family. And they were all here, safe and sound. Most importantly, my sister was alive and well. Rehashing the details of the past would only mean dredging up a bunch of he-said-she-said bullshit that I wasn't in the emotional state to handle at that time. I just wanted to be happy. I was on an exciting new career track and in love with an amazing man who never disappointed me. My family was always there for me, supporting me every step of the way. We would have the conversation once I was ready.

"So, did you sign the contract for the venue yet?" I asked Ox as we passed a yellow convertible on the highway.

"I did. The fellas wanted to go to a cigar bar for a relaxed vibe, but I opted to rent a downtown loft near my apartment for privacy. As long as I'm getting it catered and we're stocked with beer, they won't care where we link up."

I laughed, proud that he'd decided to move forward with hosting a small monthly gathering for his childhood friends to chat about life, goals, and whatever they pleased. It wasn't exactly therapy, but it was a start. "Well, if the ladies ever want to fit in some self-care while the fellas are away, I'm more than happy to arrange a trip to the spa."

"Sounds like a plan."

"Turn left at the light," I said as we got off at the Richmond Road exit. His jaw stiffened for the third time. "Anything wrong, bae?"

"Nothing, just checking the rearview mirror, hoping this fool isn't following us."

I squeezed his hand. "Bae, you shouldn't be worried about that."

He turned to glance at me like I'd said something totally outlandish. "I shouldn't be worried about Daniel following us around? Like he hasn't done this before?"

"Yes, he was tracking us, and the shit was foul. But he thought he was protecting me."

He scoffed. "He was the one you need protection from."

"Agreed. But in his warped mind, he thought I was moving too quickly with you without knowing you well enough, and he was concerned. After speaking to him about it, I believe he'll step back. I just want to extend a little grace, Ox. He's never given me a reason to question his mental or emotional stability before."

He turned at the light, gripping the steering wheel. "And if he doesn't step back?"

"Turn right here, then it's the cul-de-sac on the right," I instructed. "Then there'll be a restraining order in his future. I'll serve that ass quick and hot, like Serena."

When he didn't crack a smile, I said, "Tell me exactly what you're concerned about."

"I trust your judgment, babe. But I don't want his drama to impact us. We've been doing great, but now that I'm here, we've entered a whole new phase in our relationship. Hopefully, he realizes it's over and doesn't contact you again."

I nodded. "I understand your point. And I just want you to know that I'm not making excuses for his choices and behavior. We shouldn't have to peek over our shoulders like this. And, if he crosses the line with either of us again, you'll know about it. There won't ever be secrets between us, okay? I promise."

After a few tense moments passed, Ox nodded and said, "I don't trust Emo Ernie any further than I can toss his ass." He pulled up in the driveway, put the car in park, then turned to face me. "But, *you* have my full trust."

He leaned in for a kiss. It was gentle, sweet, and genuine. I was relieved to know he fully trusted me, even after the character-assassinating DM Daniel had sent. I was actually grateful that Ox and I had already navigated serious hardships together. As a result, we placed high priorities on deep emotional intimacy, trust, respect, and vulnerability in our relationship. Without them, it would have been easy for Daniel to come in and ransack everything we'd lovingly built. Little did he know, our little "rebound relationship" was strong enough to withstand any nonsense he tried to bring.

Ox stepped out and opened my door. Hand in hand, we walked up the driveway and rang the doorbell.

"Hey, hey, hey." Sister Perkins opened the door and pulled me in for a hug.

I blinked. Not her answering my grandfather's door. "Hey, Sister Perkins," I said, kissing her cheek. "How are you?"

"Doing just fine. Oh, and you can call me Flora now, chile." She widened her eyes, placing her hand on her chest. "And just who is this tall drink of mocha latte?"

I hadn't brought Ox to church with me yet so I still needed to make a formal introduction. "This is my boyfriend, Lennox Davenport. Lennox, this is Sister Perkins."

Ox extended his hand. "Nice to meet you, Sister Perkins."

"Mm, mm, mm. Talk about a hottie, Patience," Sister Perkins said, lowering her hand into his and fanning her eyelashes. "I mean, that chocolate nurse was nice, but this is an upgrade, girl! Come on in, young man."

Sister Perkins led the way into the house humming "Upgrade U" with an added pep in her step. Shaking my head, I left them in the living room and went to look for my family. I put the bottle of wine in the fridge after kissing everyone. Pop-Pop was setting the dining room table, my mother was buttering homemade rolls, and Chelsea was making her sherbet fruit punch. I smiled, watching them rock to Stevie Wonder's "I Just Called to Say I Love You" on Pop-Pop's record player, the music stirring up memories from my childhood. Just as I was about to wash my hands and help Chelsea slice strawberries and pineapples for the punch, my phone buzzed in my back pocket.

Dad: *Hey, sweet baby girl. Thanks for your text.*

Dad: *We don't need to revisit anything from the past. I didn't share those things with you to cause you any more pain. You've already been through enough. All I've ever wanted was to be a part of your life. Can we move on and make that happen now? If so, give your old man a call.*

Dad: *Remember, I'm always here for you, no matter what.*

Butterflies danced in my stomach. Then I thought about what I'd said to Ox about extending grace to Daniel. How could I do that for someone who'd intentionally tried to hurt me and sabotage my happiness but refuse my own flesh and blood? I glanced at Ox who was sitting on the living room couch with Sister Perkins. She was showing him pictures from a recent cruise with her book club. Then I heard her ask him how to set up a GoFundMe page for breast implants. He wasn't going anywhere anytime soon.

I stepped onto the back porch, softly sliding the door closed behind me. The pink and lavender swirls from the setting sun spilled across the sky, and a sudden warmth and sense of excitement consumed me, very much like what I'd experienced as a little girl. Reflecting on our short time together during my childhood, I remember watching the sun dip past the horizon while chit-chatting about our day. The elation I'd feel whenever he'd tickle me after a bad day, when he'd come home with a new coloring book and fresh crayons, or whistle loudly at each of my dance recitals was larger than life.

A big part of me was relieved to finally know that he hadn't stopped fighting to make his presence felt in my life and his undying love for me known. He was committed to showing me that I was worthy of his time and devotion. No matter how difficult my family may have made that for him or how much rejection I'd doled out over the years, he'd never stopped trying to convince me that—to him—I mattered.

As the sun slowly disappeared from view, I promised to be intentional about every moment and seize each opportunity to right my own wrongs. Easing onto my grandfather's favorite cushioned rocking chair, I brushed away the silent tears collecting beneath my chin. Then I said a quick prayer, took a deep breath, and with a spirit fixated on the hope of new beginnings, I made a phone call that was long overdue.

# Sneak Peek of Beauty Betrothed

*Beauty Betrothed*

As Patience steps into a new leadership role, a viral controversy threatens her company's reputation, forcing her to navigate professional turmoil while juggling school and family betrayal. Meanwhile, Lennox provides unwavering support as he adapts to his own fresh start in Cleveland.

In Brooklyn, Preston and Mia's engagement is tested by career ambitions—Preston's business decisions put him at odds with his board, while Mia fights for a game-changing opportunity in a high-stakes pitch competition.

With emotional depth, dynamic relationships, and the perfect balance of romance and real-life challenges, *Beauty Betrothed* is a must-read for fans of contemporary love stories that celebrate strength, communication, and the power of partnership.

**Sneak Peek**

"Whew, boy! I swear you're trying to kill me." I emerged from beneath the down comforter, gasping for air. We'd spent our three-day long weekend tangled in his satin sheets. Every muscle and ligament felt loose, limber, and free—he had worked wonders on my body.

Ox's large, warm hand slid over my abdomen, making me quiver.

"Well, I can't kidnap my Beauty for the weekend without cooking for her," he said, his voice low and measured, sending vibrations straight to my inner ear. "Besides, the best way to eat my breakfast is right off..." He leaned over and kissed my collarbone. "...this elegant, delicate..." He kissed my right breast. "...original sculpture that's been flawlessly crafted..." He traced a wet trail down to my navel. "...just for my daily dining pleasure..."

I moaned.

Ever since he'd moved to Cleveland a few weeks ago, every hobby, task, and personal responsibility of ours had been long neglected. Outside of work and running my side business, I spent every free moment at Ox's spacious, upscale apartment in Downtown Cleveland. It was less than five miles from each of our jobs, and when Ox took a break from cooking for me, several five-star restaurants were within an eight-minute walk in every direction.

"Ox," I whined, angling my chin toward the ceiling. "I really need to get back home. Thanks for this much-needed getaway."

He sighed reluctantly. "Okay, Beauty."

We shared a deep kiss before I slipped out of bed to get dressed.

"I'll shower at home because I don't trust you not to hop in there with me and start another round."

He chuckled, flashing those irresistible dimples. "I'd definitely go with your instinct on that one."

"I'll FaceTime you before bed. Probably around nine. Love you."

I'd almost made it to his front door before stopping dead in my tracks.

Shit. Shit. Shit.

Squeezing my eyes shut and pursing my lips, I tried to act like that didn't just happen—but it was too late. After weeks of feeling it, thinking it, and wanting to say it, the damn words were out in the open.

And now what?

I could keep walking like I'd never said them.

I could turn around and take them back.

It was too soon. He needed an explanation. I needed to—

His hands landed on the backs of my arms. "Patience, what did you just say?"

Wringing my hands, I reluctantly turned to face him. His eyes —warm, smiling, reassuring—granted me the courage to say what was on my mind.

"Ox...I said I love you."

He nodded, and a warm smile curved his lips.

I continued. "I've loved you for almost the entire time I've known you. But...you don't have to say it back. I know it's still early in our relationship, so I understand if you're not there yet. But I'm owning this moment. I want you to know exactly how I feel."

Just when the burden of concealing my feelings lifted from my shoulders, I noticed he was still nodding—almost amused. My confidence wavered. After everything I'd been through, my injured pride urged me to turn tail and run.

But I stood my ground, trembling beneath his unwavering gaze.

Soon, I found myself nodding along with him.

Then smiling.

And before long, we were both nodding and smiling like fools.

After a few moments, my bobbing head started to hurt. "Ox, why are we smiling and nodding?"

"I'm just glad you feel comfortable enough to tell me. Even though I could tell how you were feeling, after everything with your ex, I didn't want to rush you. I've been waiting for you to share this with me.

Babe, I've been in love with you since we shared that first meal you cooked for us. What was it—?"

"Chicken fajitas with cauliflower rice and cilantro avocado lime sauce," we said together.

"You're such a damn foodie," I smiled, shaking my head.

"Food's cool, but if you haven't noticed, I'm into anything that involves you. Period."

I stared up at him, blinking back a torrent of hot tears. For the past five years, I'd been existing as a shell of myself—supporting someone else's dreams while neglecting my own. I eventually realized no one had forced me to lose myself. I'd allowed it.

In a few short months, Ox had invested in learning about my passions and supporting my goals. He gave me the time and space to forge my own path.

It was a foreign—and welcomed—experience.

And while I wasn't sure if I loved him for the man he was or the woman he inspired me to become, I knew both were equally important.

Because they embodied how we showed up for each other every single day.

He kissed me long and deep, almost lifting me off my feet. After breaking the kiss, he said,

"So, in case you need to hear it officially: I love you too, Patience Christine Hampton."

I swayed, and his arms tightened around me.

Gazing at him for several long moments, I realized he no longer looked the same.

I saw him in a whole new light—like I was dreaming.

Everything about him was new, almost like I was seeing him for the first time.

"Boy, you got me swoonin'. Please," I whispered, "tell me again."

I watched his lips as he spoke the sweetest words I'd ever heard.

"I said I love you, babe. With all my heart."

My weekend bag clunked onto the kitchen floor as he swept me up into his arms, this time, with no resistance from me.

I kissed him as he carried me back into his bedroom.

Love is only the beginning...

When careers are on the line, family secrets rise to the surface, and dreams are put to the ultimate test, will Patience, Lennox, Preston, and Mia find a way to fight for their futures—and for each other?

*Find out in Beauty Betrothed, Book Two in the Beauty is Her Name series.*

*Beauty Beheld* is the first novel in the *Beauty Is Her Name* series. Be sure to check out Preston and Mia's origin story in the cute holiday novella *Mistletowed*. Patience, Lennox, Preston, and Mia's stories will continue in Book 2 in the *Beauty Is Her Name* series, *Beauty Betrothed* (released in Spring 2025). Book 3 in this series, *Beauty Betrayed* (released in Fall 2025).

Visit www.ZariahLBanks.com/bookclubbae for discussion questions, tips for starting a book club, and book club recipes. Thanks for reading!

## Acknowledgments

Thanks to my loving husband, Doug, for holding our household down so I could sneak away and find time to write. Thanks to my mother, Gail, for sparking my love of women's contemporary fiction. Thanks to my father, Charles, for always encouraging and inspiring me. As a result, a dream of over thirty years in the making has come true.

Thanks to my developmental editor, Shaundale Rénā, for pushing me to demand more for Patience's story and personal development—and for all the laughs! Thanks to my proofreader, Sherian Brown for your valuable feedback and insight. And for joining Patience and Lennox's fan club! To my writing coach, Dominique Gibson, thanks for helping me properly categorize my book and clarify the message of this story. Thanks to my Cleveland writers' dream team and fiction writing G.O.A.T.S., JJ Winston and Michael C. Payne. We're truly all we got and this is just the beginning! Michael, your brutally honest feedback and edits during the creation of Patience and Lennox's story was a game changer. I'm grateful for everyone who has beta read this story and given me unique feedback during this complicated process. It takes a spirited, committed village to help tell and spread a good story.

To anyone who's found inspiration to heal emotional wounds, self-advocate, and renew their pursuit of love because of these pages, I thank you for spending time with this story and I thank you in advance for sharing it with others.

Until our next chapter,

Z

Emotional intimacy novelist Zariah L. Banks tells stories about beautifully flawed people who are often victims of unrequited love. She is a true romantic at heart who believes that everyone is deserving of experiencing the joyful ups, downs, and topsy-turvy whirlwinds of love—despite what they've been through.

**Zariah *loves* book clubs!** As an avid book club member for most of her adult life, she would love a personal invite to attend yours. For a free Book Club Discussion Guide complete with an appetizer menu and relationship Q&A's, or to request an author appearance for your book club discussion of:

*Beauty Beheld*
*Mistletowed*
*Love in the Key of Summer*
*Covert Seduction*

please fill out a book club request form at www.Zariah-LBanks.com/bookclubbae. Zariah is also available to attend virtual book club meetings.

For tips on establishing self-love & emotional intimacy, and finding the love of a lifetime, visit: www.ZariahLBanks.-com/main-blog and follow Zariah at @authorzariahlbanks on IG, Threads, and Tik Tok, and fb.me/authorzariahlbanks.

# Also by Zariah L. Banks

Mistletowed: A Holiday Novella

Covert Seduction

Beauty Betrothed: A Beauty Is Her Name Novel

Love in the Key of Summer